FULL BLAST

FULL BLAST

Janet Evanovich

and Charlotte Hughes

St. Martin's Paperbacks

FULL BLAST

For information address St. Martin's Press, 175 Fifth Avenue, New York, NY 10010.

ISBN: 978-0-312-53157-7

Printed in the United States of America

St. Martin's Paperbacks edition / April 2004

St. Martin's Paperbacks are published by St. Martin's Press, 175 Fifth Avenue, New York, NY 10010.

15   14   13   12

Many thanks to Jen Enderlin aka SuperJen for giving us a great book idea! Special thanks to Eric Hughes for coming up with the title for this book.

CHAPTER ONE

JAMIE SWIFT HAD BEEN IN THE NEWSPAPER BUSI-
ness long enough to realize it was a lot like being a
waitress. You had to meet the needs of those you
served—the rich, the poor, the in-between, even the
crazies who complained no matter what you did.
And like a waitress, you had to hope the tips were
good. A big tip could make all the difference. A big
tip in her case meant headlines, and she was in the
business of finding headlines. But they didn't come
easy in a small Southern town where life was, for
the most part, uneventful, even predictable. She had
to scramble for newsworthy events.

So here she was, once again, sitting at her desk,
sifting through stories, looking for a new slant or an
idea to make it more interesting to the reading public. She was so intent on what she was doing that she
jumped when someone tapped on her door.

Sixty-year-old Vera Bankhead rushed into Jamie's

office and closed the door behind her. "You are *not* going to believe this!"

Jamie glanced up. "What is it?" she asked, straightening in her chair and trying to work the kinks out of her neck from sitting in one position for so long. She had come in early, hoping to work undisturbed. "You got a good tip for me?" she asked the woman before her. "Give me a headline, and I'll kiss the ground you walk on."

"This is even better." Vera paused, as if to add a little drama to what she was about to say. The hairpins had popped out from her gray beehive hairdo, and her glasses were askew. She shoved them high on her nose and glanced about as if to make certain they were alone. She eyed the large plate-glass window overlooking the courthouse square where automatic sprinklers were doing damage control to a parched lawn brought on by a record-breaking July heat wave. Vera marched over and snapped the blinds closed.

Jamie arched one brow. "This must be big."

"It's bigger than when Lorraine Brown caught her husband doing the nasty with Beth Toomey on a sofa in the back office of the VFW Hall."

"Wow. Wasn't she jailed for going after them with a letter opener?"

"Yeah, and Tom refused to bail her out until she signed an agreement stating she wouldn't do him bodily harm afterward. She kicked his butt anyway the minute they released her."

"So tell me."

"You're not going to believe it," the woman repeated.

"Vera, out with it already!"

Vera held up a white paper sack. She reached into it and pulled out a brownie. "Taste it."

Jamie's mouth watered at the sight of the chocolate goodie. "I really shouldn't. I've already had three doughnuts this morning. I can barely button the top of my jeans."

Vera gave her *that* look, the one that said she wasn't going to take no for an answer. And Vera could be fierce. Although she still worked as Jamie's secretary, fear and intimidation had prompted Jamie to promote her to assistant editor of the *Gazette*, as well. That and the fact Vera carried a .38 Smith and Wesson in her purse. Jamie was almost sure she wouldn't pull it on her; Vera was the closest thing she'd had to a mother, but it was best to humor her.

"Okay, okay." Jamie reached for the brownie and tasted it. "Yum, that's good." She finished it off in three bites.

"Do you feel any different?" Vera asked, eyeing her closely.

"Yeah, I want another one. I can always buy larger jeans."

"This isn't just *any* brownie," Vera said in a conspiratorial whisper. "There are rumors floating around that Lyle Betts is putting aphrodisiacs in them."

Jamie arched one brow. Lyle Betts owned Sunshine Bakery, and was considered a pillar of the community. He was president of the Jaycees, coached Little League, and played Santa Claus for the children's unit at the hospital every year. "No way," she said.

Vera crossed her heart. "As God is my witness."

Jamie pondered it. Vera was a strict Southern Baptist; she only lied when absolutely necessary.

"Do you have any more?"

"Yeah, I bought extra. I figured we should do a little experimenting. We'll eat a couple more, and then compare notes."

"Oh, Lord," Jamie said, as Vera divvied them up. The last thing she needed was to start feeling horny. It had been three weeks since she'd laid eyes on sexy and mysterious Maximillian Holt, the man who blew into her life from time to time just long enough to turn her world upside down and inside out. The same man she had already voted most likely to climb beneath the sheets with first chance she got.

"I've already had three," Vera said, "and I don't

feel a thing except for a little indigestion. Chocolate does that to me."

"I'm sure it's just a bunch of hype to sell brownies," Jamie said, hoping she was right. Lately she'd been having X-rated dreams where she and Max played starring roles. They did things she was certain were illegal in most states.

"And get this," Vera said. "Maxine Chambers quit her job at the library and just opened a lingerie shop right on Main Street. And guess what she named it? Sinful Delights."

Jamie couldn't hide her surprise. She couldn't imagine the prim librarian doing such a thing.

"And that's not all," Vera went on. "Folks say she's got a whole display of unmentionables hanging in her window where God and everybody can see them. She just undraped it today. Elbert Swank said his jaw fell open so hard when he saw them that he almost lost his dentures on the sidewalk out front. I would have given anything to see that."

"A new lingerie shop," Jamie mused. "Imagine that." She tried to keep her excitement at bay. Beaumont needed a good lingerie store, a place where cotton panties and practical bras weren't the order of the day.

"Of course I got my information secondhand so I'll have to get over there and check it out personally. You know how I am about getting my facts straight."

"Maybe she'll advertise with us," Jamie said. "We can always use the business."

"Oh, pooh. We're going to make money on that new personals section you started. How many people have written in so far?"

"We must have about ten total; seven from men, three from women. Pretty good for a small-town newspaper, don't you think?" Jamie had hoped the ads would bring in well-needed revenue and attract more readers. It was too early to tell, but she remained confident.

"I'm keeping my fingers crossed," Vera said. She stepped closer. "One ad in particular caught my attention," she almost whispered. "It was in yesterday's paper. The heading read 'Ready, Willing, and Able.' Sounds like a winner to me, seeing as how most men in my age bracket have a little trouble in the *able* department."

Jamie laughed out loud. "Vera Bankhead, I am *shocked*!"

Vera grinned. "Hey, even a woman my age has needs."

"Perhaps you should respond to the ad."

"What if he's ugly? You know I can't abide an ugly man. Maybe you should give me his name first."

Jamie shook her head. "You know the ads are strictly confidential."

"I'll bet I could figure out who he is. I know everybody in this town."

Which was why Jamie had insisted on handling the personals section, she reminded herself. She kept the ads locked in a file cabinet in her office. As much as she loved Vera, it was a well-known fact the woman was the biggest gossip in town. Jamie shrugged as though it made no difference. "I would see that your letter reached him."

"I'll have to think about it."

Jamie sighed wistfully. "Well, one thing is certain. Love is definitely in the air in the town of Beaumont, South Carolina. I think it's romantic." Jamie had only recently come to realize just what a romantic she was, and she knew Max Holt was responsible. She had begun to daydream about their relationship, had begun to wonder where it was going. She wanted him in her life permanently, and that scared the hell out of her.

"Sounds more like L-U-S-T to me," Vera replied. "It's the heat. Everybody in town is acting strange. If they start eating these brownies, they're going to be out of control."

Jamie didn't want to talk about lust because, once again, it brought Max to mind. Max, who was too gorgeous for his own good and knew it. Max, who clearly lusted after her but kept his true feelings to himself. Not that she didn't have a bad case of lust, as well; it's what drew them together like iron shavings to a magnet, what made her skin literally ache for his touch.

It had been that way from the moment they'd first laid eyes on each other, when Max had come to Beaumont to aid his brother-in-law, now the mayor, in an attempt to clean up town corruption. Max had ridden in on his white horse, or in his case, a two-million-dollar car with enough technology to run a small country. Max's investigation had dragged Jamie right into the middle of it; she'd found herself dodging bullets from hit men, almost getting blown to smithereens by a car bomb, and landing in the path of a monster-sized alligator.

Okay, so maybe she was exaggerating the size of the alligator, but all alligators looked big when you were treading water and happened to be in their path.

Most women with half a brain would have grabbed their purses and said, "See ya," but not Jamie. She had followed Max to Tennessee to find the person responsible for hiring the hit.

Simply put, Max was a philanthropist with brains and money, and as long as there was a cause or an injustice, he would be there, come hell or high water.

"My stomach feels funny," Vera said. "I think I ate too many brownies."

Jamie looked up. "Yeah?" She wouldn't tell Vera she was having a bad case of butterflies. The woman would attribute it to the brownies, but Jamie knew better. She was thinking about the last time she and Max were together in what could only be described as a compromising position. Sooner or later, things were bound to come to a head.

She and Max couldn't go on this way forever, but she was afraid to hope for more. She could fantasize all she wanted about a lasting relationship, but Max did not impress her as a man who could be tied down to any woman for very long.

"It's probably all in my mind," Vera said. "Lyle Betts most likely started the rumor just to get people into his bakery." She glanced about the office. "Where is Fleas, by the way?"

"Huh?"

"Are you even listening to me? Where is your dog? You know, that ugly hound you bring to work with you every day because he sulks if you leave him at home?"

"He's at the vet. And he's not ugly."

"I hope he's getting his anal glands expressed. I can't live with that flatulence problem much longer."

Jamie had *inherited* Fleas, a wrinkled, forlorn-faced bloodhound some weeks back. At the time she had desperately needed a vehicle, and, trying to save money, had bought a rust bucket of a pickup truck.

The car salesman, who claimed the dog was attached to the truck, had knocked fifty bucks off the price of the truck as an incentive for her to take the dog. They were bonding rather well, or at least as well as could be expected with a dog that had chronic gas.

"He's being neutered today," Jamie said. "Poor thing," she added. "I'll bet Dr. Adams has his nuts on a chopping block as we speak."

Vera shuddered. "I don't even want to think about it."

They were interrupted when someone tapped on the door. "Pardon me," a female voice said.

Vera and Jamie glanced toward the door. Jamie felt her jaw drop to her collarbone. Vera gaped, as well.

"I'm sorry to disturb you," the woman said, "but there was nobody out front."

Jamie continued to stare. The woman had coal-black hair that fell to her waist. Sparkly blue eye shadow colored her lids, and her lashes were long enough to paint the side of a barn. "May I help you?" Jamie managed.

The woman stepped into the room. Her skirt was short and tight; her low-cut blouse, emphasized perfect oversized breasts. Jamie decided either God had been very generous in the boob department or the woman was stuffed to the gills with silicone.

"My name is Destiny Moultrie," she said in a husky voice. "I'm here about the job."

Vera tossed Jamie a suspicious look. "What job? You've decided to replace me, haven't you? You'd rather have some Elvira–Erin Brockovich look-alike with big knockers sitting out front."

"I don't know anything about this," Jamie said, holding out both hands. She looked at the woman. "What job?" she asked, echoing Vera's question.

"The advice columnist. You've been turning it over in your mind for weeks."

"I have?"

Vera looked at Jamie. "You have?"

Jamie shifted in her seat. "Um, well—"

"You never mentioned it to me," a very peeved Vera interrupted. "You've always come to me with your ideas."

The woman looked from Vera to Jamie. "I didn't mean to cause friction. Perhaps we should discuss this in private, Miss Swift."

Vera took offense. "*Miss Swift* doesn't keep secrets from me. I know more about what's going on around here than anyone else." She tossed Jamie a dark look. "At least I thought I did."

Jamie couldn't mask her confusion. "Vera, please, not now."

But Vera was not deterred. "First, you take the

personals section away from me because you don't trust me, and now *this*. I should quit. I should hand in my resignation and go on one of those senior citizens' cruises that serves seven meals a day. I could meet a nice widower, and sow a few wild oats. I still have a few oats left, you know."

"Vera—" Jamie fought the urge to crawl beneath her desk. They were acting anything but professional. But she knew better than to argue. In Vera's mind, Jamie was still an unruly kid who'd never been properly disciplined by her father.

"Seven meals a day?" Destiny said. "That's a lot of food. I would bust right out of my clothes."

"You're *already* busting out of your clothes," Vera said. She turned to Jamie. "On second thought, I'm *not* quitting, because I've been here longer than anyone, and I'm not going to risk losing my benefits. Furthermore, you *can't* fire me. It was your daddy, God rest his soul, who hired me, not you." She gave a huff and marched from the room, but not before slamming the door behind her.

"Uh-oh, I blew it," Destiny said.

Jamie turned to her visitor. She was intrigued. "Please sit down, Miss Moultrie," she said, using her professional voice. She smiled serenely, as though it were an everyday occurrence for her secretary to pitch a fit. Okay, so it *was* an everyday occurrence, she reminded herself. Vera was probably out front right now polishing her .38.

"Please call me Destiny," the woman said. She took one of the chairs directly across from Jamie's desk. "I'm sorry for barging in like this, but I sensed you would be making a decision soon, and I wanted to be the first to apply."

Jamie merely looked at her.

"You *have* been thinking about starting an advice column, right?" Without warning, the woman smacked her forehead. "Oh, man, I hope I'm not in the wrong place."

"The wrong place?" Jamie realized she was repeating a lot of what was being said.

Destiny pulled out a small notebook and flipped through several pages. "Is your middle name Leigh?"

Jamie nodded. "Yes. It was my mother's first name." Now why had she gone and given out personal information to some stranger she'd probably never see again?

"Yeah, I know about your mother. She walked out when you were still in diapers."

Jamie arched both brows. "Excuse me, but I don't see the point of all this."

Destiny looked up. "Sorry. I shouldn't have mentioned the part about your mother. I know you still find it painful at times."

"What else do you know?"

"There's an old tire swing hanging in your back yard, am I right?"

Jamie snapped her fingers. "I've got it. You're a private investigator, aren't you? Who hired you, and for what reason?"

"No, I'm not. Just answer this one last question. Do you have a bar of Dove soap in your lingerie drawer?"

Jamie felt the color drain from her face. "Who are you? How do you know about the soap?"

"I just do."

Jamie leveled her gaze at the woman. Her astonishment had an edge of anger to it. "Tell me more about the soap."

"Are you sure?" When Jamie nodded, she went on. "The scent reminds you of your mother, even though you remember little else about her."

Jamie felt the goose bumps rise on her arms. She was quiet for a moment. "I'm going to ask you again. How do you know this?"

The woman sighed. "I'm psychic. Sort of."

Jamie did a gigantic eye-roll. "Sort of? What does that mean?"

"I have visions, and I'm right a lot of the time, unless I'm under a lot of stress, then I might make a mistake now and then. It's a simple case of performance anxiety; sort of like sex. But I get it right more often than not."

Jamie sighed. It was really turning out to be a weird morning. First Vera with her brownies, and now she was conversing with a woman who claimed to be psychic. She had time for neither because she had to concentrate on getting a newspaper out. "Miss Moultrie, um, Destiny—"

"I'm working on getting better," Destiny said. "I practice every night." She paused. "You don't believe in psychics, do you?"

"Not exactly."

"See, I knew that." The woman licked the tip of her finger and drew a short imaginary line in the air as though marking her success. Turquoise rings circled every finger, bracelets jangled on her wrists. "There are a lot of phonies out there. Some claim to be one hundred percent accurate. There's no such thing."

"I wasn't, um, looking for a psychic. Just an advice columnist." There. She'd gone and admitted it.

"You've already got 'Dear Abby.' "

"My column was going to be for locals only. To sort of complement—"

"Your new personals section," Destiny said. "People would be more intrigued by a psychic. And I've got the perfect name for it. 'The Divine Love

Goddess Advisor.'" She pulled out an envelope and handed it to Jamie. "Why don't you look over my résumé and give it some thought. I wouldn't be able to start for a day or two since I just moved here and have to unpack. But I travel light."

Jamie shifted uneasily in her chair. "Why Beaumont, South Carolina?" she asked. "This town isn't exactly a booming metropolis. And the *Gazette* is rather small."

"I was sent here for a reason," Destiny said. "I'd never even heard of this place, but it came to me in a vision. So I used a small pendulum, and Beaumont came up on the map. I had to use a magnifying glass to see it, but now I'm sure I'm in the right place. Well, pretty sure."

Jamie simply nodded. She figured it was best to humor the woman until she could get rid of her.

Destiny smiled. "I know it's a lot to take in, but you can rest easy, my column will bring in many new readers."

"You know this for a fact?"

"Yep. I also have a very good feeling you're going to hire me. This interview is just a formality."

Jamie had no intention of hiring her. The last thing she needed was some kook working for her. "I'll have to think about it. I'll keep your résumé on file in the meantime."

"I know you have doubts," Destiny went on as

though she hadn't heard. "And I don't blame you. This newspaper is very important to you after what you've been through. You've struggled for so long to keep it going. I admire your tenacity, Jamie, but you have to stop comparing yourself to your grandfather."

Once again, Jamie felt the tiny hairs on her arm prickle. "What do you know about my grandfather?"

"He started this newspaper from nothing and did extremely well. He passed it on to your father when he died, but your father didn't fare so well. He never wanted to be a newspaperman to begin with."

"You're pretty good," Jamie said, "but this is a small town where everybody knows everybody's business. You'd only have to ask around to get your information." Even as she said it, she wondered how the woman had found out about the soap in her dresser drawer. She decided to humor her. "While you're at it, tell me this. There's this man in my life."

"Yeah, I know all about him. He sort of saved your behind when you had financial problems so he's a silent partner. You're afraid of falling in love with him, but I would advise you to follow your heart."

"How does *he* feel?" Jamie surprised herself by asking.

Destiny looked thoughtful. "He's hard to read." Suddenly, she sneezed.

"Bless you," Jamie said.

Destiny's eyes watered, and she sneezed again. "You'll have to forgive me. This always happens when I start picking up on stuff. Do you have a tissue?"

"Don't you know?"

"Look, I can't be expected to know *everything*."

Jamie reached into her side drawer and pulled out a small box of tissues and handed it to her, just as Destiny let out another sneeze.

"I have to go before it gets worse." The woman stood and wiped her eyes. "Oh, by the way, I'm not going to charge you for my services. I've been married five times so I get plenty of alimony. This is just a hobby."

"Five husbands, huh?"

Another sneeze. "Yeah, and I'm not even forty years old. A girl has to work fast to rack up that many husbands in such a short period."

Jamie sat back and studied her. "Didn't you know the marriages were going to fail?"

Sniff, sniff, sneeze. "I was in love with them at the time, so what could I do? How about you call me when you're ready for me to start? My new number is on my résumé." She made for the door, and then paused. "This man you're thinking about?"

Jamie remained silent.

"He's going to be back in your life very soon."

Jamie perked. "And?"

"Fireworks."

Jamie arched one brow. "Fireworks?"

Destiny smiled. "Fireworks."

CHAPTER TWO

VERA EYED DESTINY SUSPICIOUSLY AS SHE STEPPED into the reception area. "It was very nice meeting you, Vera," Destiny said, dabbing her nose with a tissue. She sneezed several times as she made her way toward the front door. She opened it, and then turned. "By the way, I'm sorry you're having car trouble."

Vera hitched her chin high. "Excuse me? There's not a darn thing wrong with my car."

Destiny shrugged. "Whatever." She hurried out.

"What was all *that* about?" Vera demanded when Jamie stepped out of her office. "Am I fired?"

"Don't be ridiculous, you'll still be here when I'm dead and gone. I was thinking about starting an advice column now that our personals section is doing so well."

"Why wasn't I told?"

"Because I haven't made up my mind."

Vera frowned. "Then how—"

Jamie was beginning to feel weary. "Destiny Moultrie is psychic. Or so she says."

Vera pursed her lips. "Oh, good grief, you don't believe in that hocus-pocus, do you?"

"She was very convincing, but, no, I think it's all a crock." That didn't mean she didn't feel uneasy about some of what Destiny had told her.

"Hogwash, that's what it is," Vera said. "And that woman needs to get on allergy medication. One of these days she's going to sneeze too hard, and those T-I-T-S are going to pop a button, and somebody is going to get hurt."

JAMIE WAITED UNTIL AFTER LUNCH TO CHECK ON Fleas. The vet's assistant assured her the surgery had gone well. "You can pick him up in the morning," she said. "We'll give you a list of things to look out for during his recovery. You're going to have to make sure his stitches don't pull free, and he's not going to be able to go for walks for about ten days."

"That shouldn't be a problem," Jamie said, "since all he does is eat and sleep."

Jamie hung up a moment later. Stitches? Recovery? She did a mental eye-roll as she imagined Fleas lying on her sofa with an IV of ice cream dripping into his veins. Once again, she reminded herself she was not the perfect pet owner. But what could she do? The animal refused to eat the healthy dog food she bought for him. He preferred cheeseburgers, fries, butter pecan ice cream, and Krispy Kreme doughnuts. And Jamie, who practically lived on junk food, ate the same things.

She told herself that despite their bad eating habits, as best she could figure, they were close to getting in the four food groups.

THE REST OF THE DAY PASSED QUICKLY FOR JAMIE, approving layouts for the newspaper and getting it to print. She had begun working for her father at the newspaper—performing small jobs after school like emptying wastepaper baskets and keeping pencils sharpened—since first grade, earning three dollars per week. Looking back, she realized he'd preferred bringing her to the office instead of leaving her with a baby-sitter.

As she'd grown, so had her duties, and, until she'd gone off to college to study journalism, she'd worked in every department, earning little money but loving the work so much that she would have done it for free. She'd earned extra cash by selling subscriptions, which her father claimed she had a knack for, what with her big blue eyes, blond hair, and winning smile.

"You're like your grandpa," her father had told her not long before he'd died. "You've got ink running through your veins. You love this newspaper as much as he did. You'll do well by it."

Jamie smiled fondly at the thought, the good old days, when she and her father had worked side by side in order to make deadlines. And thinking of her father brought Destiny Moultrie to mind once more. The woman was about as strange as they came, but just thinking about all she'd known of Jamie's life gave her a bad case of heebie-jeebies. Jamie's father had *not* wanted to be a newspaperman, and the paper had suffered as a consequence. Jamie had begged and pleaded for permission to leave college in order to relieve him of some of the work, but he had absolutely refused to let her quit. Somehow his staff, all of them as devoted as Vera, had been invaluable in seeing that the paper made it to print on time.

Jamie couldn't help but wonder how Destiny had managed to get as much information as she had, but she knew there had to be a logical explanation. There were gossips in town who would be only too happy to share what they knew.

Except for one thing, she reminded herself, the soap in her drawer. That couldn't be explained.

JAMIE AND VERA HEADED OUT THE FRONT DOOR shortly after five P.M. Jamie lingered beside Vera's car, in no hurry to go home to an empty house. She hadn't realized just how much she'd come to depend on Fleas's company.

"You headed any place in particular?" she asked Vera as the woman slid into the driver's seat of her old Buick.

"We usually have church on Wednesday night," Vera said, "but we're having Vacation Bible School so that's out. Maybe I'll bake a cake for my sick neighbor. What about you?"

"Oh, I've got a million things to do," Jamie lied. "You know me, busy, busy." Jamie tried to think of what she could do to pass the evening.

Vera closed her door and rolled down the window. "This car is hotter'n Hades. Next car I buy is going to have a decent air conditioner."

Jamie continued to stand there. "Well, then, you have a nice evening."

Vera nodded, stabbed her key into the ignition, and turned it. Nothing happened. "What in the world? It was running fine this morning." She tried again. The car didn't respond.

"Uh-oh," Jamie said. "Sounds like you're having car trouble. Sounds like the starter."

Jamie's eyes widened. The two women locked gazes. "Uh-oh," she said.

"Don't be ridiculous," Vera said, as if reading her mind. "It's just a coincidence."

• • •

AN HOUR LATER, JAMIE LED VERA INTO HER GARAGE where a red 1964½ Mustang convertible sat. With the exception of the color, it was an exact replica of the one Jamie had received from her father as a graduation present years before, only hers was white. Even though she'd spent a lot of money maintaining it, she still drove it with pride and wouldn't have thought of replacing it. It was in that very garage that Jamie had helped her father rebuild old cars, and each time he sold one, he'd tucked the money into her college fund.

Vera stepped up to the car and ran her hand along the hood. "It looks like it just rolled off the show-room floor. Are you sure Max won't mind if I borrow it? I mean, he bought it for you. It was a gift."

Jamie shrugged. "He only bought it because it was his fault mine was riddled with bullet holes." Luckily, it had since been repaired.

Vera shook her head sadly. "Do you know how strange that sounds? How many people send their cars to a body shop with bullet holes? That is precisely why I think Max Holt is the wrong man for you. I appreciate what he did for this town, but trouble seems to follow him everywhere."

Jamie figured it was best not to get into a debate with Vera over Max. Not that Max couldn't charm Vera's Hush Puppies right off her feet, mind you, but nobody had ever been good enough for Jamie as far as Vera was concerned. It didn't matter that Max was filthy stinking rich and turned every female's head between the ages of eighteen and eighty; he was a moving target for con men, bad guys, and the mob.

What Jamie also wouldn't tell Vera was that Max was more dangerous to her heart than any other body part. The three weeks she'd gone without seeing him seemed like forever. She knew he was a busy man—his company, Holt Industries, had offices all over the world—but surely he could have found time to pick up a telephone.

"So, you wanna take it for a spin?" Jamie said, chasing Max from her thoughts.

Vera opened the door. "Oh, Lord, it's a stick shift. I haven't driven one of those in years."

"All you need is a little practice."

Twenty minutes later, they were cruising Main Street with the top down, Vera grinning like a sixteen-year-old who'd just gotten her driver's license. "Hey, I'm pretty good at this," she said, shifting the gear into first after pausing at a stop sign.

Jamie grinned, as well. "See, I told you you'd pick it up in no time."

Vera glanced at her. "I don't look silly, do I? I mean, me driving around in such a snazzy car at my age. I'm no spring chicken, you know."

Jamie looked at her. Vera's beehive had already

lost its hairpins and fallen to her shoulders, but the excitement in her eyes made up for her mussed hair. "You look great. And, no, you do not look silly." If anything she looked younger.

The woman hitched her chin high. "I want to take it around the courthouse square again. Maybe I'll see somebody I know."

Jamie smiled at Vera's enthusiasm. She had to admit it was more fun riding around town with her than sitting home alone worrying about Fleas.

Vera circled the square. The downtown area had received a face-lift in the past couple of years. Each shop owner had painted his or her store in what was referred to as an historic color. They'd added awnings and massive flowerpots out front, hoping to draw business from the strip mall on the outskirts of town.

Jamie knew the town well. Despite changes to the outside, the Downtown Café still served the best coffee in town, and she knew the regulars who gathered first thing in the morning for the $2.99 breakfast special of eggs and bacon and the best homemade biscuits she'd ever tasted. There was Coot Hathaway's doughnut shop where you could buy glazed doughnuts straight from the oven and sticky buns that stuck to the roof of your mouth and chocolate mocha doughnuts that were her personal favorite. And nobody made better sandwiches than

Donnie Maynard, who owned the local sandwich shop. He bought his bread fresh from Sunshine Bakery, and his meat-loaf sandwiches, served cold, always drew a crowd. He used a secret ingredient that he swore he would take to his grave, and no matter how hard folks tried they couldn't figure it out.

The courthouse square was as quaint as it had been in Jamie's younger days. People still fed pigeons or read the daily newspaper or gathered in small groups to catch up on the latest gossip. The Garden Club had replaced the old shrubbery with new—in late spring, the azaleas blazed with color in every imaginable hue. Fall brought with it colorful mums, and pansies were planted in winter. Even the bandstand had been given a fresh coat of white paint.

"Oh, look!" Vera said. "There's Robyn Decker and Betty Hamilton from my Sunday school class. Wait'll they get a look at me in this hot car." Vera braked and tapped the horn several times, and the women looked up. They gaped in surprise and hurried over. Both wore lightweight jogging outfits and sneakers.

"Vera, is that you?" Betty said. She was tall and slender and wore a mop of short gray curls that had obviously been sprayed into place because not one strand strayed.

"What in heaven's name are you doing in that

car?" Robyn asked. Her hair was the same light gray, on the frizzy side, tucked back with hair combs. She was on the heavy side. A sheen of perspiration coated her forehead.

"I'm taking a test-drive," Vera said, winking at Jamie. "Ya'll want to cruise with us?"

The two women looked at one another. "Sure," Betty said. "It's too hot to try to get our exercise."

Jamie had to agree. Not only was it hot, the humidity hung over the town like a woolen blanket. She got out of the car, and pulled back the seat so the two women could climb in. "Fasten your seat belts," she said, once they'd settled themselves and Jamie reclaimed the front seat.

"You sure you know how to drive this thing?" Robyn asked.

"Vera drives it like a pro," Jamie told her.

They shot off, and the women in the back seat giggled like teenagers. "Hey, maybe we can pick up some guys," Betty said.

Robyn Decker gasped. "Why, Betty Hamilton, I don't believe what just came out of your mouth. You know we can't fit any men into this back seat, what with the size of my rear end." More giggles.

"Holy marolly," Vera called out. "There's Maxine Chambers's new store." She whipped the Mustang into a parking slot directly in front.

All four women leaned forward as if trying to get

a closer look from where they were sitting. Finally, Jamie opened her door.

"Where are you going?" Vera asked.

"I want to check it out."

Double gasps from the back seat. "What if somebody sees you?" Betty said.

Jamie shrugged. "Aw, come on, ladies. The ground is not going to open up and swallow us just for looking."

"I don't care if the ground does swallow me up," Vera said. "I figure it's worth it." She pulled the seat forward, and the two in back reluctantly climbed out.

All four women hurried to the front of the store and gazed at the window display.

"Oh, my," Betty said. "I can't believe a proper Southern woman like Maxine would fill her window with unmentionables. What are our young people going to think? It might be dangerous. It might raise the testerone level in some of the boys, and that could spell trouble."

"Testosterone," Jamie corrected. "And I seriously doubt it's something they've never seen before. You know how inquisitive boys can be."

Vera eyed the merchandise. "I don't think I would even know how to wear some of this stuff."

Jamie perused the items in the window, making a mental list of what she planned to buy. "Maybe Maxine provides a list of instructions." But she was as surprised as the others that Maxine Chambers would actually open a sexy lingerie shop. Maxine had always been on the prudish side.

"What are those lacy things hanging over there?" Vera asked. "Between the garter belts and the see-through bras."

Jamie followed her gaze. "Those are thong bikini underwear."

Vera arched both brows. "They don't look as though they would do much good in covering your behind. Why, if a cold wind blew up your skirt—"

"Oh, Lord, ya'll are *not* going to believe who is heading our way," Robyn said.

Betty turned. "Oh, heavenly days, it's Agnes Aimsley and her grandson. The jig is up."

Jamie turned as Agnes, frail and white-haired, inched her way toward them. Her sneakers looked out of place with her prim dress. The man beside her, a twenty-something preppie type, had her arm tucked through his protectively. His brown hair was cropped short, and he wore oversized tortoiseshell glasses that had gone out of style long ago.

Vera looked grim. "Agnes teaches our Sunday school class," she told Jamie. "You may have heard she had a heart attack last year. She's such a devout Christian that she'll have another one if she sees what's in Maxine's window."

"We're talking de-vout," Betty emphasized. "If

she dies, Jesus is going to have to move over and let her sit next to God. I'll bet that's her grandson. I hear he's one of those religious fanatics. I hear he can be a real cuckoo clock at times."

"Hello, ladies," Agnes called out pleasantly. "I see you're taking advantage of the nice weather the good Lord has provided."

"Um, hello, Agnes," Vera said.

Jamie tried to suppress a smile as Vera, Betty, and Robyn backed against the store window, no doubt attempting to block it from Agnes's view.

"Have ya'll met my grandson, Brent Walker? He's visiting for the summer while on break from Emory University where he is studying to be one of God's messengers."

They all shook hands. "Very nice to meet you, ladies," Brent said politely. He glanced up at the sign hanging over the window. Agnes looked up as well.

" 'Sinful Delights,' " she read aloud, and suddenly smiled. "I didn't know we had a new chocolate shop in town. I hope they sell Godiva, that's my favorite. Scoot over, I want to see."

She and Vera did a little jig as Vera tried to stop her from looking past her.

"Believe me, Agnes, you're better off not knowing," Betty said.

Jamie cleared her throat and tried to remain straight-faced. The grandson looked confused.

"Perhaps we should move on," Brent said, as if taking his cue from the looks on the women's faces.

Agnes wasn't deterred. "Would you ladies please step aside so I can see what's in the window?"

It was like the parting of the Red Sea, Jamie decided, watching Vera, Betty, and Robyn clear the way so Agnes could step closer. "Oh, my," she said. Her eyes glazed over in shock.

Brent's face turned a deep red. "What is the meaning of this?" he demanded. "Who would open such a place?"

Vera started to answer, but he cut her off and pulled a small tablet from his back pocket.

"I demand to know the name of the owner."

"Maxine Chambers," Betty supplied. "Actually, we're shocked, as well."

He scribbled the name on his pad. "This place looks like something straight out of Sodom and Gomorrah. I'm going to have a talk with this Chambers woman. I feel it's my Christian duty."

"Would somebody please explain what *those* are," Agnes said, pointing to a pair of underwear.

"They're edible undies," Jamie said, only to have Brent glare at her. Jamie shrugged. "Well, she asked."

"Edible undies?" Agnes said. "I don't understand." Suddenly, as if a lightbulb had gone off in her head, she gasped and covered her breast with both hands as if to keep her heart from leaping out. "Oh, my."

"Let's go, Gram," Brent said, taking her by the arm. And not a moment too soon. Agnes swayed and fell into a dead faint.

Brent caught her in his arms. "Somebody call 911!"

"WELL, THANK GOD IT WASN'T A HEART ATTACK," Vera said when she dropped Jamie off at her house two hours later, after sitting in the ER waiting on word of Agnes's condition.

"It was probably a good idea that her doctor decided to keep her overnight for observation anyway," Jamie said. "I'll tell you, that grandson of hers is a nut."

"Yeah, he's a real fruitcake," Vera said, putting the gear into neutral. "Oh, by the way, you're not feeling a little weird, are you?"

"What do you mean?"

"You know, from eating those brownies?"

"You mean horny?"

Vera rolled her eyes. "Yeah, that."

Jamie decided she wouldn't tell Vera she got horny every time she thought of tall, dark, and drop-dead gorgeous Max Holt. "Yeah, I'm feeling a little frisky," Jamie confessed, although she suspected it was just her imagination. "I'm thinking maybe a cold shower is in order."

Vera sighed. "I'm thinking the same thing. Must be my wild oats acting up."

JAMIE ARRIVED AT WORK THE NEXT MORNING, JUST as Destiny Moultrie climbed from a cream-colored Mercedes. The woman hurried over.

"I know I promised to give you a day or two to think about the column," she began, "but I'm anxious to get started."

Moultrie was dressed in silk khaki-colored slacks and a matching jacket that hung open to expose a tight purple bustier that barely contained her breasts. "Cleavage" seemed to be Destiny's middle name.

"I'm really busy," Jamie said.

"I was hoping we could talk it over this morning. And I'd like to discuss another matter with you. It's pretty important."

Jamie did a mental sigh. That meant all the doughnuts would be eaten by the time she got to the small kitchen in back, but she figured she at least owed Destiny the truth. She had no intention of hiring a psychic for her column, even if there was to be a column, which she hadn't decided on one way or the other.

"I can only afford a few minutes," she said.

"I knew you'd say that." Destiny followed her to the front double-glass doors.

Vera looked up the minute they stepped inside. Her gaze immediately fell on Destiny. "How did you know I was going to have car trouble?"

Destiny shrugged. "I just had a feeling. I didn't want you to find yourself stranded."

"You didn't tamper beneath my hood, did you?"

"Vera!" Jamie said. "That was not a nice thing to say."

"It happens all the time," Destiny said. "People don't want to believe in things they can't see."

Vera gave a grunt. "So what's it going to cost me to get my car repaired?"

Destiny shrugged. "I have no idea."

Vera looked at Jamie. "See, I told you there was nothing to this psychic stuff."

"What I meant to say," Destiny began slowly, "is I have no idea how much a new engine costs."

"A new engine!" Vera cried.

"Man, that's going to cost you," Jamie said, then caught herself. What was she thinking?

"New engine, my foot," Vera said. "There's not a darn thing wrong with my engine."

"Maybe we should step into my office," Jamie said, motioning Destiny inside.

The woman followed. Jamie paused at the door and glanced back at Vera. "Has Mike come in yet?" Mike Henderson was Jamie's fresh-out-of-college editor. She was trying to raise him to be a real newspaperman since he was organizationally challenged and spent much of his time chasing women.

"He's covering the city council meeting, and then he has an appointment to interview the new high school football coach."

Jamie nodded and closed the door. She turned and almost bumped into Destiny.

"I have something to tell you," the woman said.

Jamie took the chair behind her desk and motioned for Destiny to sit. "What is it?"

"Last night I had a vision. You were in it. There was a man with you."

Jamie perked up and thought of Max. "Oh, yeah? Were we naked?" She slapped her hand against her forehead. Now why had she gone and said something like that? The last thing she needed to do was encourage the woman.

"It wasn't that kind of vision," Destiny said. "This man was in uniform, and he was asking you a lot of questions."

Jamie remained quiet.

Destiny didn't seem deterred by her silence. "The situation was, um, dire, because I had this heavy feeling in my chest afterward."

Jamie figured any woman with Destiny's breasts would have a heavy feeling in her chest. She sighed. "Okay, Destiny, I'll play along. Who was asking these questions and what were they?"

"I don't know." At Jamie's look, Destiny went on. "Hey, I'm doing my best here, okay? I can't give you every little detail." All at once she glanced to the chair beside her. "Shut up, okay? I don't need your help."

Jamie's eyes widened as she followed Destiny's gaze to the empty chair. "Uh, Destiny, who are you talking to?" she asked.

The woman didn't hesitate. "His name is Ronnie. He's from the spirit world. He doesn't have enough sense to know he's dead. Follows me everywhere."

Jamie gripped the arms on her chair as chills raced up her spine. Time to bolt, she told herself.

"He's just an old redneck, don't worry, he's harmless." She glanced back at the empty chair. "Yes, you heard me right, Ronnie, you *are* a redneck. Anybody who gets sloppy drunk and falls out of the back of a pickup truck doing sixty miles per hour is a bona fide redneck in my book." She looked at Jamie. "That's how he died. He's kinda between worlds."

"Oh, well, that certainly explains it." Jamie glanced at the door. It would take her less than three seconds to reach it if she ran like hell.

"Hey, I know it sounds crazy," Destiny said, "but

that's the way it is. I have dead people show up all the time. They don't usually stay long. So, when do you want me to start?"

Jamie blinked. "Huh?"

"The job? I got a lot of my stuff unpacked last night so I'm ready to roll."

Jamie decided the woman had enough problems so she tried to let her down easy. "I'm thinking maybe I should hold off on the column," she said. What Jamie was actually thinking was that Destiny needed to be hauled off in a straitjacket.

"I suggest you announce the new column in your newspaper as soon as possible."

"Well, like I said—"

Destiny sighed in exasperation. "Dammit, Ronnie, would you *please* stop yakking and let me finish this conversation?" She shifted in her chair and regarded Jamie. "Look, I don't have all day. Let's do this. Run the announcement. If you don't get a substantial amount of responses, I promise I won't bother you again."

Once again, Jamie glanced at the chair beside Destiny. "Does he follow you everywhere?" she asked, thinking it would be best to have all the facts before she reported the woman to the authorities.

"Who, Ronnie?" Destiny sighed. "Hell, I can't even take a shower without the pervert getting in there with me. But don't worry; as soon as his pea brain realizes he needs to move on, he'll be out of my life." She rolled her eyes. "Dead people," she said on a sigh. "They can be such a pain in the ass." All at once, she sneezed. "Uh-oh, gotta run before I go into a sneezing frenzy." She stood and made for the door. "I'll call you later."

Jamie stopped her. "Um, Destiny?"

She turned. "Yeah?"

Jamie almost felt sorry for her. "How about I call you when I've made my decision? In the meantime, don't tell Vera about your friend, okay?"

"VERA, I NEED TO RUN AN ERRAND," JAMIE SAID, shortly after Destiny left. "I won't be long."

"No problem, I'll hold down the fort."

Jamie picked up her pocketbook and left the building, hurrying down the street toward Maxine Chambers's shop. She couldn't wait to see what was inside. She opened the door and stepped in, and was greeted by the smell of lavender.

Maxine was standing behind the counter. She had changed her mousy brown hair to a flattering red and wore makeup, something she had never bothered with when she'd worked at the library.

"Well, Jamie Swift, it's wonderful to see you again, only this time we don't have to whisper like we did at the library."

"I just came by to offer my congratulations on your new store," Jamie said.

Maxine smiled. "Well, you're the first. Everyone else is shocked that I would do such a thing, and some preacher wannabe is calling constantly, accusing me of corrupting the town. And get this; he wants to meet with me so he can pray for my soul. I told him to take a hike."

Jamie knew Brent Walker had been the one to call. "I'm sure it's going to take time for some folks to adjust. I'd just ignore him." She glanced around. "Now then, why don't you show me around? I've been dying to come in."

"What did you have in mind?"

"I'm not sure. Something a little sexy." She thought of the edible underwear. "Without going overboard," she added.

"Come on and let me show you my new European lace collection. They're elegant but simple. Sexy *and* classy," she added.

Jamie followed her to an aisle where Maxine held up the most beautiful bras and panties she'd ever seen. "Oh, my," she said.

"Aren't they lovely?" Maxine said proudly. "And look at this baby doll sleepwear in satin. Think how nice that would feel against your skin."

Jamie ran her hand against the material. "I've never felt anything so nice."

"I agree," Maxine said. "This is top-of-the-line. Oh, and I've got these beautiful teddies and body suits. Aren't they wonderful? And you've got just the figure for them."

"Why, thank you, Maxine." Jamie paused and studied the woman. "I don't mean to be nosy, Maxine, but what made you decide to open a lingerie store?"

The woman smiled. "I guess I'm the last person in the world people would expect to find running a store like this, but it's always been a secret fantasy of mine. So one morning I woke up and reminded myself I wasn't getting any younger, and that's when I started getting serious about it. Unfortunately, I haven't had a lot of customers since I opened."

"Then you'll have to let me write an article about your store," Jamie said, "along with a nice advertisement. It'll be my celebration gift to you."

"Why, thank you, Jamie. That's very kind of you. You know, I've always liked you. You were so careful with your library books. You never dog-eared the pages like some folks, and you always brought them back on time." She sniffed. "Not all people respect books like you do. Why, I could tell you stories—"

"Show me what else you've got," Jamie said, wanting to change the subject. Maxine probably did have a lot of stories, but she didn't have time to listen to them.

Maxine gave her a complete tour of the store. In the end, Jamie selected a number of items from the European collection.

"Good choice," Maxine said, "and since you're one of my first customers, I'm going to give you a ten percent discount." She rang up the merchandise, then wrapped the bras, panties, sleepwear, and body suits in tissue paper and put them in a beautiful lavender-colored bag.

Jamie handed her a check. "Why don't we meet for lunch early next week so we can talk about your store?" she said. "In the meantime, I'll send my editor over to get a picture of you for the ad."

Maxine looked pleased. "Well, now, I think that would be quite nice. You just call me when it's convenient."

"I'll check my calendar and get back to you." Jamie left the store a few minutes later with her purchases and walked by the bakery, thinking how good a brownie would taste right about now. She didn't really believe they contained an aphrodisiac, but on the off chance they did, she'd better steer clear of them. Her libido was giving her enough trouble these days.

And that made her think of Max. She wondered when she would see him again. At the same time, she questioned why she had allowed herself to become so involved. She knew very little about the man except that he was a gazillionaire who owned a whole slew of companies and had dated his share of celebrities. She knew he'd once been married, but that it hadn't worked out, and it was probably one of the reasons he wasn't in a hurry to marry again.

What she didn't know was how she felt about their situation. After an engagement gone badly, Jamie had pretty much decided marriage wasn't in the cards for her, at least not in the near future. But now she was beginning to have second thoughts, and it was all because of Max. Knowing herself as she did, she was aware that she wasn't cut out for the short-term flings Max was accustomed to. She wanted more.

Damn. She had tried so hard not to fall for him. She had fought her growing attraction to him every step of the way, only to realize that she was beginning to entertain thoughts of a possible future with him.

As she saw it, she had two choices. She could try to get the man out of her system and wonder for the rest of her life if anything would have become of them or she could continue to wait.

Neither option sounded particularly appealing.

CHAPTER THREE

HAPPY PAWS VETERINARY CLINIC WAS DECORATED with vinyl chairs and floors, obviously to make it easier to clean up after nervous cats and dogs. Which explained the strong disinfectant smell, Jamie thought upon entering the reception area shortly after lunch. Some furry friend had either suffered a sudden loss of bladder control or heaved up a helping of meat chunks. From somewhere in back, a cacophony of barking persisted.

As Jamie waited for the receptionist to get off the telephone, she studied the large bulletin board that served as a lost-and-found center. Another bulletin board listed a variety of puppies and kittens to sell or give away.

She thought of adding Fleas's name to the list. Owning a pet was more trouble than she'd thought. Only, she couldn't think of a person who'd want to take on a dog with emotional problems and missing hair.

When the receptionist hung up the phone, she smiled at Jamie. "Oh, you're Fleas's mommy, aren't you?" the woman said in a voice that sounded too small and squeaky for someone who appeared to be at least one hundred pounds overweight.

"That's me," Jamie said.

"Hold on one sec, hon, and I'll get him."

Fleas did not look happy to see Jamie, but then the sagging brown skin and folds along the hound's face and jowls gave him a perpetual look of sadness and discontent. This time it seemed to be mixed with outright annoyance.

Oh, great, she thought. He's pouting.

"Okeydokey," the receptionist said. "His heartworm test was negative, so you can give him his first dose today, then he has to take one every month. You'll need to mark your calendar."

"He won't eat it," Jamie said dully. "Unless I can hide it in his ice cream."

The woman laughed as though it were the funniest thing she'd ever heard. "Oh, dogs love them," she insisted. "It comes in a meatlike treat."

"Can I put it between a hamburger bun with cheese on top?"

More laughter. Which was rather annoying for Jamie since she was serious.

"And then there's the flea preventive. You'll want to apply it once a month. It'll be easier to remember if you do it at the same time you give him his monthly heartworm medicine. I gave you a six-month supply of each. That's what people usually request." She hesitated and looked about the room as if to make sure nobody was listening. "Have you ever owned a pet, hon?" she whispered.

Was it that obvious? Jamie wondered. "This is my first, um, experience."

"There's a booklet inside his goody bag. It'll give you all sorts of information. And you can call us if you run into problems."

Jamie pulled out her checkbook and pen. "How much do I owe?"

"Well, now, let's see." The woman pulled up the information on the computer. "He had a full exam, we clipped his toenails, took blood for the heartworm test, performed the surgery—" She looked up. "We expressed his anal glands. I have to tell you, it wasn't pretty. Our technician had to go home for the rest of the day." She burst into giggles. "Just kidding."

Fleas sank to the floor and covered both eyes with his paws.

Jamie tightened her grip on the pen as she prepared to write the check. This was going to be bad.

"Oh, and there was a charge for anesthesia, of course, and his nerve pills."

"Nerve pills?"

"You mentioned he had a bad case of separation anxiety. Don't worry, Dr. Adams started him on a teensy-weensy dose, but it should take the edge off. Try giving it to Fleas with peanut butter. It's easier that way."

Jamie looked at Fleas. The dog had serious emotional problems, including shell shock from his coon-hunting days.

The woman behind the counter looked up from her computer. "Okeydokey, it comes to four hundred and eight dollars."

Jamie's eyes almost popped out of her head. She looked at Fleas. "You realize I paid less than that for the truck."

Fleas rose up on his front legs and shook hard. His long ears flapped annoyingly. Finally, he sat back on his haunches and began to lick himself.

Jamie cringed.

POLICE CHIEF LAMAR TEVIS WAS WAITING FOR Jamie when she arrived back at the office, Fleas on her heels. The serious look on the man's face told her something was wrong. He held his cap in his hands, and his sandy-colored hair was still flat from wearing it. Vera was on the telephone. She shrugged at Jamie as though she had no idea why the chief of police wanted to see her.

"Hello, Lamar," Jamie said. "May I help you?"

He glanced at the bloodhound beside her. "Wow, that's about the ugliest dog I've ever seen. Is he a stray?"

"He belongs to me," Jamie said.

"Sorry, I didn't know he was yours. How come he's missing hair on his back?"

"A raccoon attacked him."

"I didn't know you liked to hunt coons. Why, me and my buddies—"

"It happened before I, um, came into ownership." Jamie saw that Lamar was still staring at her dog as though he were ugly. She hitched her head high. "Actually, he's pure bloodhound. Comes from championship bloodline," she added. It was a lie she told often.

"No kidding. What's his name?"

This was the part Jamie hated most. "Fleas."

"Uh-oh." Lamar stepped back.

"He doesn't actually *have* fleas, somebody just named him that. So what brings you to this neck of the woods, Lamar?"

Lamar glanced at Vera, then back to Jamie. "Perhaps we should talk privately. No offense, Vera."

Vera hung up the telephone. "Like I won't find out," she said. "So you can just kiss my royal behind, Lamar."

"Spoken like a true Southern Baptist," Lamar said with a chuckle.

"Any word from Mike?" Jamie asked, wishing her editor would check in more often. He was probably sweet-talking one of the counter girls at Dairy Queen.

"He called while you were out. Said he was working a hot story and would be in shortly. He wouldn't give me the details, he was acting real secretive and all. You know how dramatic he gets."

Jamie nodded. "Pray for a decent headline." She led Lamar inside her office and closed the door. He waited for Jamie to sit before he took the chair in front of her desk. Fleas plopped down beside Jamie's feet and gave a huge sigh.

"I guess you haven't heard the news," Lamar said. "Luanne Ritter was found murdered in her home late this morning. Suffered a fatal blow to her head," he added.

"Oh, my God!" Jamie said. Luanne Ritter owned Ritter's Loan Company.

"Yup. That's where your editor has been all morning. At the murder scene," he added. "I didn't want to say anything in front of Vera. Not until I gave you the news."

"Do you have a suspect?"

"It's too early to tell. Her neighbor, Elaine something-or-other—" He paused and reached for notes. "Elaine Brewer is her name. Anyway, she went over to Luanne's house to borrow some coffee, knocked several times, but there was no answer. She found the door unlocked and almost tripped over Luanne's body on the kitchen floor. Coroner said Luanne had been dead at least ten or twelve hours. Sounds a little suspicious to me," he added.

"Oh, yeah?"

Lamar leaned closer. "Get this. The neighbor drinks decaf. Luanne drinks only regular coffee. I'd think after being neighbors for ten years this Brewer woman would have known. We've taken her in for questioning."

Jamie just looked at him. Lamar was a good honest man, but he wasn't the smartest investigator she'd ever met. "This is unbelievable," Jamie said.

Lamar glanced up quickly. He looked defensive. "You don't think I'm making this up, do you? The murder, I mean? My men will vouch for me. Your editor, too."

Jamie blinked. "What I meant was it's hard to believe someone just murdered Luanne in cold blood."

"I have the body to prove it. I can take you over to the morgue if you want to see for yourself."

Jamie did a mental eye-roll. "Let's start over, Lamar. What can I do for you?"

Lamar reached into his shirt pocket and pulled out a small section of newspaper. He unfolded it and handed it to Jamie. "This was on Luanne's night table. Nobody knows about it except the responding officer and me. I'd like to keep it that way for now." He pretended to zip his lips. "Get my drift?"

Jamie found herself looking at a copy of her personals section that had been cut out of the newspaper. She glanced at Lamar. "You're not thinking my personals section had something to do with Luanne's murder?"

"There may be nothing to it, but I thought you should know." He leaned back in his chair and crossed one leg over the other. Fleas sat up and began to scratch. Lamar watched, an uneasy expression on his face. "Luanne wasn't very popular in this town," he went on, "what with her line of work. Way I heard, she could lean pretty hard on someone if they were late on their loan payment."

Jamie shook her head as she continued staring at the ads. Her hands trembled. "It has to be business related, Lamar. I think this—" She paused and held up the section of newspaper. "This is just a coincidence."

"Could be. I've sealed her place of business, and we're planning a full investigation. Like I said, I don't want this ad stuff getting out. I just wanted to make you aware." He took it from her, refolded it, and stuffed it into his pocket. "Also, I need your help."

Jamie knew where he was headed. "You know I

can't give you the names of those who've submitted an ad without a court order."

"No judge is going to give me an order to look into every name on your list," he said. "All I'm asking is that you keep an eye out for anything that looks suspicious. In case we have some kook on our hands."

"Yes, of course."

"I do have one other question. Did Luanne run an ad?"

"No."

Lamar shifted in his seat. "She had a message on her answering machine from a man regarding an ad. Said he'd call her back. Unfortunately, Luanne didn't have caller ID, and the tape must've been old because the voices weren't that clear."

"She must've answered his ad."

"She had another call from a fellow who claimed he was a man of God, said he wanted to meet with her immediately. He didn't leave his telephone number, told her he'd call back. Once again, it was hard to make out the message."

"Wonder why he didn't leave his name," Jamie pondered aloud.

"We also found religious literature stuffed inside her mailbox so he obviously knew where she lived."

"Was there any indication of forced entry?"

"No. Luanne opened the door for the person who killed her, so whoever it was must've not presented a threat. She might have opened the door for a preacher. This is all speculation, of course."

Jamie nodded. She thought of Agnes Aimsley's grandson, Brent Walker, then pushed it aside. Brent might be a bit on the kooky side, he might even leave religious material in Luanne's mailbox, but he wasn't a murderer. But she kept quiet, knowing how quickly Lamar could get sidetracked.

"By the way," Lamar said. "Where's Max Holt?"

Jamie would have loved nothing more than to say, "Geez, last time I saw Max he had my skirt shoved to my waist and his hands on my thighs." Instead, she shrugged. "Who knows? He's a busy man."

"He's your partner."

"Max is my *silent* partner, Lamar. I run the newspaper."

"Max is good at this sort of thing. Investigative work," he added.

Jamie was not surprised by the remark. Lamar had witnessed firsthand just how good Max was when he'd almost single-handedly discovered who was involved in the town's corruption, which had bled taxpayers of their dollars for years. "You thinking of hiring him on as a deputy?" she asked, grinning, if for no other reason than to lighten the mood.

Lamar grinned back. "I tried, but he turned down the job. I reckon he has bigger fish to fry."

Despite her attempt at flippancy, Jamie could feel her stomach knotting. "Lamar, tell me you don't really think Luanne's murder is connected to my personals section, because if you think it is, I'll stop running the ads immediately."

"Then we risk losing the killer *if* it's connected. Are you going to help me?"

"I'll do what I can legally."

"That's all I'm asking," Lamar said. He left a few minutes later.

Jamie reached for the telephone. It was time to call Max.

MAX HOLT WAS IN THE BOARDROOM OF HOLT INdustries when he received Jamie's call. He immediately excused himself and hurried into his private office. "What's up, Swifty?"

Jamie had not forgotten the sexy pitch of his voice, or the teasing lilt he often used with her. Just hearing his voice again did all sorts of soft and fuzzy things to her insides. And that reminded her of how little she knew about the man. He moved in mysterious circles, dined with royalty, and made business deals that ended up on the pages of the *New York Times*.

"Max, do you have any idea what I had to go through to reach you?" Jamie said. "I had to bypass a receptionist, a secretary, and your personal assistant, all of whom insisted on knowing my business with you."

"What did you tell them?"

"I said I had a small oil-rich country for sale and that you might be interested in buying it."

He chuckled. "Well, I'm glad you were able to reach me. What's up?"

Jamie wondered how he could sound so casual when every nerve ending in her body was tingling at the sound of his voice. She wondered if he'd thought about her these past weeks. "I have a problem on my hands," she said. She told him about the personals section she had started, Luanne Ritter's murder, and the fact Police Chief Lamar Tevis suspected the two might be connected. She figured, as her partner, Max should know. Okay, so maybe there was more to it than that. It was a good excuse to call him.

"And here I thought you were calling to say you missed me," Max said. "You and I have some unfinished business, you know."

Jamie felt a thrill of delight race up her backbone at the thought. They had come so close the last time. She shook her head, trying to push the image from her mind. "Max, this is serious," she said, wondering how he could just pick up where they'd left off after three weeks of no word.

"Does Lamar Tevis have proof the two are connected?"

"No. But what if they are?"

"Don't assume the worst before we have time to look into the facts," he said. "Listen, I'm driving down tomorrow for Frankie's surprise birthday party. I can't believe my brother-in-law is reaching the big five-oh."

Jamie had received her invitation the week before. Jamie had met Frankie and his wife, Dee Dee, when they'd moved to Beaumont some ten years prior, after Frankie had retired from wrestling as Frankie-the-Assassin. They'd become fast friends, but it was hard to believe Max and Dee Dee were brother and sister. "Of course I'm going," she said.

"My schedule will be tight," Max said, "but I can swing by your house and pick you up on the way."

Jamie took her time in answering. It was no surprise that Max would just assume she would attend the party with him. And on a Friday night of all nights when most reasonably attractive single women had dates. She almost preferred cutting her tongue out with her dull letter opener than telling Max she was dateless.

Be cool, she told herself.

"I, um, didn't know you were coming, Max, so I sort of made other plans," she said, then wanted to smack her own mouth. Her and her dumb pride, she thought. But Max had a way of bringing out the worst in her when it came to male-female stuff.

"Oh, yeah?" He sounded more amused than annoyed. "Well, if we put our heads together I'm sure we can think of a way to ditch him. I have to get back to a meeting and wrap things up here so I can leave, but do me a favor. Wear that blue dress you wore the first night I met you."

Jamie heard a dial tone. She hung up. She felt something nudge her foot and glanced down at Fleas who was watching her. "Okay, so I made up that part about having a date," she said. "Sometimes things just fall out of my mouth before I have time to think about them. Especially when it comes to *that* man," she added.

The dog thumped his tail against the floor.

"It's complicated with Max and me," she went on. "I never know where I stand with him." She couldn't tell Fleas the truth, that she couldn't get Max out of her mind, that she was just itching for the chance to be alone and naked with him. It wouldn't be fair to discuss sex in front of the poor animal since he'd just been neutered. Not that she could imagine Fleas interested in chasing a female dog, since it would take effort on his part. And Fleas was allergic to effort.

Jamie gave a huge sigh. Suddenly, her thoughts took a drastic turn, and she snapped her head up. Holy cow! Destiny Moultrie had warned her she would be talking to a man in a uniform, and it would be bad. She had been right on the money. Jamie picked up the telephone and dialed the woman's number. Destiny answered on the first ring.

"We need to talk," Jamie said.

"I DEMAND TO KNOW WHAT'S GOING ON," VERA said, standing in the doorway of Jamie's office. "And I'm not going to take no for an answer."

Jamie noted the determined look on Vera's face. "You're not armed, are you?" she said.

Vera pressed her lips into a grim line and ignored Jamie's question. "You've never kept secrets from me. Why was Lamar Tevis here? What'd you do now? Are you in trouble with the police?"

Jamie gave a sigh. Why did the woman always assume she'd done something wrong? "Luanne Ritter was murdered."

Vera's brows shot up in surprise. "No kidding? Well, I'm sure she had it coming."

"Vera!"

"Nobody liked her anyway. Folks only borrowed money from her when they were desperate. And Luanne liked to talk. If someone's credit rating was low, she blabbed it all over town. Why, I heard that one of Luanne's employees roughed up a couple of customers who fell behind on their payments. And to think, Luanne's husband, God rest his soul, was such a nice man. If he knew how Luanne treated her customers, he'd have reached right out of his grave and snatched her bald-headed."

"Well, now, that's something to think about," Jamie said, not knowing how to respond.

"I'm telling you, that woman was no better than a loan shark. So why did Lamar come to you?"

Jamie didn't meet her gaze. She didn't like lying to Vera. "Um, Mike was on the crime scene, and Lamar doesn't want vital information printed in the paper."

Vera suddenly looked indignant. "Why didn't Mike call me? I'm the assistant editor. I should have been there to take photos."

"I suppose he felt he had to move fast since it was a murder investigation." Jamie was proud that Mike had made it to the scene. He was a good editor, but his poor time-management skills and sexual exploits had interfered with his work in the past. He now made a concerted effort to get to work on time.

Vera didn't look placated. She sniffed, a definite

sign of annoyance. "Well, I have to leave for a hair appointment," she said. "Helen is going to cover the phones. Besides, I want to be the first to tell everybody at the beauty shop about Luanne."

Five minutes later, Mike rushed into Jamie's office. As usual, his clothes looked as though he'd slept in them. His light brown hair was mussed, as though he'd finger-combed it on his way out of the house. "Have you heard the news?" he asked.

"Yes. Lamar was here earlier."

"I'm going to get right on the story. We're going to have a kick-butt headline. Oh, and you're not going to believe this one. They were hauling Luanne out of her house on a stretcher, and the body bag slipped. Luanne hit the ground."

"Oh, geez. Please don't mention it in your article."

"Lamar almost had a stroke."

"So did Vera when she found out you didn't call her to take pictures."

"Uh-oh. Maybe I should leave town for a couple of days," he said. "By the way, are you going to Frankie Fontana's birthday party tomorrow night? It's the talk of the town, what with him being the new mayor and just turning fifty and all."

"Yeah, I'm going."

"You should take me with you. I could get pictures for the society column."

Jamie hadn't thought of that. Frankie's wife,

Dee Dee, would go all-out for the party, and the photos would fill up space. With the exception of Luanne Ritter's murder, there just wasn't enough going on in Beaumont these days. "You'd have to rent a tux."

"I've already got one. Come on, Jamie, I need a night out. My life is as boring as yours."

"My life is not boring."

"Whatever. So, what do you say?"

Jamie pondered it. At least it meant she wouldn't have to show up alone. Not that she'd ever let that stop her before, but this was different since she'd already told Max she had a date. She had to save face. "Okay, you can go as my escort."

"Your escort? Oh, I get it. You couldn't find a date."

Jamie gave him a look.

"Hey, I understand. It's not like I've never had to scramble to find someone to go with me at the last minute. It's harder for women to go alone, though. They tend to look desperate."

Jamie drummed her fingers on her desk. "Mike, don't you have an article to write?"

"Hello?" a voice called out.

Jamie looked up to find Destiny standing in the doorway. Mike looked, as well. "Well, hello to you," he said, straightening his tie and squaring his shoulders as if to make himself appear taller. "May I help you?" His eyes were fixed on her breasts.

"I'm here to see Jamie."

He went on as if he hadn't heard. "I'm her editor, Mike Henderson." He rubbed a hand over his head, smoothing out his rumpled hair. "You've probably seen my byline."

"Destiny Moultrie," she said in her husky voice. "And, no, I haven't had the pleasure of reading your articles. I've just moved to Beaumont."

"You just moved here?" he repeated. "Well, then you probably haven't had a chance to dine at our best restaurants or see the sights. I could—"

"I don't eat out much," Destiny said. "I'm a vegetarian."

Mike smiled broadly. "A vegetarian? Well, now, isn't that a coincidence. It just so happens I'm a vegetarian, too."

Jamie tried to suppress a smile. Mike lived on fast food and probably wouldn't recognize a zucchini from a cucumber. "Um, Mike, about that article—"

"Yeah, yeah." He reached into his pocket. "Here's my business card, Miss Moultrie."

"Call me Destiny," she said, taking the card.

"If you should find yourself in need of a tour guide, I'm the man for the job. Oh, and use my pager. That's quicker."

"Thank you, Mike."

He was still smiling as he backed from the room and closed the door.

"Nice man," Destiny said to Jamie.

"Yes, Mike can be very, um, charming," Jamie said. She motioned for Destiny to take a seat. "Thank you for coming right over," she said. "I have something I want to discuss with you."

"Have you decided about the job?"

"I'm still thinking about it." She paused. "Something terrible has happened." Jamie debated whether or not to tell her about Luanne and decided to hold off.

Destiny leaned forward. "Oh, my, what is it?"

"I was hoping you could tell me."

Destiny shook her head. "I haven't had any more visions if that's what you're asking."

"Nothing about the man in uniform who was supposed to question me?"

"No, nothing. Why?"

Jamie leveled her gaze on the woman. "I was questioned by the chief of police this morning about a murder that took place last night."

Destiny simply looked at her. "I'm not surprised. Who was the victim?"

Jamie told her what she knew.

Destiny listened carefully. "I'm not getting anything on it, but that doesn't mean it won't come to me later." She suddenly glanced behind her. "Ronnie, I asked you to wait in the car."

Jamie looked up at the vacant spot behind her. "Your dead spirit came with you?"

"Sorry. Just ignore him."

Jamie nodded as though it were an everyday occurrence to have a dead spirit in her office. "Destiny, I don't know anything about psychic ability; in fact, I don't really believe in such things."

"I know that, but I hope you won't let it stand in the way of giving me a job. I am perfect for it. I have feel for what people really need help with. I *can* help them, Jamie. I've done this sort of thing before with a lot of success."

Jamie considered it. If an advice column pulled in more readers, it could only mean more revenue for the newspaper. "Tell you what. I'll announce the new column in an article and see if we get any responses. If we get a significant number, the job is yours. As long as you realize I have editorial control on what goes out," she added.

"Are you going to announce to your readers that I'm psychic?"

"The jury is still out on that one." Jamie wasn't sure how the citizens of Beaumont would accept it.

"Don't forget, I want to be referred to as the Divine Love Goddess Advisor. I think it's catchy, don't you?"

Jamie didn't have a clue. Probably folks would laugh her right out of town. "You realize I'm going out on a limb here."

"I won't let you down," Destiny promised.

VERA WALKED THROUGH THE DOOR TWO HOURS later. Jamie sat back in her chair and stared, her mouth agape. "Wow!" The gray was gone, and her hair cut in a flattering style.

Vera preened. "Susie colored it, added a light frosting, and then cut it. She says this haircut is the rage in Hollywood. Susan Sarandon and Sharon Stone are wearing this style. Mitzi, the cosmetologist, did my makeup. Of course, I ended up buying fifty dollars' worth of foundation, powder, and eye shadow from her, but she showed me how to use it to enhance my best features."

"You look great," Jamie said and meant it. "In fact, you look ten years younger."

"That's what everyone said. It sort of made up for the fact they already knew about Luanne Ritter. News travels fast in this town." She paused. "Um, Jamie, would you mind if I kept the Mustang for a few more days? It's going to cost a fortune to fix my old car."

"What's wrong with it?"

"Don't ask."

"It's the engine, right?"

"Yeah, but that doesn't mean your psychic friend is on the up-and-up."

"You're saying it's just another coincidence?" Jamie asked.

"I'm saying my car is old, and the engine was bound to give out sooner or later."

Jamie just looked at her.

"Frankly, the car is not worth what it would cost to replace the engine so I need to look around, see if I can find something affordable."

"You're welcome to keep the Mustang as long as you need it," Jamie replied.

"You're a doll. By the way, I hear your friend Dee Dee is throwing a big birthday party for Frankie tomorrow night. You plan on going?"

"I wouldn't miss it."

"Who are you going with?" Vera asked.

Big pause. "Mike."

"*Our* Mike? What's wrong, couldn't you find a real date?" She didn't wait for Jamie to respond. "Well, I don't blame you for not wanting to go alone. Not with people still talking about your broken engagement and all."

Jamie felt her ego plunge to her toes. "That wasn't my fault." Which was true. She'd broken up with Phillip Standish because his mother had been the ringleader of the town's corruption scandal. "Besides, I didn't love him." That was true, too. She'd simply wanted to belong to a real family for once. Security and predictability had been important to her at the time. Seemed those days were gone forever. Her life was about as predictable as a tornado. And that tornado had a name: Max Holt.

"Oh, nobody is blaming you," Vera said. "It's just, well, I don't want folks feeling sorry for you. I wish you could have found a better date than Mike. I mean, he's so young. He can't be more than twenty-four or five."

"I'm hoping he'll look older in his tux," Jamie said.

"I'm hoping he'll remember to wash behind his ears."

Leave it to Vera to make things worse, Jamie thought. "It's not a *real* date, okay? He's just acting as my escort. Besides, he wanted to go so he could snap some pictures for the society column." Jamie regretted the words before they left her mouth. Snapping pictures was supposed to be Vera's job.

"I've already heard about the birthday cake your friend Dee Dee chose for Frankie," Vera said, as if she were more interested in the latest gossip than she was in snapping pictures. "Lyle Betts baked it if that tells you anything."

Jamie leaned back in her seat. "Oh, yeah?"

"The way I heard it, Lyle has an *adults' only* book to order from. The cake is supposed to be of a naked woman."

Jamie chuckled. It sounded like something Dee Dee would do; she could be outlandish at times. Which was why some of the more genteel families had had trouble accepting the couple when they'd first moved to Beaumont. Dee Dee had arrived wearing rhinestone outfits, and Frankie had shocked the town when he'd invited his old wrestling buddies for a visit. Jamie had taken them under her wing and invited them to all the social events, and the two had become a hit. It was a known fact they could liven up even the dullest party with their presence. And when Frankie had run for mayor, promising to clean up town corruption, he'd won hands down.

"And get this," Vera said. "People are lining up at Lyle's bakery to buy brownies. Wouldn't surprise me if half the women in this town ended up pregnant before long," she added with a knowing look.

Jamie promised herself to steer clear of the brownies.

THE FOLLOWING NIGHT, JAMIE SLIPPED ON HER blue silk dress, and checked herself in the mirror. Her makeup and hair were perfect. She had taken a long bubble bath, slathered herself with lotion from head to toe, and then given herself a manicure and a pedicure. She tried to convince herself it had nothing to do with Max.

She'd even tried to convince herself that her trip to Maxine Chambers's lingerie shop had nothing to do with Max, but beneath her clothes she wore a body suit that was designed to make a man's tongue fall to the floor. The fact that she'd spent close to two hundred dollars in the shop had almost caused her to swallow her own tongue.

The doorbell rang at precisely six forty-five. Jamie opened the door and found Mike on the other side. He wore a baby-blue tux that was outdated, and at least one size too small. Ruffles peeked out from his sleeves. "Oh, geez," she said.

"I know it's a little snug," he told her. "My parents bought it for my high school prom. I guess I've filled out."

"You look fine," Jamie told him, not wanting to hurt his feelings. She knew he tried to help his parents financially from time to time, and odds were he couldn't afford to rent a tux. Probably nobody would notice his white socks anyway. Besides, it wasn't a date. Mike was going as part of his job.

"Hey, you look gorgeous," he said, taking a long look. "You should dress up more often, and you wouldn't have so much trouble finding a date. Hey, speaking of gorgeous, what's your friend Destiny doing tonight? I'm here to tell you, that woman is hot. You should fix us up."

"Don't you think she's a little, um, mature for you?" Jamie asked.

"Age is not an issue with me. I'm taking you out, aren't I?"

Jamie shot him a dark look. "May we leave now?"

JAMIE DID NOT SEE MAX AMONG THE CROWD OF people when she and Mike came through the door at Frankie and Dee Dee's, and her heart sank. What if he'd been unable to get away? Or maybe he'd had a better offer in the way of female companionship. Max Holt would naturally have his share of offers. Jamie pushed the thought aside. Max would not renege on a promise to be at his brother-in-law's fiftieth birthday party. She craned her head, trying to see above the tall heads in the room.

Max spotted Jamie the minute she stepped through the front door. He smiled at the sight of her so-called date, who immediately headed toward the dining room where the buffet was set up. His smile broadened when he noticed she was looking for him, but he was hidden from view at his place beside one of the round, floor-to-ceiling columns inside the house. He simply stood there for a moment watching her. Finally, he moved toward her until he was standing directly behind her.

"Looking for someone?"

Jamie felt the hairs stand on the back of her neck at the sound of his voice. Every nerve in her body sprang to life as she turned and found herself looking into Max Holt's handsome face. For a moment all they could do was stand and stare at each other. It was as though all the people in the room had evaporated.

"Hello, Max," she said, trying to sound cool. But cool wasn't easy, what with her heart beating like a conga drum in her chest. Damn, he looked good in his black tux, which, unlike Mike's, was simple and elegant and probably tailor made. Of course, the man looked good no matter what he wore.

Max was all male—sinewy muscle, gorgeous olive complexion, hard jaw. He was as polished as they came, with an underlying air of danger that oddly made her feel safe in his presence.

His smile was slow and lazy as a winding river. "You amaze me, Swifty. I thought you couldn't get any prettier. I was wrong."

Jamie offered him a benign smile, meant to make him feel as though she were immune to his charm. "Thank you, Max. Coming from a world-renowned womanizer I consider that quite a compliment."

He grinned. "So, who's the boy?"

"Excuse me?"

"Your date?"

"You know Mike Henderson. I hardly think he qualifies as a boy. He's, um, not exactly a real date, he just escorted me. He's here to take pictures for the society column."

"If he were any younger, I'd have to report you to the authorities."

"Same old Max."

"Tell you what, Swifty. I'm going to be a gentleman about this, seeing as how you probably think I took you for granted. I assumed you wanted to see me as badly as I wanted to see you. But let's get something straight." His tone dropped, and there was a slight huskiness to it. "You leave the party with me."

CHAPTER FOUR

JAMIE'S STOMACH QUIVERED AT THE THOUGHT OF going anywhere with Max. "I don't know if that's wise."

He stroked one finger down her arm. Her skin prickled.

"There you go again," he said. "You're thinking too much." He gave her a private smile. "You're wearing the blue dress. I can't wait to see what's under it."

Jamie gulped. Yikes, the man was seducing her right there on the spot. And damned if there was anything she could do about it because her tongue had suddenly become plastered to the roof of her mouth.

And now, here she was, wondering what *he* was wearing, if anything, beneath that dignified-looking tux.

"I need a drink," she said, if for no other reason

than to change the subject. Max knew what he did to her, and he was probably enjoying every minute of it.

Max motioned, and a waiter appeared instantly, carrying a tray of white wine in tall, long-stemmed glasses. "Would you like a glass of chardonnay?" the man asked.

Jamie concentrated on keeping her hand steady as she reached for one of the goblets. She could feel the perspiration beading her upper lip, and she hadn't put any tissues in the small bag she'd chosen to bring.

"Are you hot?" Max asked.

Jamie tried to play it down, suspecting Max was enjoying her discomfort. "There are too many people crammed into this place. I think your sister invited half the town."

"Dee Dee does have a way of going overboard," Max said, looking about the room.

Mike returned balancing a plate stacked high with food, camera dangling from his neck. "Hi, Max. Hey, nice tux. I'll bet you didn't rent it in Beaumont." He looked at Jamie. "Why is your face all sweaty?" He didn't give her a chance to answer. "I haven't eaten all day. I hope I don't make a pig of myself." He bit into a finger sandwich. "Wow, check out the brunette who just walked through the door. The one in the red dress," he added. "I should go over and introduce myself. Maybe she'll let me take her picture." He winked at Jamie. "Don't tell Destiny. I'm saving myself for her." He hurried away.

Jamie shook her head as she caught the amused look on Max's face. He pulled a handkerchief from his pocket. "May I?" When Jamie merely shrugged, he very carefully mopped her forehead and upper lip. "There now, good as new."

Jamie drained her glass. "I should find Frankie and wish him a happy birthday."

"Great, we can go together."

Dee Dee Fontana and her assistant Beenie appeared out of nowhere. "Oh, Jamie, I'm so glad you could come!" she cried, hugging her tightly. "You too little brother." She and Max hugged, as well.

"You look beautiful," Jamie said, noting Dee Dee's ankle-length, Kelly-green cocktail dress. It set off her green eyes and red hair. Jamie was certain Beenie had handpicked the outfit for her; he'd long ago tossed her slinky rhinestone garb, before husband Frankie had been elected as town mayor. Beenie was dressed in Ralph Lauren, his dark hair combed straight back, emphasizing a perfect oval face.

"Frankie will be thrilled to see you," Dee Dee said in her Betty Boop voice that gave the former beauty queen a childlike quality most people found endearing.

"We wouldn't have missed it for the world,"

Jamie said, and then wished she had used a singular pronoun. She didn't want anyone, least of all Max, to think she was his date for the evening. "You look gorgeous as always," she told the woman quickly, hoping no one had caught the slip. Dee Dee seemed to sparkle. Well into her forties, she passed for thirty, thanks to a plastic surgeon in Hilton Head that she kept on call.

"Where *is* Frankie?" Max asked.

Dee Dee giggled. Coming from anyone else, it would have sounded silly, but Dee Dee's little-girl quality and naïveté made people, especially her husband, want to take care of her. "He and several of his old wrestling buddies are at the bar. Snakeman, Big John, Choker, and Dirty Deed Dan flew in to celebrate with us."

Jamie recognized some of the names as Frankie's old wrestling buddies. Snakeman had toured with a twenty-foot boa during his wrestling days. "Is there a snake in residence?" Jamie asked, hoping that wasn't the case.

Another giggle from Dee Dee. "No, the snake died a while back, and Snakeman decided not to replace him because it made traveling difficult. The snake was just part of the show."

Jamie tried to hide her sigh of relief. The last thing she wanted was something wrapping itself around one of her ankles.

Dee Dee offered them a conspiratorial grin. "Wait till you see the cake I ordered."

Beenie rolled his eyes and tapped his fingers against his lips. "It's designed to look like a naked woman. It starts at the shoulders and ends at her navel, and get this, she's wearing a nipple ring. Tacky, tacky, tacky."

Dee Dee pretended to pout, something else she pulled off very well. "You didn't think the one that looked like a man's buns was tacky."

Beenie struck a pose. "Now that was a work of art." He shrugged. "Besides, I like men's buns." He went on. "Anyway, as I told Dee Dee, this is *not* the time or place for such decadence. We have visiting dignitaries, and they will probably be offended. I would have chosen something elegant but simple. Less is always more."

The waiter came by. Jamie grabbed another glass of wine. Max grinned.

"Oh, Beenie, stop acting like an old maid and loosen up a bit," Dee Dee said. "It's not going to kill you to have a little fun now and then."

Jamie couldn't help but smile as Dee Dee and Beenie continued to fuss. Dee Dee had hired Beenie away from an exclusive spa in Hilton Head. They were inseparable, but they tended to argue like brother and sister.

"And guess what else we ordered from the bakery?" Dee Dee said in a conspiratorial whisper. "Aphrodisiac-laced brownies. Everybody in town is shocked that Lyle Betts is making them, but he claims he can't bake them fast enough. Isn't that a scream?"

Jamie wasn't about to tell her she had already tried them. "Oh, here's the birthday boy now," she said as Frankie joined them. Standing well over six and a half feet, with a barrel of a chest, Frankie Fontana struck an imposing figure. Jamie had not known Frankie in his wrestling days, but as a teenager, Max had seen him in the ring a number of times and assured her he had been quite formidable. Now, having been retired more than ten years, Frankie wore a good-natured smile and easygoing attitude that made him appear as harmless as a kitten.

"Glad you could come," Frankie said, pumping Max's arm enthusiastically and giving him a hearty slap on the back. He hugged Jamie lightly as though realizing his own strength.

"Happy birthday," Jamie said and Max seconded it.

Frankie grinned from ear to ear, looking much like an overgrown kid despite his graying temples. "I guess Dee Dee told you about the cake. Snake-man is going to remove the nipple ring with his teeth, and then we're going to have arm-wrestling matches in the kitchen. Better place your bets while there's still time."

Beenie looked aghast. "Do you realize the lieutenant governor is here?" he hissed.

"Yeah, he's the one taking up the bets," Frankie said.

Dee Dee patted her husband's hand. "Well, I'll put my money on you any time, sweetie," she said. He kissed her lightly on the lips although it was obvious he would have preferred something more passionate. Twenty years of marriage had not dampened their desire for each other.

Frankie looked at Jamie. "I'm especially glad to see you. Dee Dee has a dilemma."

"Frankie's right," Dee Dee said. "I need to find a cause."

"A cause for what?" Jamie asked.

Dee Dee giggled. "You know, a cause. Now that Frankie's the new mayor, I think I should make some sort of contribution to this town."

"That's a wonderful idea," Jamie told her friend. "You could volunteer at the hospital."

"Eeyeuuw!" Dee Dee shuddered.

"Dee Dee doesn't like being around sick people," Frankie explained. "We wouldn't want her to catch any germs."

"There's a telephone number in the phone book

for people wanting to volunteer their time," Jamie offered. "You could call them and see what they need. I'm sure you'll find something that interests you."

Dee Dee suddenly brightened. "I could work for a hotline service. You know, help people out who have personal problems. I'm a good listener."

Jamie and Max exchanged looks. Jamie couldn't imagine Dee Dee trying to solve anyone's problems. God bless her, but Dee Dee's answer to everything was a new piece of fine jewelry or a shopping trip to New York.

"I don't know about the rest of you, but I'm hungry," Frankie announced. "Let's grab some grub."

A few minutes later, Max and Jamie carried their plates and glasses of wine to one of the love seats adorned in faux leopard. Dee Dee had decorated the room in a jungle theme, complete with animal-skin sofas, banana plants, and wooden giraffes. Max sat close enough so that their thighs touched. It didn't go unnoticed by Jamie.

"Max, we really need to talk," she said, trying to ignore the tingling that started at her hip bone and spread right down to her painted toenails. Her stomach took a nosedive as she imagined his hair-roughened thighs touching hers without benefit of clothes. Lord, what the man did to her!

"You smell nice," he said.

"Thank you." She didn't want to think about how

good he smelled. She tried to remember what she had been saying before he'd touched her and her mind had taken leave. "I'm, uh, really concerned about Luanne Ritter's murder and that the personals section may be connected to it. I told Lamar I'd pull the ads, but he disagreed. He's afraid if the murder had something to do with the ads, we might lose the killer. I think it's too risky."

"Give me a few more details," he said.

Jamie told him about her conversation with Lamar, trying not to leave anything out.

"We're going to have to work fast, Swifty," he said.

"We'll have to work at night, after the office is closed. Nobody is supposed to know. Not even Vera."

"What about the production staff?"

"They never come up front. Besides, even if they did, they'd have no idea what we were working on."

"You have records of the people who've written in?"

Jamie nodded. "I keep them locked in my office for confidentiality's sake. Vera pitched the fit of all fits when I told her she wasn't privy to the information, but you know how she loves to gossip." Jamie paused. "By the way, I lent her the red Mustang. Her old car gave out on her."

He grinned. "Does she drive it with the top down?"

God, if only he wouldn't smile like that, Jamie thought. She could handle almost anything but those bone-melting smiles. "Yes. She even got a new haircut so the wind wouldn't mess up her hair so badly."

"I can't wait to see that." He glanced around the room. "Tell you what. We'll wait until the birthday cake is served, then slip out and drive to the office." He suddenly smiled. "Unless you need to get your date home in time for his curfew."

Jamie shot him one of her looks.

FRANKIE'S CAKE WAS ROLLED OUT ON A SERVING cart an hour later, and the guests gathered around and sang "Happy Birthday," even as some gasped at the sight of the naked figure of a woman with size-D breasts. Frankie blew out his candles and hugged Dee Dee as everyone clapped. Snakeman made a production of removing the nipple ring with his teeth and received a rousing applause.

"Speech!" someone shouted from across the room.

Frankie laughed. "I'd have thought you guys had heard enough of my speeches during the mayoral campaign," he said. "Okay, but I'll make it short. First of all, I'd like to thank you all for being here to share my birthday. Dee Dee and I are very lucky to have so many friends. And because we consider all of you friends, I would like to make an important announcement."

Max and Jamie looked at each other and shrugged.

Frankie paused and smiled tenderly at Dee Dee. She beamed. "After all these years, my wife and I are expecting a baby."

Everyone clapped. Jamie looked at Max. "Well, there goes that perfect figure she's worked so hard to keep," she said, knowing Dee Dee went bananas if she gained a pound.

Max merely grinned. "Sounds like she and Frankie have been eating brownies."

MAX AND JAMIE LEFT THE PARTY SHORTLY AFTER-ward, but not before they'd offered Frankie and Dee Dee their congratulations.

"I'm going to be an uncle," Max said, his tone incredulous, as they pulled away from the Fontana house, which was really an estate. An estate on which sat a salmon-colored house that Frankie claimed was pink and caused a lot of snickering from his wrestling buddies who referred to it as the Pink Palace.

Jamie still couldn't believe the news. "Dee Dee is going to have to give up her rigid dieting. She's eating for two now."

"Hello, Jamie," a voice called from the dash-board. "What's this about Max being an uncle?"

Jamie smiled. "Hey, I've missed you, Muffin," she said to the voice-recognition computer that ran Max's business from a dashboard that was more complicated than most jets; thanks to a team of first-rate computer whizzes. Max had hired them away from top government contractors, and with his help, they'd created the car's instrumentation using state-of-the-art equipment.

Spread out among luxury automotive goodies like a tachometer, an altimeter, and a global positioning satellite system were a highly enhanced PDA, a keyboard, a digital speech-recognition module, a photo-quality printer, fax, satellite phone, HDTV display screen, and a full video-conferencing suite, all operated by a high-powered computer that was smaller than an ashtray. "She" had a Marilyn Monroe voice, but because she was constantly fed information from a team of experts, she was the only one capable of matching Max's genius.

Not only that, Max had created in her technology that was able to make judgment calls, not based on data but on simple human emotion. His competitors, including the federal government, claimed it couldn't be done. Now they wanted to buy that technology.

"Dee Dee's pregnant," Jamie said at last.

"Uh-oh."

"My thoughts exactly," Max said. "We can expect drastic changes in the Fontana household."

"Wait a minute," Muffin said, "I thought she was going through menopause."

Jamie smiled, although she was still stunned by the news. "You ever heard of a change-of-life baby? It happens."

"How's she taking the news?"

"She looked thrilled," Jamie said, "and I think she'll make a wonderful mother. Dee Dee is very softhearted. And Frankie is going to enjoy spoiling the little tyke."

"I'm going to start looking into all the best baby books," Muffin said. "I'll get every piece of data I can, then Dee Dee and I will talk."

"I can't wait to see her in maternity clothes," Jamie said. "I'm sure Beenie will insist on the best designer money can buy."

Max gave her one of his slow easy smiles. "You sound a little exuberant there, Swifty. Sounds like you wouldn't mind having a little bambino of your own. You might need to give it some thought, what with that ticking biological clock thing that women worry so much about."

"My clock is ticking just fine, Max," she said, "and no, I don't think I'm ready for motherhood. I can't even raise a dog properly, but at least he won't be sitting in some therapist's office thirty years from now complaining what a crummy job I did."

"Ah, Jamie, you'd be a great mom," he said.

"Really?" The sincerity in his voice touched her.

"Excuse me," Muffin said. "I think we're missing something here. A father, maybe?"

Max and Jamie locked gazes. "How *is* Fleas, by the way?" Max asked.

Jamie thought he'd done a clumsy job of changing the subject. "I just had him neutered."

"See, that makes you a responsible pet owner," Max said.

"Uh, Muffin," Jamie began, "back to love and marriage and baby carriages, how's your love life?" Muffin had been having an on-again off-again on-line romance with a laptop computer at MIT. Max had also programmed Muffin with a personality. She had attitude.

"We're sort of taking a break from each other," Muffin said. "I think I intimidate him. I think he's chatting with someone else."

"He'll be back," Max said. "A smart man never walks away from a good thing."

Jamie felt his eyes on her, but she didn't dare look his way. As she had told Fleas, their relationship was complicated. "I suppose you told Muffin what's going on in Beaumont," she said, realizing she had been the one to change the subject this time. Each time things got too personal between them, one or both of them backed off. Besides, if Max started sweet-talking her, they'd never make it to the newspaper office.

"Yeah, what do you think?" Muffin asked.

"I think I'm going to feel guilty for the rest of my life if my personals section is involved in that poor woman's murder."

"You can't take everything Lamar Tevis says as fact," Muffin said. "We're not dealing with Colombo. Do you have backup info on the people writing the ads?"

Jamie felt herself nod even though she knew Muffin couldn't see her. "Yeah, I have to keep the letters on file in case someone gets a response."

"Anybody else have access to them?" Muffin asked.

"Not even Vera."

"Oh, man, I'll bet that pissed her off. So, here's what we do," Muffin began. "You give me the names and any other pertinent info, and I check them out. If I find anyone who looks suspicious, we'll take a closer look."

Twenty minutes later, Max pulled into the parking lot of the *Beaumont Gazette*. A cream-colored Mercedes was parked in one of the slots. "Boy, you must've given somebody on your staff a really good raise," he said.

"Oh, no, that's Destiny Moultrie," Jamie said with a sigh as the woman climbed from her car. Destiny had not picked a good time to show up. "She's going to be our new Divine Love Goddess Advisor."

Max frowned. "Come again?"

"I'll explain later."

Destiny raced around to the passenger door as Jamie climbed out. The woman was wearing her bathrobe and bedroom slippers. "Oh, thank God I found you," she cried. "I drove by your house, but you weren't home. I figured I'd check here just in case."

Jamie could see the woman was upset about something. "Um, Destiny, this is my partner, Max Holt."

Jamie didn't miss the knowing look in Destiny's eyes as she looked his way. "It's about time you showed up," she said. Max arched both brows in question, but Destiny turned to Jamie and grasped her hands tightly. Jamie was surprised to find them icy cold.

"I had a vision." Destiny glanced to her side. "Ronnie, get lost, this is important."

Jamie winced inwardly. Just what Max needed to hear, she thought.

"The name is Max Holt, not Ronnie," Max told her.

"Destiny isn't talking to you," Jamie quickly said. "Ronnie is from the spirit world."

"Actually, he's between worlds," Destiny said. "He doesn't know he's dead, so he follows me everywhere."

Max simply nodded as though it made complete sense. "Okay."

"I've been eating garlic pickles all day," Destiny told Jamie.

Which explained her breath, Jamie thought.

"I know it sounds crazy, but when I eat garlic pickles I dream a lot." She looked from Jamie to Max. "Sometimes I have waking dreams or visions where I see things."

"Destiny claims she's psychic," Jamie told Max. She wasn't sure what kind of reaction she expected, but she was surprised when Max merely smiled politely.

"Nice to meet you, Destiny."

"Same here." Once again, she turned to Jamie. "Anyway, I awoke about an hour ago, and—" She paused and shuddered. "I saw this woman. Her skull was crushed."

"You're right, Destiny," Jamie said. "A woman *was* found dead this morning. Remember, we discussed it."

"No, Jamie. You don't understand. I'm talking about another woman. A second victim," she added. "It hasn't happened yet."

CHAPTER FIVE

JAMIE FELT A SENSE OF FEAR, A FEELING OF DREAD wash over her. Then she reminded herself she didn't believe in psychics. Yes, but Destiny had told her things, things that couldn't be explained. She suddenly realized Destiny was shivering, despite the warm night. "How do you know these women are not one and the same?" Jamie challenged.

Destiny sneezed. "I just do. The second woman will put up a fight. There will be scratches on the killer's arms."

"Did you see the victim's face or the face of the killer in your vision?" Max asked, surprising Jamie.

"Believe me, I tried."

"This sounds a little far-fetched," Jamie said, no longer knowing what to think about the woman's predictions.

"It's true," Destiny said.

Max looked thoughtful but remained silent.

Jamie wanted to send Destiny on her way, but the woman appeared too upset to drive. "Destiny, we need to get you inside," she said. "You don't look so good."

Max followed them. Jamie noticed he didn't seem a bit skeptical when Destiny announced that Ronnie was right behind her. Jamie turned and eyed Destiny suspiciously. "If you're so certain this murder is going to take place, why can't you see the killer?"

Destiny paused and looked at her. "I'm blocked, okay? Everything is murky. I don't know where or when the murder is going to take place, but one thing is for sure—" She suddenly sneezed. "It's only a matter of time."

IT WASN'T UNTIL JAMIE HAD GOTTEN DESTINY IN-side and sat her down in the small kitchen with a fresh cup of coffee that she stopped shivering. "All I keep seeing is this poor woman," she said. "Fighting for her life," she added, followed by another sneeze.

Jamie grabbed several tissues and handed them to her.

Max leaned in the doorway listening. Jamie gave him a cup of coffee and he quietly thanked her, all the while watching Destiny closely, as though trying to make up his mind about something. Jamie wondered if he was trying to decide whether Destiny was the real thing, and she couldn't help feeling surprised. Did Max actually believe what she was saying? Of all the people in the world, Max Holt struck her as the last person on earth who would believe in psychics.

Jamie joined Destiny at the table. She had her eyes closed. "What are you doing?" Jamie asked.

"Looking for a face," Destiny said. "All I'm getting is a view of her, the victim, from her shoulders down. Struggling and fighting for her life."

"Is she wearing something unusual?" Max asked. "Maybe something with a monogram on it?"

Jamie glanced up quickly. Was Max merely trying to humor her?

"I'm not getting anything." A fat tear rolled from Destiny's left eye and slid down her cheek. "There's no use trying to force it. It either comes to me or it doesn't."

"What about the garlic pickles?" Jamie asked.

Destiny shrugged. "That's something my grandmother used to do. It sometimes works, but not always."

Jamie tried to think, tried to open herself up to what she was hearing. What she knew about psychic phenomena was next to nothing. But she was certain Destiny believed somebody was about to die.

Max put down his coffee cup. "Jamie, may I have a word with you?"

Jamie looked at Destiny.

"I'm okay. Besides, I need a minute to myself."

Max and Jamie didn't speak until they'd reached her office and closed the door. "Max, I know all this sounds and looks strange, but—"

"Not really."

Jamie couldn't hide her astonishment. "Are you saying you believe in this sort of thing?"

"I don't disbelieve. I think there are some things in this world that can't be explained. And I believe the woman saw something. She's obviously hysterical."

"She spooks me, Max. I mean, she shows up in my parking lot in her bathrobe with stories of visions and murder and some guy named Ronnie from the spirit world. You don't think that's strange?"

"Have any of her predictions come true?"

Jamie told him about Destiny's vision concerning Lamar. "I want to believe her, but she has a ghost following her around, for Pete's sake. I don't know whether to take her seriously or call a doctor."

Max put his hand on Jamie's shoulder. "Listen, I'm not saying she's the real thing, but I think she bears listening to. That doesn't mean I'm not going to put Muffin on the case. I think we should use every possible means to catch the killer before he strikes again. If what Destiny says is true," he added.

"I'm scared, Max," Jamie said. "I honestly can't bear the thought of my column being responsible for Luanne Ritter's death. I don't care if everybody in this town *did* hate her; she was still a human being. And the thought of somebody else getting killed is more than I can handle."

Max took her in his arms. "Then we'd better get to work."

JAMIE UNLOCKED THE FILE DRAWER IN HER OFFICE and pulled it out. She found what she was looking for right away. She joined Max and Destiny.

"Max and I thought maybe you could look through some of these ads and see if you get a feel for them."

Destiny looked doubtful. "I've never been real good at psychometrics, but I'll give it a try."

Max slid forward in his chair. "Jamie, before you get started, I'd like for you to make a copy of the ads so I can fax them to Muffin."

"Sure, Max. It won't take but a couple of minutes. Please help yourself to more coffee if you like. Also, there are soft drinks in the refrigerator and maybe a couple of stale doughnuts." Jamie hurried into the reception area where the copy machine and fax were situated along one wall near Vera's desk. She felt like she had stepped into a bad science fiction movie.

When she returned, she found Max and Destiny talking softly. He seemed genuinely interested in what she was saying. "Here are the copies." Jamie handed them to Max, and showed him to the fax machine. "Call me if you need me."

He nodded and went to work.

Finally, Jamie joined Destiny on the sofa. "Okay, here's what we've got."

"There's only one problem, Jamie," Destiny said. "Even though I've never been really good at this sort of thing, it works better if the object is handled by the original person only."

Jamie gave her a blank look. "Come again?"

"In this case, the actual author of the ad." She reached for one of the sheets of paper. "The way psychometrics works is that you feel the energy from the person who touched the object."

Jamie tried to hide her skepticism. "You're saying since I was the last one who touched these ads they will hold my energy?"

Destiny nodded. "At least some of it. What we can do is look at the ads and see if anything stands out. Maybe something will come to me. It might help later in a vision, who knows?"

Max returned and reclaimed his seat. "Okay, I faxed the info to Muffin, and she's already at work on it."

"I'm afraid we're not having much luck," Destiny said. Jamie nodded in agreement. "We're just looking through the ads, seeing if anything sounds unusual or, um, ominous. For example, the heading on this ad reads 'Looking for discreet relationship. Must be open to new experiences.' "

"You're right, that's scary," Max said.

Jamie realized he was teasing her. "We don't know what it means," she said. " 'Open to new experiences' could mean he's into kinky stuff."

Destiny pondered it and finally shrugged. "Or maybe he just likes sailing or horseback riding," she said. "That could be one way of looking at new experiences."

"But why would he insist on discretion?" Jamie asked. "Doesn't that sound a little paranoid?"

Max shrugged. "It could mean he doesn't want people to know he found a date through a personals ad. That doesn't mean we don't check him out, though."

"How many ads do you have there?" Destiny asked.

"Only seven, since I just copied the ones from the men. I have all their addresses and phone numbers. The way it works is, they pay for the ad, which includes a couple of dollars extra for postage, and when I get a reply I forward it to them. It's a new feature, of course, and I'm hoping it'll catch on. As least I was until I heard about Luanne Ritter's murder."

"Did you happen to notice any return addresses from those who responded to the ads?" Max asked.

"There weren't any," Jamie told him. "They obviously wanted to keep it confidential. Small town and all," she added.

"Take a look at this ad," Max said after a minute.

Jamie shuffled through the pages. "Yeah, I remember that one."

Destiny leaned forward and read, " 'Till Death Do Us Part.' "

"Did you not think that sounded strange when you read it?" Max asked.

Jamie shook her head. "No. It could simply mean this person is looking for a lifetime partner, which is what a couple of the ads say. Now that someone has been killed it sounds pretty menacing, and we definitely need to check it out."

"Don't you have anyone who sounds like a guy I'd want to meet?" Destiny asked, surprising them both. "Hey, I'm new in town; I wouldn't mind meeting a nice guy. He'd have to be open-minded, of course."

Jamie almost welcomed the change of subject. "My editor Mike Henderson has a crush on you."

"Oh, yeah?"

"He's a little young."

"Young is nice. Two of my husbands were old and died on me. It's such a hassle planning a funeral."

Max cleared his throat. "I believe we have work to do, ladies," he said.

Jamie nodded. "Okay, this ad reads, 'Don't Pass Me By,' and another one, 'Walking on Sunshine.'" She suddenly chuckled. "Oh, listen to this. 'Offer Good for a Limited Time.'"

Even Max chuckled at that one.

"They all seem to be searching for the same thing," Jamie said. "A woman looking for a good time who might be interested in a long-term relationship." A sheet of paper fell to the floor. "Oh, I almost missed one. Listen to this. It reads, 'Deeper Than the Night.'"

"That sounds nice," Destiny said.

"Yeah, listen to his ad. He says, 'No matter what path you choose, keep it simple, but throw your heart into it.'"

Destiny sighed. "Wow, that's deep." She glanced to an empty space in the room. "Oh, stop acting jealous, Ronnie. Remember, you're dead? It's not like I can go bowling or coon hunting with you." She rolled her eyes at Jamie. "That's Ronnie's idea of a good time, if you can believe it. At least the last guy that attached himself to me had a little class. He was an English professor."

Jamie just stared at her.

"How old is this guy who claimed to be deeper than the night?" Destiny asked.

"Thirty-five and never been married."

"Which means he doesn't have children," Destiny said. "Believe me, I've had my share of stepchildren. I should take the ad home and put it beneath my pillow tonight. Maybe something will come to me. You should give me his name and address. I could drive by his house; see if I get any vibes."

"These are confidential."

"You didn't mind letting me hold them a few minutes ago," Destiny objected.

"That was different. I was seeking your, um, professional opinion. If you want to meet this guy, you'll have to go through the proper channels like everybody else. Only, I'd hold off until we look into the murder."

Max checked his wristwatch. "It's after midnight. We need to go home and get a good night's sleep. By morning, Muffin will have a lot of the information I requested, and we can start from there."

They left the building a few minutes later, once Jamie had locked up. Destiny pulled away in her Mercedes as Max helped Jamie into the passenger's side of his car. He joined her in the front seat a moment later.

"Max, we need to talk about Destiny," Jamie said. "I know she sounds convincing, but surely you don't believe in the supernatural."

"I simply try to keep an open mind," he said. "I've seen and heard of instances where psychics have taken investigators right to the crime scene. In fact, I was personally involved in one of those instances."

Jamie looked at him. "You were involved with a psychic?"

"The son of a close friend of mine was kidnapped for ransom five years ago. A woman just appeared at his front door with all the information the police needed to find the boy. They still call on her from time to time."

Jamie felt the goose pimples rise on her arms. "But what about this Ronnie, this dead spirit that Destiny claims follows her everywhere?"

Max grinned. "Yeah, that's pretty strange, but from what I've read, and this is only what I've read, some people get lost between worlds when they die suddenly or violently because they're confused and don't know they should go to the light."

"The light?" Jamie shook her head. "Max, do you know how that sounds?"

He laughed. "Yeah, I know, but there have been cases reported. Some priests believe in it. Why do you suppose exorcisms are performed? It's believed that a dead spirit can attach itself to a live human. I read all this stuff when I was a kid. I was really fascinated with that sort of thing."

"You're really scaring me now." Jamie said shuddering. "I don't think I want to talk about it anymore."

"I know it all sounds far-fetched like you said, but I believe the woman in your office tonight saw something that frightened her. I don't think she was faking it."

"I've lived in a small town too long," Jamie said. "I believe in what I can see. Could we change the subject?"

"Yeah." Max looked at the dashboard. "Muffin, are you there?" he asked.

"Yes, and I've been listening to every word. I'm with Jamie. This whole thing gives me the creeps."

"Then let's talk facts. You got anything yet?"

"Do you know what time it is?"

"I know it's late, but—"

"So, go to your hotel and get a good night's sleep. I should have something for you in the morning."

Jamie was glad they were headed in a different direction. That's exactly what she wanted to hear: facts. "You're not staying at Frankie and Dee Dee's?" she asked.

Max shook his head. "I need a place to work while I'm in town, and I wouldn't be able to think straight with Frankie and his wrestling buddies around. Besides, I'm not into arm wrestling."

"Where are you staying?"

Max shrugged. "Where am I staying, Muffin?"

"You have reservations at the Carteret Street Bed and Breakfast."

"It's really nice," Jamie said. "Probably not as nice as you're accustomed to," she added, suspecting Max had stayed in some of the best hotels in the world. "But you should be comfortable there."

"You have a suite on the first floor," Muffin said. "It has a sitting room, courtyard, and private entrance on the east side. Guaranteed late arrival; you'll find a key waiting for you beneath the doormat."

Max looked at Jamie. "You should stay with me tonight."

"Uh-oh, here it comes," Muffin said. "I'm outta here."

"I can't stay with you," Jamie replied. "I know the owners. I went to school with their daughter. I wouldn't feel right."

"I have my own private entrance, remember?"

It sounded so tempting. And Jamie hated to waste the body suit she'd spent forty bucks on. And in all honesty, she wasn't sure she wanted to stay by herself after hearing about dead spirits and exorcisms. But she had a dog to care for.

"You're going to have to show me how to get to the place anyway," he said. "I'll get lost."

Jamie looked at him. "Oh, puh-lease. You could find your way to Mars in this car, Max."

"Yeah, but—"

"Why don't you ask Muffin for directions to the Carteret Street Bed and Breakfast?"

"Because she doesn't have beautiful blue eyes like you." He stopped at a red light. "C'mon, Swifty, what d'you say?"

She sighed. "Oh, Max—"

"You're doing it again, Jamie. You're thinking too much. You're doing the 'what-if' thing."

She knew he was right. It was time she stopped doing so much thinking and just enjoyed being with Max because, well, in all honesty, she wanted him as much as he wanted her. And it wasn't like she had to stay all night. She could go home later and let Fleas out. Later, after she got over her case of the heebie-jeebies.

"Turn left at the light."

CHAPTER SIX

CARTERET STREET BED AND BREAKFAST WAS A massive, two-story Colonial with verandas on both floors. Oversized rocking chairs and baskets of ferns gave it a welcoming look. Once Max had parked his car and grabbed a bag from the trunk, Jamie pointed him toward a narrow, flower-laden path where old-fashioned street lamps lit the way. They found themselves standing at the door to his room. Sure enough, a key had been placed beneath the doormat. He unlocked the door, opened it, and motioned for Jamie to go through first.

Fresh daisies sat on a highly polished cherry coffee table. The rust-and-cream-colored furniture was comfortable looking while maintaining a look of simple elegance. The ornate crown moldings and woodwork were a deep mahogany, and repeated in the oversized fireplace. A tasteful rug covered heart-pine floors. Max opened a set of French doors and found a sink, small refrigerator, and microwave.

"Nice," he said. "Where's the bedroom?"

Jamie's stomach dipped to her toes. "Through that door."

He took her hand in his and led her in that direction. An old four-poster rice bed and matching highboy, both in cherry, greeted them. The comforter was pure linen, as were the curtains. Jamie had visited the bed-and-breakfast several years ago when it had been redecorated, and she had praised it in an article. She was glad Mrs. Hobbs had given Max the nicest suite.

The Hobbses were an older couple—short and stout as teacups, as Vera liked to say, but Mrs. Hobbs was worse than Vera when it came to gossip. Vera did most of her gossiping on the church lawn after Sunday services; Myrna Hobbs preferred holding court at the local Piggly Wiggly grocery store, where she could often be found picking up food items for her guests. Vera claimed Myrna exaggerated, that a soul couldn't believe a word that came out of the woman's mouth. Vera believed in sticking to the facts.

Max reached for Jamie.

"I, um, thought maybe you'd like to see the garden first," she said quickly. "It's really very nice.

Mrs. Hobbs hired a man who designed a garden at one of the old plantations in Charleston."

Max suddenly smiled. "You're nervous, aren't you, Swifty? You're remembering last time. I have to tell you, you're all I've thought about the past few weeks."

She smiled. "Really? Gee, I wish I'd known." Jamie hated to bring up the fact he hadn't contacted her in the three weeks since that time, but she figured it needed saying. It had to be the wine talking. She'd had three glasses at Frankie and Dee Dee's, which was well over her quota.

"I was out of the country most of that time. I'm not real good at sending postcards." When she didn't say anything, he went on. "I guess I could do better." He sighed and raked his hands through his hair. "Do you still want to look at that garden?"

Jamie opened the French doors leading from the bedroom. Taking Max's hand in hers, she led him down a brick walkway and across a small footbridge that covered a pond. Once again, old-fashioned street lamps lighted the way. Jamie was glad Mrs. Hobbs had left them burning for Max's arrival.

"The pond actually has goldfish in it," Jamie said. "Huge ones."

Max studied his surroundings with only a hint of

interest. "So, can you tell me the names of these plants?"

"Sure." Jamie glanced around. "That tree is a hemlock. And the plants growing beneath it are hosta plants. Or plantain lilies as they're sometimes called," she added. "They're shade plants." She pointed. "And that's caladium, and growing next to it is ostrich fern." She caught sight of Max's grin. "What?"

"How do you know this?"

"Just because I never have time to mow my lawn or weed my flower beds doesn't mean I don't know about plants. I planted a whole bunch of daylilies around the pickup truck in the back yard to try to make it look more attractive."

"Did it work?"

"No. But you know how attached Fleas is to that truck."

"Does he sleep in it?"

"Are you kidding? He has this giant pillow that I bought for him so he can sleep on the floor in my bedroom, but when I wake up each morning I find him sprawled across the foot of my bed."

"That's going to present a real problem for us."

Jamie's stomach fluttered. "I think he's become somewhat spoiled since you last saw him," she said, changing the subject.

Max stroked her arm. "I'd like to go inside and spoil you."

More fluttering. "Okay, but you didn't get to see the entire garden."

This time, Max captured her hand and led her through the French doors into the bedroom. A breeze blew in from the doorway, bringing with it the scent of magnolia. Moonlight dappled the room. Max pulled Jamie into his arms and kissed her.

Jamie leaned against him, delighting in the solid planes of his body and his scent. He offered more than a mere distraction from spending part of the evening talking about bogeymen, and she had been waiting for this moment all evening. No, she had been waiting much longer than that. Common sense had told her it was sheer folly, but her heart refused to listen. She returned Max's kisses with a hunger that surprised even her.

Max cupped her hips in his hands, pressing her flat against him so there was no doubt that he was as eager for her as she was for him. He slid his fingers through her hair, anchoring her head between his palms as he kissed her more deeply. Jamie clung to the jacket of his tux.

She slipped her arms around his neck and tilted her head back, parting her lips beneath his so his tongue could explore the inside of her mouth. Max's hands moved to her breasts, warming them through the clothes she wore.

"I want you, Jamie," he whispered. "I have since the first time I saw you."

Damned if she didn't want him too. She just wasn't sure she could get him out of that tux quickly enough. "I need to use the powder room first," she said.

He gazed down at her, a promise in his eyes.

Jamie slipped from his arms and stepped inside the bathroom, purse in hand. An old claw-foot bathtub dominated the room. The mahogany woodwork had been softened with beige linen wallpaper and ivory towels. Still a bit rattled, Jamie checked behind the shower curtain, and then told herself she was being silly. From the next room, she heard soft music and realized Max had turned on a radio. She swayed to the sound as she reached for the zipper of her dress, slid it down and shrugged out of it. She gazed at her flushed face in the mirror, noted the worry lines on either side of her mouth.

She wished she weren't so edgy.

She reached into her purse for the minibottle of Kahlúa that she had stuffed into her pocketbook before leaving the house that evening. Dee Dee had given it to her, as well as a raw-silk jacket, when she and Beenie had returned from a shopping trip in New York. Jamie had suspected things might turn romantic with Max before the evening was over, and she'd hoped the Kahlúa would settle her nerves. She opened the small bottle and took a sip. What if she was making a mistake? What if she fell head over heels in love with Max, knowing how reluctant he was to make a long-term commitment? What if? Oh, the hell with it, she thought. She drained the small bottle.

Bravery had never tasted so good. She could feel her shoulder muscles relaxing, and the knots loosening in her stomach.

It was about time she took a few chances in life.

MAX UNDID THE KNOT OF HIS BOW TIE AND WALKED into the sitting room. He opened the small refrigerator and reached inside for a container of bottled water. He turned and started for the bedroom when a light tap at the door stopped him. He unlocked it and opened it, finding a squat, gray-haired woman on the other side. She held a tray of food.

"I hope I'm not disturbing you, Mr. Holt," she said quickly, "I know it's terribly late—I've been up watching old black-and-white movies, and I heard you come in and thought you might enjoy a light snack from the kitchen."

"You must be Mrs. Hobbs," Max said, backing away so the woman could enter.

"Yes, but you can call me Myrna." She set the tray on the coffee table. "I trust you've found everything you needed."

"Everything is fine."

"I hope you like croissants. I also brought several cheeses and grapes. Fruit and cheese always go together so well, don't you think?"

"You wouldn't happen to have a bottle of champagne handy, would you?" Max asked.

Mrs. Hobbs sniffed. "I don't keep alcoholic beverages on the premises, Mr. Holt. I guess it comes from my strict Baptist upbringing, but I've always been a teetotaler. My husband accuses me of being far too prim and proper, but I'm afraid it's a little late in life for me to change."

"I understand, Myrna, and I respect your beliefs. Thank you for bringing me the snack." The woman didn't seem to take the hint.

"Tell me, Mr. Holt," Myrna said, her eyes bright with curiosity. "What's it like being a big-time celebrity with all that money?"

Max laughed and shook his head. It didn't look like Myrna was in a hurry to leave.

JAMIE HAD FRESHENED HER MAKEUP AND SPRAYED perfume in places she was certain would shock Vera's church friends. She fluffed her hair, hoping it gave her a wild, untamed look.

She turned for the door, felt her head swim. She was loose as a goose. Maybe she shouldn't have drunk the whole ounce of Kahlúa, especially since she'd had more than her share of wine at Frankie and Dee Dee's party. Not only that, she'd barely touched her food.

Oh, well, it was too late to worry about it now. Besides, she was single and over twenty-one, and if she wanted to act a little wild and crazy every now and then, so be it. Max accused her of thinking too much, of being too predictable.

Let him get a look at the new Jamie Swift.

The music was coming from the alarm-clock radio on the bedside table; Johnny Mathis singing "Chances Are." The bed was empty. Jamie wondered why Max wasn't already naked and in it. Maybe he'd sensed just how nervous she was and wanted to take his time. She turned for the short hall leading to the sitting room, almost tripping over her own two feet.

Okay, so she was a little tipsy.

" 'Chances are,' " she sang off-key as she started down the hall, failing miserably at her attempt to walk straight. Finally, she called out. "Okay, here I am, ready and willing." She stepped inside the sitting room, did a little dance routine, and then froze when she found Max standing at the door with Myrna Hobbs.

The woman looked Jamie's way, and her mouth formed a gigantic O.

. . .

"JAMIE, I'M SORRY YOU'RE SO EMBARRASSED," MAX said, once he'd packed her inside his car and pulled away from Carteret Street Bed and Breakfast.

"I'll get over it."

Max shook his head. "I can't believe Myrna Hobbs kicked me out of my room."

Jamie wasn't surprised. "Oh, that's nothing. Myrna will beat it to the Piggly Wiggly the minute they open tomorrow. By noon, everyone in town will know what happened." She did a massive eye-roll. "Did you hear what that woman called me, Max? She called me a drunken floozy."

"Yeah, well, I think I got it across to her that I didn't appreciate it."

Jamie had to admit it was true. Max had called Myrna Hobbs on the carpet for that one, which was why the woman had asked him to leave the premises. "Thank you for defending me."

He grinned. "I'll have to admit, you *did* sort of look like a drunken floozy, but I liked it. You looked cute."

Jamie groaned.

"Hey, I think it's great you've loosened up, Swifty." He gave a low whistle. "And that thing you're wearing under your dress," he added. "Where can I buy you ten more just like it?"

So he'd liked the body suit. At least one good thing had come of the evening.

A voice sounded from the dashboard. "Excuse me? What are we up to *now*?"

Jamie put her finger to her lips in an obvious attempt to stop Max from telling Muffin what had just occurred. He smiled and turned down the volume switch. "Wait a minute. You're worried about what my computer will think of you?"

"Muffin is not just *any* computer," she whispered.

Max turned up the switch.

"Hello?" Muffin called out. "Is anyone home?"

"I'm here," Max said.

"Why'd you hit the volume switch?"

"None of your business," he said, grinning.

Silence. Finally, "Don't piss me off, Max. You need me. I make you look good."

"Yeah, yeah, yeah. I need the name of another hotel. Something with a work station so I can go on-line. You know the routine."

"What was wrong with the last one?" Muffin asked.

"Too stuffy. See what you can find."

Jamie was only vaguely aware of the conversation between the two. She didn't feel well, her stomach was churning and her head hurt, no doubt from the alcohol she'd consumed. She was glad when

Max turned into her driveway. She waited until the safety bar rose before reaching for the doorknob. "Well, I'd invite you in, but I have to go throw up."

"Rule number one: never mix your alcohol."

"Geez, I could have used that information earlier."

FLEAS NUDGED JAMIE AWAKE THE NEXT MORNING at five A.M. She rubbed her eyes and looked at him. "Gee, thanks for rescuing me from the possibility of sleeping late on a Saturday." Since becoming housemates with the bloodhound, she rarely slept until the alarm clock sounded during the workweek, and she never slept late on weekends.

"This must be what it's like to have kids," she grumbled, knowing Fleas probably had to go to the bathroom. After that he would want something to eat. She sighed.

The doorbell rang. Max, no doubt. The man was like a vampire. He could live on four hours' sleep. She stumbled from the bed and into the living room. Her head hurt, and her eyes felt gritty. She checked the peephole, and sure enough, Max stood on the other side.

She opened the door. How could he look that good in the morning? "What?"

"How's your head?"

She noted the amused look. "I think a couple of aspirin might help. Is that why you stopped by?"

"I know you don't like getting up before seven," he said. "That's why I brought coffee and dough-nuts. To sort of soften the blow."

"Chocolate doughnuts?"

"Chocolate mocha cream."

Damn the man for knowing her every weakness. She opened the door. He stepped inside and fol-lowed her into the kitchen, staring at her wrinkled sleep shirt. "I was kind of hoping you'd still be wearing that black thing this morning," he said, set-ting down her coffee and the folder he carried under one arm.

Jamie reached for the aspirin bottle beside her sink. She popped two in her mouth and followed it with a sip of water. "I burned it," she said.

"God, please, no."

"Okay, I'm *thinking* about burning it."

"Don't do it, Jamie. Burn that shirt instead."

She took a sip of her coffee. Naturally, Max knew just how she liked it. He grinned at Fleas and the two reacquainted themselves, Max giving the ani-mal a hearty rub on the head. "Have you taught him any tricks yet?" he asked Jamie.

She looked into the bag of doughnuts and pulled one out. Fleas licked his chops. "Yeah, he's learned to wait until I leave the house before getting on my sofa so he doesn't get yelled at."

"Good dog." Max offered the dog a sympathetic

look. "Sorry to hear she had your gonads cut off, guy. You're looking a little depressed."

"Speaking of his unmentionables, he needs to go out." Jamie unlocked the back door, opened it, and Fleas ambled outside as though he had all the time in the world. "Don't pee on my rosebush," she said, as he hiked his leg on a small bush of tiny yellow tea roses.

Max chuckled. "Yeah, you've trained him real well."

Jamie carried her coffee and doughnut to the kitchen table and sat down. "Not that I'm not thrilled to see you, Max, but is there a specific reason you felt you had to visit the minute the sun came up?"

He grabbed his folder and joined her. "Yeah, Muffin has all kinds of information for us. I figured you'd be interested."

"I'm all ears," she mumbled.

"Remember the ad that read 'Till Death Do Us Part'?"

"Yeah, that was spooky," Jamie said.

"He's a minister who performs a lot of marriage ceremonies. He obviously doesn't believe in divorce."

Jamie glanced up quickly. "A minister? Lamar said someone called Luanne saying he was a man of God. Max, we could be on to something."

"That's why I told Muffin to dig deeper."

"Anything else?"

"All the men are either single or divorced. We've got an auto mechanic, a dentist, a chef, and—" He paused and chuckled. "Remember the ad that read 'Offer Good for a Limited Time'?"

"Yeah."

"He's a car salesman."

Jamie laughed. She had finished her doughnut and was debating having a second, but she wouldn't rush. She didn't want Max to think she lacked discipline. She sipped her coffee, counted to ten.

"Just get the doughnut and be done with it," he said, as though reading her mind. "I bought extra."

Jamie got up, grabbed the bag and carried it to the table. "I don't normally eat more than one, but—"

"Save it, Swifty. This is me you're talking to. I've seen you go through a dozen doughnuts in two days flat."

She frowned at Max but took a bite from the second doughnut nevertheless. "I was under a lot of stress at the time. So the guys you mentioned seemed to check out okay?"

"Yeah. Their ages vary, but most of them just want to meet someone who likes to go to a movie or dine out, that sort of thing."

"Um, what about the guy Destiny and I thought was so cool. You know, the ad that read 'Deeper Than the Night'?"

"I was waiting for you to ask about him. What do you know about Samuel Alister Hunter, or Sam Hunter as he's called?"

Jamie arched both brows. "I didn't recognize the name until just now, but then I'm not used to seeing his full name. And I can't tell you much about him except that he was a hunk in high school. Unfortunately, I was in middle school at the time so I didn't stand a chance. He went off to college, and eventually went to work on Wall Street. I haven't seen him since. I had no idea he'd returned to Beaumont."

"He just moved back. He's semiretired after making his money in the stock market, but he's looking to buy land which he plans to develop."

"No kidding? I wonder if he's still a hunk."

"Control yourself, Swifty. You're hot for me, remember?"

"I should probably try to set up a date with him," she said. "Just in case he's the murderer," she added.

"You're a brave and admirable woman," Max said, "to put yourself in harm's way in order to protect others."

"That's me, Max, brave and admirable. Willing to risk life and limb for the safety of others."

Max leaned back in his chair and regarded her with a half-smile. "You didn't sound so brave last night when we were discussing the supernatural."

"I hope we're not going to get on that subject again," Jamie said.

Fleas scratched at the back door. Jamie let him in, gave him a doughnut and poured him a bowl of milk.

"That's the most ridiculous thing I've ever seen in my life," Max said. "He should be eating meat."

"He has a cheeseburger every day for lunch." Jamie put on a fresh pot of coffee, hoping it would ease her throbbing head. She leaned against the cabinet.

"Back to the subject of Sam Hunter," Max said. "We don't really know much about the guy, and he returned to Beaumont three days before running his ad."

"Why would a guy with his looks be interested in someone like Luanne Ritter?" Jamie pondered aloud.

"Maybe he didn't know her."

"That's hard to believe, everybody knew Luanne."

"What did she look like?"

"She was so-so," Jamie said, trying to think of a nice way to describe the woman.

"I've got all the addresses, information, every-thing. We need to check these people out. You're go-ing to have to arrange a date with them. Quickly," he added.

"I can't date all these men that fast," Jamie said.

"You're only going to contact the ones who allowed their phone numbers to be printed," Max said. "Unless you want to tell them that you were processing their ads at the newspaper office and liked what you saw. Maybe we can enlist Destiny. She can contact half of them. Besides, she already knows what's going on."

"That's a great idea," Jamie said, sarcasm slipping into her voice. "Ronnie can chaperone."

"Yeah, well, we'll have to talk to her about bringing Ronnie. We don't want to spook these guys. But I think between the two of you, we'll be able to get the job done quicker. I'll be close by, of course."

"We're not going to be able to find out who the murderer is in one date," Jamie said.

"You're right. We're going to have to watch them. If I have to call in some of my people, I will."

"We don't have a minute to waste, Max. We need to get to work on this immediately."

He stood, crossed the distance between them, and pulled Jamie against him. "It's still early. We could toss out that shirt."

Jamie's stomach fluttered in response. He had a point there. It wasn't even eight o'clock. Murderers usually waited until after dark to strike. She was about to respond when the doorbell rang several times.

"So much for that idea," Max said, releasing her with a sigh.

Jamie hurried into the living room and peered through the peephole. "Oh, damn. It's Vera," she called out to Max. "She's probably already heard the news. Myrna works fast."

the
... as long as I've lived.
LADY WHY ...
Yeah, I'm ... pretty ... threw me out of the
... livestock to have me around, if I didn't
have ... entered a ... contest because I
have to know ... ... for Aunt Almira to

CHAPTER SEVEN

JAMIE REACHED FOR THE DOORKNOB AND OPENED it. "Good morning, Vera. Max and I were just having coffee and doughnuts. Won't you join us?"

The woman stepped through the front door. "I just ran into Myrna Hobbs at the Piggly Wiggly. Were you really drunk and doing the hootchy-kootchy in one of her suites last night?"

"Aw, Jamie was just having a little fun," Max said, coming up behind her. "Mrs. Hobbs overreacted."

"Yeah, I was just having a little fun," Jamie echoed.

"At least you're being honest with me," Vera told her, "which is a good thing. I couldn't bear the thought of your being a slut *and* a liar."

Jamie rolled her eyes. "I'm not a slut. There aren't enough eligible men in this town for me to be a slut, even if I wanted to."

Vera looked at Jamie. "Well, for your information, I slapped Myrna's face and told her she'd better never make another derogatory comment about you as long as she lived."

"Good for you," Max said.

"You actually slapped her?" Jamie asked. "In the Piggly Wiggly?"

"Yeah, the security guard threw me out of the store, threatened to have me arrested if I didn't leave. I can't afford to go to the slammer because I have to teach Sunday school for Agnes Aimsley tomorrow. She's still in shock after seeing all those unmentionables hanging in the window of Sinful Delights." Vera had to pause to suck in a deep breath.

"Myrna Hobbs will think twice before she decides to pull me over in frozen foods and start talking trash about you. I told her it was okay if I called you a slut, but she'd better keep her fat mouth shut."

"Thank you for defending me," Jamie said. "I think."

Vera shrugged as if it were no big deal. "Look, I know you're all grown-up, but if you insist on sleeping around you're going to have to be discreet. I hope you're on the pill and practicing safe sex. I probably should have had this talk with you long before now. I probably shouldn't have fed you all those brownies."

Max regarded Jamie. "You never mentioned you were promiscuous."

Jamie pressed the ball of her hand against her forehead. "Vera, could we talk about this later? I have a small headache."

"She's hungover," Max said. "She mixed wine with Kahlúa."

"Yeah, Myrna mentioned you had an alcohol problem," Vera said. "You might want to get help with that."

Fleas came up beside Jamie and nuzzled her leg as though he sensed she was in need of his support. Jamie sighed. "Would you guys give me a break? I have less sex than this dog, and he's been neutered. And I'm *not* an alcoholic."

"She's in denial," Max said, obviously enjoying the whole thing.

Vera turned to him. "Now that we've got that settled, I want you to come outside and look at this Ferrari I'm test-driving. I thought maybe you'd take a ride with me, see what you think."

Max shrugged. "Sure."

"You're test-driving a Ferrari?" Jamie said incredulously. "Why?"

"Because I'm thinking of buying it. I can buy a Ferrari if I want to."

Jamie had just realized Vera was wearing Capri

pants. Vera, who never wore anything other than dresses. "Do you have any idea how much they cost?"

"Yeah, but it's ten years old, and the guy is going to cut me a deal. I'm thinking I need something a little sporty. I'm thinking I need to reinvent myself. I've signed up for a class on line dancing. I might meet someone. All the men at church are on their last legs." Vera started out the door, then paused and glanced over her shoulder at Jamie. "You might want to change into something else. That shirt you're wearing isn't very flattering."

BY THE TIME MAX RETURNED, JAMIE HAD SHOW-ered and changed into shorts and a cotton T-shirt. She wore only a hint of makeup, and had pulled her wet hair into a ponytail. Luckily, her headache had dulled.

Max paused when he saw her. "Damned if you don't have the best set of legs I've ever seen on a woman. No wonder you have such a reputation with men."

Jamie gave him one of her looks. "Tell me Vera isn't really going to buy a Ferrari," she said.

"I think I convinced her not to. The mileage was too high, and it's kind of beat-up. I told her I could probably find her a good deal on a car if she'd give me a few days, but I think she's having a good time looking. Now, why don't we get to work?"

"Okay, I'll call Destiny and see if she can help," Jamie said, although she wasn't thrilled at the prospect.

DESTINY ARRIVED AN HOUR LATER. "HERE ARE THE ground rules," Max said, addressing both women. "You meet the guy in public, and you carry a cell phone that I will provide for each of you, complete with a GPA."

"What the heck is a GPA?" Destiny asked.

Jamie answered. "It's a device that lets Max know where we are at all times."

"You two have done this sort of thing before, haven't you?" Destiny asked.

Jamie nodded. "Yeah, and we always get the bad guy in the end." She paused. "Um, Destiny, Max and I didn't want to bring this up, but it might be distracting if you start talking to Ronnie on your, um, dates."

Destiny turned to the empty chair beside her. "Did you hear that, Ronnie? We're trying to find a killer. You're going to have to keep your mouth shut." She paused. Finally, she turned to Max and Jamie. "He promises to cooperate if I'll hang out with him at the bowling alley afterward. That's Ronnie's idea of a good time." She rolled her eyes.

"Okay," Max said. "Muffin, my assistant, was able to get much of the information we need. The guy with the 'Till Death Do Us Part' ad is a minister. We just found out he does a lot of marriage counseling, even has a little wedding chapel and provides everything a couple needs for the auspicious occasion, right down to the flowers and catering. He's very antidivorce and insists on counseling couples for an extended period of time before he'll agree to marry them. He accepts fairly large donations for the sessions, and the use of his chapel. I think Jamie and I should check him out just in case. We could pose as an engaged couple."

"That'll never work," Jamie said. "He'll see right through us."

"Not if you act like a real fiancée," Max said. "You're going to have to be nice to me, hold my hand, and simper at me a lot. That's what engaged couples do. It isn't until after the marriage that they learn to dislike each other."

Jamie just looked at him. Leave it to Max to make marriage sound like a prison term.

"Aw, come on, Swifty, it'll be fun," Max said, as though he hadn't realized he'd made a blunder. He reached for a cell phone in his pocket and punched a button. "Muffin, why don't you see if the Reverend Heyward can schedule us after lunch," he said. "In the meantime, Jamie and I are going to check out one Larry Johnson, author of 'Offer Good for a Limited Time.'"

"I'm on it," Muffin said. "What else?"

"Just hold tight." Max turned to Destiny. "I want you to call the dentist. He takes Saturday-morning appointments. Can you fake a toothache?"

She shrugged. "I've faked orgasms, that's gotta count for something. Besides, my wisdom teeth have been bothering me for months. I can kill two birds with one stone."

LARRY JOHNSON OWNED AND OPERATED BEAUMONT Used Cars and reminded Jamie of a weasel with his beady, close-set black eyes. He held a hand-flex exerciser in one fist and pumped it furiously as he questioned Max about his Porsche look-alike. "That didn't come off an assembly line," Johnson said.

"You're right," Max said. "I had it custom designed."

Johnson changed the flex device to his other hand before taking them on a tour of the lot.

"My therapist advised me to use this," Larry told Jamie when he caught her staring. "I work out every morning at the local gym. It's supposed to help with stress."

"Does it?"

"No." He chuckled. "The only thing that works is a double shot of scotch straight up."

Jamie and Max pretended to find his words amusing. "I can certainly relate to that," Jamie said, thinking it was a good way to break the ice. They needed to get a fix on the guy, and in order to do that they needed good rapport. "I prefer Kahlúa," she added with a grin.

Larry smiled at her but didn't let up on his flexing. "That's a girlie drink."

She batted her lashes, something Dee Dee would have done with ease but which she found taxing. "So, I'm a girl."

Larry paused and gave her a long, hard look. "Yeah." He cleared his throat. "So, do you folks see anything you like?" It was obvious Larry had seen what he liked.

"I want to take a second look at the white Chevy Corvette convertible," Max said.

Larry nodded. "Good choice. Just so happens that's my old car, and I took damn good care of it. Low mileage, too," he added. He hitched his shoulders high. "Just bought me a brand-new one. Unfortunately, it's about the only nice thing I own since my divorce. Child support payments, you know? But I'm real proud of it. Got a security system on it that'll wake the dead."

They walked over to the used Corvette, and Max climbed in. "You mind if I take it for a test drive?"

"No problem, pardner." Larry dropped the keys into Max's hand. "It runs like a charm."

"I'll stay here and wait for you," Jamie said, giving Max one of her looks. She glanced Larry's way. "I might just find something on the lot I like."

The comment seemed to fly right over Larry's head, Jamie noticed, but then he probably thought she and Max were a couple. Jamie figured she could change that easily enough. She looked at Larry. "You got any coffee inside?"

"Sure."

Max took off in the Corvette, and Jamie followed Larry inside a small building. The dark paneled walls were adorned with pictures of race cars. Jamie noted a nondescript woman sitting before a computer. "This is my secretary, Mabel," Larry said. The two women nodded, and Mabel handed Larry several messages. "Come into my office and I'll pour you a cup of java," he told Jamie.

"Actually, Larry, I don't care for coffee," Jamie said once he'd closed the door behind them.

"Well, then, we'll just chat until your, um"—he glanced at Jamie's ring finger, which was bare—"until your significant other returns."

Jamie sat on a fake-leather couch. "Max and I are just friends. You know, good buddies."

"Oh, well, that's nice." Flex, flex. "You can never

have too many friends in this crazy world," he said. "Me? I'm a loner."

"Sometimes it's good to have someone to talk to after you've ended a relationship. I speak from experience."

"Sorry to hear that, Jamie. Is it okay if I call you Jamie?"

She nodded. "I know what you're feeling right now because I've gone through it. The pain and emptiness." She sighed heavily. There were times she thought she would have made a damn good actress. "The loneliness," she added.

He was flexing triple time. "I can't imagine a woman with your looks being lonely. Maybe you should get out more."

Jamie gave a grunt of disgust. "Most of the men in this town are either married or downright ugly. It's not every day a woman meets a guy who owns his own business and is attractive to boot."

He nodded. Finally, he jerked his head up as though a lightbulb had just gone off inside. "Oh, were you talking about me?"

Jamie wagged her finger and made a tsking sound with her tongue. "You're playing games, Larry. I don't like games."

He sat up straighter in his chair. The man's eyes registered interest. "Maybe you and I can get together for a drink sometime. Soon," he added, after a few seconds.

"How about this evening?" Jamie asked.

He looked surprised. "Well, sure. I usually leave here around six. I could meet you in the lounge at the Holiday Inn around six-fifteen. They have happy hour until seven-thirty. Free food, half price on drinks." He gave a self-deprecating smile. "That's usually where I eat my dinner. Not that I can't afford to take a lady someplace nice once in a while and buy her a real meal," he added quickly. "Why, we could—"

"The Holiday Inn will be fine, Larry. Six-fifteen," she added.

The Corvette reappeared, and Max climbed from it. Jamie watched him walk toward the building. She wondered if Max had any idea just how good-looking he was, how no men came close in comparison.

Jamie and Larry rejoined Max. "What'd you think of the car?" Larry asked.

"I like the looks of it," Max said. "Let us talk with our friend. If she's interested, we'll bring her over."

"I look forward to hearing from you," Larry said. He winked at Jamie. He seemed so excited at the thought of meeting her later that he didn't even bother with a sales pitch.

Max and Jamie climbed into Max's car and pulled from the car lot. "I'm meeting Mr. Johnson for a drink at six-fifteen," Jamie said. "The lounge at the Holiday Inn."

"Boy, you work fast," Max said. "I didn't even have time to get the VIN number off the car so Muffin could check it out. No wonder you've got such a reputation in this town."

Jamie rolled her eyes.

Muffin came on. "Make sure you don't get into Larry Johnson's car," she warned Jamie. "He's got a couple of DUIs on his record."

"Hmm," Max said. "And I'd stay away from the Kahlúa tonight, Swifty, or you'll be doing the hootchy-kootchy on the tables at the Holiday Inn."

Jamie looked at him. "Go ahead and have your fun. I, on the other hand, have a job to do." She paused. "Speaking of which, have you heard from Destiny?"

"Yeah, she's waiting to see the dentist."

DR. KEVIN SMALLS, A THIRTYSOMETHING MAN, WAS almost completely bald, and his belly tugged at the buttons on his shirt. The examining room was decorated in a pale blue-green; obviously to make patients feel less anxious, but it wasn't working on Destiny as she drummed her long nails against the arm of her chair.

"Just relax," the dental assistant said and smiled. "We haven't lost a patient yet."

Finally, Dr. Smalls pulled the small mouth mirror from Destiny's mouth. "Okay, I'm done here. I'll meet you in my office." He got up and left the room.

Destiny was shown to his office a moment later. Smalls shook his head sadly. "It's no wonder your wisdom teeth have been bothering you, Miss Moultrie," he said. "You know, most people have them extracted at a much earlier age."

"Really?" Destiny asked, not looking too pleased. She glanced around the office, her eyes resting on a bag of golf clubs.

"They're crowding the back of your mouth. I suggest we set you up with an oral surgeon as soon as possible."

"Do you play golf, doctor?" she asked.

He glanced at the bag of clubs. "When I have time. My wife and I share custody of our children so my weekends are pretty much taken up with them."

"So, what do you do for fun?" she asked.

"Well, I hadn't really thought much about it."

"Maybe it's time you started taking care of your own needs. You could start by inviting me to lunch."

MAX AND JAMIE GRABBED AN EARLY LUNCH AT Maynard's Sandwich Shop where Donnie Maynard convinced Max his meat-loaf sandwich was the best thing in the world next to indoor plumbing.

"I'll give it a try," Max said.

"Make that two," Jamie told Donnie and wondered if Max had ever eaten a meat-loaf sandwich.

Max paid for the order, and they carried their drinks to a table. The walls inside the shop were of old brick, the tables and chairs battered and scarred, yet sturdy. Max took a sip of his iced tea. As if noting the curious look on Jamie's face, he arched one brow. "What?"

"When's the last time you had meat loaf?"

"Are you kidding? My cousin's wife, Billie, used to cook it all the time."

"The people who practically raised you?" she asked, remembering he'd mentioned them before.

"Right. I was sixteen years old when I moved in with them. Nick taught me everything I know about the newspaper business and horses; Billie taught me to focus my energy."

"You lost me on the last part."

"I was pretty much a juvenile delinquent from the age of five."

"Too smart for your own good, I'll bet."

"Nick was instrumental in breaking my bad habits by having me muck the stalls each time I got into trouble. You ever mucked a horse stall?"

"Nope. Don't want to, either."

"Builds character."

Their sandwiches arrived. Jamie thanked Donnie and waited until he walked away before saying anything. She knew that Max's parents had pretty much given up on their son; that the only attention he'd gotten was from the servants and during his summer vacations with his cousin Nick. "Do you ever see your parents?"

"I swing by now and then if I'm in the vicinity. They're older and have more time for me than they used to." He took a bite of his sandwich and nodded his approval. "Hey, this is good," he said.

Jamie bit into her sandwich, as well. As usual, Donnie had outdone himself on the meat loaf. "He has a secret recipe. Neither love nor money will get him to part with it." But her thoughts were elsewhere. She pondered what Max had just said about his parents having time for him now. There had been no bitterness in his voice. He'd obviously come to terms with their relationship. "What about Nick and Billie?" she asked. "Do you see them often?"

"I usually spend holidays with them. They have two kids; Christie and Joel." He chuckled. "Well, they're not really kids anymore, Christie is probably about thirty, and Joel is a couple of years younger. They both work for the newspaper. We're all pretty close." He smiled.

"Why are you smiling?" Jamie asked.

"I'm thinking about Billie. She goes all out decorating the house for Christmas, and every year she swears it's going to be her last. Somehow, she ends up doing even more the next year." He paused. "You would like her. She's simple and down-to-earth. So is Nick."

"I'll bet they're proud of you."

Max looked surprised. "Thank you. I believe that's the nicest thing you've ever said to me."

"Well, look at all you've accomplished, Max."

He shrugged. "Nick taught me to go after what I wanted. The only time he disagreed with me was when I told him I was getting married. He and Billie didn't feel I was ready. It didn't take me long to realize they were right."

"Is that why you're dead set against marriage now?"

"Let's just say I learned my lesson. I'm in no hurry to repeat that mistake."

"Don't you think you're being a little harsh?" Jamie asked. "I mean, look at Frankie and Dee Dee. After twenty years they're still madly in love."

"I'd say they're the exception, as are Nick and Billie."

They concentrated on their lunch after that, although Jamie realized she didn't have much of an appetite. She wondered how long it would be before Max became bored with her and moved on, and the thought was not a pleasant one. But she couldn't think about that right now because she had to work with him to solve Luanne Ritter's murder.

In the meantime, she needed to protect her heart.

Once they'd finished lunch, they thanked Donnie and headed out the door. Muffin was waiting for them.

"Good thing I don't take lunch breaks or we wouldn't get anything done," she said.

"What's up?" Max asked.

"The Reverend Heyward claimed he was much too busy to see you, but I was able to get you in at two o'clock, once I hinted that a hefty donation would change hands."

"Great," Max said. "That'll give us time to check out a couple of addresses." Max reached for a folder beside his seat. He handed it to Jamie. "How about looking at the ad entitled 'Open to New Experiences' and giving me the address," he said. "You know, the guy looking for a discreet relationship?"

Jamie flipped through the file of names and printouts that Muffin had supplied. "Here we go. John Price, age fifty-five, new to Beaumont, recently opened his own accounting firm. He lives on the edge of town. I know the area. Just stay on this road until you hit the main highway."

Max followed her directions, and they ended up in a rural area. They found the house, a two-story frame with NO TRESPASSING signs on the property, and a Doberman pinscher on a long leash that was attached to the porch rail.

"Well, now, Mr. Price obviously doesn't want company," Max said. "What else have we got on him?"

Jamie glanced back at the file. "Like I said, he's new in town, lived here about three months," she said. "Been divorced about a year from his second wife. He has a daughter by his first wife; she's in college. No police record. He left a high-paying position in Atlanta to come here. He's renting the house."

Max picked up a pair of binoculars and trained them on the man's residence. "Interesting. He's installed a fairly expensive security system on a piece of rental property, and he's got a man-eating creature guarding the front door. Wonder what he's got guarding the back?"

"I'm not going to go look," Jamie said. "I don't want to arrive at my date with half my face ripped off. Besides, he's accustomed to living in a large city where the crime rate is high."

Max looked at her. "Or maybe he's hiding something. Muffin, do what you have to do, but I want to know if Mr. Price is at work today. I want to have a look inside."

Jamie gaped. "You're not going in there?" When

Max didn't respond, she went on. "See, this is why I should never have called you. I should have let Lamar Tevis handle it. You remember Lamar Tevis, our chief of police? He's the man who's going to throw you behind bars for breaking and entering."

"Just for the record, Max," Muffin said, "I want you to know I'm taking Jamie's side on this." She paused for a few minutes, and then came back on the speaker. "Mr. Price is with a client," she said.

Max grinned. "Perfect. Now, here's what we're going to do."

CHAPTER EIGHT

JAMIE WATCHED MAX SLIP AROUND THE SIDE OF the house and disappear. The dog out front barked ferociously. "I hate this," she said to Muffin. "Max has absolutely no respect for the law. He's either hacking through firewalls or breaking and entering, and I can't believe I always find myself in the middle of it. One day we're going to get caught, and they're going to lock us up and throw away the key."

Three minutes later, Muffin came on. "He's in." Then, a quick, "Uh-oh."

Jamie's heart leaped to her throat. "What is it?"

"There's another Doberman inside. A mean one."

"Holy Toledo!" Jamie cried. All at once, the dog out front began barking out of control.

"Hang on, Max," Muffin said. "I'll cover you."

"What's going on?" Jamie demanded.

"I just blasted both animals with an ultrasonic frequency that should draw their attention for a few minutes. Max and I have done this sort of thing before. Max," Muffin said. "Are you okay?"

Jamie's nails bit into the palms of her hands. "Put him on the speaker," she said. "I want to know that he's okay."

Max came on. "I managed to lock the dog in the bathroom. I'm going to search the place."

"Oh, boy," Jamie said. "Muffin, how do you plan to get him out?"

"Same way I got him in."

Jamie counted the minutes. "How long has he been in there?"

"Less than five minutes," Muffin said. "There's nothing we can do but wait."

"I wish I hadn't quit smoking," Jamie said. "I could use a cigarette about now."

"Don't worry," Muffin told her. "Max is good at this sort of thing."

Jamie watched the clock on the dashboard. The next ten minutes seemed to drag on forever. Once Max was finished searching the house, he alerted Muffin, and she hit the dogs with the high-frequency sound once again. Max emerged from the house looking calm. He started the car and pulled away. "The place is clean," he said. "I didn't find anything out of the ordinary, but that doesn't mean we're not dealing with a killer."

Jamie leaned her head against the seat and

closed her eyes, waiting for her heartbeat to return to normal.

Once Max had driven a distance, he looked at her. "Are you okay?"

"I am now."

"So you were worried about me, huh?"

She just looked at him.

Max grinned. "Muffin, Jamie was worried about me. That says a lot about our relationship."

"What relationship?" Muffin asked.

"Thank you, Muffin," Jamie said, "for not feeding his enormous ego. He knows darn well why I was worried. I don't look good in stripes, and if I go to prison, what's going to happen to Fleas? Nobody wants a dog with emotional problems and missing hair."

"You guys need to stop arguing," Muffin said. "You have an appointment with the Reverend Heyward in half an hour. You're supposed to be in love."

THE REVEREND JOE HEYWARD WAS A BIG MAN, standing well over six feet, with a broad chest that made Jamie think of Frankie. He looked to be in his early sixties. "So you two are thinking of getting married," he said, once Jamie and Max had joined him in his office. The paneled walls were adorned with pictures of happy brides and grooms.

"Yes, sir," Max said. "We're in love."

"Madly," Jamie said.

"Sometimes, love is not enough," the reverend replied. "There are trials and tribulations in this world that can tear a couple apart unless they are determined to work on their relationship every single day, every single hour, every single minute. You must be one hundred and fifty percent dedicated."

"Wow, that sounds like a lot of work," Max said.

"It certainly is," the reverend replied. "Otherwise, you'll end up in divorce court like half the couples in this country, and—" He paused and leaned forward. "I do not believe in divorce." He clasped his hands as if in prayer. "What God hath joined together let no man put asunder. Till death do you part," he added.

"We agree, don't we, honey?" Max said to Jamie.

"Huh? Oh, right."

The reverend went on as though he hadn't heard. "I was married to my wife for thirty years before the Lord took her. Do you think it was always easy? No, it was not. Oh, she looked real nice when I first met her, all dolled up at the church social. Prettiest thing I'd ever seen. But people change over the years, and you have to accept change."

The man pointed to Jamie. "She's a beauty right now, but what are you going to do when she gets fat and starts nagging with every breath? 'Cause you can count on that happening, son. Women love to nag. They can nag in their sleep. You fantasize about putting a pillow over their face and shutting them up for good." He paused and cleared his throat, as if realizing he'd made a blunder. "Not that I would ever consider such an act, mind you."

Jamie almost shivered at his last sentence. The man sounded off his rocker. Why on earth Luanne had contacted him was beyond her; the woman had obviously been desperate for male attention. Was he the one who'd called her the night of her murder? What if he'd decided to stop by and meet Luanne personally? Would she have opened the door if he'd mentioned he was a minister? So many unanswered questions.

"This marriage business sounds tougher than I thought it would be," Max said. He looked at Jamie. "And you *do* eat a lot of doughnuts. You keep that up, and you're going to be the size of a freight train."

"That's how big my wife was," Heyward said.

Jamie gaped at Max. "I don't eat *that* many doughnuts. And I don't nag."

"Oh, yes you do," Max told her. He looked at the Reverend Heyward. "And she can be disagreeable at times. It's not always easy."

"I'm not disagreeable," Jamie said. "You're just stubborn and arrogant."

Heyward shook his head sadly. "I can see that we have our work cut out for us." He reached for his appointment book. "Let me see when I can fit you in."

"Would you mind if we get back to you?" Max said. "I need to check my calendar." He handed the man a hefty cash donation.

Heyward's eyes widened at the sight of the money. "I suggest we begin as soon as possible, maybe meet a couple of times a week. Call me as soon as it's convenient. And don't be discouraged; a good solid marriage makes for a lot of happiness. As a matter of fact, I hope to marry again one day soon. I'm definitely in the market for a good wife."

Max was grinning when he and Jamie climbed into the front seat of his car a few minutes later. "What do you think?"

"I think the man is wacko. I don't think many women are going to jump at the chance to become the next Mrs. Heyward. And that business about putting a pillow over someone's face to shut them up." She shuddered. "I don't like it."

"I wouldn't mind knowing how his wife died," Max said.

"Muffin, are you there?" Jamie asked.

"Yeah, what's up?"

"How did the Reverend Joe Heyward's wife die?"

"She choked on a chicken bone," Muffin replied.

Jamie rolled her eyes. "No, seriously."

"I'm telling you, the woman choked on a chicken bone."

Jamie sat there for a moment. She felt Max's smile before she glanced over and saw it. "How can you possibly think that's funny?"

"Well, he said she was as large as a freight train. I'll bet she could put back a whole truckload of fried chicken."

"Max, that's not one bit funny." Nevertheless, Jamie could feel the corners of her mouth twitching. Max reached over and tickled her.

"Lighten up, Swifty. We're not letting Heyward off the hook that easily."

"I don't like being tickled."

"I plan to find all your ticklish spots before long," he said.

Jamie tried not to let her mind run amuck. "So what's next?"

Max didn't hesitate. "I think we need to pay Lamar Tevis a visit and see if he's got the tape of the phone messages Luanne received the night of her murder. Muffin, call the police department and see if the chief is in."

LAMAR GREETED MAX WITH A HANDSHAKE. "GOOD to see you again, Max," he said. He nodded at Jamie and invited them to sit. He reclaimed his chair. "Now, then, may I ask *why* you want to hear the tape?"

Jamie answered. "A minister ran an ad with me, Lamar, and you said a man called Luanne claiming to be a man of God. She must've contacted him and left her telephone number."

"Well, like I told you, the tape must've been old and worn because the voices aren't very clear. But I'll be glad to play it." He popped a small cassette into his answering machine and pushed a button. There were several brief messages, along with a lot of crackling on the tape. They were followed by the voice of the man who claimed to be a man of God and needed to meet with Luanne immediately.

Jamie felt the hairs rise on her arms. She looked at Max.

"It's not Heyward," he said.

"No, but I think I recognize the voice. It sounds like Brent Walker."

Lamar stopped the tape. "Who is Brent Walker?"

"Agnes Aimsley's grandson. He's visiting her from the seminary."

"Are you sure?" Lamar asked.

"Could you play the tape again?" Jamie asked.

Lamar did as she requested. He cut off the machine once the tape ran out. "What do you think?" he said.

"I've only met this Walker guy once, and you're right, the voices aren't very clear, but I'm almost positive it's him. I can't imagine why he'd be calling Luanne, though. He didn't run an ad."

Lamar leaned back in his chair. "I reckon I'll have to pay him a visit and find out."

"I'm curious," Max said. "Was Luanne robbed?"

Lamar looked at Jamie. "We haven't released this information, so this is off the record."

"Of course."

"I think it was made to look like a robbery," he said. "Her jewelry box was cleaned out, but she was wearing several expensive rings. A burglar would have noticed."

THE LOUNGE AT THE HOLIDAY INN WAS DOING A good business when Jamie arrived. Obviously, the free hors d'oeuvres were a big plus; people were lined up at the two tables that had been set up with chafing dishes. Larry Johnson was sitting at the bar. He looked surprised to see Jamie, as if he'd expected her not to show.

He stood as she crossed the room. "You dressed up," he said. "I'm flattered."

"Of course I did," Jamie said. "I wanted to look my best."

"You succeeded very well. Would you rather get a table?"

"A table would be nice," Jamie said, thinking he

would be more open to conversation if they had privacy. She needed him to feel comfortable with her.

Larry grabbed his drink and led Jamie to a table that was situated in a dark corner. A cocktail waitress appeared a moment later. Jamie ordered a club soda and lime; Larry a double scotch.

"I thought you liked Kahlúa," Larry said, once the waitress left them.

Jamie noted he looked disappointed that she hadn't ordered a drink. After what Muffin had said about his drinking history, she suspected Larry preferred hanging with boozers, and, despite all the ribbing Jamie had received about how she'd acted at Myrna Hobbs's place, she seldom touched alcohol. But once again, she needed Larry to feel comfortable around her or he wouldn't say what was on his mind.

"Actually, I love the stuff," she said, "but I'm still recovering from a hangover I got at a friend's birthday party."

He grinned. "I hope you don't mind if I have another."

"No, please, I insist."

"I'm afraid I'm not in the greatest mood tonight," he confessed. "I received a call from my ex-wife, and we got into it over the telephone so I closed the dealership at five and got the hell out of there."

Jamie hoped it meant he'd had time to belt back

several scotches. "I take it the split was not amicable."

He gave a grunt. "Hardly. She got everything, including the house, and I'm paying child support out the ass. My apartment is crap, and I barely have any furniture. All I have to show for years of hard work is a decent car."

"I'm sorry." Jamie didn't know the man well, but she suspected he'd gotten exactly what he deserved. "I'm sure you feel a lot of animosity toward your ex right now, but perhaps it'll pass in time."

"Don't count on it. She put the screws to me. But I'm here to tell you, she's going to get hers."

Jamie caught the menace in his voice. "What do you mean?"

His answer was guarded. "As they say, what goes around comes around, know what I mean?" He suddenly looked apologetic. "I'm sorry. I have no right to unload on you. I invited you here for a good time."

"I *am* having a good time," Jamie said. "I don't get out much."

He looked doubtful. "A woman with your looks? I find that hard to believe."

"Remember, I mentioned I was involved with someone for a while? He didn't like to go out much."

"I go out every night." Larry shrugged. "Here, mostly, but it's better than sitting at home. The ex got the only decent TV set, too. I was mad as hell over that one. A guy shouldn't have to give up his TV."

They were interrupted when the cocktail waitress appeared with their drinks.

Larry shoved several bills at her, told her to keep the change, and she walked away. He stirred his drink. "My ex claims I have an anger problem, among other things. The judge ordered me to get counseling on anger management if I wanted to see my children. I think that sucks." He raised his glass, but it slipped from his hand, and his entire drink spilled on him, soaking the front of his shirt. "Oh, shit, now look what I've done."

Jamie tried to help him mop the spill with a napkin, but it was useless.

"I've got to get out of this shirt," Larry said. "It's sticking to me." He looked at her. "I only live a couple of miles from here. Why don't we run by my place, let me clean up, then we can grab a bite to eat someplace. I'll take you to a real restaurant so you can show off that nice dress."

Jamie hesitated. Max had specifically told her and Destiny not to leave a public area with the men.

"Hey, this isn't a pickup, okay? I just want to get out of this wet shirt."

Jamie knew Max would be mad as hell if she left

the premises with Larry, but what could she do? If she refused to go, she might lose her one chance of finding out whether he had ever met Luanne Ritter, much less visited her the night of her murder. He certainly had an anger problem, and his alcohol abuse made him a walking time bomb.

Besides, she owed Max for having scared the life out of her when he'd broken into John Price's house. "I'll follow you in my car," she said.

They left the lounge. Jamie climbed into her car and followed Larry from the parking lot, wondering if Max could see her from his vantage point at the other end of the lot. She grabbed her cell phone and punched in Max's number. He answered on the first ring.

"Okay, Max, I know you're not going to like this, but I'm following Larry Johnson to his place so he can change shirts." She explained about the spilled drink.

"Bad idea," he said. "I specifically told you—"

"I know what you told me, but I think I'm on to something here. This guy looks suspicious."

"All the more reason to turn your car around and head in the opposite direction. I don't want you alone with him."

"Listen, Max, I can't see him intentionally killing Luanne Ritter, but he has serious problems. I think he feels he can talk to me."

"Oh, so you think you're going to get a full confession out of him?"

"Not exactly, but—"

"Turn your car around, Jamie," he ordered. "It's not worth the risk. I'll follow you to Frankie and Dee Dee's."

"No way, Max. Not when I'm this close. Trust me on this one, okay? And call Frankie and Dee Dee and tell them we can't make it for dinner. I'll be dining with Larry."

She hung up the phone in order to avoid arguing with him. The cell phone rang. She knew it was Max. She ignored it, knowing he would never agree to let her enter Larry's apartment. But she was determined to find out what she could. Besides, something told her she had nothing to fear with Larry Johnson. As long as she played along, she reminded herself.

Finally, the cell phone stopped ringing.

Five minutes later, Jamie followed Larry into the parking lot of a generic-looking apartment complex. She parked beside his car and climbed out. He hit a button on his key chain, and his Corvette beeped. "I don't trust the teenagers around here," he said. "If I ever catch them messing with my car, I'm going to take a crowbar to them. Matter of fact, I keep one behind the seat of my car and another one beside the front door in my apartment."

Jamie suppressed a shiver. Luanne Ritter had

died from a blow to the head. She tried to make light of it. "A crowbar would certainly scare me away," she said with a laugh. At the same time, she wondered what Larry's wife had found appealing about him. "Yes, sir, a crowbar would definitely get my attention," she added, causing him to grin.

She followed Larry to a door and paused beside him while he unlocked it. He opened it, stepped inside and flipped on a light switch, then motioned for Jamie to enter. "It's not much, but it's home."

Jamie followed him into a sparsely furnished living room. Larry had obviously found a good deal on fake-leather furniture because the couch and chair matched those in his office. The apartment smelled of stale food and booze. Sure enough, there was a crowbar leaning against the wall beside the front door. "It's not so bad," she lied. "A few pictures on the wall, and the place would be really homey."

"I'm not much of a decorator."

No kidding, she thought.

"Hey, and I'm sorry about the mess, but I wasn't expecting company." He grabbed a pile of clothes from the sofa. "Have a seat."

Jamie sat down. He went about turning on more lights, then headed into the kitchen and made himself another scotch. "My shirt is plastered to me," he said. "Would you mind if I grabbed a quick shower and changed? Then I'll take you to dinner."

"No problem," she said.

He hurried into the next room. Several minutes later, Jamie heard the sound of running water. She stood and tiptoed into the bedroom and immediately started searching through Larry's dresser drawers. She was looking for jewelry. If Larry had indeed killed Luanne and tried to make it look like a robbery, he could very well have hidden his stash until he could dispose of it. A man with his financial problems would probably try to sell it when he felt it was safe.

If he'd been the one, she reminded herself. *If* the murder was actually tied to her personals ads. There were a lot of ifs, but Jamie knew she wouldn't have any answers unless she checked.

Nothing unusual in the drawers. Jamie glanced at the closet. She sometimes kept money tucked inside an old coat pocket. She heard a noise and turned.

Larry was standing in the doorway, a towel draped around his midsection.

She froze. Damn, damn, damn.

"Why are you in my bedroom?" he asked.

Jamie stared back at him for a full minute as she tried to find her tongue. She had been so engrossed in her search that she hadn't heard the sound of the shower being turned off or the bathroom door opening. Finally, she smiled. "Why do you think?"

• • •

"I SHOULD HAVE KNOWN JAMIE WOULD PULL SOME-thing like this," Max said, having followed her car to Larry's apartment complex and watched her enter through one of the doors.

"What are you going to do?" Muffin asked.

Max stared at the door to the apartment. He noted Larry's Corvette out front. "She thinks she's so smart. Let her figure it out." He sat there for about twenty seconds. "Dammit," he muttered. He opened his car door and climbed out.

LARRY SMILED AT JAMIE AND STEPPED CLOSER. "Why am I surprised?" he said. "I knew we had chemistry the minute I laid eyes on you."

Jamie wanted to tell him she felt about as much at-traction for him as she did for an eel. "Yes," she said in a husky tone meant to sound sexy. "I felt it, too."

"We don't have to go out," Larry said. "Besides, I'm hungry for you."

"Yes. I mean, no," Jamie said hurriedly. "On sec-ond thought, I think we should still go out. Some-place romantic," she added. "We shouldn't rush things."

"I could order pizza. Is that romantic enough?"

"Um, I was sort of hoping for soft music and candlelight. Maybe we could go dancing."

"Baby, we don't need all that." He suddenly pulled her against him. "Why put off the inevitable? You want it as bad as I do." He dropped his towel to the floor and pressed himself against her.

Jamie's skin crawled. The last thing she wanted to see was a naked Larry Johnson. He pulled her face close, studied her with those beady eyes. Oh, hell, he was going to kiss her, she thought.

He lowered his head, and their lips touched. Jamie felt herself stiffen.

"Relax," he whispered against her lips. "I'll go slow."

Jamie closed her eyes. It would be easier to let him kiss her if she didn't have to look at him. She braced herself. Think; think. His kiss deepened, and she started bargaining with God.

Please don't let him stick his tongue in my mouth. I'll even start going to church with Vera if I have to.

Larry pressed his tongue against her lips, trying to prod them open. "Come on, baby," he crooned.

Jamie's heart sank to her toes. She flattened her hand against his bare chest, hoping to push him away gently, when, all at once a loud siren split the night. They both jumped.

"Sonofabitch!" Larry yelled. "Someone is messing with my car."

Jamie's head spun. "What?"

"That's my alarm system. Some asshole is trying to break into my car." He searched the room frantically and grabbed a pair of pants. He danced about, trying to get his legs into his slacks. He didn't bother zipping them as he raced from the room.

"Oh, thank you, God," Jamie whispered as she heard the front door of the apartment being flung open. She hurried into the living room, grabbed her purse, and ran out. She stood there for a moment, disoriented. Finally, she bolted toward her car.

And bumped into Larry and his crowbar.

"My car's okay," he said, and then gave her a funny look. "Where are you going?"

"I just remembered I have to go home and feed my dog."

"Feed your dog?" he said in disbelief. "Can't that wait?"

"He's hypoglycemic. If he doesn't eat every four hours, his blood sugar level drops and—"

"Lady, what the hell are you talking about?" Larry scowled and began flexing his fists. "You get a man hard enough to break concrete blocks, and then you come up with this bullshit story about having to go home and feed your dog? What's with that?"

Jamie suspected he was on the verge of erupting. "Larry, things were getting out of hand. It's my fault. I haven't, well, you know, it's been *sooo* long since I've been with a man, and I'm really attracted to you, but I need more time. I don't want to do something I might regret later, you know? Especially since—" She paused, hoping she sounded convincing. "We might want to keep on seeing each other."

His facial muscles relaxed. "You're worried I won't respect you in the morning, is that it?"

"Something like that. You know how it is."

He seemed to ponder it. Finally, he nodded. "Okay, then, I can wait. I'll call you."

"No. I'll call you. Just give me a couple of days."

He flexed a fist. "Well, okay."

Jamie covered the short distance to her car, climbed in, and punched the lock.

MAX WAS WAITING NEAR THE ENTRANCE TO THE apartment complex. He drove forward slowly as Jamie approached in her Mustang. She followed him for several miles before he pulled into the parking lot of the Piggly Wiggly supermarket. He slammed out of his car.

The look on his face told her she was in deep doo-doo. She rolled down her window. "Max, I—"

He jerked her car door open. "Get out."

Jamie gave a huge sigh but did as he said. "Okay, go ahead and yell at me so we can get it over with."

"Just what the hell were you thinking?"

"I was trying to get information." She wasn't about to tell him she'd ended up in Larry's bedroom.

"You're off the job."

CHAPTER NINE

JAMIE BLINKED FURIOUSLY. "EXCUSE ME?"

"I'm calling in my own people. It's too dangerous, and I can't trust you to follow directions."

"You *can't* pull me off the job," she almost shouted. "I'm the one who called you. Besides, who are you to talk about taking chances when you broke into John Price's house today? At least I didn't break any laws."

"I knew what I was doing or I would never have gone in," Max said. "You acted irrationally by entering Johnson's apartment when we don't know if he's the killer or not. Jesus, Jamie, the man could have overpowered you. You're not thinking straight because you're emotionally involved in this."

"You're not taking me off the *job*, as you call it, but you're right—I *am* emotionally involved. My personals section could be connected to Luanne Ritter's murder. *That's* why I took the chance I did. If Larry Johnson killed Luanne, I want to know."

"At the risk of causing harm to yourself?" he asked.

"If I had felt threatened by him, I would never have gone in. Besides, I got out before anything happened, didn't I?"

"I got you out by tripping the alarm system in his car."

She wasn't about to tell him how grateful she was for that or let him see how shaken she was over her ordeal. "It's a moot point now," she said, raising her voice. "I'm safe."

"You need to settle down."

"I *can't* settle down. Nobody in this town seems to care that a human being died. They keep thinking of the Luanne Ritter who ran a loan company and wasn't liked. Well, she may not have been the most popular person in town, but she didn't deserve to die. I don't know how I'll live with myself if my newspaper is involved."

"Well, you just might have to face that fact, so get over it."

"Gee, thanks."

"I'm being realistic. If you want to spend the rest of your life beating yourself up over something you had no control over, then do it."

"I shouldn't have called you. I should have let Lamar handle it."

"Then why *did* you call me?"

She hesitated, and her voice broke when she answered. "Because I was afraid Lamar couldn't handle the job. I knew you could. Satisfied?"

Without warning, Max pulled her against him. For a moment, he simply held her, waiting for Jamie to calm down. He sighed heavily. Finally, he pulled back so that he was looking into her eyes. "Look, I'm sorry I got angry with you, babe, but I was worried as hell. Promise me you won't try anything like that again."

"I have to know the truth, Max."

"And we're doing everything we can." He released her. "Did you see anything in his place that looked suspicious?"

She told him about the crowbars. "He carries one in his car. If we could get our hands on it—"

"No way," Max said. "If he looks like our man, I'll have Lamar Tevis check him out and send the crowbar to the crime lab. Also, I'm going to have Muffin check his and Luanne's telephone records."

"Luanne's picture was recently in the newspaper. We could take it to the Holiday Inn and show it around. See if anybody remembers her being there with Larry."

"He might find out, and we'll blow our cover. We

just need to have him watched closely for the next couple of days until we can rule out the others. I suppose I could put Destiny on it."

"That's fine." Jamie had no desire to lay eyes on the man again.

Max checked his wristwatch. "We still have time to make dinner at Frankie and Dee Dee's."

Jamie was glad he hadn't canceled. She needed the diversion after what she'd been through. "I'll follow you."

VERA BANKHEAD STARED AT HERSELF IN THE MIRror as she tried on the new dress. On the bed behind her were two new pantsuits she'd purchased, as well.

Vera reached inside the little pocket of her purse and pulled out the ad she had cut out of the newspaper that day. " 'Open to New Experiences,' " she read aloud. She often talked to herself, a result of living alone most of her life. " 'Interested in discreet relationship with woman in fifties,' " she continued. "Okay, I'm a tad older, but I look pretty good, and I can be as discreet as the next person. Lord knows I wouldn't want my preacher finding out that I was responding to a personals ad."

She hurried into her living room where she kept her old Remington typewriter. She typed the address on a plain white envelope and chuckled. "Jamie will never suspect a thing," she said.

• • •

MAX AND JAMIE ARRIVED AT FRANKIE AND DEE Dee's house around eight P.M. to find Dee Dee in tears.

"It's because of the lobsters," Frankie said miserably. "We had a tank installed in the kitchen. You may have noticed it when you were here for the party. Anyway, I had a bunch of lobsters flown in from Maine, and we were going to have them for dinner tonight, but Dee Dee—"

Dee Dee interrupted. "The chef was going to drop them live into a pot of boiling water, Max." Her bottom lip trembled.

"Honey, how do you think they cook lobster?" Frankie asked.

"Well, there *are* more humane ways to prepare them," Max said, "but I'm sure your chef knows that."

"I don't want to hear about it!" Dee Dee cried, palms pressed to her ears. "I want them sent back. Or find homes for them."

Max and Jamie exchanged looks. Jamie tried to imagine where one would find a good home for a lobster. It wasn't like they could drop them off at the local animal shelter and hope someone would adopt them.

Beenie had his arms crossed and was tapping his foot impatiently. "Well, I, for one, had my heart set on a nice lobster dinner, but Dee Dee said there will be no murders committed in this house so we'll all probably end up eating bologna and cheese sandwiches."

"I'd rather have a big old rare steak anyway," Snakeman said. "Come on, Big John. You and me can run to the store and pick up a load of 'em."

"I guess that will be okay," Dee Dee said. "Since the cows are already dead."

Jamie walked over to her friend. Dee Dee looked delicate in a cream-colored georgette dress that fell to her ankles. "Honey, I don't care what we eat as long as it doesn't distress you. You're just feeling a little sensitive now that you're pregnant, and you have every right."

Dee Dee sniffed. "I told them I wouldn't mind eating the lobsters once they grew old and died. I'm trying to cooperate."

"Does anyone know the life span of a lobster?" Beenie asked sarcastically.

No one had heard the chef come into the room. "This is nonsense, waiting for a lobster to die before we can cook him," the man said. "A lobster must be alive when you cook him or he's no good. I can put them in the freezer to numb them before I drop them into boiling water."

Dee Dee burst into tears.

"Scrap the lobster," Frankie said. "Snakeman is going to buy steaks."

"This is a crazy house," the chef muttered under his breath and pushed through the swinging door leading to the kitchen.

"Would you like to go upstairs and lie down for a while before dinner?" Jamie asked Dee Dee.

Beenie softened at the sad look in Dee Dee's eyes. "Of course she would. Come on, honey, you need to rest a bit, and then I'll repair your makeup."

"The rest of the guys are in the game room playing pool and darts," Frankie said to Max. "Why don't we join them?"

BEENIE VERY GENTLY PLACED A LAVENDER-scented satin eye mask over Dee Dee's eyes as she half reclined on a settee, holding her Maltese, Choo-Choo, against her breasts. "I know everyone thinks I'm being foolish," she said, "but the thought of killing those poor lobsters is more than I can bear." She sniffed. "I was beginning to think of them as pets."

Beenie caught Jamie's eye and shook his head sadly. "Our Dee Dee has been feeling out of sorts all day," he said. "Tired and weepy," he added. "She was real upset over that woman's murder."

"That poor woman," Dee Dee said, removing her eye mask. "It's all I can think about."

"We're all very saddened by it," Jamie told her, "but I'm sure the police are doing everything they can to find the killer." She offered Dee Dee the closest thing she had to a smile and changed the subject. "You'll be relieved to know that Muffin is already doing research on pregnancy and child care. She's ordered a few books for you. By the time this baby comes into the world we'll all be experts."

Beenie did a quick repair job on Dee Dee's eyes. "I just hope I don't gain a lot of weight," Dee Dee replied. "You know how I am about my weight."

"Oh, pooh," Beenie said. "For once in your life stop worrying about your waistline. Besides, that new fashion designer I selected assured me you'd be the best-looking pregnant woman in town. In the country, even," he added. "You know what I think? I think a lot of celebrities out there will have their own designers trying to copy your style."

Dee Dee seemed to perk up at the thought.

"And of course the baby's nursery will look like something off a magazine cover," Beenie said. "I'm talking to interior designers who have been commissioned by the biggest names in show business."

"It sounds so exciting," Jamie said. "I can't wait."

Dee Dee touched her still flat tummy. "Eeyeuuw, I'm going to look like I'm carrying a giant melon," she said suddenly. "I won't be able to let Frankie see me in the buff."

"I've heard that a lot of men find pregnant women very sexy," Jamie said.

"But some women never totally regain their figures after having a baby," Dee Dee pointed out.

"That's not going to happen," Beenie said. "Your plastic surgeon can perform liposuction as soon as you deliver the baby. We'll have him on standby."

Jamie suppressed a shudder. It sounded rather drastic.

"And what do I know about being a mother?" Dee Dee said. "I've never raised anything but a Maltese." She sat up. "I have to speak to Muffin."

"Now?" Jamie asked.

"Yes. She always has the answers to all my questions, and I have a lot of questions."

"You want me to come with you?" Jamie asked.

"Yes. You can take notes." She glanced at Beenie. "You want to come?"

"No, I'm going to join the guys. I get hot being around all that testosterone."

"SO YOU'RE SAYING YOU'VE BEEN EXPERIENCING morning sickness for some weeks now?" Muffin said a short while later.

Dee Dee sniffed. "Yes. It isn't very pleasant."

"Your doctor has probably told you to keep soda crackers on your night table, right?" Muffin replied.

"I have trouble keeping them down."

"The nausea should go away after the first couple of months," Muffin told her. "There are medications to help you through it if you like."

"I just hate taking anything while I'm pregnant," Dee Dee said. "What bothers me even more is the fatigue. I get up in the morning and several hours later I'm ready for a nap."

"It happens to a lot of women," Muffin told her. "The first three months or trimester, as it's called, is the worst. Odds are, once you get into your fourth and fifth month you'll start feeling better. Of course, you're going to be the size of a refrigerator."

"Eeyeuuw!" Dee Dee cried.

Muffin chuckled. "Just kidding."

"Hey, pregnant women are cool," Jamie said. "Once you start getting big, everyone opens doors for you and waits on you like a princess."

Dee Dee seemed to ponder it. "But people already do that."

Muffin spoke up. "Hey, I'll bet Frankie will start buying you more jewelry."

Jamie looked up from her notes. "Muffin, what a materialistic thing to say."

Dee Dee looked at her. "Maybe if I play my cards right I'll get that new ten-karat solitaire from Tiffany's I've been wanting." She looked thoughtful. "This pregnancy thing might just end up being the best thing that's ever happened to me, and when it's all over, I'll have a precious little baby boy or girl. It's a win-win situation."

"Do you plan on breast-feeding?" Muffin asked.

"Eeyeuuw, I hadn't thought of that." Dee Dee was quiet for a moment. Finally, she looked at Jamie. "What do you think?"

"Don't ask me, I can't even raise a bloodhound properly. Maybe you're trying to make too many decisions at once. You've barely had time to get used to the thought of being pregnant, much less buying maternity clothes, decorating a nursery, and deciding whether you should breast-feed. You need to relax."

"How come Frankie isn't worried about these things?" Dee Dee asked. "I feel like I'm going through most of it alone."

Jamie grinned. "He's too happy to be worried. The woman he loves more than anything in the world is going to have his baby. He's passing out cigars."

"Are you happy for me, Jamie?" Dee Dee asked.

"Of course I am. Why wouldn't I be?"

"It's silly, but I just wanted to make sure I had your support. And because I'm a little nervous. I want to be the best mother I can be. I never thought I'd feel like this about a baby. It's a miracle that I got pregnant after all these years, and I don't want to botch it."

Jamie reached across the seat and hugged her.

"Dee Dee, you are going to be a wonderful mother. And Frankie will be a great father. I think this is one lucky baby."

"How far along are you?" Muffin asked.

"Six weeks."

"Well, that'll give us plenty of time to learn everything we can about babies," Muffin said.

Dee Dee smiled almost dreamily at Jamie. "You know, I never thought I would be facing motherhood, but this would more fun if you were going through it with me. I mean, you're my best friend. We'd have a blast if we were both pregnant at the same time. We could shop together."

Jamie almost swallowed her own tongue. "Um, maybe I should just concentrate on raising Fleas right now."

IT WAS SHORTLY AFTER ELEVEN P.M. WHEN MAX and Jamie arrived back at her house. Fleas was spread-eagled on the sofa. He didn't move as they came into the house.

"That's some watchdog you've got there," Max said.

Jamie walked up to the animal, hands on hips. "Excuse me, but are you supposed to be on the sofa?" she asked.

The dog didn't budge.

"Okay, play your games, but Max and I are going to have ice cream."

One of Fleas's eyes popped open. He raised his head.

"I figured that would get your attention," Jamie said, going into the kitchen.

Max followed. "You don't really feed him ice cream, do you?"

Jamie was already pulling a carton of butter pecan from the freezer. "Yeah. He won't go to bed for the night without his treat."

Fleas climbed from the sofa and walked into the kitchen. He sat and waited, watching Jamie's every move. She dipped ice cream into his doggie bowl, and then put some in bowls for Max and her. Fleas had eaten his by the time they carried their bowls to the kitchen table. For a moment, Jamie and Max enjoyed their dessert in silence. Max looked at her.

"I'm sorry I came down so hard on you earlier," he said. "I almost lost it when you went into Larry Johnson's apartment. I think he's dangerous."

"Or he could just be angry because he had to give up everything in the divorce. He's hard to figure, but it's obvious he doesn't have much respect for women. Still, I have a hard time believing he's a cold-blooded killer, but then I can't imagine anyone murdering another human being." Not that she hadn't witnessed killing during their trip to Tennessee, she reminded herself. She'd watched the FBI gun down two notorious mob figures, and she still had nightmares about it from time to time.

"Johnson definitely has two things against him," Max said. "Anger and booze. That can make for a deadly combination. Also, if he has financial problems, he might have taken Luanne Ritter's jewelry."

"Assuming, of course, that he killed her," Jamie added quickly.

They finished their ice cream. Jamie picked up the bowls and carried them to the sink where she rinsed them out. She didn't hear Max get up, but all at once she felt his arms slide around her waist.

"I really missed you while I was away, Swifty," he said, his mouth at her ear.

Jamie tried to suppress the shiver that raced up her backbone and reached for the towel to dry her hands. "I missed you, too, Max," she said.

He turned her around so that she was facing him, and the two gazed at each other for a moment. Finally, Max kissed her.

Jamie could taste the ice cream on his tongue as he explored her mouth. She slipped her arms around his neck and drew him even closer. She had been waiting for Max to kiss her for most of the evening, and now she opened her mouth wider to receive him.

Max broke the kiss and studied her. "Remember that unfinished business back in Tennessee?"

Jamie blushed in spite of herself. Her with her skirt shoved high on her hips, Max's mouth on her, tasting. "Yes." The word was little more than a whisper.

"I'd like to finish it."

He took her hand and led her to her bedroom. He walked over to the nightstand and switched on the light. At Jamie's look, he smiled. "I want to be able to get a good look at you." He pulled her into his arms once more; this time there was a look of sheer determination on his face. Jamie welcomed his hands on her breasts and closed her eyes as her nipples contracted, despite the clothing that separated them. She gave in to the wonderful sensations his touch created.

Max reached around and unzipped her dress, kissing each shoulder as he bared it. He released the garment and it fell to her feet. Jamie kicked off her heels and was left standing there in her bra and panties, the ones she'd bought at Sinful Delights.

"Jesus, Swifty," Max said, his voice suddenly husky. "I'd like to know where you buy your lingerie."

She smiled coyly and reached for the buttons on his shirt, but her fingers trembled as she undid them. Finally, she pulled the shirt free, and Max stood there with his chest bare, looking better than anything she'd ever laid eyes on. She ran her hands over him. Her stomach fluttered. If she'd known he looked this good, she would have jumped into the sack with him sooner.

Max reached around and unfastened her bra. He tossed it aside and pulled her into his arms. Skin met skin. Jamie's body responded immediately.

Max cupped her breasts in his hands and then he lowered his head and kissed the spot between them. Jamie held his head tightly against her as she felt her insides swoop upward. Max's hands suddenly appeared at her hips. He kneaded the flesh before pulling her against him where she could feel his hardness. Something hot flashed low in her belly.

Jamie whimpered his name as he buried his face against her throat. "Oh, Max."

"I know, Jamie. I know." He picked her up and carried her the short distance to the bed.

Jamie reached for his belt, fumbled with it until she was able to unfasten it. "I could use some help, Holt."

He grinned and pulled off his socks and shoes. Finally, he unzipped his pants. It took only seconds for him to dispense with them. His boxers followed. Jamie's breath caught in her throat at the sight of his lean but slightly muscular body.

Max joined her on the bed, pulled her into his arms once more, and kissed her deeply. He pulled back slightly. "Birth control?" he whispered.

"We're covered," she managed.

He removed her panties and sought the area between her thighs with his fingers. Jamie pressed herself against his hand.

Max teased her with his fingers, even as he continued kissing her. He began to inch his way down her body, kissing her abdomen, her tummy. He parted her thighs to receive his tongue.

The doorbell rang.

Max jerked his head up. "What the hell?"

Jamie blinked furiously, trying to awaken her dulled senses. "I wonder who that could be."

"Ignore it."

She sat up. "I can't ignore it, Max. It's almost midnight. Something must be wrong. It could be Vera."

He gave a huge sigh, climbed from the bed, and reached for his slacks. "This had better be good." He tugged them on and zipped them.

Jamie grabbed her bathrobe. She hurried into the next room, Max right behind her. Fleas was on the sofa sleeping soundly. Jamie shot him a dirty look as she made for the door. She checked the peephole. "It's Destiny."

"You're kidding. What's she doing here?"

Jamie opened the front door. Destiny was dressed in skintight faux-leather shorts and a rhinestone tee that was molded to her oversized breasts.

"Don't you ever check your answering machine?" the woman asked frantically. Her eyes darted to Max then back to Jamie.

"I was out all evening," Jamie said. "I only returned home a little while ago. Do you know what time it is?"

"Of course I do," Destiny said. "I wouldn't be here if it weren't important. I've lost Ronnie."

CHAPTER TEN

JAMIE GAPED AT DESTINY. "YOU'RE SERIOUS, AREN'T you?"

"Of course I am. I feel responsible for him. I was wondering if he was over here."

"Why would he be here?" Jamie asked.

"He likes the two of you. He told me. He especially likes your hound because he had one similar. Ronnie used to be an expert coon hunter," she added, shaking her head sadly. "I can't let him go off on his own because, well, because he needs my help. I'm the only one who can convince him to cross over to the other side. To the light," she added.

Jamie gave a massive eye-roll. "I don't believe we're having this conversation," she muttered.

Destiny looked past both of them. "There you are, dammit," she said to an empty space. "Ronnie, what are you doing here this time of night? I've been searching all over for you."

Jamie and Max glanced around the room. "Where is he?" Jamie asked.

"Sitting next to your dog." Destiny walked over to Fleas, once again staring at an empty space. She put her hands on her hips. "It's time to go home, Ronnie," she said. "If you don't go to the light, you'll keep wandering around lost. I know you're not anxious to see your dead mother, but you've got to face her sooner or later." Destiny paused and looked at Max and Jamie. "Ronnie knows his mother is going to read him the riot act for getting drunk and falling out of that pickup truck."

Max and Jamie exchanged glances.

Finally, Destiny sighed. "Okay, I'll let you hang around my place for a while longer, but you can't go running off like this because I'll worry."

Jamie was intrigued. "How come you can see Ronnie, but we can't?"

Destiny shrugged. "Everyone has some psychic ability," she said, "but they don't use it."

"What does he look like?" Jamie asked.

"He's short and bald with a beer gut." Destiny gave a grunt. "Yes, Ronnie, you do have a beer gut. Now are you coming with me or not?" She glanced at Max and Jamie. "Ronnie can be stubborn at times."

"Well, I'm sure the two of you will work things

out," Max said. He walked into the bedroom for the rest of his clothes.

Jamie couldn't hide her irritation. "Destiny, you're going to have to keep up with your dead spirit. I can't have him showing up here at all hours of the night." She suddenly remembered what Max had said about dead spirits attaching themselves to other people. "Ronnie isn't, um, an evil spirit, is he?" she asked, and then realized how strange her question sounded.

"Oh, no, he's quite friendly," Destiny said, "even if he is a real pain in the ass." She paused. "Yes, Ronnie, you *are* a pain in the ass, and I don't know why I put up with you. Now let's go home and let these people get some sleep." She crossed her arms and tapped her foot impatiently. "I'm waiting."

Max reentered the room, still buttoning his shirt. "You haven't come up with any more information, have you?"

Destiny shook her head. "Sorry. I think I'm still blocked."

"Max said you didn't think the dentist looked suspicious."

Destiny shrugged. "He seemed harmless to me, but he did have golf clubs in his office, and I suppose one of them could have been used to kill that poor woman. Maybe something will come to me soon. In the meantime, I'll be in the office early Monday morning to pick up my mail."

"Your mail?"

"I assume I'll have responses to the new column you mentioned to your readers."

Jamie doubted it, but she didn't want to hurt Destiny's feelings. She had almost been too embarrassed to run the announcement and couldn't imagine anyone in Beaumont writing in for advice from the Divine Love Goddess Advisor, but for some insane reason she had posted it anyway.

Max stepped forward. "By the way, I was hoping you could follow one of the suspects around for a couple of days."

Destiny shrugged. "Sure."

"I don't want you to get too close, but he needs to be watched."

"How will I know what the guy looks like?"

Max described him. "Do you have a pair of binoculars?" he asked.

"They're easy enough to buy."

"His name is Larry Johnson, and he owns a local car dealership. It would be best if you parked across from his place of business. He'll probably be at the car lot all day tomorrow. He'll be easy to spot since he's the only salesman on the lot. He also hangs out in the lounge at the Holiday Inn at night. Like I said, I don't want you to get too close."

"What am I looking for?"

"I'd just like to know who he's spending his evenings with."

"Okay." Destiny suddenly glanced sideways. "No, Ronnie, I don't think that's a polite question to ask."

"What does Ronnie want to know?" Jamie said.

"I'm almost too embarrassed to say, but he is asking what happened to your dog's hair."

"Coon attack," Jamie said, irritated that people were always finding flaws with her pet. "Um, it's getting late, Destiny, and I don't mean to be rude, but do you think you could take your dead spirit home now?"

Max looked amused.

"Okay, I'm out of here," Destiny said. "Come on, Ronnie." She turned for the door, and then glanced over her shoulder. "We need to figure out who the murderer is right away because I have to have oral surgery next week. The dentist said my wisdom teeth have to come out."

Jamie watched Destiny pull away in her Mercedes. Max came up beside her and put his hands on her shoulders. "That woman needs help," Jamie said. When Max chuckled, she went on. "And you're only encouraging her."

"I'm just trying to find a killer. Any way I can," he added.

"You don't think it's strange for a woman to show up at my door at midnight looking for a ghost?"

He grinned.

"It's not funny, Max," she said. "If you want to play ball with her and her imaginary playmate, go for it, but I'm out." He removed his hands from her shoulders, and Jamie wished she hadn't been so brusque with him.

"If you don't want her around, tell her," he said. He glanced at his wristwatch. "Look, I need to be going. I've got to make a few phone calls."

"At this hour?"

"I'm calling countries in a different time zone. Besides, we're both tired. How about I catch up with you tomorrow?"

Jamie felt her jaw drop. He was leaving? Just like that? She didn't want him to go.

Or maybe they needed a little distance. If Max stayed, they would finish making love, and if that happened she was a goner. Once she made love with Max Holt she would fall hopelessly in love with him. She didn't have time to fall in love, not with a murderer on the loose.

"Maybe that's best," she said at last.

MAX CLIMBED INTO HIS CAR AND STARTED THE ENgine. Muffin came on. "Boy, that was quick. I figured the two of you would go at it all night."

"Very funny."

"Uh-oh," Muffin said. "I can tell by the sound of your voice it didn't go well. Did you guys have an argument?"

"No."

"I'm confused," Muffin said. "What's the problem? Why this constant tug-of-war? It's obvious the two of you are hot for each other."

"Okay, Muffin, I'll level with you. I'm beginning to worry that Jamie might want more out of this relationship than I can give her."

"So is this the part where you tell the woman in question that you can't possibly make a commitment and you try to soften the blow with flowers?"

Max didn't answer.

"Because if it is I'm telling you right now it's not going to work," Muffin went on. "You're not willing to let Jamie go. Face it, Max. You've got it bad."

Max didn't respond at first. "Do me a favor, Muffin," he said, changing the subject. "I want you to check out a Destiny Moultrie for me. I want to know everything you can find on her."

"So we're not going to talk about it, is that it?"

He didn't try to keep the irritation from his voice when he spoke. "I don't want to talk about Jamie right now if it's all the same to you."

A few minutes later, Max pulled into the parking lot of his hotel and parked. He sat there for a moment before getting out of the car and making his way to his room. He gazed at the empty bed. "Shit."

JAMIE AWOKE TO THE SMELL OF FLEAS'S BREATH ON her face. "Oh, God!" she cried, shoving him away. "I hope you haven't been licking yourself again."

He simply stood there, watching and waiting.

"You need to go out, is that it?" She dragged herself from the bed and headed for the back door with him on her heels. She paused to unlock the door, and he bumped into her. Dog and master exchanged looks. "You do that every time," Jamie said. "You know I'm going to have to stop and unlock the door, but you insist on running into me. Why is that?"

He thumped his tail once.

"And why am I in such a sour mood this morning?" Suddenly she remembered. She frowned as she opened the door so Fleas could go out. Max had just walked out on her the night before. Just walked out. She wished it didn't bother her so much. She wished she knew where she stood with him.

"Stop kidding yourself," she said aloud. "You know exactly where you stand." That's what hurt. It didn't matter that they were just itching to climb into bed together; the fact was Max didn't want anything permanent, and she was just going to have to accept it.

It was time she faced facts.

Fleas made straight for Jamie's one rosebush. Worse, he glanced back at her as if to say, "So what're you gonna do about it?" He hiked his leg and whizzed right on it. Jamie gave a sigh, went inside and turned on her automatic coffee maker. It gurgled to life.

Her stomach growled. She wondered if Max was going to show up with doughnuts. She wasn't counting on it; it was already seven o'clock, and he would have been there by now. He was probably sitting in his hotel room practicing his great rejection speech. Well, he could shove it, as far as she was concerned. She didn't need him any more than he needed her. She had her pride.

Still, it hurt. They had been through so much together. How could a man look at her the way Max did and not feel something? How could he touch her and kiss her and remain so casual about it? Well, she wasn't made that way.

Fleas scratched at the door, and Jamie let him in, then she went into the bathroom. Fleas followed. Jamie stared at her reflection. Her hair was a mess, her mascara smudged. Her sleep shirt bore more wrinkles than Fleas's face. She glanced down at the dog.

"Would you just look at me?" she said. "I've let myself go."

Fleas cocked his head to the side as though trying to understand.

"We can't continue living on junk food," Jamie went on. "We're both at the age where we need to start taking better care of ourselves or our arteries are going to need Drano to get them unclogged. You know what that means? No more doughnuts and ice cream."

Fleas sank to the floor and put a paw over one eye. Jamie knew he didn't understand a word she said—he mainly reacted to her tone of voice—but one would have thought he was capable of taking in her every word.

"Yep, this means I need to start eating more vegetables, and you need to eat that expensive dog food I buy you. I'm serious, pal," she said, trying to convince herself as much as him. "I'm going to turn over a new leaf today, and I'm going to get Max Holt out of my system if it kills me. I'm going to stop eating those brownies."

Jamie went into her bedroom and changed into a pair of sweats, an old T-shirt, and running shoes. Fleas watched her, as if he expected something big was about to happen. Jamie tried to remember when she had last done anything that resembled jogging. Geez, she would probably have a heart attack before she cleared the driveway.

Fleas followed her outside. It was already muggy, the air thick with humidity. She could literally feel it on her face and arms. If only the weather would break. Jamie regarded Fleas. "You can't go jogging because you just got neutered," she told him. "Besides, it requires physical activity, and we both know that's not your strong suit."

As if he understood, Fleas walked over to the nearest tree and plopped down in the shade. Jamie began doing a few stretches to prepare her poor body for what she was about to put it through.

She did not see the French poodle dash across the yard, but the next thing she knew Fleas was howling in protest, and a poodle was trying to mount him. Fleas darted behind Jamie as if hoping she could protect him.

"Oh, good grief!" a woman cried. "Precious, you stop that this instant!"

Jamie glanced in the direction of the voice. The woman wore a tight polka-dot dress and spike heels, had big blond hair, and she was doing her best to walk through the high grass in Jamie's yard. "Dammit, Precious, I said stop!"

Jamie stared in disbelief as the poodle chased Fleas around a large oleander bush. Finally, Fleas skirted around the back of the house with the poodle right behind him.

"Miss, I am so embarrassed," the woman said. "Precious tries to mount everything in sight. It's like he has just gone off the deep end. It's so embarrassing."

"Your dog is a male?" Jamie asked. "So is mine."

"Yes, he's a male, but that wouldn't stop him. It's humiliating." She sighed heavily.

"I'd better check on my dog," Jamie said, worried that Fleas would pull his stitches out running from the poodle. The last thing she needed was another vet bill. She hurried around the back of the house with the woman behind her. Fleas had found refuge in the old truck Jamie had parked in her back yard. The poodle was jumping up and down like a yo-yo trying to reach the tailgate.

"I think it'll be okay now," Jamie said. "Your dog doesn't seem to be able to reach the bed of the truck." She took another look at the blonde, who seemed to be in her early forties. "I don't recall see-ing you before. Are you new in the neighborhood?"

"Oh, yes, I'm renting the house next door. My name is Barbara Fender."

"Jamie Swift." Jamie saw the woman's eyes sud-denly widen, and she turned. Max had arrived with coffee and doughnuts.

"Who is that hunk?" Barbara whispered.

"His name is Max."

"Is he your boyfriend?"

"Well, um, it's complicated."

"All relationships are complicated," the woman said sourly. "You ask me, they're not worth it."

Jamie found herself nodding in agreement.

"Sorry I'm late," Max called out. "I had to make a lot of calls this morning." His eyes combed her in her baggy sweats. "Nice outfit."

Jamie felt like crawling beneath the truck, but she was afraid the poodle would start humping her. "I was about to go for a run."

"Why? Is your car on the blink?" Max looked at the woman beside Jamie. "Hi. I'm Max."

"Barbara."

All at once, the poodle raced toward Max and started humping his leg. "Nice to meet you, Barbara," he said, trying to shake the poodle off. "Is this your dog? I have to admit I've always had a fondness for poodles. My grandmother raised them. I just can't remember any of them liking *me* this well."

Barbara tried to get her dog under control. Finally, she grabbed him and picked him up. "Precious is going through a difficult time right now. I'm so sorry."

"No need to apologize," Max said.

"Barbara is moving in next door," Jamie explained. Max nodded, and they were all silent, each of them obviously at a loss for words. "Would you like to join us for a cup of coffee?" Jamie asked, although she knew she didn't sound sincere. She was eager for the woman to take her dog home.

As if sensing Jamie was only trying to be polite,

Barbara shook her head. "I think I need to get Precious home," she said, "but thanks just the same."

Max and Jamie waited until she'd disappeared inside her house before trying to convince Fleas to get down from the bed of the truck. Finally, Max pulled out a doughnut, and the hound climbed down, took the doughnut and almost swallowed it whole before racing toward the house.

"Wow, I've never seen Fleas run like that," Jamie said.

"How come you didn't want your neighbor to have coffee with us?" Max asked.

Jamie looked at him. "What makes you think I didn't?"

"You're usually friendlier. Even to people you've just met."

"I think it had a lot to do with her kooky dog."

"You don't like her."

Jamie didn't respond because he was right. It could have been her imagination, but she hadn't appreciated the way Barbara had looked at Max. But then, he always drew stares from the opposite sex.

Oh, geez, she had been jealous. She had all the symptoms of being in love. She could try to convince herself otherwise, but she knew better.

Problem was, Max probably knew, as well. That was the worst part.

CHAPTER ELEVEN

MAX FOLLOWED JAMIE INSIDE THE HOUSE WITH the bag of doughnuts. "About last night," he began.

"I'd rather not discuss last night," Jamie said, avoiding eye contact. "We've got a murder to solve."

"I'll grant you that, but we probably need to discuss what's going on between us."

Jamie looked at him. "And what *is* going on between us, Max?"

"It's complicated."

"Funny, that's the same word I'd use."

"I have very strong feelings for you, Jamie. The last thing I want to do is hurt you."

"Save it, Max. I think I know where this is going."

He stepped closer. "I don't think you do."

"Then tell me."

He hesitated. "I don't want to lose you. But I'm not sure what our future holds. I spent most of the night thinking about you. I need time."

Jamie knew better. Time would not change anything. "I really have a lot on my mind right now," she said, wanting to change the subject. Max did not have to spell it out for her.

"I know," he said softly. He was quiet for a moment. "So, you were going jogging, huh? You look like you're in pretty good shape to me."

She shrugged.

"I have doughnuts," he said.

Damn the man. He knew doughnuts were her weakness.

"Would you rather I leave?"

That was the last thing she wanted. "No."

Max offered Fleas another doughnut. The dog inhaled it. So much for her plan for the two of them to start eating healthy, Jamie thought.

The doorbell rang, and Jamie stood. Max looked at her. "What is this, Grand Central Station? Don't you ever have time to yourself?"

"Vera's test-driving another car," Jamie said. "She called earlier, wants me to have a look." Jamie opened the door before Vera had time to ring the bell a second time. The woman was dressed in a purple pantsuit and hot-pink scarf. It was obvious she'd taken a lot of time with her hair and makeup.

"What do you think?" she asked Jamie, turning around so Jamie could get a better look at her outfit. "My preacher's going to have a hissy fit when he sees me coming down the aisle for communion this morning."

"You look great," Jamie said.

"I feel great. I figure age is just a state of mind, know what I mean?" She didn't wait for a response. "Quick, come check out the cool wheels I'm test-driving. I don't have much time because I'm going to the early church service, then a bunch of us girls are attending the singles breakfast. Let the guys get a load of me in this outfit. 'Course, they're too old to do anything about it if you get my drift."

Jamie glanced past Vera and found herself looking at a white Jaguar. "Oh, geez."

"It's eight years old," Vera said, "but you'd never know it. Isn't it beautiful? The dealer said he can give me a really good deal on it."

Jamie looked at her. "Why can't you buy something sensible?"

"Because I don't want to ruin my new image," Vera said. "Besides, I can afford a car like this as long as it's not brand-new."

"I think you'd better have Max look at it," Jamie said. She turned, almost bumping into an amused Max.

"A Jag, huh?" he said to Vera.

"Yeah. Would you mind taking a look at it?"

Max followed her outside where he spent a few minutes checking it over before Vera pulled away.

"I shouldn't have lent her the red Mustang," Jamie said. "I've created a monster."

"She's just having fun," Max said. "Speaking of which, why don't you and I spend the day investigating a few of the guys, then have dinner tonight."

Jamie wrestled with the thought. It was tempting.

"Say yes, Jamie."

She wanted to go in the worst way. "What should I wear?"

"Something a little dressy," he said. "And wear that black thing underneath it."

Jamie's stomach fluttered. She was playing with fire, and she was likely to get burned.

DESTINY ARRIVED AT JAMIE'S HOUSE AN HOUR later.

"I'm sorry if I sounded rude last night," Jamie said. "I still don't believe in all this otherworldly stuff, but we do need your help."

Destiny shrugged. "Like I said, I'm used to it." She looked at Max. "I drove by Larry's car lot on the way over and saw the new Corvette you mentioned parked beside the building so he's obviously working. I also picked up a pair of binoculars."

Max handed her a photo of Johnson. "This should help."

Jamie arched a brow. "How'd you come up with such a good picture in so little time?"

"Holt Technology, Swifty."

"Why aren't you going to the police with your suspicions?" Destiny asked.

"And tell them what?" Max said. "We don't have anything on him. Yet," he added.

"He's very angry," Destiny said. "I sense that about him even though I haven't seen him."

"You've got that right," Jamie said, then realized it was the first time she had agreed with anything Destiny said.

"Oh, by the way," Max said, "I'd like for you to try and meet with the chef today if you have time."

"What excuse is she going to use?" Jamie asked.

Destiny smiled. "I'll come up with something. I don't have trouble meeting men."

"Dumb question," Jamie said.

Max grinned. "I'm going to have Jamie pretend to have car trouble so we can get a look at the mechanic, then we'll try to set up a meeting with John Price, the accountant."

"What about the other guy? Mr. 'Deeper Than the Night'?"

"Don't worry, I've been saving him for you," Max said. "Why don't you call him today and see what you can work out?"

"Tell me this," Destiny said. "If he's rich and good-looking, why would he run an ad in a personals section?"

"He just moved back to town and is obviously looking for a way to meet women. He appears clean, but the fact that Luanne Ritter died only a week after he moved back to Beaumont makes him a suspect. *If* the murder had anything to do with the personals section. Plus, I have his cell phone record proving he and Luanne talked. She must've written to him the minute his ad hit the paper. I suspect she contacted everyone who ran an ad."

"She must've been very lonely," Destiny said.

Jamie spoke. "They could have met for drinks or dinner, but Sam decided she wasn't his type."

"Not a very good reason to kill her," Destiny said. She suddenly looked annoyed.

"What is it?" Jamie asked.

"Oh, it's just Ronnie being a pain in the ass as usual. Like I told you, he doesn't like the fact that I might actually meet a man and find him attractive. It's like I'm supposed to be content hanging out with spooks all the time. This Sam Hunter sounds like a real catch to me."

"If he's not a killer," Max reminded.

Destiny nodded. "Yes, well, a woman has to draw the line somewhere."

"We have to work out a plan so that I'll be available at all times for each of you," Max said. "The rules remain the same. You each carry cell phones, and you avoid being alone with these men at all costs." He looked at Jamie. "Understood?"

She nodded.

Max checked his wristwatch. "Jamie, I'm going to need the keys to your car. I'm going to pull it out of the garage and make a few adjustments under the hood so you'll have a reason to call the mechanic."

"I'm confused," Destiny said. "Why can't Jamie just call him, like I did the dentist?"

"This guy didn't list his telephone number in the ad," Max said, "so my, um, assistant had to find him through other sources."

"John Price didn't list his phone number in his ad," Jamie pointed out.

"We're going to use a different angle. You'll tell him you own the newspaper and that you were intrigued by his ad."

"Is that what you told Larry Johnson?" Destiny asked.

"No. He thought we were looking for a car."

Jamie went for her car keys while Destiny called the chef and made a date for later that day. When Jamie returned, she called the mechanic, who promised to be there in an hour, mentioning there would be an extra fee for coming out on his day off.

Jamie then called John Price, explained she owned the *Gazette* and had gotten the information from his ad. At first he was cool toward her, but he finally agreed to meet for coffee later in the day. "I don't think Mr. Price appreciated me contacting him the way I did," she said after she hung up. "Perhaps I should have written him via our post office box."

"That would have taken too long," Max said. "What other impressions did you get?"

"He sounded very cautious. I have a funny feeling he's hiding something."

BY THE TIME JAMIE WALKED INTO THE DOWNTOWN Café for her meeting with John Price, the mechanic, a good old boy by the name of Carl Edwards, had made the necessary repairs to her car and had asked her out. She'd taken his phone number and promised to get back to him. "Edwards might be a flirt," she'd told Max once the man left, "but he didn't come off as a murderer."

Max had shrugged. "Since when do murderers wear signs?"

John Price was in his mid to late fifties, a tall man with salt-and-pepper hair, dressed in neat slacks and a golf shirt. He looked embarrassed when Jamie approached the table.

"I was afraid of this," he said, standing until she was seated.

"I beg your pardon?"

"I thought you sounded a little young on the telephone. I probably should have asked your age."

"Is age an issue with you?"

"It is when the woman you're meeting for coffee is the same age as your daughter."

"I doubt that," Jamie said. "I'm thirty years old, not exactly a kid."

The waitress appeared and took their order for pie and coffee. "So, you own the local newspaper," Price said.

"Yes. It has been in my family for years."

"I'm sorry if I sounded rude to you on the telephone, but I was very surprised to get your call since I hadn't listed my number in the newspaper."

"I took it off the information you sent with your ad," Jamie said. "I didn't mean to infringe on your privacy," she added, "but I was intrigued. Your ad said you were open to new experiences. What exactly does that mean?"

He chuckled. "My doctor has accused me of showing signs of a midlife crisis," he said. "First thing I did when I turned fifty was buy a brand-new Harley and start dating younger women. My second wife was fifteen years my junior. Bad move on my part; we've since parted ways." He quickly changed the subject. "Now, I'm thinking of taking flying lessons."

Jamie noticed he had an easy smile. "Sounds interesting," she said.

The waitress appeared with their order.

They talked for an hour. Finally, John picked up the check. "Jamie, I had a delightful time, but I suggest you try meeting someone your own age. With your looks, you shouldn't have any trouble."

She glanced up in surprise. "Am I being rejected?"

He laughed. "No, but I would feel silly dating a woman twenty-five years younger than me. Please don't take it personally."

They said goodbye with a handshake. Max waited just down the street at Maynard's Sandwich Shop. "Mr. Price dumped me after the first date."

Max shrugged. "That's okay, you still have me."

Jamie didn't respond.

Destiny showed up later that afternoon. "The chef is about a hundred pounds overweight. Naturally, he's looking for a long-term relationship. I think he's already found one in food. I spent the rest of the day watching Larry Johnson. He didn't leave his car lot. He was the only one working today. I'm not surprised, since it's Sunday."

The three sat around the table discussing their findings and brainstorming. Finally, Destiny left.

Max stood to leave a few minutes later. "I need to go back to my hotel and make some calls," he said. "How about I pick you up around six?"

"Sounds good," Jamie said. "Where are we going?"

"It's a surprise."

Jamie walked him to the front door. He paused and looked down at her and for a moment she thought he might kiss her. Instead, he turned and headed for his car.

She sighed and leaned against the doorjamb. Now, why, when the timing had been perfect, hadn't he kissed her? She looked at Fleas. "See what I mean? I never know where I stand with that man."

Fleas responded by walking over to the refrigerator and glancing up at the freezer. "You're right," Jamie said. "When the going gets tough, the tough eat ice cream."

MUFFIN WAS WAITING WHEN MAX CLIMBED INTO the car. "I've taken care of everything you requested for your date tonight," she said. "Your plane will be here within the hour, and I made reservations at your favorite restaurant in New York City. Once you get off the plane, a limo will be waiting to take you there."

"Thanks," Max said. "You think Jamie will be impressed?"

"I think Jamie would be happy eating a barbecue sandwich at a local restaurant," Muffin said, "but if this is the way you want to play it, go for it."

Max was quiet. "You think I'm going overboard?"

"Hey, what do I know? She'll either think you're showing off or she'll be flattered. And since when do you worry what a woman thinks?"

"This is different."

"If I know Jamie, she'll be touched by your efforts."

"Were you able to get anything else on Sam Hunter?"

"I found nothing to indicate the man is not who he seems to be. No police record." She paused. "I'm beginning to wonder if Luanne's murder had something to do with her business. She had a lot of enemies."

"Lamar Tevis is checking into it."

"Which means we could be looking in the wrong place."

"I hope you're right, Muffin, but if you're not there's a good chance we're going to have another murder on our hands before long."

CHAPTER TWELVE

JAMIE WAS READY AND WAITING FOR MAX BY QUARter of six. She wore a simple black dress with spaghetti straps, matching heels, and carried a small purse. The see-through body suit beneath it, her purchase from Sinful Delights, was strapless and hugged her tightly. After her talk with Max she wondered why she was wearing it.

She was taking a big chance, and she knew it. She was risking a broken heart. Max Holt had made it plain he didn't know what their future held; he had not promised her happily-ever-after. But he had a hold on her heart, and there wasn't a damn thing she could do about it.

"How do I look?" she asked Fleas, who was napping in front of a kid's TV show since she did not allow him to watch anything with sex or violence. He didn't budge, didn't bat an eye. Jamie knew he was pouting because she was going out. It didn't take a genius of a dog to realize she didn't wear her best black dress every day.

And Fleas was no genius.

"Okay, be that way," she said, "but I deserve a night out once in a while. It's not like I don't try to take you with me everywhere I go. Lord, you even go to work with me."

Still Fleas made no movement.

"And I was going to give you another bowl of ice cream before I left. That's two in one day for you, pal."

Fleas suddenly raised his head. He might not be a genius, but he had learned to recognize the words *ice cream* and *doughnuts*.

"I knew that would get your attention," she said.

He thumped his tail and pulled himself into a standing position. Jamie watched him make his way into the kitchen where he sat down in front of the refrigerator and waited.

The doorbell rang. Jamie had been so busy trying to get a response from her dog that she hadn't heard Max pull up. Her stomach did a series of tiny flip-flops as she opened the door. Max stood on the other side looking like something off a magazine cover in a dove-gray suit and blue shirt and tie.

Several seconds passed before either of them said anything.

Finally, Max spoke. "Are you wearing anything under that dress?"

Of all the questions he might have asked, Jamie had not expected that one. "Um, not much."

"You know, Swifty," he said, stepping inside, "we could always stay in and order takeout."

"You look pretty good yourself, Holt."

"If we don't leave soon—"

"I just need a couple of minutes," she said. "I promised Fleas he could have ice cream."

"Of course."

Max followed her into the kitchen where Jamie dipped out a healthy serving of butter pecan ice cream into Fleas's bowl. The dog never took his eyes off her. Finally, she set it down before him. "There now. He's had his dinner, and I let him out, so he should be okay until I get back." Jamie grabbed her purse, and they started for the door.

"Aren't you going to turn off the TV?" Max asked.

"No, he likes having it on while I'm gone. It helps with his separation anxiety." Max shook his head sadly as they stepped outside. He took the keys from her and locked her door while Jamie waited, then he walked her to his car. She was nervous. This seriously smacked of a date, and she and Max weren't in the habit of dating. What did it mean?

Was she reading more into it than she should? Max was right. She did too much thinking. Couldn't she for once allow herself the luxury of enjoying herself without all the what-ifs? Just for once?

Max helped her into the car and closed the door. He climbed in beside her.

Lord but he smelled good, she thought.

They were on their way in minutes. "It's quiet in here," Jamie said. "Where's Muffin?"

"She's not feeling well so I gave her the night off."

"What do you mean she's not feeling well? She's a computer."

He shook his head. "She's been researching all this pregnancy stuff for Dee Dee so she's suffering the same symptoms."

"Tell me you're kidding." Not that Jamie should have been surprised. Muffin had gone through menopause when it seemed as if Dee Dee were suffering the symptoms and Muffin had researched it. "That is the craziest thing I've ever heard," she added.

He smiled. "So is feeding your dog ice cream in front of the TV set. It's a strange world in which we live, Swifty."

Max reached over and took her hand. He raised it to his lips, and his gaze met hers. "Have I told you lately that you're beautiful?"

Jamie felt her heart in her throat. Was it her imagination or did he seem different tonight? His eyes searched her face. What was he looking for? Did he suspect the depth of her feelings? She was the first to look away. "Thank you, Max," she said at last.

It was almost as if they'd unconsciously agreed not to discuss Luanne Ritter's murder and their investigation as Max drove through town. Instead, he filled her in on what was happening at Holt Industries. Jamie was amazed at what she heard. Not only was Max on the cutting edge of technological research, he was involved in biomedical research and pharmaceuticals, among other things. He had offices all over the world. She listened as he described where some of his research could actually lead. It seemed there was nothing the man wasn't interested in exploring.

Jamie arched one brow when he took the road that led to the small airport.

"Where are we going?" she asked.

"I told you, it's a surprise."

Jamie's jaw dropped clear to her collarbone when Max pulled up near the runway where a medium-sized jet waited with the words "Holt Industries" emblazoned on the sides. Lights were flashing, and airport personnel hurried about. Two pilots stood near the steps of the plane, each dressed in khaki slacks and navy blazers.

"Good evening, Mr. Holt," one of them said as

soon as Max pulled to a stop and stepped from the car.

Jamie's door was immediately opened, and the other pilot helped her out. "It's a beautiful night for flying," he told her with a smile.

Max held out his elbow as Jamie, still gaping, took it and walked with him toward the jet. "We've filed the flight plan," the older pilot said. "We're ready to go. Out ETA at LaGuardia is eight-thirty."

"LaGuardia?" Jamie asked as Max prodded her up the steps leading inside the luxury cabin. He nodded. "But that's in New York City," she said.

"I told you I wanted to take you someplace nice."

Jamie stepped inside the cabin and found herself enveloped in luxury. The sizable sitting area was done in a rich tan, but there were touches of navy blue that set it off.

She turned and looked at Max as the pilots disappeared through a curtain in the cockpit. "I've never been on a jet like this."

"It's perfectly safe if that's what you're worried about. I'll show you around if you like."

They took a tour of the front area first, the lavatory, a small galley, and a built-in cabinet that held a stereo, DVD player, satellite phone, and whatever else Max might need in order to relax or conduct business during his flight. Finally, he led her to the back of the plane where a small but more than adequate bedroom was situated, complete with a lavatory that included a small tub.

"Holy mackerel," Jamie said. "It's got everything."

"I specifically designed it so I could rest during international flights." He studied the look on her face. "How about a glass of champagne?" he said. "I usually have a flight attendant on board when I travel on business, but I wanted us to be alone tonight."

Jamie smiled. She felt like Cinderella. Someone had even thought to put out a plate of hors d'oeuvres. "Except for the pilots, of course," she said.

Max nodded. "Yes, I'm afraid there was no getting around that, but they won't bother us. Please—" He motioned toward one of the sofas. "Sit down and relax, and I'll open the champagne."

Jamie did as he asked, but it was all she could do to keep from gawking. The jet should come as no surprise, she reminded herself. Any man who drove a two-million-dollar car was bound to have a nice jet.

Lord, if Vera could see her now.

She jumped when she heard the champagne cork pop. A moment later, Max carried in an ice bucket holding a bottle; in his other hand were two flute glasses. He poured them each a glass and toasted her, just as one of the pilots told them to fasten their seat belts for takeoff.

"To you, Swifty. For bringing so many good things into my life."

She didn't want to think what that meant. "From the looks of it, you already have a lot of good stuff." The plane started moving.

"A man can have all the material things he needs and still be lacking. You fill up that empty space."

Jamie couldn't have been more surprised. What did it mean? "That's the nicest thing you've ever said to me, Max." They touched glasses and took sips of their champagne.

"Maybe I should start saying more nice things," Max said. "Seems we spend all our time chasing bad guys."

"You may have something there, Holt. Feels like we're always knee-deep in trouble."

"Yeah, but you'll have to admit we make a great team. The bad guys don't stand a chance."

She laughed. "Yeah, but we've had our share of close calls."

"I like that you're adventurous."

"I haven't had much of a choice since you came into my life."

"True. But you'll have to admit I'm not boring."

"I'd settle for boring once in a while. I'm allergic to bullets."

"I guess I like a challenge now and then."

"Now and then, Max? You would never be happy living a normal life."

"What do you consider normal?"

A house surrounded by a picket fence came to mind, but Jamie suspected the thought would scare him to death. It would smack of settling down, and she doubted Max would ever be satisfied with such an existence. "Maybe there's no such thing as normal after all," she said after a moment.

"You know what I think?" Max said. "I think you need to be challenged, too. And you know what else? I want to kiss you." He took her glass and set it on the coffee table in front of the sofa.

She didn't protest as he placed his hand beneath her chin and lifted her head slightly before gently touching his lips to hers. Jamie found herself leaning into the kiss, and she welcomed it when he took her in his arms and held her close. He kissed her temple and her eyelids and pressed his lips against the hollow of her throat before capturing her lips once more.

Jamie clung to him, loving the taste and smell and feel of the man who held her. She reached up and curled her hands around his neck. The kiss deepened, and Max slipped his tongue past her lips, exploring the inside of her mouth, tasting her thoroughly. Jamie boldly met his tongue with hers. She felt him draw a quick breath of excitement.

Max gathered her up in his arms and stood, tugging off her heels as he went. Jamie knew where they were headed, knew she wanted Max Holt as much as he wanted her.

It had been that way from the beginning. Their gazes locked as Max carried her into the bedroom. He dipped his head forward and kissed her again. Just like in the movies, she thought. Once again, lips parted, tongues mingled. Jamie could feel her insides growing as soft as warm butter. For once she didn't think about what tomorrow or the next day might bring.

She was willing to take a chance.

She felt the bed sink beneath her as Max gently laid her on the mattress. He turned long enough to close the door and lock it, and then he began removing his clothes. He draped them over a chair. He never once took his eyes off her face.

He was naked and already aroused when he joined her. He raised her up slightly, just long enough to unzip her dress, which he draped over his own clothes. "Oh, Jesus," he said, staring at the filmy black body suit. "I'm going to buy stock in the company that makes those things."

Once again, he was beside her, kissing her, running his hands over her body. Using his tongue, he teased her nipples through the fabric of the body suit.

"Oh, Swifty." He smoothed one hand over her hip, her belly, then slid one finger along the lace edge of the body suit, slowly, leisurely.

Jamie moaned and arched against him. She

reached for him, but he smiled. "We're in no hurry, sweetheart. Just lie back and enjoy."

Jamie closed her eyes as he pulled the wispy fabric from her body and kissed his way down, pausing only briefly between her thighs before touching her with his tongue. She cried out softly. He flicked his tongue lightly over her before parting her with his fingers and tasting her fully. Jamie's breath caught at the back of her throat.

When she could no longer stand it, Max entered her, and it was all she could do to keep from crying out.

Max paused for a moment as if he needed time to get himself under control. "Damn" was all he could say in a shaky voice.

They began to move together, slowly at first, but each thrust from Max's body brought them closer to the edge. Jamie could feel the intensity building with sweet anticipation, even as Max's brow beaded with sweat, and he gritted his teeth in an obvious attempt to restrain himself.

Jamie was the first to feel the burst of pleasure, a pleasure so intense that she called out to Max who immediately joined her in the last frenzied moments.

They clung to each other long afterward, waiting for their heartbeats to slow, waiting for the fog of passion to lift. Jamie snuggled against Max, knowing as long as she lived she would never want another man the way she did the one beside her.

"Max?"

He pulled her close. "Yeah?"

She wanted to tell him how she felt, confess her love, but fear alone prevented it. "I've never felt this way before," she said instead. There, she'd said it.

He kissed her forehead. "I knew we'd be good together, Swifty. I knew it the first time I saw you."

It was probably the closest she was going to get to what she'd wanted; an admission of love, but Jamie said nothing. Instead, she made to get up.

Max tightened his grip on her. "Where do you think you're going?"

"I saw a small tub in the bathroom. I thought—"

He interrupted her with a kiss. "There's plenty of time for that." He pulled her face close to his for another kiss.

Lord, she was a goner.

JAMIE WAS TOUCHING UP HER MAKEUP WHEN MAX reentered the bedroom and told her they needed to prepare for landing. She followed him into the sitting room, fastened her seat belt, and waited until the plane touched down and came to a halt, and the captain gave them the okay to move about the cabin.

Max checked his wristwatch and ushered her off the jet into a waiting limo. Jamie had never felt so pampered. The driver immediately whisked them away.

"I've never been to New York City," she said.

"You live in one of the prettiest towns I've ever seen," he said. "Why would you want to leave it?" Max hit a button, and a window slid up, separating them from the driver. He grinned and pulled Jamie onto his lap. "It's only half an hour from here to the restaurant," he whispered. "I'm putting you in charge."

Jamie shivered when his tongue made contact with her ear. "In charge of what?" she asked.

"Not letting us get carried away back here."

"You're talking to the wrong person, pal," she whispered as she snuggled against him and raised her lips to his for a kiss.

EMILIE'S WAS AN INTIMATE FRENCH RESTAURANT with tiny white lights attached to a dark ceiling that gave one the feeling of dining beneath the stars. After sharing an appetizer of pâté de foie gras and wafers, Max and Jamie ordered filet mignon with a béarnaise sauce that Jamie claimed was to die for. Max teased her unmercifully as Jamie ordered chocolate pecan pie for dessert, but it was obvious he enjoyed watching her while he sipped his coffee.

"You remind me of a little girl sometimes," he said, when she caught him staring. "I don't think you ever had the chance to be a little girl when you were growing up."

A slight shadow crossed Jamie's face. "It often feels like I grew up too fast, but my dad and I had some pretty good times together."

Max smiled. "Tell me."

Jamie looked wistful. "He took me to Charleston from time to time, and we would eat at nice restaurants and visit the art gallery or the museum. I would wear my prettiest dress. My dad was the best. I don't remember a time he scolded me, except when I wanted to leave college and work full-time at the newspaper. He wouldn't hear of it."

"I'm glad you have so many good memories of him," Max said.

"Vera said he spoiled me shamelessly, and I guess he did."

"Why do you suppose he never remarried?"

Jamie's eyes clouded. "I don't think he ever got over my mother leaving him. He kept her clothes for the longest time. Vera finally made him give them to the Salvation Army."

"He never dated?"

"No. And it wasn't because he didn't have the opportunity. My father was a handsome man. Would you like to see a picture?" Jamie didn't wait for a response; she was already reaching into her purse for her wallet. She flipped it open to the image of a dark-haired man and handed it to Max.

"I can see the resemblance," Max said. He returned the picture. "You must've loved him very much."

Jamie nodded. "I was devastated when he died."

"Why do you suppose Vera never married?" Max asked, changing the subject.

"Vera was in love with my father, Max," she said simply.

"I guess I've always assumed as much," he said.

"She's never admitted it to me, but I knew."

"I wonder why she never told him."

"Vera's a proud woman. She would never have made her feelings known because he spent his life grieving the loss of my mother."

"Do you miss her?" Max asked.

"How can you miss someone you never knew?" Jamie pondered the question. "There were times, of course, when I wanted a mother. I envied the girls at school whose moms helped with parties or participated in school outings. Not that Vera didn't help out," she added quickly, "but it wasn't the same."

"I'm sorry, Jamie."

"Don't be. I had all the love and attention a kid could have possibly wanted. I just hope—" She paused and blushed.

Max waited. "What do you hope?"

Jamie met his gaze. "I just hope, if and when I have children, that I'm a better mother."

He smiled. "You'll be a fantastic mother, Jamie."

"I don't know," she said. "I've already spoiled Fleas something awful, and he's a dog."

Max laughed, and the two continued conversing for more than an hour before he signaled for the bill. Once he'd paid, he looked at Jamie. "Now, tell me. Is there anything in particular you'd like to see while we're in New York?"

It didn't take long for her to answer. "Times Square."

"You got it, Swifty."

The limo was waiting when they left the restaurant. Jamie stared out the window, awed by the skyscrapers that disappeared into the night sky. "I can't believe all the people," she said, noting the crowded sidewalks. When Times Square came into view, Max had the driver open the sunroof of the limo so Jamie could peer out.

"It looks just like it does on TV," she said, feeling a surge of excitement as she gazed in delight, much like a child on Christmas morning. They spent an hour riding through the streets before Max told the limo driver to stop at Sardi's where they had coffee.

When it was time to head back to the airport, Jamie turned to Max. "Thank you," she said.

Max smiled at her enthusiasm. "It was my pleasure. I'd like to bring you back during the day so you can see Central Park. I would love to take you to other places, say, Paris and Rome and Hong Kong, just to see them through your eyes."

"Don't you enjoy them?"

"Most of my travel is business related."

"Max, this is me you're talking to. I'm sure you've had your share of lovely companions."

"Does that bother you?"

It did, but she wouldn't admit it. "It's none of my business." Still, she wondered how many women he'd taken with him on his private jet.

"There are different types of relationships, Jamie. Some are more meaningful than others."

She paused and met his gaze. Her heart thumped wildly in her chest. "Yeah?"

"Some are nothing more than two people providing, as you say, companionship. Both people are mature enough to know up front that it isn't likely to last. Then there are those worth hanging on to."

Jamie stared back at him for so long she was sure her eyes had crossed. What the devil was the man trying to say? "You know what your problem is, Max?"

"Uh-oh."

"You don't know what you want."

"Or maybe it's that I want something so badly, and I don't know where it will lead," he said ruefully. "Ever thought of that?"

Was he referring to them? she wondered. "Are you scared? That's hard to believe."

"I'm human."

Jamie saw the vulnerability in his eyes. "People take risks when they fall in love," she said softly.

"Do you love me, Jamie?"

Her heart turned over in her chest. He had just asked her the million-dollar question. "I don't know," she hedged. "I keep telling myself it would be a mistake."

"Why?"

The look in his eyes was sincere. He wanted to know. "I don't think we're looking for the same thing, Max."

"Would it matter if I told you I'm looking for a way to spend more time in Beaumont? Frankie and I are discussing the possibility of bringing much-needed industry to the area."

"How come nobody told me?"

"It's still in the planning stages."

"What would you manufacture?"

"The same material my car is made of. It's a newly identified polymer that is lightweight but has the durability of the strongest steel. Think if that same material could be used on other automobiles. It could save a lot of lives. I just need to find a way to make it more affordable to the consumer."

"And you'd lower the unemployment rate in Beaumont," she said, thrilled at the prospect. "Oh, Max, this is exciting news."

"It's confidential for now," he said. "I don't want it announced until we know it's a sure thing." He paused. "The main reason I'm telling you is because I want you to know I'm hoping to be around more. If that means anything," he added.

Jamie's stomach turned somersaults at the thought. "I could probably adapt," she said.

"Yeah?"

"Yeah."

They arrived at the airport and boarded the plane. Once they'd taken off and were able to move about the cabin, Max and Jamie found themselves back in his bedroom where they made love until the captain announced they would be landing soon. They dressed hurriedly and took their seats in the front cabin. Jamie couldn't stop grinning.

"Why are you smiling?" Max said.

"Why do you think I'm smiling? I've been flown to New York on a private jet, eaten at a fancy restaurant, seen Times Square, and I've been laid three times."

Max laughed out loud. "The things you say. That's what I like best about you."

As Max drove Jamie home shortly after three A.M., she leaned her head back in the seat and sighed happily. "Thank you, Max, for a wonderful evening."

"We should do it more often," he said.

They arrived back at Jamie's house, only to find Destiny's car sitting in the driveway. Jamie frowned. "I don't believe this," she said. "What is *she* doing here at this hour? I'm beginning to think she's following me."

"I'm beginning to think the same thing," Max said in annoyance, surprising Jamie.

Jamie suddenly felt afraid. "I hope it's not what I think it is." She rushed from the car as soon as Max parked.

"Oh, thank goodness you're finally home," Destiny said.

"What on earth are you doing here at this hour?" Jamie demanded.

"I've had several visions." She suddenly sneezed. "They were awful."

"We're listening," Max said, still sounding irritated.

"It's about the next victim," Destiny said, looking directly at Jamie. "She's going to be somebody you know."

CHAPTER THIRTEEN

Jamie felt as though her breath had been knocked out of her. "Oh, my God!" she cried. "Who is it?"

"I can't get a fix on the person," Destiny said.

"Come inside," Jamie said, noting that the woman was trembling badly. There was fear in her eyes.

"Ronnie is with me."

"He can come in."

Jamie handed a silent Max the keys to her front door, and he started ahead of them as Jamie and Destiny waited. Once inside, Max, maintaining his silence, put on coffee.

"Now, tell me what you saw," Jamie said.

Once again, Destiny sneezed. "Like I told you, the victim is going to put up a fight, and she'll leave scratches on the murderer's arms. I can't get an image of a face or name. But I'm positive you know her." Destiny began to wring her hands. "Do you have any friends who might answer a personals ad?"

"No one I can think of."

They moved to the kitchen as soon as Max had the coffee ready. "Max, I think we should go ahead and notify the police," Jamie said.

"Lamar can't find out the kind of information I can. Muffin is working around the clock doing background checks."

"Muffin is out of whack right now," Jamie said, "since she talked to Dee Dee. She thinks she's pregnant, remember?"

"She's still able to do her job."

"Your secretary is pregnant?" Destiny asked Max.

Max shifted in his seat. "She just thinks she is."

"Has she seen a doctor?" Destiny asked.

"It's a long story," he said, "but she's good at background checks. As a matter of fact, she did one on you."

Jamie turned to the woman. "Max does background checks on everyone. He even did one on me."

"So you think you know all about me, do you?" she said, anger having replaced the scared look in her eyes. "If you're so smart, tell me what you've learned."

Max didn't hesitate. "I know that before you married into money you made your living as a fortune-teller in one carnival show after another. I know you were arrested more than once for operating illegally out of your home. You've changed your name several times."

"My real name is Betty Sue Jenkins," Destiny said. "Of course I changed it. Who's going to take a psychic seriously with a name like that?"

Max looked at Jamie. "She's been married five times, and the authorities exhumed the body of one of her husbands because his children suspected poisoning."

Destiny hitched her chin high. "They found nothing. His kids were a bunch of spoiled brats who resented the fact I was awarded the bulk of their father's estate. And do you know *why* I was awarded it? Because I was a damn good wife to him, and I was the one who cared for him when he was sick. His children couldn't be bothered."

Jamie realized she was staring and rubbing Fleas's head frantically. The dog seemed as agitated as she was. She stood. "I don't care about Destiny's past, Max. All I care about is finding a killer. You're the one who said we should use every means possible."

"I don't need you to defend me, Jamie," Destiny said. "I've lived with this sort of thing all my life. I'm going home now and get some rest." She paused to sneeze. "I'm sorry I bothered you."

She was gone. Jamie sank into her chair and looked at Max. "What's going on?"

"I'm beginning to have my doubts about her. She hasn't given us anything we could go on. I wasn't going to tell you what I found out at first, but I don't appreciate her barging in at this hour and scaring you. And think about this. Suppose she did get away with poisoning her husband. That would make her a murderer. Luanne Ritter's murder didn't occur until after Destiny Moultrie hit town, right?"

Jamie gaped at him. "You're not insinuating that Destiny killed Luanne? What would be her motive? She didn't even know Luanne Ritter."

"We don't know that. She could have done business with Luanne."

"She doesn't need money; her husbands left her well off."

"I just think it's possible that Destiny might have ulterior motives. I'm not certain what they are, but her past speaks for itself."

"My instincts are pretty good, and I believe Destiny has a good heart. Her only motive for contacting me was to write a column for the newspaper, but she got dragged into this situation when she had a vision about Luanne Ritter's murder. Maybe it's all been just one big coincidence after another, but I believe she saw something tonight. You saw how upset she was. The woman was terrified."

Jamie got up and let Fleas out, then went about picking up dirty coffee cups. All at once she heard Fleas yelp. She and Max raced to the door.

The poodle next door was chasing Fleas across the back yard. "Oh, it's that damn poodle again," Jamie said, racing out the door, just as her neighbor, Barbara Fender, hurried over.

"Precious, come here this instant!" the woman cried, although the dog paid no heed. She and Jamie reached the dogs at the same instant. Barbara pulled her dog free, and Fleas took off for the pickup truck parked close by.

"Jamie, I am so sorry," the woman said. "Precious woke up having to go to the bathroom."

Jamie noticed the woman had changed her big hair. It had been cut into a flattering style and colored, giving her a softer look. Jamie felt bad that she hadn't tried to get to know her better; the woman probably didn't know a soul in town. Then Jamie reminded herself she'd been too busy trying to catch a killer.

As though realizing Jamie was staring at her hair, Barbara touched it self-consciously. "What do you think?" she said. "I figured it was time for a change. New town, new people, new hairstyle."

"I think it looks nice," Jamie said. She smiled. "Tell you what. I'll call you first chance I get. We'll get together, and I'll tell you about my dog's emotional problems. Then you won't feel so bad."

"I'd like that," Barbara said.

Max joined them. "Come on, Fleas," he said, trying to coax the hound from the back of the pickup.

"He's not going to get down," Jamie said.

Max finally picked up Fleas and carried him into the house. Jamie and Barbara said good night, and Jamie headed for her house. She found Max inside feeding the dog cheese curls. "There you go, spoiling my dog."

"He deserves it after what he's been through. That's the ugliest poodle I've ever laid eyes on."

"Are you okay, boy?" Jamie asked her pet. But he was more interested in the cheese curls. Finally, Max poured the rest of the bag into Fleas's bowl.

Max checked his wristwatch. "Wow, it's almost four A.M. I'm beat, how about you?"

"Exhausted," Jamie said.

"You need to get to bed."

"I was thinking the same thing."

He slipped his arms around her waist and kissed her lightly on the lips.

"I'm just so confused, Max. I don't know what to think anymore. If Destiny is right—" She paused and shuddered. "I don't even want to think what might happen."

"I should get going," Max said, although he looked reluctant. "You need your rest."

"Yeah, like I'm going to be able to sleep. I'm afraid, Max."

His look softened. As if to ease the tension, he suddenly smiled. "If I stay, your neighbors will think you're a floozy."

She knew he was trying to lighten the mood. "Everyone already thinks I'm a floozy, not to mention the town drunk."

"Frankly, I liked seeing that side of you. I hope to see more of it." He released her.

The last thing she wanted him to do was leave. "Um, Max?"

"Yeah?"

She made a poor attempt at trying to return his smile. "If I let you stay, will you still get the doughnuts after we wake up?"

WHEN JAMIE AWOKE IT WAS AFTER TEN O'CLOCK. She bolted upright on the bed, just as Max came into the room with a tray of doughnuts and coffee.

"Don't panic," he said. "I called Vera and told her you would be late coming into the office." He set the tray on the bed. "Breakfast is served."

Jamie suddenly realized she was naked. Then she recalled that, despite both of them being tired when they'd gone to bed at four A.M., they had made love again. She had needed him desperately, had needed to feel his lips on her body, feel him inside her. Only Max could chase away the fear in her heart and give her something good to cling to. Exhaustion had forced her eyes closed afterward, but at dawn she had jerked awake in the throes of a nightmare. Max had gathered her close, coaxing her to sleep once more with his steady voice at her ear.

Now with the sun up, she felt less afraid. What she did feel was self-conscious at being stark raving naked. She pulled the sheet higher over her breasts.

"No need for that," Max said. "I've already seen every square inch of you, and I like it."

Jamie blushed and reached for her cup of coffee. "How do my eyes look?" They felt gritty from lack of sleep.

"They look very blue and beautiful, as always."

She noted Max was dressed in casual clothes. "You've been up a while."

"Yeah, I drove over to my hotel and showered. I needed to change clothes."

Jamie quickly ate two doughnuts and polished off her coffee. "I've got to grab a shower," she said. She glanced around. "What happened to my sleep shirt?"

"I have no idea."

"Max?" Her voice was stern. He'd probably tossed it in the trash. "Oh, what the hell." She climbed from the bed and turned for the door leading toward the bathroom. She could feel Max's eyes on her. "Take a picture, Holt," she called back over her shoulder.

"Don't need to. I've already burned your image in my brain."

Jamie was thankful when she reached the privacy of her bathroom. She turned on the shower, waited for the water to heat up, and climbed in. She thought of Destiny's visit the night before and experienced the same sense of dread. She tried to push it from her mind. Maybe Destiny was wrong. Hadn't she admitted that her predictions weren't one hundred percent accurate? Maybe this was one of those times. Jamie prayed that was the case, but she still remembered the look of fear in the woman's eyes.

She shook her head, trying to clear it. Since when did she believe in Destiny's visions anyway? Anybody who claimed to have a dead spirit following them everywhere they went had to be a little kooky, didn't they? Didn't they?

She was too wrapped up in the case, Jamie told herself. She and Max had done nothing but work on it since he'd hit town. She needed a break. She needed to check her schedule so she could have lunch with Maxine Chambers. Or maybe she could get together with her new neighbor. Barbara was probably anxious to start making friends; and she most likely needed a break from all her unpacking.

Jamie did not hear the door open, but the shower curtain suddenly parted and Max stepped in as naked as the day he was born.

"What the—"

He smiled. "I've often wondered what it would be like to take a shower with you."

"Isn't this your second for the day?"

"Yeah, but who's counting? Give me your soap and washcloth."

"I can do this myself, you know."

"Come on, Swifty, give a guy a break."

Jamie did as she was told. Max lathered the washcloth and started at the nape of her neck, working his way down to the heels of her feet. The feel of his hands on her body did wonderful things to her insides, made her forget things.

"Okay, turn around," he said.

She turned. Max busied himself washing her breasts, leaning forward to tongue each nipple once he rinsed them of soap. Jamie was suddenly enveloped in a world of sensations and tingling nerve endings. "I usually shower in half this time," she managed.

"Yeah, but think how dull it is to shower alone." He worked his way down her abdomen, her flat tummy, and finally between her thighs where he explored her with deft fingers. Jamie moaned; all logical thinking ceased, worries dissipated like smoke in a breeze. She grasped his shoulders for support as he brought her to the height of pleasure.

She was trembling by the time she climbed from the tub and toweled herself. She caught the glint of desire in Max's eyes, the slight tilt of his mouth. He knew damn well what he did to her. She glanced down at him.

"As you can see, the feeling is mutual," he said, drying himself. He smacked her behind lightly and chased her into the bedroom.

Jamie giggled like a schoolgirl. It felt good to laugh. "I have to go to work," she protested.

"It'll wait," he said. "Besides, I'll be there to help you."

They fell onto the bed together. Jamie suddenly felt less shy with him. She ran her fingers over his chest, and nipped one of his nipples playfully.

He shivered.

"You're asking for trouble, Swifty," he said.

"You ain't seen nuthin' yet, bubba." She toyed with his chest for a moment before lightly running her fingers down his stomach where the hair thinned slightly, and then she moved lower. She stroked him. Finally, using the very tip of her tongue, she tasted him.

"Oh, God, I'm a dead man," he said.

Jamie smiled and put him in her mouth. Max gazed down at her with a look of dazed passion. The husky moan he gave prodded her onward.

Jamie swirled her tongue around him. It was exhilarating to know she could wield so much power over a man who was accustomed to calling all the shots.

Finally, he pulled away, eased her gently onto her back, and using his own tongue, brought her to the edge of orgasm. She moaned and reached for him, and he entered her. Their sighs of pleasure rose like music.

Max moved against her slowly at first, but soon they were caught up in an erotic dance, and Jamie's cries were stifled by Max's kisses.

Afterward, Max gathered her in his arms, where Jamie snuggled against him like a soft kitten. She felt safe and secure.

"A man could get used to this, Swifty," he said.

She nodded, reveling in the fact that she had Max Holt spent and naked beside her. Her hand on his chest measured each heartbeat, and she remained quiet until his breathing slowed. She could smell the heady scent of their lovemaking mixed with Max's soap and aftershave.

Jamie rose up on one elbow and gazed down at him, a self-satisfied look on her face. His own expression was lazy and contented. "A woman could get used to this, too, Holt."

"Yeah?"

"Yeah." She knew she was grinning too broadly for any sane woman; that Max would take one look at her goofy expression and guess the truth. Just as she had expected, she had fallen head over heels in love with him, and there wasn't a damn thing she could do about it.

IT WAS ALMOST NOON BY THE TIME MAX AND JAMIE arrived at the newspaper office, with Fleas in tow. Vera was dressed in a fire-engine-red pantsuit and tall heels that she seemed to have trouble maneuvering. She handed Jamie a large stack of mail.

"I have to leave for a while," Vera said, "because a bunch of women from my church are picketing Maxine Chambers's lingerie store this morning. I want to be there to take pictures."

"Why don't people leave the poor woman alone?" Jamie said.

"Because she's displaying unmentionables in her front window," Vera said. "And wouldn't you know it; Agnes Aimsley's grandson is the ringleader. Most folks don't like Maxine anyway 'cause she was such a snooty librarian."

Jamie gave an enormous sigh. "I don't believe

this. I'm going with you, but I'll be the opposition. The woman has a right to run her business without a bunch of old church ladies interfering."

"I'm with you." When Jamie looked surprised, she went on. "After all, this is a free country. Besides, I've been thinking I might buy one of those push-up bras she has in her window. I might just give Destiny Moultrie a run for her money." She grabbed her camera. "This could be good headline material, you know."

"I need to make a few calls," Jamie said before Vera hurried out the door. "Maxine is going to need support." Dee Dee was first on her list. She was outraged and promised to call her friends. Jamie then called several old high school buddies, all of whom promised to meet her outside Maxine's store and rally their support. She even phoned Destiny.

"I've got to run," she told Max, who'd walked in on the tail end of one of Jamie's calls. "A bunch of old church biddies are going to picket our new lingerie store, and I'm going to try to put a stop to it."

"I thought we had a paper to get out."

"This won't take long," Jamie promised. "But I can't just sit back and do nothing while an army of angry women descends on Maxine Chambers's place of business." She hurried out the door.

By the time Jamie arrived at Maxine's shop there were at least fifty women gathered out front, many of them chanting, "Close this store!" Agnes Aimsley and her grandson were right in front. A nervous Maxine peered out the window. Jamie gave her the thumbs-up, and the woman looked relieved to see her.

Jamie spotted Dee Dee, Beenie, and Destiny and hurried over. "How many do we have on our side?" she asked.

"We just arrived," Dee Dee said, "but I don't think we have more than ten or twelve. Those church ladies look pretty vicious if you ask me."

Beenie appeared anxious. "I wish I had stayed home. I'm afraid they'll kick my butt."

Jamie spied Vera on the sidelines, snapping pictures as fast as she could. "I need something to stand on," Jamie said. She hurried two doors down to Lowery's Hardware and returned with a ladder. She didn't see Max pull up across the street and get out as she climbed the ladder.

"Ladies, please hear me out," Jamie said, trying to talk above the roaring crowd of female voices. "At least give me a chance to have my say."

Brent Walker looked annoyed. "The town has spoken," he said. "We want Maxine Chambers to pack her slut-wear and close shop."

Obviously feeling braver now that Jamie had arrived, Maxine Chambers stood at the front door of her shop, arms folded across her breasts, a defiant look on her face. "I have as much right to run my business as any other person," she shouted.

The crowd booed their disapproval. Jamie finally quieted them. "Maxine is right," she yelled. "As long as she pays rent she has just as much right to operate her shop as the next merchant. And without being harassed," she added.

"I can't believe you're taking her side, Jamie," Lyle Betts's wife, Lorna, said.

Jamie regarded the woman. "You don't have the right to judge Maxine," she replied. "Your husband is selling aphrodisiac-laced brownies and cakes with naked people on them."

All eyes turned to Mrs. Betts.

She squared her shoulders. "That's a lie. Lyle would never do something like that."

"Then I suggest you march right up to his bakery and demand to see his new 'Adults Only' catalog."

Brent Walker frowned. "I can't believe you're supporting this woman," he said, pointing at Maxine. "But that should come as no surprise what with your new personals ads. Men and women need to meet in church."

Jamie ignored him and turned to another woman. "And what about you, Mrs. Frazier?" she called out. "Are you going to tell me that you and Mr. Frazier don't have adult videos in your store? I know you do because I've seen them."

Mrs. Frazier looked embarrassed. "Some people enjoy watching that sort of thing. We have to keep up with our competition."

"And some people enjoy wearing pretty lingerie," Jamie said, "myself included."

The women gasped.

"There's a difference," Edna Wilburn said. "I love pretty nightgowns, but I wouldn't think of displaying that trash in my front store window. It's not fair that the rest of us are forced to see it every time we walk by."

Jamie hitched her chin high as she regarded the woman who was married to the owner of Wilburn's Garage. "You want to talk about what's fair, Edna?" she said. "Is it fair your husband charges a fortune for his work? Is it fair that he preys on women because he knows they have no idea what it costs for parts and labor to repair their cars?"

"Well, I never," Edna said in a huff.

"Jamie's right," Vera called out. "How do you think you got that new swimming pool?"

Edna looked shocked. "Why, Vera Bankhead, I never knew you felt that way about my George."

Agnes Aimsley stepped forward. "Maybe we can solve this like good Christians," she said in her fruity-textured voice.

Everyone glanced her way. "What do you suggest, Mrs. Aimsley?" Jamie asked.

Agnes didn't hesitate. "Why don't we all agree to stop bothering Maxine if she agrees to use a little more, um, decorum in her window display."

Brent looked at her in astonishment. "What are you saying, Gram?" He pointed to Maxine. "Why are you defending this, this—"

"Watch what you say, Brent," Jamie said. "You know what the Good Book says about judging people."

His face reddened. "I feel it's my Christian duty to clean up this town."

"Is that why you visited Luanne Ritter the night of her murder?" Jamie realized she'd gone too far the minute the words left her mouth.

The women went silent and fixed their gaze on the man. Brent shot Jamie a menacing look. "So you're the one," he said. "For your information the police have already visited me, and I've been cleared of any wrongdoing. Perhaps you should concentrate on running your newspaper, Miss Swift, and leave innocent people alone."

"Oh, why do we have to have all this bickering?" Agnes said. "Why can't we all get along?"

Jamie nodded. "Sounds like a good idea to me, Mrs. Aimsley."

The woman faced her grandson. "I like pretty nightgowns. I think Miss Chambers should be able to run her store as she sees fit. I don't know why everybody insists on making trouble for her. If people don't like what they see, they should just stay away."

Finally, Maxine spoke up. "If you people will agree to leave me alone, I'll take some of the more, um, offensive items out of my window."

"That sounds fair," Agnes replied.

Brent gaped at his grandmother. "Well, I for one refuse to give in to the devil's work." He looked at Maxine. "You'll pay for your actions. Mark my words." He stalked away.

Dee Dee stepped up. "I haven't been in your store before, Maxine, but Jamie has told me all about it. I plan to have a look before I leave here today."

"Me, too," Beenie said. "I love women's lingerie."

Jamie's high school friends promised to visit the store, as well.

All at once, a police car skidded to a stop and Lamar Tevis and one of his deputies stepped out. They were in uniform, but instead of wearing slacks, they wore shorts.

"What in the world?" Vera said to Jamie the minute she saw them. "Would you look at how Lamar and his deputy are dressed?"

"Oh, my," Beenie said, fanning himself. "Would you look at that deputy? I'd like some of that."

Even Jamie had to admit the shorts bordered on

indecent. "I guess they changed to shorts because of the heat," she said.

"Okay, ladies," Lamar said. "What's going on here?" He was tugging at his shorts as if he found them uncomfortable.

Jamie opened her mouth to speak, but was cut off by Lamar's deputy. "Lamar, these women are obviously picketing, and they don't have a permit. They're breaking the law. We'll have to arrest them."

This brought another gasp from the crowd. Jamie didn't know if they feared jail or were afraid the men would bust out of their shorts.

"I'm guilty," Beenie shouted, waving both hands in the air. "I insist that your deputy take me away immediately."

Lamar looked bewildered as he gazed at the crowd of women. "Are you sure about that, Joe?" he asked the deputy.

"Yes, sir."

Jamie stepped forward. "Lamar, you don't have a jail large enough to hold all these women." She tried to ignore Beenie tugging on her blouse.

"Well, that's true. But like Joe says, you're breaking the law, and I can't just stand by and do nothing."

Vera shot Lamar a dark look. "You wouldn't dare arrest us. Besides, nobody is picketing anyone.

Maxine Chambers is holding a big sale, and we're standing in line to get into her store."

"I'm confused," Lamar said.

"That's obvious," Vera said, "or you wouldn't be dressed like that."

"Huh? Oh, you mean the shorts. I think the measurements were off because they're kinda snug."

Beenie moaned and bit his hand.

Jamie called out from her place on the ladder. "Ladies, Chief Tevis has the mistaken impression that we're picketing Maxine's store without a permit, which is against the law. We could all be arrested. But Vera just assured him that we're here for Maxine's grand opening sale, so what do you say? Who wants to buy a new nightgown today?"

Everyone in the crowd raised their hand.

MAX LOOKED PLEASED WITH JAMIE WHEN SHE crossed the street to his car. "Why are you grinning?" she asked.

"I'm proud of you, Swifty. You stood up for what you believed in. And from the looks of it, the lady who owns that store is going to make a hell of a lot of sales today."

MAX AND JAMIE SPENT MOST OF THE DAY WORKING to get the newspaper out on time and pondering what information Muffin had for them. By the time they sent the newspaper to press, both were tired. They dropped Fleas off at Jamie's house, and drove to a nearby Chinese restaurant for dinner.

Jamie noticed Max was quiet. "What's wrong?" she asked.

He shrugged. "I'm disappointed that we don't seem to be any closer to solving Luanne Ritter's murder than we were in the beginning."

Jamie nodded. "I'm worried, too, Max. Especially since Destiny said there was going to be another murder, and it would be someone I know." Max remained quiet. "I know I didn't take Destiny seriously at first, and I'm probably crazy for saying this, but what if, just what if she's right? What if the killer is still out there looking for his next victim?" When Max didn't respond, she went on. "Are you listening to me?"

"Yeah. You just don't want to know what I'm thinking."

She leaned back in her seat, noting the serious look on his face. "What is it?"

Max met her gaze. "We've never discussed this, but it's been in the back of my mind all along. If Luanne Ritter's murder had something to do with her business dealings, that's one thing. If her murder involved the personals section, that's a different story.

But if he strikes again, it's a whole new ballgame, you know that, don't you?"

"What do you mean?"

"It means we're dealing with a serial killer."

VERA WAS ODDLY QUIET WHEN MAX AND JAMIE ARrived at the office the next morning with Fleas on their heels. Jamie spoke to her and grabbed the morning mail. When Vera didn't respond, Jamie looked up. The woman looked pale, the lines around her mouth drawn. "Is something wrong?" Jamie asked.

Vera glanced from Jamie to Max and finally to Jamie again. "You haven't heard, have you?"

Max and Jamie exchanged looks. "Heard what?" Jamie asked.

"Maxine Chambers was found dead in the back of her store last night."

CHAPTER FOURTEEN

Jamie dropped the mail and it scattered across the floor. She felt her stomach take a dive. All at once, her lips became numb, her knees rubbery, and she felt a blackness descending. Max noted it right away and reached for her. "Are you okay?" he asked.

"I—I need to sit."

He helped her into her office as Vera followed. "I'm sorry I just blurted it out," the older woman said, "but I haven't been myself since I heard the news."

"I think I'm going to be sick," Jamie said, sitting on the sofa.

Max immediately shoved her head between her legs. "Get some wet paper towels," he told Vera.

Fleas came to Jamie's side as though he sensed a problem. Jamie kept her head down until the nausea passed. Vera returned with the wet paper towels and handed them to her.

"What happened?" Jamie managed.

"One of Lamar's deputies saw the lights on when he drove by late last night and decided to check it out," Vera said. "The back door was open."

"How did she—" Jamie couldn't say the word.

"Same as Luanne Ritter. A fatal blow to the head."

Jamie felt sick again, mopped her face with the wet towels.

"Take deep breaths," Max said.

She gulped in air.

"I feel so bad for her," Vera said. "Especially after everybody gave her such a hard time yesterday. I tell you, something isn't right in this town. I'm wondering if the two murders are connected in some way."

Max and Jamie exchanged looks.

Vera checked her wristwatch. "Oh, darn, I'm supposed to be at the doctor's office in fifteen minutes."

"Are you ill?" Jamie asked.

"No, it's just my yearly checkup, but if I cancel there's no telling how long I'll have to wait for my next appointment. Not that I'm in much of a mind to go," she added. She studied Jamie, as if unsure what to do.

Jamie continued to breathe deeply. "You need to go," she said between breaths. "I'll be okay."

"Are you sure?" Vera said.

"I'll stay with her," Max said.

Vera left a few minutes later. Max touched Jamie's shoulder. "How are you feeling?"

"The nausea has finally passed." She felt the sting of tears, blinked them back. "It's just such a shock."

Max retrieved the mail and placed it on the coffee table before her. "Is there anything I can do?"

"Yeah, we need to find the killer." Jamie glanced at the stack of mail and shuffled through it if for no other reason than to have something to do. There were five new ads for her personals section, but more than a dozen addressed to the Divine Love Goddess Advisor. She was surprised to find they'd written in so soon. She put the mail aside and looked at Max.

"Destiny was right. Not only do we have a new murder on our hands, I knew the victim personally."

"It's a small town, Jamie. You know a lot of people."

She wasn't listening. "Brent Walker," she said suddenly. "He threatened Maxine yesterday." She jumped as someone knocked on the door. Destiny peeked in.

"I heard the news on the radio and came straight over. Are you okay?"

Jamie shrugged.

"We'll find the person responsible."

"Yeah, but how many people have to die in the meantime?" Jamie's eyes glistened. "Poor Maxine. She had so many dreams for her store."

Destiny seemed at a loss for words. The three of them were quiet for a moment. Destiny glanced at the mail. "Is any of that for me?"

Jamie swiped at her eyes. "Most of it's for you."

They were interrupted by another knock on the door. Jamie wasn't surprised to find Police Chief Lamar Tevis standing there.

He glanced at Destiny, studied her a moment, then moved to Jamie. "From the looks on your faces I take it you've heard."

Jamie nodded. "We all feel awful about it."

Lamar glanced at Destiny again. "Jamie, I need to speak to you and Max. In private," he added.

Jamie feared the worst was to come. "Lamar, this is Destiny Moultrie. She has been helping Max and me study the case. You can speak freely in front of her. But please, won't you sit down? Would you like coffee?"

Lamar shook his head as he sat on the sofa. "I've been up all night, had my quota of caffeine." He hesitated. "I'm afraid I have some more bad news for you. We searched Maxine's store and her house, and we found a clipping of the personals section from your newspaper on her kitchen table. We don't know if she actually called anyone, because none of the ads had been circled, but—" He paused and reached into his shirt pocket. He pulled out a sheet of paper and unfolded it.

Just what Jamie had been dreading.

"I have a court order here," he said, handing Jamie an official document, "for you to hand over any information you have on those who've placed or answered ads in your column. In the meantime, I'm going to request that you stop running the column. At least until we get to the bottom of this."

"I'll need to make copies for you," Max said, reaching into his briefcase for the file they'd started.

Jamie stood. Her knees still trembled. "I'll make them," she said, needing to do something. She hurried out to the reception area, thankful that Vera was not around to ask questions. When she returned with the copies, she handed them to Lamar.

He glanced through them. "Larry Johnson. Now there's a name I recognize. We've already had a few run-ins with him, a domestic-violence charge being one of them. Unfortunately, his wife dropped the charges."

"He has a serious alcohol and anger problem," Jamie said.

Max nodded. "When he's not working, he hangs out at the lounge at the Holiday Inn."

"I see you've made notes on the rest of these guys," Lamar said. "That will be real helpful for us since me and my men have been focusing on Luanne's business dealings instead of the personals section."

"Destiny and I set up dates with these men," Jamie said. "At first blush they seemed harmless. Except for Larry Johnson."

Destiny spoke. "Don't forget he keeps a crowbar handy," she reminded Jamie.

Jamie looked at Lamar. "One in his car and one just inside his front door."

"You should probably check them for trace evidence," Max told Lamar.

"And let's not forget about Brent Walker," Jamie said. "He publicly threatened Maxine yesterday. I could be wrong, but I think the man has a few loose screws."

"He's been preaching on street corners, scaring folks half to death with talk of doom and gloom," Lamar said. "One of my deputies threatened to haul him in if he didn't stop. 'Course, Walker started yapping about freedom of speech and all that.

"We suspect he visited Luanne Ritter the night of her murder," he went on, "but we have no proof. He claims he was home reading Scripture. It's not exactly an airtight alibi; Agnes wasn't feeling well that night and went to bed early. I mean, who else would have left all that religious material in her mailbox?"

"There is one other person who could have put

that religious literature in Luanne's mailbox," Max said. He told him about the Reverend Heyward. "He ran an ad. He's strange."

"Do you know if Luanne contacted him?" Lamar asked.

Max shook his head. "I managed to get my hands on Luanne's cell phone records, did a cross-check on the phone numbers, but I got nothing. She obviously made the calls from her home or office phone."

"Any return addresses on the envelopes of those who responded to the ads?" Lamar asked Jamie.

She shook her head. "Like I told Max, they would have wanted it confidential."

Lamar shuffled through the ads. "You've met with all these men?"

"Except for Sam Hunter," Max said.

"I've left several messages on his answering machine," Destiny said. "He must be playing hard to get."

Lamar looked at her. "If you don't mind my asking, what is your involvement in this case?"

"She's psychic," Max said.

"Oh, Lord, not one of *those*," Lamar said with a sigh.

"Actually, she has visions," Jamie told him. "She knew there would be another victim, but since we had nothing specific—"

"The scratches," Destiny interrupted. She looked at Lamar. "Maxine Chambers put up a fight before she died. She left deep scratches on the killer's arms."

Lamar looked from Jamie to Max. "Several of her fingernails were broken. I had my men bag her hands for nail scrapings. I'd like to have a look at Larry Johnson's and Brent Walker's arms. Would ya'll excuse me just a minute?" He got on his radio while Jamie and Destiny headed to the small kitchen for coffee.

"Maybe I could help you, Chief Tevis," Destiny said, once she and Jamie had returned with their coffee. "If I could take a look at the murder scene, you know, I might get a feel for something. I can't make any promises."

Lamar seemed to struggle with the idea. "The guys would laugh me right out of my job."

"But what if it works?" Max said. "What if it saves another woman's life? You won't know until you try."

Lamar finally relented. "Oh, okay, you can come with me, but don't tell the guys why you're really there. I'll think of something on the way over." They started for the door.

"I'll have to bring Ronnie."

"Who's Ronnie?" Lamar asked.

Jamie cleared her throat.

"Never mind," Destiny said.

. . .

AGNES AIMSLEY AWOKE IN HER EASY CHAIR WITH a start. She felt tired and haggard after a fitful night. She had awakened when Brent had come in after midnight, only to toss and turn for hours. She had finally given up on sleep and had risen at four A.M. She glanced at the clock, reached for her remote control, and turned on the midday news where the top story of the day brought a gasp from her lips.

Brent found her there when he came through the front door several hours later. The TV was off. Agnes hadn't moved from the chair except to answer the door once and make a cup of tea.

"What's wrong, Gram?" he asked.

She didn't answer.

"Gram?"

"The police came by earlier."

He gave an exasperated sigh. "What do they want this time?"

"They didn't say. Brent, the most awful thing has happened. Mrs. Chambers was murdered last night."

"Who?"

"Maxine Chambers from the lingerie store."

"Oh, great, the police probably want to pin that on me, too."

Agnes looked at him. "What are you talking about?"

He sank onto the sofa and raked his hands through his hair. "They questioned me about that Ritter woman. I left some spiritual literature in her mailbox so they naturally assume I killed her."

"I don't understand. What was your business with Mrs. Ritter?"

Brent gaped at her. "Surely you know that she was hounding several members of the church, Gram. They had taken out loans with her and were having a hard time making payments. Ritter sent a couple of her goons out to scare them. These guys scared one of the members pretty bad. I'm surprised you haven't heard."

"I thought they were just rumors."

"Somebody had to take the woman to task," Brent said. "I felt it was my Christian duty."

"You visited her?"

Brent nodded.

"Do the police know this?"

He hesitated. "I don't want to involve you, Gram. The less you know the better."

"You've always been able to talk to me."

Brent clasped his hands together and stared down at the floor. "I had to lie to the police, Gram. I told them I never set foot inside Ritter's house. That's not true."

Agnes went deathly still. "What happened?"

"She let me in, said she'd give me five minutes to

have my say. It turned into a yelling match. I was so mad." He raked his hands across his face. "I don't want to talk about it."

"You should have told the police the truth, Brent. It's not like you to lie."

"I had no choice. They're desperate to pin this thing on someone. And now they're going to come after me over that Chambers woman. I lost my temper yesterday, said some things I probably shouldn't have. My guess is somebody reported it. Probably that newspaperwoman."

Agnes suddenly looked afraid. "The police asked me if you went out last night. I told them yes, that you didn't come home until late."

Brent paled. "I was out driving around," he said. "Driving and thinking. I might as well tell you things aren't going well at school."

"Then I suggest you return immediately and straighten them out, young man," Agnes said sharply.

Their gazes locked. "Yes, of course," he said. "I can be packed and out of here in less than an hour."

VERA WAS NOT HAPPY. "I CAN'T BELIEVE YOU'RE going to pull the personals section to give that crazy woman more space for her Divine Love Goddess Advisor column."

"It's just temporary," Jamie said. "Did you see the stack of mail Destiny received?"

"Yes. It just goes to show you people aren't thinking straight if they're seeking information from somebody like her. They must be spending too much time in the sun. Or maybe they're eating too many of Lyle Betts's brownies."

Dee Dee and Beenie came through the front door. It was obvious Dee Dee had been crying. "We heard the news about Maxine, and we just stopped by to make sure you were okay. I know you liked her."

"Thank you," Jamie said. "It came as a real shock."

"And we wanted to invite you to lunch," Beenie said.

Dee Dee nodded. "That's right. We haven't had lunch together in ages. We used to do it all the time when I first moved here."

It was obvious they were trying to cheer her up. "I wish I could join you," Jamie said, "but I've been so upset over Maxine that I haven't been able to concentrate on my work, and it's going to be difficult enough meeting today's deadline. I need to stay here."

"Do you know if the police have any suspects?" Dee Dee asked nervously. "Do you know if Luanne Ritter's death was connected?" she added, without waiting for an answer. "I shudder to think we have a killer walking the streets. I mean, what if he strikes again?" She had to pause to catch her breath.

"Dee Dee didn't take the news well," Beenie said, meeting Jamie's gaze. "She's really trying to be brave about the whole thing."

"I'm afraid the police don't know much at this time," Jamie replied, not wanting to give out too much information. But she was just as worried as Dee Dee about the possibility of another murder.

"Well, I for one am going to make sure my doors are locked at all times," Vera said.

Dee Dee took Jamie's hand in hers, squeezed it reassuringly, but it was obvious the woman was equally distressed. "Perhaps we'll have lunch soon?" Her bottom lip quivered.

Jamie offered the closest thing she had to a smile. "Of course we will. And try not to worry. It's not good for the baby."

Dee Dee nodded. "I promise." She and Beenie left a few minutes later.

"I NEED TO TALK TO MAX," VERA TOLD JAMIE, later that afternoon.

Max stepped out of Jamie's office. "Did I hear someone mention my name?"

Vera nodded. "You're just the person I'm looking for. I've decided I like Jamie's Mustang so well that I want you to find me one."

He shrugged. "That shouldn't be a problem. Any specific color?"

"Pink."

"Then pink it is. I'll get right on it."

"Just like that?"

"Just like that."

THE REST OF THE DAY PASSED QUICKLY FOR JAMIE as she and Max worked together on the newspaper. By the time they sent it to press, Jamie was dog tired. Worry had etched lines on either side of her mouth, and when Mike Henderson had handed in his piece on Maxine Chambers, she'd asked Max to look at it.

Destiny came in for her mail as Max and Jamie prepared to leave the office. "I'm afraid I wasn't much help to Lamar. Ronnie was yakking in my ear the whole time so it sort of blew my concentration. He doesn't particularly like policemen since he had a few run-ins with the law when he was alive."

Jamie nodded as though it made complete sense.

"Oh, and guess what I did? I applied for a job as bartender at the Holiday Inn and they asked me if I could start tonight since they're short of help. I figured, what better way to watch Larry Johnson."

"Good idea," Max said.

"Do you know anything about making cocktails?" Jamie asked.

"No, but I suppose I can pick it up in no time. And here's the best news. Sam Hunter finally returned my call. He's going to come by for a drink tonight so we can meet."

"Just as long as you remember to stay in a public place with him," Max said. "Two women have died. We're not taking any chances."

Mike Henderson peeked in, and his eyes widened at the sight of Destiny. "Well, hello again. Have you thought any more about my offer to take you to dinner?"

Destiny stepped just outside the door with him. "I appreciate the offer," she said, "but I work nights."

"Oh, yeah? Well, that's no problem for me. I can pick you up after you get off."

Destiny smiled. "Look, Mike, I'm really flattered, but I'm sort of interested in someone."

He looked disappointed. "Oh, well, I guess that changes things," he said. "But, hey, if it doesn't work out you can always give me a call."

"How about we make it an early night?" Max told Jamie as they climbed into his car. "I'll call out for pizza. Besides, I need to be available for Destiny, even though I don't expect her to run into problems."

"Sounds good to me," Jamie said, although she didn't have much of an appetite. All she could do was think about Maxine and hope the woman hadn't suffered.

Muffin came on, and Max filled her in.

"Did anyone check Larry Johnson's or Brent Walker's whereabouts last night?" Muffin asked.

"Lamar said he'd put his deputies on it," Max said.

Once home, Jamie checked to make sure her neighbor's dog was nowhere in sight, then let Fleas out of the car. After they had decided what topping they wanted on their pizza, Max placed a takeout order and started a bath for Jamie.

Jamie headed for the bathroom. She stripped off her clothes, climbed into the hot bath, and sank deep into the water.

Once again, she thought of Maxine. Maxine, who'd been so proud of her new shop, had finally taken a chance in life and gone after her dreams. Jamie had admired her for it and was sure they would have eventually become good friends.

Now Maxine was dead, and it was probably related to Jamie's new personals section. That was the toughest part.

Max returned some twenty minutes later with the pizza. Having dressed in shorts and a T-shirt, Jamie grabbed plates and silverware and set the table. She placed a slice of pizza on each plate, only to sit there and stare at her piece.

"Are you okay?" Max asked.

She looked at him. Tears pooled in her eyes. "I'll be fine."

Max pushed his chair from the table and reached

for her. Jamie immediately went to him, and he pulled her onto his lap. She let her head rest against his chest.

"I feel responsible for all of this," she said.

Max pressed his lips against her hair. "Jamie, we don't know if the newspaper is involved, and even if it is, I've already told you, you can't control the actions of a cold-blooded killer." He paused. "You know, I've been thinking. Maybe we should leave Lamar to his investigative work and go away for a few days."

She gaped at him. "I can't leave while there's a killer on the loose." She didn't realize she'd raised her voice. "I can't believe you'd even suggest it. We have to find out who's behind this, Max."

"You're taking it pretty hard," he said. "I've never seen you like this."

Jamie opened her mouth to respond, but the doorbell rang. "Oh, damn, who could that be?" she said. She got up and made her way to the front door.

Beenie and Dee Dee stood on the other side.

"Oh, Jamie, I am so glad to see you," Dee Dee said, in her little-girl voice. "When you're in trouble, the first person you want to see is your best friend." She walked into the living room with Beenie on her heels. He held Dee Dee's Maltese, Choo-Choo. Behind them stood a bevy of servants carrying luggage.

"What's wrong?" Jamie asked, noting Dee Dee's

eyes were swollen. She'd obviously been crying again. "Did something happen?"

"It's Frankie and all his wrestling buddies," she said. "They're driving me crazy."

"Dee Dee needs peace and quiet in her, um, fragile condition," Beenie said. "She's not getting it at home, not with all those wrestlers around. They can be loud and obnoxious."

"So I've left Frankie," Dee Dee said. "I was hoping it would be okay if Beenie and I stayed with you until we found a place of our own. It is okay, isn't it?" Her staff began stacking expensive suitcases in the living room as Dee Dee spoke.

Jamie blinked back her astonishment. Of all times for Dee Dee to show up. "I, um, of course it's okay, honey. Come on in." She was only vaguely aware that Max had entered the room.

"What's wrong, Dee Dee?" he asked.

Beenie answered for her. "Frankie has totally lost interest in Dee Dee," he said. "All he does is hang out with his wrestling buddies."

Dee Dee burst into tears. "Beenie's right. Frankie doesn't seem to know I exist."

Fleas walked into the room and sniffed her dress. "Eeyeuuw! Is that your new dog? The one that came with the truck?" she added as she backed away.

"Yes," Jamie said, hoping Dee Dee wouldn't ask

about the missing hair on his back. "I'm very attached to him. In fact, he sleeps with me."

"Eeyeuuw!" Dee Dee's jaw dropped clear to her collarbone. "What happened to his hair?"

Jamie sighed. "It's a long story, honey, but if you plan to stay, you'll have to get used to him. He's really very sweet."

Dee Dee attempted a smile. "What's his name?"

"Fleas."

"Eeyeuuw!" Both Dee Dee and Beenie huddled together. Even one of the staff carrying in the luggage paused.

"You're joking, right?" Beenie said.

"I didn't name him that, and he doesn't really have fleas." Jamie paused. "You'll have to sleep with me," she told Dee Dee. Beenie can use the other bedroom."

"I thought you had three bedrooms," Dee Dee said.

"I converted one of them into an office a long time ago."

"I still think we should go to a nice hotel," Beenie said, staring at the dog with disdain.

Dee Dee almost snapped at him. "I can't go to a hotel. How would it look if the mayor's wife just up and left her husband? Especially after we've announced my pregnancy to half the town."

Max stepped forward. "Dee Dee, I'm sure you

and Frankie can work this out. It's not often he and his wrestling buddies get together."

"Yes, but they've decided to stay a month. I can't take it. All they do is talk about the good old days and eat Vienna sausage, potted meat, and sardines right out of the can. They claim that's what they lived on before they became famous wrestlers." She shuddered. "And that's not the worst of it. Snakeman and Big John have tons of girlie magazines lying about. That's the last thing Frankie needs to be looking at since I'm going to blow up to the size of a watermelon soon." She suddenly burst into fresh tears.

Beenie patted her shoulder. "There, there," he said. "You'll only ruin your makeup, and tomorrow your eyes will be twice as puffy. You're going to have to be brave for the baby's sake."

Max tried to calm her, but it was obvious he was accustomed to her dramatics. "Beenie's right," he said. "You need to calm down. For the baby's sake."

"How will I support myself?" she cried. "The only thing I've ever done is jump out of cakes at bachelor parties."

"Oh, that *is* going to be a problem," Beenie said. "You certainly won't be able to pay my salary on that." He suddenly brightened. "Oh, pooh, your husband will still take care of you. It's his child you're carrying."

"Excuse me, but where am I supposed to put these suitcases?" one of Dee Dee's staff asked.

Jamie pointed toward her bedroom. "How many bags do you have?"

"Only seven or eight."

Only seven or eight. Jamie realized she should be grateful there weren't more.

"Does Frankie know you've left?" Max asked.

Dee Dee shook her head. "He and his buddies went bowling. They'll probably go to Charlie's Sports Bar after that. No telling when they'll get in."

"He's going to call here looking for you the minute he finds out you're gone," Jamie told her.

"We won't answer the door," Dee Dee said.

"If he wants to see you badly enough, he might break it down."

"You really think so?" Dee Dee looked hopeful.

"That sounds so romantic," Beenie said.

Max put his hand on Jamie's shoulder. "Listen, I hate to break up the party, but I think I'll just go back to my hotel. I have a lot of work to do. Besides, I know you're anxious to get your guests settled." Then he kissed his sister on her forehead and left.

"Well, now," Dee Dee said. "I suppose we should order something to eat."

"There's pizza in the kitchen that hasn't been touched," Jamie said, perturbed that Max had left her to deal with his histrionic sister. As if she didn't have enough on her mind.

"Pizza!" Dee Dee cried. "Eeyeuuw, that is so fattening. Do you have any lettuce?"

"You can't just eat lettuce," Beenie said. "You're pregnant. One slice of pizza isn't going to hurt you."

Jamie nodded. "Come on in, and I'll fix you a plate."

"Would you mind if I turned in early tonight?" Dee Dee asked. "Having all those wrestlers in my house has been exhausting, and I've been thinking about poor Maxine all day. I just want to rest."

"I second that motion," Beenie said on a sigh. "If she rests, then I can finally get some rest."

Jamie nodded. "You can turn in any time you like." She figured the sooner she got them to bed the better. At least it would give her time to think about how she could arrange a quick reconciliation between Dee Dee and Frankie.

JAMIE WAS AWAKENED AT MIDNIGHT BY THE RINGing of the doorbell. It didn't take a rocket scientist to figure out who it was.

Dee Dee opened her eyes. "It's Frankie," she said. "Would you please tell him I'm never coming home?"

"Never is an awfully long time for a woman who is deeply in love with her husband and carrying his child," Jamie said. "As I see it we have two problems here."

"Oh, yeah?" Dee Dee looked at her.

"We have a woman going through hormonal changes which are perfectly normal, and we have a houseful of wrestlers who have overstayed their welcome."

"I'm too tired to go anywhere right now," Dee Dee said.

Jamie climbed from the bed and searched her closet for a bathrobe as Frankie began pounding on the door. The best she could come up with was a raincoat. She slipped it on and hurried into the living room. She spotted Frankie's worried expression through the peephole of her door.

"Jamie, I'm sorry to wake you," he said once she opened the door, "but I need to talk to Dee Dee."

He looked distraught. Jamie smiled and touched his shoulder. "Everything is okay, Frankie, so stop looking so concerned. Dee Dee is just very tired and needs a break from your wrestling buddies."

"She left me. She's never left me, not in twenty years of marriage."

"She's never been pregnant, either."

"It's because I haven't been giving her enough attention," he said mournfully, "but all that is about to change. My buddies are going home tomorrow, and everything will be back to normal." He took in her attire. "Is it supposed to rain?"

"I couldn't find my bathrobe. Listen, why don't you let Dee Dee sleep here tonight, and you can come over tomorrow and talk to her."

"Do you think she'll come back home?"

"Perhaps you should send roses before your visit. You know how Dee Dee loves roses."

It was as if a lightbulb had gone off in his head. "Yeah, that's what I'll do. And I'll start reading those baby books with her. I've been so busy with my friends I haven't had time for my own wife. Thank you, Jamie, for helping us out."

"Good night, Frankie."

Jamie closed the door and went back into her room. She shucked off her raincoat, draped it on a chair, and lay down. Dee Dee had already drifted off to sleep once more, her Maltese snuggled beside her. Sprawled across the foot of the bed, Fleas raised his head. He glanced at Dee Dee's dog, and gave a disgruntled sigh. "It's okay, boy," Jamie said. "Go back to sleep."

The dog needed no further prodding.

JAMIE WAS PACING THE FLOOR, AND DEE DEE sleeping soundly when the first of the roses began arriving. Beenie stumbled into the room in a satin

Ralph Lauren dressing gown. He took one look at the roses and shrugged as though it were an everyday occurrence to find a living room half-filled with long-stemmed red roses.

"Coffee?" he whispered, sounding desperate.

"In the kitchen," Jamie said. "You'll find everything you need beside the automatic coffee maker."

Max arrived shortly after the second load of roses was delivered. He whistled under his breath. "Well, there goes the Rose Bowl parade this year. Have you heard from Frankie?"

Jamie told him about Frankie's visit the night before.

"Eeyeuuw!" Dee Dee cried from Jamie's bedroom. She appeared in the doorway a moment later in a lavish Christian Dior nightgown and robe. "Your dog is taking up half the bed." She paused at the sight of the flowers. "Are those for me?"

"Yep," Jamie said. "Compliments of Frankie. I don't know where or how he was able to find so many red roses, but it must've cost a king's ransom. Personally, I think you got his attention."

The doorbell rang. Max opened it, and Frankie stepped in looking handsome in a dark gray suit. His eyes immediately sought out his wife, and he hurried to her. "Dee Dee, I just dropped the guys off at the airport. Things will be back to normal now. Please come home."

"Things will never be completely normal again, Frankie," she said in her Betty Boop voice. "Don't you understand? We have a baby on the way." Her bottom lip quivered. "I'm not ready to come home. Please have the rest of my luggage delivered."

Jamie sighed inwardly. This was not going the way she'd hoped.

"Dee Dee, are you crazy?" Beenie said. "Frankie has put his friends on an airplane. He's willing to jump through hoops to get you back. This place is too small for three people, two dogs, *and* your luggage."

"I'll come back home when I'm darn good and ready," Dee Dee announced to Frankie, "and not a moment sooner."

A crestfallen Frankie left several minutes later, and Dee Dee disappeared into the bathroom for what she termed a well-deserved bubble bath.

Beenie shook his head sadly. "I'm going to have another cup of coffee," he said and made his way toward the kitchen, leaving a baffled Max and Jamie in the living room.

"Of all times for this to happen," Jamie said. "We've got a murderer to catch, and your sister and companion decide to move in. Are there any normal people in your family?"

"Yeah, a whole bunch of them. But they're up in Virginia. Remind me to introduce them to you someday."

. . .

LAMAR TEVIS SHOWED UP AT THE NEWSPAPER OF-fice shortly after Jamie and Max arrived. "Okay, here's what we've got so far. I have an eyewitness who claims he saw Maxine Chambers leave her shop with a man night before last. Unfortunately, it was dark so the witness couldn't give me a description of him. He recognized Maxine when she stepped beneath a streetlight, but the guy obviously kept to the shadows."

"Did the witness notice what kind of car the man was driving?" Max asked.

Lamar shook his head. "He didn't look since he saw nothing out of the ordinary. What we think happened is Maxine had a date with this man, and he took her back to the shop afterward, probably so she could pick up her car. Maxine went back inside her shop, I believe, to pick up her deposit bag since it was her habit to make her deposits at the bank first thing each morning. Also, we found the deposit bag next to the body."

"Any sign of forced entry?" Max asked.

"Nope. She probably just ran inside to pick up the bag, not bothering to lock the door. She entered through the back. The killer had to have entered only seconds after she went in. Either her date followed her in or somebody was there waiting for her and slipped in right behind her."

"Anything taken from the bag?" Jamie asked.

"No. Which means robbery was not the motive."

"What kind of weapon was used?" Max asked.

"We found a baseball bat in a nearby Dumpster with blood and hair on it. We checked it out in the crime lab, and it's definitely the murder weapon. Unfortunately, there were no fingerprints."

"I don't know if this is going to help," Jamie said, "but Destiny Moultrie started working in the lounge at the Holiday Inn last night. Both Larry Johnson and Sam Hunter had a couple of drinks, but they left right after happy hour."

"Yeah, one of my deputies followed Johnson home. He was alone, and he didn't go back out. Could be he suspected he was being watched and decided to lay low." Lamar sighed. "I shouldn't have wasted so much time looking into Luanne Ritter's business dealings. This latest murder sheds a whole new light on things. Two murders in a week. We don't know if and when this person is going to strike again."

Jamie felt a chill race up her spine.

CHAPTER FIFTEEN

Vera's pink Mustang arrived later that day, looking as though it had just come off the showroom floor. The woman was ecstatic.

"I don't believe it," Jamie said to Max. "She only asked you yesterday, and you've already found one. How did you manage to find one so quickly?"

Max smiled as he watched Vera circle the car in delight. It was obvious he was enjoying her excitement. "Muffin and I had already made a lot of contacts when I was picking out the red one for you. It was just a matter of getting it here overnight." Max had already sent the driver to the airport in a taxi; the man would be flown home courtesy of Holt Industries.

Vera couldn't stop grinning. "It's perfect," she told Max, "and it fits the new me to a T. Wait till my friends see me driving it." She paused and suddenly looked worried. "Can I afford it?"

Max suddenly looked ill at ease. "I was hoping you would accept it as a gift. For all you've done for Jamie."

It was the first time in Jamie's life that she could remember Vera being speechless. Finally, the woman hitched her chin high. "I can't do that. It would feel as though I were accepting charity, and I've always worked for what I wanted."

"It's a gift plain and simple," Max said. "If you don't want it, then I'll have to go to the expense of sending it back. Now, why don't you take a spin in it and see how it runs?"

Vera thought long and hard. "I don't know what to say," she said, looking genuinely touched.

"Just say thank you," Jamie told her.

"Thank you doesn't seem to come close," Vera replied, eyes suddenly tearing, "but thanks just the same." She hugged Max. "I can't wait to get behind the wheel."

Jamie was glad they had something to smile about after the past week. Luanne's and Maxine's murders had left a dark cloud hanging over everyone's head. But Vera, more than anyone, deserved to be happy.

Jamie raised her eyes and met Max's gaze. His look seemed to reach right out and touch her. She offered him a silent thank-you, and was rewarded with a tender look.

That's what love is, she thought.

• • •

THEY WERE STILL STANDING IN THE PARKING LOT of the newspaper office when Lamar Tevis pulled up. Vera showed him her new car, and although he tried to look excited about it, Jamie could tell his thoughts were elsewhere. She hoped it wasn't more bad news as she ushered him inside her office a few minutes later.

"You were right about Larry Johnson," he said. "I visited his ex-wife, and she told me he could be rather heavy-handed with his fist at times. The only reason she didn't file for a divorce on the grounds of physical cruelty was because Larry agreed to all the terms of the divorce, which means he walked away with the clothes on his back. Guess he didn't want folks to know he was a wife beater."

"I knew he was scum from the beginning," Jamie said.

"Yeah, he's real tough where the ladies are concerned," Lamar said, "but he didn't act so tough when we questioned him. He and Maxine Chambers had drinks together the night of her murder."

"So that's who the witness saw lurking in the shadows," Jamie said. "Maybe there was a reason Larry didn't want to be seen."

"Of course, Larry claims he never went inside her place of business," Lamar went on. "Said he met her at the door and drove her to the Holiday Inn. They had a couple of drinks and left. Said they didn't hit it off. Not a very good reason to kill someone if he's the one," Lamar added.

"Does he have an alibi for later that night?" Max asked.

Lamar shook his head. "Nope. But he offered to let us have a look at his apartment and car, so my deputies are combing them now."

VERA GLANCED AT HERSELF IN THE REARVIEW MIRror and tried to smooth the frown lines on her forehead. She was clearly irritated as she followed the highway that led to Moseley, the next town, and the restaurant where she was to meet her date.

She sighed aloud. "This is ridiculous driving almost twenty-five miles for dinner," she told her reflection. "Whoever heard of such?"

Still a bit peeved, Vera turned off the highway a half hour later and located the restaurant. She checked her lipstick and stepped from the car. The air hung thick with humidity, but she didn't seem to notice as she smiled at her new Mustang. She stepped inside the cool restaurant a moment later and made her way toward the lounge where her date had suggested they meet. It was not yet six o'clock. John Price had agreed to meet for an early dinner so Vera wouldn't have to drive home in the dark.

The lounge was empty except for a couple at one

end of the bar, and a man with broad shoulders and salt-and-pepper hair. He was neatly dressed in a navy blazer and white slacks. He stood and hurried over.

He smiled warmly. "You must be Vera. I'm glad you could make it."

She offered her hand. "I just want you to know I don't usually do this sort of thing, and I've most certainly never been in a bar, but your ad sounded so interesting I felt I should respond."

"I promise you won't regret it," he said.

"SO WHAT I'M THINKING, ONCE WE FIND THE killer—and we will find him, Jamie—we need to get away," Max told her once they left the newspaper office shortly after seven. It had been a long day, trying to deal with a murderer on the loose and meet deadlines, as well. They'd been late finishing up, but the production manager, who normally would have complained about it, had taken one look at Jamie's face and kept quiet.

Now, Jamie was exhausted.

"We could fly up to my place in Virginia," Max said. "You need the rest and a little pampering. It'll take your mind off things."

Jamie didn't respond to his suggestion; she had more pressing matters on her mind. "Do you think Dee Dee had a change of heart and went back to Frankie today?" she asked.

"Oh, man, I'd forgotten about her," Max said. "Who knows?" Five minutes later, they had their answer when they found a catering truck in the driveway. The grass had been cut, the flower beds weeded and filled with pansies.

"Wow, would you look at that?" Jamie said, glancing at her house to make sure they were at the right one. "Are you responsible for this?"

He shook his head. "No, but it's pretty impressive. Looks like my big sister has been busy. Probably trying to keep her mind off her troubles." He parked and they went inside.

"Surprise!" Dee Dee said.

Jamie glanced around. "Dee Dee, what have you done?" Jamie asked, going from room to room. Most of the furniture had been replaced, and new window treatments put up.

"I called my decorator as soon as you left for the office this morning, and I told her you needed all new stuff. You'll have to admit yours was old and worn. I described your house, and she immediately sent a truckload of furniture in from Charleston. She's been here all day, just finished putting up the new curtains before you arrived. She left not five minutes ago. Isn't it to die for?" Dee Dee said.

Jamie shook her head, trying to take it all in. How Dee Dee had managed to get it all accomplished in one day was beyond her. Of course, she'd probably had a dozen people working as hard as they could. "I don't know what to say."

Beenie spoke. "I told Dee Dee you wouldn't appreciate her barging in and changing everything." He had his hand on one hip. "I just want you to know I had nothing to do with it. Oh, I did insist that Dee Dee not get rid of a couple of pieces that looked like antiques."

"This must've cost you a fortune," Jamie told her friend. She and Max went into the kitchen where they found two men filling cabinets and her refrigerator with various food items.

Dee Dee waved off the remark as she followed them. "I'm rich so I can afford it. You were out of groceries. Don't you ever buy food?"

"Fleas and I eat out a lot."

"Well, from now on you can eat healthy food. My chef is coming over soon to cook. We're having salmon with cream sauce, new potatoes, and Caesar salad. I've decided to go off my diet for the baby's sake."

Jamie looked at Max. "May I have a word with you?"

"Sure."

"Don't let us stop you," Dee Dee said. "We've got plenty left to do." She went back to supervising the men.

Max and Jamie stepped outside. "Has your sister lost her mind?"

"Probably," he said, "but you'll have to admit it was a nice gesture, and everything looks great."

"But I liked my place the way it was. I mean, I don't want to sound ungrateful, but it's going to take some getting used to. I'll be afraid to sit on the sofa."

"Do you like what the decorator chose?" he asked.

"It's beautiful."

"Then let Dee Dee do this for you," he said. "I'm sure it means a lot to her. When you've been given a lot in life, it feels good to give something back."

"Is that why you gave Vera the Mustang?"

"I wanted her to have the Mustang and not worry about paying for it," he said. "But I was truthful when I told her the main reason. She's been like a mother to you. I can't help but appreciate that kindness."

"I guess I owe Dee Dee a genuine thank-you," Jamie said. "But that still doesn't solve the immediate problem. My place isn't large enough to accommodate three people and two dogs."

"So tell her."

"I can't tell her."

"Then I'll tell her."

"No, you can't tell her, either," Jamie said quickly. "It'll hurt her feelings. Plus, I'd feel like a real jerk after all she's done."

"Okay, Jamie, what do you want me to do?"

"I want you to think of a way to get her and Frankie back together right away. I can understand that Dee Dee is going through all these hormonal changes, but why hasn't Frankie been a little more insistent about her coming home?"

"His pride has probably been hurt, plus he could be embarrassed. I'll drive over and see if there's something I can do. Frankly, I'm getting tired of worrying about everyone else. It leaves us little time to worry about what's really important here, namely us. And I want more time alone with you."

"I'm beginning to think that'll never happen."

"We have to make it happen."

"Things should settle down once all this is behind us," she said.

"I'm going to drive over and talk to Frankie now," he told her, a resigned look on his face.

Max headed for his car and Jamie turned toward her house. Beenie met her at the door. "Oh, darn, I wanted to ask Max if he'd stop by the store for me."

"Do you need something?" Jamie asked.

"Yes. Dee Dee made me pack in such a hurry that I didn't get a chance to bring all my toiletry items, and I really need to exfoliate."

"Can't you borrow what you need from Dee Dee?"

"I'm allergic to the products she uses." He tapped his lips with his index finger. "Oops, I almost forgot. Lamar Tevis called only minutes before you arrived.

Wants you to call him right back. I hope he solves those two murders soon because I'm afraid to go out at night and Dee Dee is beside herself with worry."

Dee Dee came up behind him. "Beenie, why would you even bring up those poor women at a time like this? You know how upsetting it's been for me. I'll never get to sleep tonight thinking about it."

Jamie reached into her purse for her cell phone. She didn't want to make the call where she could be overheard, but the phone wasn't in her pocketbook, and she couldn't remember using it that day. Must've left it in her car, she thought.

"I have to run out to the garage," she told them. "I'll be right back."

Jamie hurried through the laundry room that led to her garage. Since Max had arrived, she'd spent most of her time riding with him and using his cell phone, which probably meant hers was dead. She opened the door to her car and found the phone lying on her console. She reached for it.

All at once, she felt the hairs on the back of her neck prickle. She jumped and turned and found herself staring into Larry Johnson's face. A rush of adrenaline hit her.

"Hello, Jamie," he said.

She blinked several times. "What are you doing here?"

"I want to know what you told the cops. They've been on my ass ever since our date."

Jamie could smell the alcohol on his breath. "I don't know what you're talking about," she said, knowing it was best to lie.

"They questioned me about those two women who were murdered, and then they proceeded to search my car and apartment. They took both crowbars." He stepped closer. "Don't you think that's a coincidence?"

"What I think is that you have no right hiding in my garage," she said, knowing he'd had to pick the lock on the door that led from the garage to the back yard. "You're trespassing."

"You're not only a tease, you're a bitch. Just like my ex-wife." He flexed both hands. "Somebody needs to teach you a lesson."

Jamie stiffened. "Are you threatening me? Because if you are, I'm going to scream this house down over our heads. My guests will come running. Now, get out of here and stay off my property or I'll have you arrested." Jamie punched the automatic garage door opener, and the door swung open. "Now," she ordered.

Larry's look turned menacing. "I'm not done with you yet, lady. You cause me any more trouble, and I promise you'll regret it." Jamie waited until he'd cleared the door before closing it. She suddenly realized she was trembling. She reached for the phone and called Lamar.

"I just wanted to let you know we didn't find anything on Larry Johnson," he said.

Jamie's voice quavered as she spoke. "He just paid me a visit." She told Lamar what had happened.

"Do you want me to pick him up?" Tevis asked.

"No, I think it would be better if your men just kept a close eye on him."

"Try not to go anywhere alone if you can help it," he said. "I think Johnson's dangerous, but I can't pin anything on him. I promise we'll keep trying."

"THAT WAS A WONDERFUL DINNER, JOHN," VERA said to the man sitting across the table from her. The hostess had seated them in the dining room where all the tables were draped in crisp white tablecloths and napkins were folded fanlike at each place setting. "Thank you for inviting me."

"You only took a few bites of your prime rib."

"I guess I'm a little nervous," Vera confessed, her gaze falling on the small glass-enclosed candle between them.

John reached across the table and touched her hand. "I feel very fortunate to have met you."

Vera shifted in her seat. "John, may I ask you a question?"

"Of course."

"In your ad, you said you wanted to meet a woman for a discreet relationship. Why are you so concerned about discretion?"

He didn't answer right away. "I'm a very private person, Vera, and the last thing I want people to know is that I ran an advertisement in the newspaper to meet a woman. I know it's silly, but that's how I feel."

"Yes, well, my minister would certainly frown on that sort of thing."

"I've dated a couple of women in town, and I could tell up front that nothing would come of it, but I must say, you and I seem to have a lot in common." He grinned. "Anybody who drives a pink Mustang is definitely my kind of woman."

Vera smiled. "It's a new acquisition."

"Plus, if I might say so, you're very attractive."

Vera patted her hair. "Why, thank you, John."

The waiter brought their check. John Price pulled out a credit card and handed it to him, and the man hurried away. "I hope we can get together again soon," John said.

"I'd like that, too."

"Is tomorrow night too soon?"

Vera laughed. "Well, gee, I guess tomorrow is okay." She paused in thought. "You know, I wouldn't normally do this, and I don't wish to sound forward, but how would you like to come to my house for pot roast tomorrow evening? Everybody always brags about my pot roast."

"Wow, a home-cooked meal. It sounds great to me since I eat out so much. I'm afraid I'm not much of a cook."

Vera pulled a small notebook from her purse on which she wrote out her address. "I'll expect you around seven."

John walked Vera to her car and waited until she climbed in. "I'll see you tomorrow night," he said.

She started her engine and pulled away. She was humming a tune under her breath as she turned onto the highway leading home. She did not notice that she was being followed.

"I CAN'T BELIEVE DEE DEE JUST UP AND LEFT ME," Frankie told Max. "We've never had a serious argument in our life."

"Your wife is pregnant," Max said. "She's going to be moody once in a while. She needs you right now more than she's ever needed you before."

"What can I do when she refuses to come home?" Frankie asked.

"Jewelry might help."

Frankie seemed to ponder it. "I'll take care of it first thing in the morning. I need to run by the bank as soon as it opens. I've got something in my safe-deposit box that just might do the trick."

. . .

MAX, JAMIE, DEE DEE, AND BEENIE SHARED A gourmet dinner in Jamie's small kitchen that evening. Once the chef and his assistant finished up, Max suggested he and Jamie take a walk. It wasn't until they had cleared Jamie's yard that Max spoke. "You've been awfully quiet this evening," he said. "I can tell something is wrong."

Jamie told Max about Larry Johnson's visit. She sensed his anger before he even responded.

"I'd like to get my hands on Johnson and show him what it's like to fight a man," he said, "but I have a feeling I wouldn't stop until it was too late."

"Too late for what?" Jamie asked.

"Never mind." He stopped walking. "Look, Jamie, I want you to come back to the hotel with me tonight."

"And leave Beenie and Dee Dee?"

"Larry Johnson isn't interested in hurting them. I'll ask Tevis to keep an eye on the place. Besides, Frankie is coming over in the morning, and I think he'll be able to convince Dee Dee to come home this time."

Jamie smiled. "Meaning diamonds will exchange hands."

"Something like that," Max said, but he didn't look amused. "Either way, I'm not leaving you alone tonight. You'll have to stay with me or I'm camping out on your sofa."

"I'll go to your place," she told him, "as long as you don't mind having Fleas along. I don't think he likes sharing our place with Choo-Choo."

"BUT I'D FEEL GUILTY RUNNING YOU OUT OF YOUR own house," Dee Dee said when Jamie broached the subject of staying with Max at his hotel. "It's bad enough that we just showed up on your doorstep without warning."

"Not to mention completely redecorating her house without her permission," Beenie said.

"Which was very sweet of you," Jamie told her. Even though it would take her time to adjust to her new surroundings, Jamie knew her friend had had good intentions. "You're my best friend," Jamie told her. "Of course I would expect you to come here."

Dee Dee suddenly looked sad. "Frankie hasn't even called me."

Jamie could see that her friend was truly in pain, but she was sure Dee Dee's pride would not let her call him. "I think Frankie's feelings are just hurt," she said. "I wouldn't be surprised if he showed up on my doorstep tomorrow. In the meantime you need to rest."

Dee Dee nodded. "I think it's great that you and Max will have a chance to spend some private time together. Will you be taking Fleas?" she asked hopefully.

"Yes. I'll make sure you and Choo-Choo have the bedroom all to yourselves tonight."

Jamie packed a small bag and climbed into Max's car a few minutes later. Fleas sat in the back seat. "They're not going to allow us to have a dog in the room," Jamie said when she saw that Max had booked a room in one of the nicer hotels.

"See, that's where being rich comes in handy," Max said. They went inside the hotel with Fleas on his leash, and although they were awarded several stares from the staff, nobody said anything.

"How much did you have to pay to get permission to bring my dog in?" Jamie asked Max.

Max looked at her. "Don't worry about it."

"Not everything comes with a price tag," she said as they waited at the elevator.

"You're right," he said. "You can't pay for what's really important. I did what I had to do because I wanted you with me tonight. I was afraid for you."

Max's cell phone rang as soon as they stepped inside his room. From the conversation, Jamie could tell it was Destiny calling. Max hung up a few minutes later. "Destiny said Larry hasn't been in tonight. I'm calling Lamar to make sure they've got someone on his tail." Max placed the call. Once he was finished, he hung up and faced Jamie. "Brent Walker left town today. Agnes Aimsley told Lamar he had to return to school."

"I don't know whether to be worried or relieved," Jamie said.

"Lamar has already informed the police in Atlanta. Walker will be questioned." He paused. "You look exhausted." He pulled her into his arms and kissed her softly on the lips. Finally, he raised his head and smiled. "I'm crazy about you, Swifty," he said. "What do you think of that?"

CHAPTER SIXTEEN

JAMIE STARED BACK AT HIM. SHE DIDN'T KNOW what to make of it. *Crazy* was a not the word she hoped for. "It's the sex," she said, trying to sound flippant so he would not read the disappointment in her eyes.

"The sex is fantastic, but that's not why I like you so much. I like your spunk, and the fact you've never been a quitter. I like that you stand up for what you believe in, like when you rallied to keep Maxine's store open."

"I suppose you know the feeling is mutual," she said, determined to keep it light.

"Like I said, you're going to be seeing a whole lot more of me in the future. No more three-week intervals." He kissed her again. "So what do you think? Think you'd like to see more of me?"

She nodded. It was a start.

. . .

FRANKIE ARRIVED AT JAMIE'S HOUSE BEFORE EIGHT A.M. the following morning. "Dee Dee, I can't live without you," he said to his wife, who was still in her nightgown. They both looked tired from lack of sleep. "I promise to get more involved with the preparations for the baby, but I need for you to come home. It's where you belong."

Dee Dee gazed lovingly into his eyes. "I feel the same way. I've been miserable without you."

He reached into his pocket and pulled out a small velvet box. "I brought you a gift."

"Oh, Frankie, you didn't have to do that. I would have come home anyway." Dee Dee opened the box. "Oh, my, it's the ring I saw in Tiffany's."

"I've had it for some time," he said. "I was saving it for a Christmas gift, but this seems the perfect time. After all, we're celebrating a baby on the way."

Dee Dee looked genuinely touched. "I have a lot of luggage with me."

"I brought some of the staff," Frankie said. "They're waiting outside."

"You're mighty sure of yourself," she teased.

"Oh, I was planning to convince you to come home no matter what," he told her. "Even if I had to pick you up and carry you out."

"Oh, Frankie, that's so romantic."

He pulled her into his arms for a kiss.

Beenie came into the room, still wearing his silk pajamas. "Oh, thank God you've made up. I'm ready to go home. I can't sleep on cotton sheets. They irritate my skin."

MAX AND JAMIE HAD AWAKENED EARLY AND MADE love, only to spend the next hour cuddling and talking. As Jamie showered, Max ordered room service, and they took their time enjoying breakfast together. It was almost nine by the time they climbed into Max's car and started for the office. Muffin came on right away.

"I've done some more digging on John Price, and I think I may have hit on something."

"I'm listening," Max said.

"Price was questioned by the Atlanta PD six months ago about a murder that took place in his neighborhood. The woman lived two doors down from him. The reason it didn't show up when I checked to see if he had a police record is because he was one of about ten who lived in the area that were questioned. I would never have found it had I not thought to look for murders in Atlanta over the last couple of years. And get this. Same MO. Somebody bashed in her head."

Max looked at Jamie. "Very interesting."

"Not only that, I found the service provider he uses for his cell phone. The reason it took so long is because the company is brand-new. It's called In Touch Communications. They weren't in the telephone book; the Better Business Bureau doesn't even have them listed yet."

"Oh, crap," Jamie said. "I completely forgot about them. They ran an ad with me a couple of weeks ago offering free phones for those who signed up. Muffin's right, they just opened for business. As a matter of fact, they've got salesmen going door to door."

"They obviously convinced Price to try their service because that's who he's using," Muffin said. "But I've been saving the best for last. Price was in touch with Luanne Ritter only three days after his personal ad hit the newspaper. She must've written to him immediately, probably the same day his ad came out."

"Bingo," Max said. "What about Maxine Chambers?"

"No record of a call placed to her number, but he could have called from another phone. I haven't found her name listed with any service provider in the area. As hard as it is to believe in this day and age, she must not have had a cell phone."

"Anything else?"

"I followed up on the dentist, the chef, and the mechanic. The dentist and chef checked out fine, but the mechanic, Carl Edwards, had had a run-in with the police. Seems he and another guy got into a fist-fight outside a bar a couple of years ago. Nothing serious; just a couple of good old boys who had too much to drink and one of them accused the other of cheating in a pool game."

"How come it didn't show up on his record?" Max asked.

"I suspect the cops just talked to them and sent them on their way because neither of them was officially charged. I found the information by checking on calls made to the dispatcher in the last three years. They list complaints in the computer, even if there are no arrests made."

"Good work, Muffin," Max said. "From here on out I want you to make Price your top priority. Find out why he left Atlanta so soon after the murder in his neighborhood."

"Will do."

"By the way, did you happen to get anything else on Sam Hunter?"

"Nothing looks suspicious. No police record, not even a parking ticket. He kept the same job for ten years. His cell phone records indicate that he was somewhat of a ladies' man, but all his ex-girlfriends are alive and well and working in New York City. Max?"

"Yeah?"

"After we figure out who committed these murders, I'm taking some time off. I don't feel so good."

"Muffin, you are *not* pregnant," Max said. "You're just having the symptoms because Dee Dee fed you the information."

"Then why are my hormones acting up?"

Max sighed. "You don't have hormones, you're a computer."

"Yeah, and you programmed me to have emotions. I do too have hormones. Just ask my friend at MIT. He's accused me more than once of having PMS. Just this morning, as a matter of fact."

"I thought the two of you broke up."

"You know how it is, on again, off again. I can't get him to make a commitment. I think I intimidate him, but what can I say? Besides, he's just a laptop, and he's not being fed information from experts around the clock like I am. He needs an upgrade; somebody needs to install more memory in him."

"Let's just try to concentrate on the case, okay?"

Muffin sounded testy when she spoke. "I've never once let my personal feelings get in the way of my work, but I do need a life." With that she was gone.

Max looked thoughtful. "I'll inform Lamar about Price, but I think it would be a good idea to drive by his house tonight and see if there's any activity."

"Only if you promise not to break in again,"
Jamie said. "I don't think my nerves can take it."

"Deal," Max said.

"Well, Destiny will be relieved that Sam looks
clean," Jamie said, changing the subject. "I think she
has a crush on him."

"Don't get her hopes up," Max said. "Until we
find the murderer, everybody is a suspect."

MAX AND JAMIE WORKED THROUGHOUT THE DAY,
breaking only for lunch, which consisted of sandwiches at Maynard's.

"Is it me or does Vera seem to be in a really good
mood today?" Jamie asked as they left the sandwich
shop and walked back to the office.

Max grinned. "Maybe she's getting laid."

"Max!"

"Well, you asked."

THEY LEFT THE OFFICE AT SIX P.M., ONLY TO FIND
that the night had not cooled.

"This has been the hottest summer I can remember," Jamie said. "No wonder people are acting
kooky in this town, Vera included. There's definitely
a change in her." Jamie was almost certain the
woman was wearing padded bras.

They arrived at Jamie's house and found a note

from Dee Dee saying she had made up with Frankie and gone home. "Well, that's one less thing to worry about," Jamie said.

"Frankie must've taken my suggestion and bought something nice for her," Max said with a grin.

"I don't think Dee Dee is as materialistic as you think, Max," Jamie said. "She genuinely loves Frankie. Twenty years is a long time to stay married these days."

"Not if two people work at it," Max said. "Do you think you'd want to be with somebody that long or longer?"

Jamie couldn't have been more surprised with his response. Had Max Holt just made a favorable comment about marriage and commitment? She felt like pinching herself to make sure she wasn't dreaming, and then realized he was waiting for her answer. "I wouldn't get married unless I was prepared to do just that," she said.

There was plenty of food in Jamie's cabinets and refrigerator, thanks to Dee Dee. Once they'd eaten, Jamie took a shower and changed into shorts while Max made calls to Holt Industries. They waited until dark before getting into Max's car. "We're going by John Price's house," he told Muffin.

"Speaking of Price, I discovered a few more things you might find interesting," Muffin said. "His divorce a year ago was less than amicable."

"Most divorces aren't real friendly," Max said, although his had been, thanks to his generosity.

"Yeah, but listen to this. Price swore out a warrant shortly after the separation, claimed his ex was stalking him. The police checked into it but no charges were filed for lack of proof."

Max looked thoughtful. "How soon can you get me a complete file on her?"

"I'm about to send it through the printer now. She has an apartment in Atlanta, but her employment history is spotty. She obviously quit work after she married Price because I can't find anything after that."

Max was thoughtful. "If Price thought she was stalking him, that might explain the guard dogs and the expensive security system."

"I wonder if he's afraid she'll find him," Jamie said. After a moment, she changed the subject. "We should probably check in with Destiny." Max made the call. He was frowning when he hung up. "Larry Johnson is there with a woman."

Jamie felt a chill race up her spine. "I hope she's armed."

"Sam Hunter is sitting at the bar. Destiny says they've really hit it off."

"I wonder what Ronnie is making of Destiny's crush on Sam," Jamie said, if for no other reason than to lighten the mood. She could see that Max had a lot on his mind. "Maybe Ronnie will finally take the hint and be on his way. Toward the light," she added with a smile.

They drove by John Price's house twenty minutes later and found it dark. Max frowned.

"What's wrong?" Jamie asked.

"Something doesn't seem right here. I get the feeling we should be someplace else."

JOHN PRICE ARRIVED AT VERA'S HOUSE AT PRE-cisely seven o'clock carrying a bouquet of flowers.

"Oh, John, how thoughtful," she said, as she put them into a vase with water. Vera had put the pot roast in a Crock-Pot that morning before leaving for work, then cut up new potatoes, carrots, and onions and placed them in the pot on high so they'd be ready in time. Although her house was kept neat, she'd dusted and vacuumed before freshening her makeup. It was obvious she'd wanted to make a good impression.

"May I offer you a glass of sweet tea?" she asked John.

"I would love something cold after coming in from that heat," he told her, wiping his brow. "I took a shower before I left the house, but I was perspiring before I got to my car."

"This has been the hottest summer we've had in years," Vera said, "and the humidity doesn't help. I dread seeing my power bill because I've used my air conditioner so much this season. Now, why don't you take a seat on the sofa, and I'll get us both something cold to drink. Dinner should be ready soon."

"I'm in no hurry," John said. "I'd much rather get to know you better."

"I'm afraid my life would sound boring to you," Vera said, returning with two tall glasses of iced tea with lemon. She took the chair opposite him. "I've lived in Beaumont all my life. Never traveled more than a couple of hundred miles away, and that was with my church friends. I'm sort of a homebody."

"I used to do a lot of traveling with my job," John said. "My ex-wife didn't like my being gone so I tried to cut back as much as I could."

"She obviously missed you while you were gone."

John shifted uncomfortably in his chair. "She was somewhat, um, possessive. She liked being able to put her finger on me at all times." He took a sip of tea. "I'm sorry; it's rude of me to discuss her with you."

"Oh, no, I don't mind. How long were you married?"

"A year."

Vera looked surprised. "That's all?"

"The marriage was doomed from the beginning,

but I fancied myself in love. She was quite a bit younger than me. Plus, it was a second marriage. I hadn't been divorced all that long before I met her. I was married to my first wife for twenty-seven years. I regret that we drifted apart." He sighed. "Anyway, I married Celia less than three months after I met her. I guess I was just lonely after the divorce and wasn't thinking straight."

"Do you have children?"

"Oh, yes, a beautiful daughter by my first wife. She studied business at college and graduated with honors, and then decided she wanted to go into nursing. She graduates in the fall." He glanced around. "Your place is very cozy. You have a real eye for decorating."

"Thank you. I study the latest magazines for ideas. Luckily, I sew," she added proudly. "I was able to make the slipcovers for the sofa and I made all the draperies, as well. But you're probably not interested in hearing all that."

He smiled. "On the contrary," he said. "You sew, you cook, you decorate, and you're a devoted employee. I'm beginning to think there's nothing you can't do."

Vera blushed. "Oh, I have my faults," she said. "I'm a very impatient woman. I want things done right away because I don't believe in wasting time.

People at the office will tell you I can be quite demanding at times."

Price nodded. "You're obviously a hard worker." He paused. "Vera, I'd like to continue to keep our friendship discreet for a while longer."

She gave him a funny look. "Well, of course, if that's the way you want it."

"Maybe we could continue to meet privately for a while," he said.

"I suppose so." But Vera was frowning as she got up to check the vegetables. "Dinner is ready," she called out. "I hope you're hungry."

BUSINESS WAS SLOW IN THE LOUNGE AT THE HOLIday Inn, which didn't seem to bother Destiny at all since Sam Hunter was the only one at the bar.

Sam watched Destiny closely, as though trying to size her up. His eyes followed the way her short skirt lifted each time she reached high for the bottle of Johnny Walker Red which two men at a nearby table were drinking, to the way her oversized breasts bounced as she washed glasses. Finally, Destiny sashayed toward Sam, took one of his hands in hers, and turned it over so that she was looking at his palm. "I didn't tell you I was a palmist, did I?" she asked.

He smiled, showing off his good looks. His thick

brown hair had not begun to gray at the temples like that of a lot of men his age. "You failed to mention it," he said.

"I'll be happy to give you a reading," she said. "No charge, of course."

He chuckled. "Of course."

"This is your lifeline," she said, tracing one of the lines that ran across his open palm. "It shows that you're going to live a long life."

"That's good to know."

"And this line—" She paused and gave him a coy smile. "It says you're going to meet a beautiful woman. You will quickly become smitten with her."

Sam smiled and captured her hands in his. "I think I already have. What time do you get off?"

Destiny didn't respond. If Sam noticed her staring across the room at the couple leaving, he didn't say anything. "Would you excuse me," she said. "I need to make a quick phone call."

Max's cell phone rang, and he picked it up. Destiny spoke from the other end. "Damn," he said. "How long ago?" He listened. "Okay, thanks."

"What is it?" Jamie asked.

"Larry Johnson just left the Holiday Inn with a woman. I hope Lamar is doing his job." He looked thoughtful. "Maybe we should drive over."

"And do what?" Jamie asked. "We can't exactly knock on his door."

Max looked thoughtful. "If he took her to his place, I think she's relatively safe. Johnson isn't dumb enough to try anything at his apartment. My concern is he'll take her home. That might put her in danger. We might be wasting our time, of course," he added. "I think Johnson suspects he's being watched. If that's the case, he's not going to take any chances."

"Unless he gets drunk enough and lets down his guard," Jamie said. "Then anything is possible."

"VERA, THAT WAS THE BEST POT ROAST I'VE EVER had," John said. "I can't believe you never married, what with your looks and cooking skills."

Vera waved off the remark. "Flattery will get you everywhere. Wait until you see what I've made for dessert."

"Dessert? I'm already busting out of my pants from that meal."

Vera got up and cleared their dishes away before cutting them each a slice of Key lime pie and filling two cups with coffee. She carried them to the table on a silver tray.

"You shouldn't have gone to so much trouble," John said.

"It wasn't any trouble. I love to cook."

John waited until she sat down before he spoke. "Tell me something," he said. "How come you never married?"

Vera shrugged. "I was in love once, but he wasn't able to make a commitment."

"I find that hard to believe."

Vera looked sad for a moment. "I wasted a lot of years hoping he'd change." Finally, she shrugged. "But I had a job with the newspaper that I loved, and I was always busy with church activities so it wasn't like I sat around moping about it."

John shifted in his chair. He suddenly looked nervous. "You didn't mention our date to anyone at the *Gazette*, did you?"

"Of course not."

He looked relieved as he took a sip of his coffee. He watched her closely from over the rim of his cup. He didn't make a move for his pie.

"Aren't you going to eat your dessert?" Vera asked.

"Could you make it to go?"

"Oh, are you leaving so soon?"

"I'm afraid my day has caught up with me," he said. "I was at the office before six, and what I need right now is a good night's sleep. I hope you don't mind."

"Well, of course not. Actually, I was thinking of turning in early myself."

John left a few minutes later after promising to call the next day. Vera locked up after him, and began cleaning the kitchen. The phone rang, and she answered.

There was no response.

"Is anyone there?" she said after a moment.

Finally, a click.

"Well, now, that was odd," she said to herself as she hung up.

She was in the process of preparing for bed when the telephone rang for the third time. She picked it up. Once again, no answer. "Listen, I can hear you breathing, what do you want?"

Nothing.

"I'm sick and tired of you calling this house. Don't call me again, do you hear?" She slammed the phone down. "Probably a bunch of kids playing pranks," she said.

"I HAVE MORE NEWS FOR YOU," MUFFIN SAID AS Max and Jamie headed for Larry Johnson's apartment. "It concerns John Price. Do either of you know a Barbara Fender?"

"That's my new neighbor's name," Jamie said. "Why do you ask, Muffin?"

"Bad news," Muffin said. "Barbara Fender aka Celia Brown Price is John Price's ex-wife."

Max and Jamie exchanged looks. "Are you sure?" he asked.

"Am I ever wrong?" Muffin asked.

Jamie stared at Max in disbelief. "She followed John from Atlanta."

"I don't like what I'm thinking," Max said.

"Tell me anyway."

"John Price filed charges that his ex was stalking him, but there was no proof so they were dropped. And later, he was questioned about a woman murdered two houses down from him. I'm willing to bet he was involved with her." He sighed. "It never occurred to me that the killer could be a woman. What I don't understand is why she's doing it. Unless she's insanely jealous," he added.

Jamie felt the familiar sense of dread. "Or maybe she's trying to set him up for a murder rap. She must really hate him. This is scary, Max."

"We need to talk to Price right away."

"Problem is, he isn't home, and he could unknowingly be putting someone else at risk," Jamie said. She had begun to fidget with her hands. "Assuming he isn't the killer."

"First we need to find out if Barbara Fender is home." Max whipped his car around and headed back to Jamie's house, making the drive in record time. Barbara Fender's car was not in the carport.

"This isn't good," Jamie said.

"If she was really stalking Price, odds are she's somewhere watching him. Do you have his phone number handy?"

"Yes, it's in his file."

"Why don't you call and see if he's home yet?"

BARBARA FENDER DROVE SLOWLY PAST VERA Bankhead's simple ranch-style house. Darkness had descended; lights burned bright in the windows. Barbara parked her car down the street, cut her headlights, and turned off the engine.

And waited.

VERA GRABBED A QUICK SHOWER, CHANGED INTO her nightgown, and climbed into bed. "Oh, that feels good," she said, yawning wide as she slipped between the sheets. She didn't read her daily Scripture as was her custom; instead, she turned off her lamp and closed her eyes. She was asleep in minutes.

JAMIE DIALED JOHN PRICE'S NUMBER. HE PICKED up on the third ring. "Mr. Price, this is Jamie Swift from the *Gazette*," she said quickly. "I'm terribly sorry to bother you, but it's important."

"How may I help you, Miss Swift?" he asked.

"My partner and I need to speak with you. Is it okay if we come over?"

"Actually, I was just getting ready for bed. Can this wait until tomorrow?"

"It's rather urgent or I wouldn't be calling. We only need a minute of your time."

Silence. "In that case, please come over."

VERA OPENED HER EYES AND STARED INTO THE darkness as the clanging of something metal sounded from the back of her house. "It's that stray dog in my garbage can again," she muttered. "I'll have a mess to clean up in the morning." She dozed off again.

CHAPTER SEVENTEEN

JAMIE AND MAX ARRIVED AT JOHN PRICE'S HOUSE in half the time it would normally have taken. As they climbed from Max's car, they heard the dogs barking. John called out from the doorway.

"Don't worry about the dogs," he said. "I've got them penned."

Max and Jamie hurried up the front walk. John stepped back to permit them inside. "Mr. Price, I'd like you to meet my partner, Max Holt," Jamie said.

Price arched one brow. "Not the Max Holt I've read about in all the financial magazines."

"That's me," Max said.

Price looked impressed as he motioned them toward the living room. "Please come in and sit down. And call me John." Max and Jamie sat beside each other on his sofa. Price took the chair on the other side of the coffee table. "You said this was urgent. How can I help you?"

"We're here to discuss the ad you ran in the newspaper," Jamie said, "among other things."

Price glanced at Max, then back at Jamie. He looked embarrassed. "I was hoping that would be kept confidential."

"It would have been," Jamie said, "but a couple of women have been murdered, and we think it may be related to the personals section. I'm surprised the police haven't already questioned you. I was served with a court order to release the files."

Price looked annoyed at the news. "I read about the murders," he said after a moment.

"We know you were in contact with Luanne Ritter," Max said. "What about Maxine Chambers?"

Price hesitated. "I received replies from both ladies right after my ad came out. I took each of them to dinner, but that was the extent of it." He glanced from Max to Jamie. "I had nothing to do with their murders."

"You were questioned about the murder of a woman in Atlanta," Jamie said. "I believe she was a neighbor."

He looked surprised. "You've been checking on me. I wasn't the only one questioned in that incident."

"Were you involved with her?"

"We had coffee once or twice. We were both going through a divorce at the time; we sort of used each other as a sounding board. It was nothing more than friendship."

"The murder was never solved," Max said.

"I regret that. She was a nice woman."

"John, didn't you think it odd that both women you dated were murdered?" Jamie asked.

Once again, he hesitated. "Of course I did, but since I had nothing to do with it I felt no need to go to the police. I'm new in town, and I've recently started my own business. The last thing I need is to get entangled in a murder investigation."

"Why did you leave Atlanta?" Max asked.

"I had my reasons."

"Did they concern your ex-wife?" Jamie asked.

Once again, he looked annoyed. "Why all these questions?"

"It could be a matter of life or death," Max said.

Price's eyes widened. "My ex-wife was hounding me. She didn't want the divorce, and she did everything possible to make my life a living hell once I left her. My apartment was ransacked twice, and the tires slashed on my car. She even started calling my boss. I swore out a peace bond against her, but it didn't help. I couldn't prove she was behind any of it. So I decided to move away and start over."

"Does anyone know you're here?"

"Only my daughter and first wife. I still send money for our daughter's education."

"Where do you mail the checks?" Max asked.

"To my first wife's mailbox, of course. She lives in Marietta, Georgia, just north of the Atlanta area."

"Did your second wife know her address?"

"It was listed in our address book. She would have seen the address where I mailed the checks."

"That might be one way Barbara found him," Jamie told Max. "She could have gone through his first wife's mailbox."

"Who's Barbara?" Price asked, obviously confused.

"That's the name your ex-wife is using," Max said. "She's going by the name Barbara Fender."

Price instantly paled. "Oh, God."

"What is it?" Max asked.

"That's the name of the neighbor in Atlanta who was murdered."

Price stood and shoved his hands in his pockets. "Her real name is Celia." He paused and regarded them. "Look, I knew Celia had problems, but I don't think she's capable of murder."

"We don't have proof of anything," Max said, "but there are a lot of coincidences."

"She's moved in next door to me," Jamie said.

John was quiet, as though trying to take it all in. "I don't know what to think. Celia was jealous of everyone I had anything to do with, my daughter, and my friends. She followed me when I left the house. I was always looking over my shoulder because I didn't know what to expect. I asked her to get help, but she refused. When I filed for divorce, she threatened to get even."

"Does she hate you enough to try and pin a murder rap on you?" Max asked.

John met his gaze. "She could be cruel. I didn't know about her problems before we married, but it didn't take long before she began showing her true colors, so to speak. I regretted the marriage almost from the beginning, but I thought I could help her."

"You went out earlier this evening," Max said, changing the subject.

"I had a dinner engagement."

"With a woman?"

"Yes. She answered my ad."

"Do you mind telling us who the woman was?"

"I would like to keep that confidential. For her sake," he added.

"John, she may be in danger," Jamie said.

He suddenly covered his face with his hands, and his voice trembled when he finally spoke. "I thought it was finally over. I thought I could start living a normal life again. If Celia was responsible for the death of those women, then it's because I asked them out."

"John, we have to know who you were with to-night," Max insisted.

He looked at Jamie. "She works for you," he said. "Vera Bankhead."

Jamie felt the blood rush to her ears.

THE SOUND OF BREAKING GLASS WOKE VERA A SEC-ond time. She bolted upright and reached for her telephone to dial 911. The line was dead. Quietly, she climbed from her bed.

"My purse," she whispered to herself. "Where did I leave it?" She started down the hall, feeling her way. The house was bathed in shadows.

There was a click at the kitchen door, the sound of the lock being turned. A hand fumbled, found the chain, slid it free.

Vera reached the living room, her hands search-ing the sofa blindly for her purse.

The kitchen door creaked.

Vera found her purse and reached inside for her gun. She raised it, aimed it toward the dark kitchen. "I don't know who you are or what you want, but I'm holding a thirty-eight Smith and Wesson, and I know how to use it."

Suddenly, a bright light hit her face. Vera was blinded. She raised her free hand to cover her eyes, as a baseball bat came down hard on her arm. Vera cried out and dropped the gun. It hit the carpet with a dull thud. "Why are you doing this?" she cried, trying to see the face behind the light.

"It's a pity you won't live to find out," the woman said with gritted teeth. The bat came down a second time. Vera cried out again and sank to the floor.

JAMIE WAS THE FIRST TO SPOT BARBARA'S CAR parked a couple of houses down from Vera's. "There it is!" she cried. "Hurry, Max!"

Max whipped his car into the driveway. "Muffin, hit the siren, and call 911."

Barbara Fender raised the bat high, a determined look on her face as she aimed for Vera's head. She jerked around as a siren split the night, and then turned once more for Vera. She shone her flashlight on the floor as Vera reached beneath the sofa for her gun.

JAMIE FELT THE ADRENALINE GUSH THROUGH HER body as she raced toward Vera's back door with Max on her heels. "Vera!" she called out loudly.

Inside, Barbara ignored both the siren and the voice and raised the bat once more. Vera rolled away, and the bat slammed against the sofa. She raised her gun and fired twice.

The woman staggered once and fell.

Jamie reached the dark kitchen and searched frantically for a light switch. She turned it on and gasped at the sight of Vera pulling herself up and Barbara Fender, with big blond hair, sprawled on the floor. A wig, Jamie thought.

"I think I hit her in the stomach," Vera said, dropping her gun as the woman writhed in pain.

Jamie saw that Barbara had been hit; her dress was already blood soaked. "Help is on the way," she said, although she found little reason to pity her. She reached down and checked her arms. Sure enough, she found several deep scratches.

JAMIE PACED THE WAITING AREA IN THE EMERGENCY room as she waited to see Vera. Celia Price had been rushed there by ambulance and was undergoing emergency surgery; Vera had ridden in another ambulance. Lamar Tevis had arrived on the scene only minutes after the injured women had been whisked away. He sat in the waiting room with Max, Jamie, and John Price, as he waited for a chance to question Vera, who had suffered a broken arm.

"I honestly had no idea Celia would resort to murder," Price told Lamar, "but it all adds up. I feel terrible about this." He'd already told Lamar about the murder in Atlanta, and his suspicions that his ex might have been responsible.

Jamie noted the man's face was a chalky white. He was obviously in shock. "It's not your fault," she said. "You can't control the actions of others." She said it as much for herself as for him.

Lamar nodded. "I'll notify the authorities in Atlanta to reopen the case." He frowned. "Why do you suppose she did it?"

Price shook his head. "Revenge, maybe. I think part of me suspected she would find me one day." He looked at Max. "That's the reason for the dogs. Still, nothing could have prepared me for this."

A nurse stepped out. "Is there a Mr. Price here?"

"I'm John Price," he said, standing.

"Miss Bankhead is asking for you."

John followed the nurse through the metal doors leading into the ER. He stepped inside a small room where Vera wore a cast on one arm.

"Max told me everything as we were waiting for the ambulance," she said.

"Vera, I'm so sorry," he said. "I don't know how I will live with this."

"You're not responsible, John. You had no way of knowing."

"I should have put two and two together. I should have known Celia would stop at nothing to get back at me for leaving her. Those poor women." He raked his hands through his hair. The look on his face was bleak. "She could have killed you."

"But she didn't, and it's behind us now. Your ex-wife, if she survives the surgery, will never have the chance to kill again."

John stepped closer to Vera's bed and took one of her hands in his. "I'm almost afraid to ask, but where does this leave us?"

Vera hesitated. "I don't know, John. I need time."

He nodded. "I guess we both do. At least until we get through this."

"We can still be friends."

A look of vulnerability crossed his face. "Thank you. I'm going to need a friend."

DESTINY AND SAM RUSHED THROUGH THE DOORS to the ER. "What's wrong?" Destiny demanded.

"What on earth are you doing here?" Jamie asked.

"I had this feeling that something was terribly wrong. I called the police. All they would tell me was that there had been a shooting. So I asked Sam to give me a ride over. Who's hurt?"

Jamie filled her in.

Sam regarded Destiny with a look of awe. "You were right. You *are* psychic."

"I tried to tell you," she said.

"Hello, Sam," Jamie said. "It's been a long time." They shook hands, and she introduced him to Max.

"What do you think of Destiny's friend, Ronnie?" Max asked Sam, as though to lighten the mood.

Sam offered him a blank look. "Who's Ronnie?"

Destiny shot Max a look, reached for Sam's hand and patted it. "We'll talk about it later, honey." She turned to Jamie. "This is probably a bad time to bring it up, but I answered most of the mail."

"More has come in since the last batch," Jamie said. "The responses have been overwhelming."

"I knew that. I'll pick them up and give you the other letters tomorrow. After it stops raining," she added. "I like to sleep late when it rains."

"That makes two of us," Sam said. They shared a private look.

"Rain?" Jamie said. "The weatherman isn't forecasting rain. In fact, the temperatures are going to be even worse than they have been."

"The weatherman is wrong," Destiny said with a shrug. "It's going to rain and finally cool things off. And not a moment too soon, if you ask me."

Destiny and Sam stayed and chatted a while until John Price joined them and told Jamie that Vera was asking for her. Jamie joined the woman a moment later.

"How are you?"

"How the heck do you think I am? I have a broken arm. But don't worry, I'll still be able to work."

"Maybe you should take a vacation," Jamie said. "You've certainly earned it after what you've been through."

"Oh, fiddlesticks, a broken arm isn't going to stop me. Besides, who will run the newspaper if I'm not there?"

"True."

"I called you back here because I want first dibs on this story."

Jamie arched one brow. "I should have known."

"I'll give you editorial control, but I think it's high time you let me write some of the articles. I *am* the assistant editor, after all, and I'm tired of watching Mike get all the glory."

"Okay, Vera, whatever it takes to make you happy."

"So, what do you think of John?"

"He's a very nice man, but he's having a hard time dealing with all this. So am I."

Vera took her hand and squeezed it. "I know, honey. But we've gotten through tough times before, and we'll get through this." She brightened. "So, you think I should let John sleep over tonight?"

"Vera!"

"Just kidding. But if I start dating him, I'm going to need a few pointers."

Jamie was glad Vera could be so upbeat after what she'd been through. "It's always a good idea to follow your instincts. Don't do anything until you know you're ready."

Vera sat up in the bed. "I've got to get out of this place. If I stay here any longer, I'm going to catch something. Would you please find my doctor and tell him I said to get his fanny in here? He's the young one who looks like Andy Garcia. If I were forty years younger, I'd jump his bones."

"Vera?"

"Yes, dear?"

"Lay off the brownies."

JAMIE AWOKE THE NEXT MORNING TO THE SOUND OF RAIN. "Holy cow!" she said to Max. "Destiny was right."

Max smiled beside her. "You know what this means."

"Um, we're going to need an umbrella?"

"Nope. It means you're going to be late for work." He reached for her.

"I can't be late for work. Vera's got a broken arm."

"That's not going to stop her, and that's why I'm not worried about taking you back to Virginia with me for a few days. We'll take the small six-passenger plane so Muffin can have some time off."

Jamie did a bit of eye-rolling. "Max, do you know how that sounds? I've never been involved with a man who owned a fleet of airplanes and a two-million-dollar car. I'm going to have to get used to your being so rich."

"It has certain advantages."

Jamie suspected it wasn't a bad idea. She needed to get away. Somehow, she had to put the bad stuff behind her and go on, and she found solace in Max's arms. She smiled. "So you're taking me to Virginia, huh?"

"I want you to meet my family, Jamie."

"Geez, Max, that sounds serious."

He gazed back at her. "I guess it does. Maybe it's time I let down my guard and went with my feelings."

Jamie waited for him to say more. "What does that mean exactly?" she asked when he didn't elaborate.

"You're asking me to go out on a limb here." His look grew serious. "Jamie, do you love me?"

She was surprised he hadn't figured it out for himself. "Men are so dumb."

"Is that a yes?"

Jamie glanced away, afraid he would see it in her eyes.

"I haven't used that word in a long time, Jamie," he said, "and I ended up being wrong."

"So take a chance, Holt."

"I asked you first."

"Come on, Max, give it up."

"It certainly feels like love. The fact that I don't

want to be without you, and I can't stop thinking about you when you're not with me is a good indication that something serious is going on between us." He grinned. "Your turn."

"You didn't say the words, Max."

His look turned tender. "I love you, Swifty."

Jamie felt her heart turn over in her chest. "See, that wasn't so hard. I love you, too, Max. I have for some time."

He looked relieved. "This smacks of commitment, you know. I usually run as fast as I can when a woman mentions that word."

"And now?"

"I'm tired of running. I love you," he repeated. He suddenly grinned. "It gets easier every time I say it."

Jamie studied him. He was sincere; she could see the love in his eyes. "You know what else I love?"

"What?"

"Rainy days."

"It's still early. I know how we could fill the time." He kissed her deeply. Before long they were aching for each other. Max began to unbutton her gown.

"Uh-oh," Jamie said. "Something tells me I'm going to be really late for work. I'll miss out on the fresh doughnuts."

He laughed. "Those doughnuts are going to be very stale by the time you show up."

EPILOGUE

ONE WEEK LATER.

Dear Divine Love Goddess Advisor:

I'm a single gay male, and I have a crush on a policeman. Every time I see him in his shorts I get hot all over—he's got a behind to die for. I've watched him closely, and I suspect he's gay as well, but he doesn't seem to know I exist. I've tried jaywalking, not putting change into parking meters, and parking more than eighteen inches from the curb. He writes me tickets but he's all business. What I want to know is whether or not I should confess my feelings to him and risk rejection, or take a chance.

Signed,
Flaming Hot in Beaumont

Dear Flaming:

The Divine Love Goddess strongly suspects this man feels the same about you, but he is trying to come to terms with his sexuality. My advice to you is to confront him, and see where it leads before you go broke paying fines. Who knows, maybe he'll handcuff you, take you home, and show you his nightstick. You might just end up on his "Most Wanted" list.

See you at the policemen's ball!

> Signed,
> The Divine Love Goddess
> Advisor

Dear Divine Love Goddess Advisor:

I have been married for a long time to a wonderful man. I recently found out I was pregnant. I am concerned my husband won't be attracted to me once I begin to gain weight because I have always taken very good care of myself, maintaining a perfect size-six figure. How can I be certain he will love me when I'm big as a house?

> Signed,
> Growing Day by Day

Dear Growing:

The Divine Love Goddess knows that your concerns are unwarranted. Your husband loves you very much and looks forward to sharing this special time with you. Many men find pregnant women very sexy, and I suspect your husband will, as well.

I suggest you not worry so much about your figure and concentrate on the miracle growing inside of you, because your husband is going to love you even when your feet swell to twice their size, you blimp out, and start waddling like a duck.

> Signed,
> The Divine Love Goddess
> Advisor

Dear Divine Love Goddess Advisor:

I am a gay policeman who recently became attracted to another man. I think the feeling is mutual because he follows me everywhere. I think he might be trying to get my attention because he's racking up fines for parking violations. Should I come clean with this man and give him the frisking of his life?

> Signed,
> Uncertain

Dear Uncertain:

I am positive this man has strong feelings for you. (Read "Flaming Hot in Beaumont.") Don't wait until he becomes so desperate he has to call 911 to get your attention.

> Signed,
> The Divine Love Goddess
> Advisor

Dear Divine Love Goddess Advisor:

I am in love with a wonderful man who recently confessed his love for me. I feel insecure at times because he's gorgeous and filthy rich and has dated his share of celebrities. Can you tell me what the future holds for us?

> Signed,
> Head over Heels

Dear Head over Heels:

One word: Fireworks.

> Signed,
> The Divine Love Goddess
> Advisor

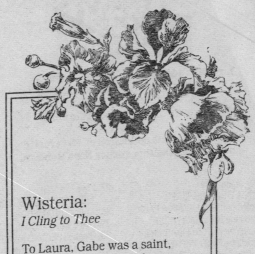

Wisteria:
I Cling to Thee

To Laura, Gabe was a saint, savior of both her and her baby. But Gabe wasn't looking for gratitude. Somehow, he'd have to convince her that two people clinging *together* meant understanding...acceptance... and love.

NORA ROBERTS
LANGUAGE OF LOVE

Love has a language all its own, and for
centuries, flowers have symbolized
love's finest expression.
Discover the language of flowers
—and love—
in this romantic collection of 48 favorite
books by bestselling author Nora Roberts.

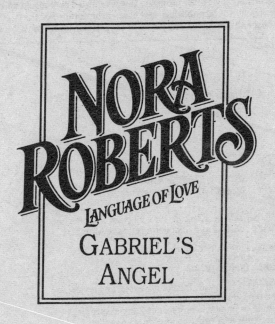

NORA ROBERTS

Language of Love

GABRIEL'S ANGEL

Silhouette® Books

Published by Silhouette Books New York

America's Publisher of Contemporary Romance

To Tom and Ky and Larry,
for having the good sense to marry well

SILHOUETTE BOOKS
300 East 42nd St., New York, N.Y. 10017

GABRIEL'S ANGEL © 1989 by Nora Roberts.
First published as a Silhouette Intimate Moments.

Language of Love edition published May 1993.

ISBN: 0-373-51032-2

Chapter One

Damn snow. Gabe downshifted to second gear, slowed the Jeep to fifteen miles an hour, swore and strained his eyes. Through the frantic swing of the wipers on the windshield all that could be seen was a wall of white. No winter wonderland. Snow pelted down in flakes that looked as big and as mean as a man's fist.

There would be no waiting out this storm, he thought as he took the next curve at a crawl. He considered himself lucky that after six months he knew the narrow, winding road from town so well. He could drive almost by feel, but a newcomer wouldn't stand a chance. Even with that advantage, his shoulders and the back of his neck were tight with tension. Colorado snows could be as vicious in spring as they were in the dead of winter, and they could last for an hour or a day. Apparently this one had been a surprise to everyone—residents, tourists and the National Weather Service.

He had only five miles to go. Then he could unload his supplies, stoke his fire and enjoy the April blizzard from the comfort of his cabin, with a hot cup of coffee or an ice cold beer.

The Jeep chugged up the incline like a tank, and he was grateful for its sturdy perseverance. The unexpected snowfall might force him to take three times as long to make the twenty-mile trip from town to home, but at least he'd get there.

The wipers worked furiously to clear the windshield. There were seconds of white vision followed by seconds of white blindness. At this rate there would be better than two feet by nightfall. Gabe comforted himself with the thought that he'd be home long before that, even as the air in the Jeep turned blue from his cursing. If he hadn't lost track of the time the day before, he'd have had his supplies and been able to laugh at the weather.

The road went into a lazy S and Gabe took it cautiously. It was difficult for him to move slowly under any circumstances, but over the winter he had gained a healthy respect for the mountains and the roads that had been blasted through them. The guardrail was sturdy enough, but beneath it the cliffs were unforgiving. He wasn't worried so much about making a mistake himself—the Jeep was solid as a rock—but he thought of others who might be traveling north or south on the pass, pulling over to the side or stopping dead in the middle of the road.

He wanted a cigarette. His hands gripping the wheel hard, he all but lusted for a cigarette. But it was a luxury that would have to wait. Three miles to go.

The tension in his shoulders began to ease. He hadn't seen another car in more than twenty minutes, and he wasn't likely to now. Anyone with any sense would have taken shelter. From this point on he could almost feel his way home. A good thing. Beside him the radio was squawking about roads closed and activities canceled. It always amazed Gabe that people planned so many meetings, luncheons, recitals and rehearsals on any given day.

But that was human nature, he supposed. Always planning on drawing together, if only to sell a bunch of cakes and cookies. He preferred to be alone. At least for now. Otherwise he wouldn't have bought the cabin and buried himself in it for the last six months.

The solitude gave him freedom, to think, to work, to heal. He'd done some of all three.

He nearly sighed when he saw—or rather felt—the road slant upward again. This was the final rise before his turn-off. Only a mile now. His face, which had been hard and tight with concentration, relaxed. It wasn't a smooth or particularly handsome face. It was too thin and angular to be merely pleasant, and the nose was out of alignment due to a heated disagreement with his younger brother during their teens. Gabe hadn't held it against him.

Because he'd forgotten to wear a hat, his dark blond hair fell untidily around his face. It was long and a bit shaggy over the collar of his parka and had been styled hastily with his fingers hours before. His eyes, a dark, clear green, were starting to burn from staring at the snow.

While his tires swished over the cushioned asphalt he glanced down at his odometer, saw that there was only a quarter mile left, then looked back to the road. That was when he saw a car coming at him out of control.

He didn't even have time to swear. He jerked the Jeep to the right just as the oncoming car seemed to come out of its spin. The Jeep skimmed over the snow piled on the shoulder, swaying dangerously before the tires chewed down to the road surface for traction. He had a bad moment when he thought the Jeep was going to roll over like a turtle. Then all he could do was sit and watch and hope the other driver was as lucky.

The oncoming car was barreling down the road sideways. Though only seconds had passed, Gabe had time to think of how nasty the impact would be when the car slammed into him. Then the driver managed to straighten out. With only feet between them the car fishtailed and swerved to avoid the collision, then began to slide helplessly toward the guardrail. Gabe set his emergency brake and was out of the Jeep when the car rammed into the metal.

He nearly fell on his face, but his boots held as he raced across the road. It was a compact—a bit more compact now, with its right side shoved in and its hood sprung like an accordion, also on the passenger side. He had another moment to think, and he grimaced at the thought of what would have happened if the car had hit on the driver's side.

Fighting his way through the snow, he managed to make it to the wrecked car. He saw a figure slumped over the wheel, and he yanked at the door. It was locked. With his heart in his throat, he began to pound against the window.

The figure moved. A woman, he saw from the thick wave of wheat-blond hair that spilled onto the shoulders of a dark coat. He watched her reach up and drag a ski cap from her head. Then she turned her face to the window and stared at him.

She was white, marble white. Even her lips were colorless. Her eyes were huge and dark, the irises almost black with shock. And she was beautiful, stunningly breathtakingly beautiful. The artist in him saw the possibilities in the diamond-shaped face, the prominent cheekbones, the full lower lip. The man in him rejected them and banged on the glass again.

She blinked and shook her head as if to clear it. As the shock passed out of them, he saw that her eyes were blue, a midnight blue. They filled now with a rush of concern. In a quick movement she rolled down the window.

"Are you hurt?" she demanded before he could speak. "Did I hit you?"

"No, you hit the guardrail."

"Thank God." She let her head slump back on the seat for a moment. Her mouth was as dry as dust. And her heart, though she was already fighting to control it, was thudding in her throat. "I started to skid coming down the incline. I thought—I hoped—I might be able to ride it out. Then I saw you and I was sure I was going to hit you.''

"You would have if you hadn't swerved away toward the rail." He glanced at the front of her car again. The damage could have been worse, much worse. If she'd been going any faster... There was no use speculating. He turned to her again, studying her face for signs of shock or concussion. "Are you all right?"

"Yes. I think so." She opened her eyes again and tried to smile at him. "I'm sorry. I must have given you quite a scare."

"At least." But the scare was over now. He was less than a quarter of a mile from hearth and home, and stuck in the snow with a strange woman whose car wasn't going anywhere for several days. "What the hell are you doing out here?"

She took the furiously bitten-off words in stride as she unhooked her seat belt. The long, deep breaths she'd been taking had gone a long way toward steadying her. "I must have gotten turned around in the storm. I was trying to get down to Lonesome Ridge to wait it out, find a place for the night. That's the closest town, according to the map, and I was afraid to pull over on the shoulder." She glanced over at the guardrail and shuddered. "What there is of it. I don't suppose there's any way I'm going to get my car out of here."

"Not tonight."

Frowning, Gabe stuck his hands in his pockets. The snow was still falling, and the road was deserted. If he turned around and walked back to his Jeep, leaving her to fend for herself, she might very well freeze to death before an emergency vehicle or a snowplow came along. However much he'd have liked to shrug off the obligation, he couldn't leave a woman stranded in this storm.

"The best I can do is take you with me." There wasn't an ounce of graciousness in his tone. She hadn't expected any. If he was angry and impatient about nearly being plowed into, and inconvenienced on top of it, he was entitled.

"I'm sorry."

He moved his shoulders, aware that he'd been rude. "The turnoff for my cabin's at the top of the hill. You'll have to leave your car and ride in the Jeep."

"I'd appreciate it." With the engine off and the window open, the cold was beginning to seep through her clothes. "I'm sorry for the imposition, Mr.—?"

"Bradley. Gabe Bradley."

"I'm Laura." She slipped out of the safety harness that had undoubtedly saved her from injury. "I have a suitcase in the trunk, if you wouldn't mind giving me a hand with it."

Gabe took the keys and stomped back toward the trunk, thinking that if he'd only left an hour earlier that afternoon he'd be home—alone—at this moment.

The case wasn't large, and it was far from new. The lady with only one name traveled light, he thought. He muttered to himself as he hefted it out of the trunk. There was no use being angry with her, or being snotty. If she hadn't managed to skid quite so well, if she hadn't avoided him, they might have been needing a doctor now instead of a cup of coffee and dry feet.

Deciding to be more civil, Gabe turned to tell her to go across to the Jeep. She was standing, watching him, with the snow falling on her uncovered hair. That was when he saw she was not only beautiful, she was very, very pregnant.

"Oh, God" was all he could manage.

"I'm really sorry to be so much trouble," Laura began. "And I want to thank you in advance for the lift. If I could call from your cabin and find a tow truck, maybe we could clear this whole thing up quickly."

He hadn't heard a word she'd said. Not one. All he could do was stare at the ripe slope beneath her dark coat. "Are you sure you're all right? You didn't tell me you were— Are you going to need a doctor?"

"I'm fine." This time she smiled, fully. The cold had brought the color back into her face. "Really. The baby wasn't hurt. He's annoyed a bit, I'd say from the way he's kicking me, but we hardly felt the impact. We didn't ram the guardrail, we sort of slid into it."

"You might have..." What? he wondered. "Jarred something."

"I'm fine," she said again. "I was strapped in, and the snow, though it started it all, cushioned the hit." Noting that he still seemed unconvinced, she tossed back her snow-covered hair. Her fingers, though they were tucked into subtle, silk-lined leather, were going numb. "I promise, I'm not going to give birth in the middle of the road—unless you plan on standing here for a few more weeks."

She was all right...he hoped. And the way she was smiling at him made him feel like an idiot. Deciding to take her word for it, he offered her a hand. "Let me help you."

The words, such simple words, went straight to her heart. She could have counted on her hands the number of times she had heard them.

He didn't know how to deal with pregnant women. Were they fragile? It had always seemed to him that the opposite must be true, given what they had to go through, but now, faced with one, he was afraid she'd shatter at a touch.

Mindful of the slippery road, Laura took a firm grip on his arm as they started across. "It's beautiful here," she said when they reached the Jeep. "But I have to admit, I'm going to appreciate the snow more from inside." She glanced at the high step below the door of the Jeep. "I think you're going to have to give me a bit of a boost. I'm not as agile as I used to be."

Gabe stowed her case, wondering exactly where to grab her. Mumbling, he put a hand under her elbow and another on her hip. Laura slid into the seat with less fuss than he'd expected.

"Thanks."

He grunted a response as he slammed the door. He skirted the hood, then took his place behind the wheel. It took a little maneuvering, but with a minimum of effort they inched back onto the road.

The dependable Jeep started up the hill. Laura uncurled her hands as they moved along at a steady pace. They'd finally stopped shaking. "I wasn't sure anyone lived along here. If I'd known, I'd have begged a roof long before this. I wasn't expecting a snowstorm in April."

"We get them later than this." He said nothing for a moment. He respected other people's privacy as zealously as his own. But these were unusual circumstances. "You're traveling alone?"

"Yes."

"Isn't that a little risky in your condition?"

"I'd planned on being in Denver in a couple of days." She laid a hand lightly on her belly. "I'm not due for six weeks." Laura took a deep breath. It was a risk to trust him, but she really had no other option. "Do you live alone, Mr. Bradley?"

"Yes."

She shifted her gaze just enough to study him as he turned down a narrow, snow-covered lane. At least she assumed a lane was buried somewhere under all the white. There was something tough and hard about his face. Not rugged, she thought. It was too lean and fine-boned for that. It was coldly sculpted, as she imagined a mythic warrior chief's might be.

But she remembered the stunned male helplessness in his eyes when he'd seen she was pregnant. She believed she'd be safe with him. She had to believe that.

He felt her gaze and read her thoughts easily enough. "I'm not a maniac," he said mildly.

"I appreciate that." She smiled a little, then turned to look out the windshield again.

The cabin could barely be seen through the snow, even when he stopped in front of it. But what Laura could see, she loved. It was a squat rectangle of wood with a covered porch and square-paned windows. Smoke puffed from the chimney.

Though it was buried under snow, there was a path of flat rocks leading from the lane to the front steps. Evergreens mantled with white trooped around the corners. Nothing had ever looked as safe and warm as this snow-decked little cabin in the mountains.

"It's lovely. You must be happy here."

"It does the job." Gabe came around to help her down. She smelled like the snow, he thought, or perhaps more like water, the pure, virginal water that poured down the mountain in the spring. "I'll take you in," he told her, knowing both his reaction and his comparison were ridiculous. "You can warm up by the fire." Gabe opened the front door and waved her in. "Go ahead. I'll bring in the rest."

He left her alone, snow dripping wet from her coat onto the woven mat inside the door.

The paintings. Laura stood just where she was and stared openmouthed at the paintings. They covered the walls, they were stacked in corners, they were piled on tables. Only a few were framed. They didn't need the ornamentation. Some where half finished, as though the artist had lost interest or motivation. There were oils, in colors vivid and harsh, and watercolors in soft, misty hues that might have sprung from dreams. Shrugging out of her coat, Laura moved in for a closer look.

There was a scene from Paris, the Bois de Boulogne. She remembered it from her honeymoon. Looking at it made her eyes swim and her muscles tense. Breathing deeply, she forced herself to look at it until her emotions settled.

An easel was set near the window, where the light would come in and fall on the canvas. She resisted the temptation to go over and steal a look. She already had the sensation that she was trespassing.

What was she going to do? Laura gripped her hands together tightly as she let the despair come. She was stranded, her car wrecked, her money dwindling. And the baby— The baby wasn't going to wait until she made things right.

If they found her now...

They weren't going to find her. Deliberately she unlaced her hands. She'd come this far. No one was going to take her baby, now or ever.

She turned as the door to the cabin opened. Gabe shifted the bags he'd carried inside, leaving them jumbled together in a pile. He, too, shrugged out of his coat and hung it on a hook by the door.

He was as lean as his face had indicated. Though he might have been a bit under six feet, the spare toughness of his build gave the illusion of more height, more power. More like a boxer than an artist, Laura thought as she watched him kick the clinging snow from his boots. More like a man of the outdoors than one who came from graceful mansions and gentle blood.

Despite what she knew of his aristocratic background, he wore flannel and corduroy and looked perfectly suited to the rustic cabin. Laura, who came from humbler stock, felt fussy and out of place in her bulky Irish knit sweater and tailored wool.

"Gabriel Bradley," she said, and gestured widely toward the walls. "My brain must have been scrambled before. I didn't put it together. I love your work."

"Thanks." Bending, he hefted two of the bags.

"Let me help—"

"No." He strode off into the kitchen, leaving Laura biting her lip.

He wasn't thrilled to have her company, she thought. Then she shrugged. It couldn't be helped. As soon as it was reasonably safe for her to leave, she would leave. Until then... Until then Gabriel Bradley, artist of the decade, would have to make do.

It was tempting just to take a seat and passively stay out of his way. Once she would have done just that, but circumstances had changed her. She followed him into the adjoining kitchen. Counting the baby she carried, there were three of them in the little room, and it was filled to capacity.

"At least let me make you something hot to drink." The ancient two-burner stove looked tricky, but she was determined.

He turned, brushed against her belly and was amazed at the wave of discomfort he felt. And the tug of fascination. "Here's the coffee," he mumbled, handing her a fresh can.

"Got a pot?"

It was in the sink, which was filled with water that had once been sudsy. He had been trying to soak out the stains from the last time he'd used it. He moved to get it, bumped her again and stepped back.

"Why don't you let me take care of it?" she suggested. "I'll put this stuff away and start the coffee, and you can call a tow truck."

"Fine. There's milk. Fresh."

She smiled. "I don't suppose you have any tea."

"No."

"Milk's fine, then. Thank you."

When he left, Laura busied herself in the kitchen. It was too small for it to be complicated. She used her own system in storing the goods since it appeared Gabe had none. She'd only emptied the first bag when he reappeared in the doorway.

"Phone's out."

"Out?"

"Dead. We lose service a lot when there's a storm."

"Oh." Laura stood holding a can of soup. "Is it usually out for long?"

"Depends. Sometimes a couple hours, sometimes a week."

She lifted a brow. Then she realized that he was perfectly serious. "I guess that puts me in your hands, Mr. Bradley."

He hooked his thumbs in his front pockets. "In that case, you better call me Gabe."

Laura frowned down at the can in her hand. When things got bad, you made the best of them. "Want some soup?"

"Yeah. I'll, ah . . . put your things in the bedroom."

Laura simply nodded, then began to search for a can opener.

She was a piece of work, all right, Gabe decided as he carried Laura's suitcase into his room. Not that he was an expert when it came to women, but he wasn't what anyone would have called a novice, either. She hadn't batted an eye when he'd told her that the phone was dead and they were effectively cut off from the outside world. Or, to put it more precisely, that she was cut off from everyone but him.

Gabe glanced into the streaked mirror over his battered dresser. As far as he knew, no one had ever considered him harmless before. A quick, cocky smile flashed over his face. He hadn't always been harmless, when it came right down to it.

This, of course, was an entirely different situation.

Under other circumstances he might have entertained some healthy fantasies about his unexpected guest. That face. There was something haunting, something indefinable, about that kind of beauty. When a man looked at it, he automatically began to wonder and imagine. Even if she hadn't been carrying a child, the fantasies would have remained only that. Fantasies. He'd never been enthusiastic about flings and one-night stands, and he certainly wasn't in any shape for a relationship. Celibacy had been the order of the day for the last few months. The desire to paint had finally seduced him again. Gabe needed no other love affair.

But as for more practical matters, he did have a guest, a lone woman who was very pregnant—and very secretive. He hadn't missed the fact that she'd told him only her first name and hadn't volunteered any information about who she was and where and why she was traveling. Since it was unlikely that she'd robbed a bank or stolen secrets for the Russians, he wouldn't press too hard right now.

But, given the strength of the storm and the seclusion of the cabin, they were likely to be together for a few days. He was going to find out more about the calm and mysterious Laura.

What was she going to do? Laura stared at the empty plate in her hand and saw a hint of her reflection. How could she get to Denver or Los Angeles or Seattle—or any huge, swallowing city that was far enough away from Boston—when she was trapped here? If only she hadn't felt that urgent need to move on this morning. If she'd stayed in that quiet little motel room another day she might still have had some control over what was happening.

Instead, she was here with a stranger. Not just any stranger, Laura reminded herself. Gabriel Bradley, artist—wealthy, respected artist from a wealthy, respected family. But he hadn't recognized her. Laura was certain of that. At least he had yet to recognize her. What would happen when he did, when he found out who she was running from? For all she knew, the Eagletons might be close family friends of the Bradleys. The gesture of her hand over the mound of her stomach was automatic and protective.

They wouldn't take her baby. No matter how much money and how much power they wielded, they wouldn't take her baby. And if she could manage it they would never find her or the child.

Setting down the plate, she turned her attention to the window. How odd it was to look out and see nothing. It gave her a nice, settled feeling to know that no one could see in, either. She was effectively curtained off from everyone. Or nearly everyone, she corrected, thinking again of Gabe.

Perhaps the storm had been a blessing. When there was no choice, she found it best to look on the bright side. No one could follow her trail in this kind of weather. And who would think of looking for her in some tiny, out-of-the-way cabin in the mountains? It felt safe. She would cling to that.

She heard him moving around in the next room, heard the sound of his boots on the hardwood, the thud of a log being added to the fire. After so many months alone she found even the sound of another human being a comfort.

"Mr. Bradley...Gabe?" She stepped through the doorway to see him adjusting the screen in front of the fire. "Could you clear off a table?"

"Clear off a table?"

"So we could eat...sitting down."

"Yeah."

She disappeared again while he tried to figure out what to do with the paints, brushes, canvas stretchers and general disorder on the picnic table that had once served as a dining area. Annoyed at having his space compromised, he spread his equipment throughout the room.

"I made some sandwiches, too." Using a bent cookie sheet as a makeshift tray, she carried in bowls and plates and cups. Embarrassed and edgy, Gabe snatched it from her.

"You shouldn't be carrying heavy things."

Her brows lifted. Surprise came first. No one had ever pampered her. And certainly her life, which had rarely been easy, had been hardest over the last seven months. Then gratitude came, and she smiled. "Thanks, but I'm careful."

"If you were careful, you'd be in your own bed with your feet up and not snowbound with me."

"Exercise is important." But she sat and let him set out the dishes. "And so's food." With her eyes closed, she breathed in the scents. Hot, simple, fortifying. "I hope I didn't put too much of a dent in your supplies, but once I got started I couldn't stop."

Gabe picked up half a sandwich that was thick with cheese, crisp bacon and sliced hothouse tomatoes. "I'm not complaining." The truth was, he'd gotten into the habit of eating right out of the pan over the kitchen sink. Hot food made with more care than hurry tasted one hell of a lot better from a plate.

"I'd like to pay you back, for the bed and the food."

"Don't worry about it." He scooped up clam chowder while he studied her. She had a way of sticking out her chin that made him think of pride and will. It made an interesting contrast with the creamy skin and the slender neck.

"That's kind of you, but I prefer paying my own way."

"This isn't the Hilton." She wore no jewelry, he noted, not even a plain gold band on her finger. "You cooked the meal, so we'll call it even."

She wanted to argue—her pride wanted to argue—but the simple truth was, she had very little cash, except for the baby fund she'd scrupulously set aside in the lining of her suitcase. "I'm very grateful." She sipped at the milk, though she detested it. The scent of his coffee was rich and forbidden. "Have you been here long, in Colorado?"

"Six months, seven, I guess."

That gave her hope. The timing was good, almost too good. From the looks of the cabin, he didn't spend much time poring over the newspapers, and she hadn't noticed a television. "It must be a wonderful place to paint."

"So far."

"I couldn't believe it when I walked in. I recognized your work right away. I've always admired it. In fact, my— someone I knew bought a couple of your pieces. One of them was a painting of a huge, deep forest. It seemed as though you could step right into it and be completely alone."

He knew the work, and, oddly enough, he'd had the same feeling about it. He couldn't be sure, but he thought it had been sold back east. New York, Boston, perhaps Washington, D.C. If his curiosity about her persisted, it would only take a phone call to his agent to refresh his memory.

"You didn't say where you were traveling from."

"No." She continued to eat, though her appetite had fled. How could she have been foolish enough to describe the painting? Tony had bought it, or rather had snapped his fingers and arranged for his lawyers to buy it on his behalf because Laura had admired it. "I've been in Dallas for a while."

She'd been there almost two months before she'd discovered that the Eagletons' detectives were making discreet inquiries about her.

"You don't sound like a Texan."

"No, I suppose I don't. That's probably because I've lived all over the country." That was true enough, and she was able to smile again. "You're not from Colorado."

"San Francisco."

"Yes, I remember reading that in an article about you and your work." She would talk about him. From her experience men were easily distracted when the conversation centered on themselves. "I've always wanted to see San Francisco. It seems like a lovely place, the hills, the bay, the beautiful old houses." She gave a quick gasp and pressed a hand to her stomach.

"What is it?"

"The baby's just restless." She smiled, but he noted that her eyes were shadowed with fatigue and her complexion was pale again.

"Look, I don't know anything about what you're going through, but common sense tells me you should be lying down."

"Actually, I am tired. If you wouldn't mind, I'd like to rest for a few minutes."

"The bed's through here." He rose and, not certain she could get up and down on her own, offered her a hand.

"I'll take care of the dishes later if..." Her words trailed off as her knees buckled.

"Hold on." Gabe put his arms around her and had the odd, rather humbling sensation of having the baby move against him.

"I'm sorry. It's been a long day, and I guess I pushed it further than I should have." She knew she should move away, pull back on her own, but there was something exquisite about leaning against the hard, sturdy body of a man. "I'll be fine after a nap."

She didn't shatter as he'd once thought she might, but now she seemed so soft, so delicate, that he imagined her dissolving in his hands. He would have liked to comfort her, would have liked to go on holding her like that while she leaned into him, trusting, depending. Needing him. Calling himself a fool, he picked her up.

Laura started to protest, but it felt so good to be off her feet. "I must weigh a ton."

"That's what I was expecting, but you don't."

She found she could laugh, even though the fatigue was smothering her. "You're a real charmer, Gabe."

His own awkwardness began to fade as he moved through the door to the bedroom. "I haven't had many opportunities to flirt with pregnant ladies."

"That's all right. You redeemed yourself by rescuing this one from a snowstorm." With her eyes half closed, she felt herself being lowered onto a bed. It might be nothing more than a mattress and a rumpled sheet, but it felt like heaven. "I want to thank you."

"You've been doing that on an average of every five minutes." He pulled a slightly ragged comforter over her. "If you really want to thank me, get some sleep and don't go into labor."

"Fair enough. Gabe?"

"Yeah."

"Will you keep trying the phone?"

"All right." She was nearly asleep. He had a moment's attack of guilt for wanting to press her while she was vulnerable. Right now, she didn't look as though she had the strength to brush away a fly. "Do you want me to call anyone for you? Your husband?"

She opened her eyes at that. Though they were clouded with fatigue, they met his levelly, and he saw that she wasn't down for the count yet.

"I'm not married," she said, very clearly. "There's no one to call."

Chapter Two

In the dream she was alone. That didn't frighten her. Laura had spent a large portion of her life alone, so she was more comfortable in solitude than in a crowd. There was a soft, misty quality to the dream—like the seascape she had seen on the wall of Gabe's cabin.

Oddly, she could even hear the ocean, purring and lapping off in the distance, though a part of her knew she was in the mountains. She walked through a pearl-colored fog, listening to the waves. Under her feet sand shifted, warm and soft. She felt safe and strong and strangely unencumbered. It had been a long, long time since she had felt so free, so at ease.

She knew she was dreaming. That was the best part. If she could have managed it, she would have stayed there, in the soft-focused fantasy of it, forever. It would be so easy to keep her eyes closed and cling to the utter peace of the dream.

Then the baby was crying. Screaming. A pulse began to beat in her temple as she listened to the high, keening wails. She started to sweat, and the clean white fog changed to a dark, threatening gray. No longer warm, the air took on a chill that whipped straight to the bone.

The cries seemed to come from everywhere and nowhere, echoing and rebounding as she searched. Sobbing for breath, she fought her way through the mist as it circled and thickened. The cries became louder, more urgent. Her heart was beating in her throat, and her breath rasped and her hands shook.

Then she saw the bassinet, with its pretty white skirt and its lacy pink and blue ruffles. The relief was so great that her knees sagged.

"It's all right," she murmured as she gathered the child in her arms. "It's all right. I'm here now." She could feel the baby's warm breath against her cheek, could feel the weight in her arms as she rocked and soothed. The fine scent of powder surrounded her. Gently she cradled the child, murmuring and comforting as she began to lift the concealing blanket from its face.

And there was nothing, nothing in her arms but an empty blanket.

Gabe was sitting at the picnic table, sketching her face, thinking of her, when he heard her cry out. The moan was so long, so desperate, that he snapped the pencil in two before he jumped up and raced to the bedroom.

"Hey, come on." Feeling awkward, he took her by the shoulders. She jerked so hard that he had to fight back his own panic, as well as hers, to hold on to her. "Laura, take it easy. Are you in pain? Is it the baby? Laura, tell me what's going on."

"They took my baby!" There was hysteria in her voice, but it was a hysteria that was laced with fury. "Help me! They took my baby!"

"No one took your baby." She was still fighting him, with a strength that awed him. Moving on instinct, he wrapped his arms around her. "You're having a dream. No one took your baby. Here." He clamped a hand around her wrist, where her pulse was beating like a jackhammer, and dragged her hand to her belly. "You're safe, both of you. Relax before you hurt yourself."

When she felt the life beneath her palms, she slumped against him. Her baby was safe, still inside her, where no one could touch him. "I'm sorry. It was a dream."

"It's okay." Without being aware of it, he was stroking her hair, cradling her as she had cradled the baby of her imagination, rocking her gently in an age-old comforting motion. "Do us both a favor and relax."

She nodded, feeling protected and sheltered. Those were two sensations she had experienced very rarely in her twenty-five years. "I'm all right, really. It must have been the shock from the accident catching up with me."

He drew her away, angry with himself because he wanted to go on holding her, shielding her. When she had asked him for help, he had known, without understanding why, that he would do anything to protect her. It was almost as though he had been dreaming himself, or had been caught up in her dream.

The snow was still falling in sheets outside the window and the only light was what came slanting through the bedroom door from the main cabin. It was dim and slightly yellow, but he could see her clearly, and he wanted to be certain that she saw him, as well. He wanted answers, and he wanted them now.

"Don't lie to me. Under normal circumstances you'd be entitled to your privacy, but right now you're under my roof for God knows how long."

"I'm not lying to you." Her voice was so calm, so even, that he nearly believed her. "I'm sorry if I upset you."

"Who are you running from, Laura?"

She said nothing, just stared at him with those dark blue eyes. He swore at her, but she didn't flinch. He sprang up to pace the room, but she didn't shudder. Abruptly he dropped down on the bed again and caught her chin in his hand. She went absolutely still. Gabe would have sworn that for an instant she stopped breathing. Though it was ridiculous, he had the odd sensation that she was bracing for a blow.

"I know you're in trouble. What I want to know is how big. Who's after you, and why?"

Again she said nothing, but her hand moved instinctively to protect the child she carried.

Since the baby was obviously the core of the problem, they would begin there. "The baby's got a father," he said slowly. "You running from him?"

She shook her head.

"Then who?"

"It's complicated."

He lifted a brow as he jerked his head toward the window. "We've got nothing but time here. This keeps up, it could be a week before the main roads are open."

"When they do, I'll go. The less you know, the better off we'll both be."

"That won't wash." He was silent a moment, trying to organize his thoughts. "It seems to me that the baby is very important to you."

"Nothing is or can be more important."

"Do you figure the strain you're carrying around is good for it?"

He saw the regret in her eyes instantly, saw the concern, the almost imperceptible folding into herself. "There are some things that can't be changed." She took a long breath. "You have a right to ask questions."

"But you don't intend to answer them."

"I don't know you. I have to trust you, to a point, because I have no choice. I can only ask you to do the same."

He moved his hand away from her face. "Why should I?"

She pressed her lips together. She knew he was right. But sometimes right wasn't enough. "I haven't committed a crime, I'm not wanted by the law. I have no family, no husband looking for me. Is that enough?''

''No. I'll take that much tonight because you need to sleep, but we'll talk in the morning.''

It was a reprieve—a short one, but she'd learned to be grateful for small things. With a nod, she waited for him to walk to the door. When it shut and the darkness was full again, she lay down. But it was a long, long time before she slept.

It was silent, absolutely silent, when Laura woke. She opened her eyes and waited for memory to return. There had been so many rooms, so many places where she'd slept, that she was used to this confusion upon waking.

She remembered it all . . . Gabriel Bradley, the storm, the cabin, the nightmare. And the sensation of waking in fear to find herself safe, in his arms. Of course, the safety was only temporary, and his arms weren't for her. Sighing, she turned her head to look out the window.

The snow was still falling. It was almost impossible to believe, but she lay and watched it, thinner now, slower, but still steady. There would be no leaving today.

Tucking her hand under her cheek, she continued to watch. It was easy to wish that the snow would never stop and that time would. She could stay here, cocooned, isolated, safe. But time, as the child she carried attested, never stopped. Rising, she opened her suitcase. She would put herself in order before she faced Gabe.

The cabin was empty. She should have felt relieved at that. Instead, the cozy fire and polished wood made her feel lonely. She wanted him there, even if it was just the sound of his movements in another room. Wherever he had gone, she reminded herself, he would be back. She started to walk into the kitchen to see what could be done about breakfast.

She saw the sketches, a half dozen of them, spread out on the picnic table. His talent, though raw in pencil or charcoal drawing, was undeniable. Still, it made her both uneasy and curious to see how someone else—no, how Gabriel Bradley—perceived her.

Her eyes seemed too big, too haunted. Her mouth was too soft, too vulnerable. She rubbed a finger over it as she frowned at the drawing. She'd seen her face countless times, in glossy photographs, posed for the best angle. She'd been draped in silks and furs, drenched in jewels. Her face and form had sold gallons of perfume, hawked fortunes in clothes and gems.

Laura Malone. She'd nearly forgotten that woman, the woman they'd said would be the face of the nineties. The woman who had, briefly, held her own destiny in her hands. She was gone, erased.

The woman in the sketches was softer, rounder and infinitely more fragile. And yet she seemed stronger. Laura lifted a sketch and studied it. Or did she just want to see the strength, need to see it?

When the front door opened, she turned, still holding the pencil sketch. Gabe, covered with snow, kicked the door shut again. His arms were loaded with wood.

"Good morning. Been busy?"

He grunted and stomped the worst of the snow from his boots, then walked, leaving a wet trail, to the firebox to dump his wood. "I thought you might sleep longer."

"I would have." She patted her belly. "He wouldn't. Can I fix you some breakfast?"

Drawing off his gloves, he tossed them down on the hearth. "Already had some. You go ahead."

Laura waited until he'd stripped off his coat. Apparently they were back on friendly terms again. Cautiously friendly. "It seems to be letting up a little."

He sat on the hearth to drag his boots off. Snow was caked in the laces. "We've got three feet now, and I wouldn't look for it to stop before afternoon." He drew out a cigarette. "Might as well make yourself at home."

"I seem to be." She held up the sketch. "I'm flattered."

"You're beautiful," He said offhandedly as he set his boots on the hearth to dry. "I can rarely resist drawing beautiful things."

"You're fortunate." She dropped the sketch back on the table. "It's so much more rewarding to be able to depict beauty than it is to be beautiful." Gabe lifted a brow. There was a trace, only a trace, of bitterness in her tone. "Things," she explained. "It's strange, but once people see you as beautiful, they almost always see you as a thing."

Turning, she slipped into the kitchen, leaving him frowning after her.

She brewed him fresh coffee, then idled away the morning tidying the kitchen. Gabe gave her room. Before night fell again, he would have some answers, but for now he was content to have her puttering around while he worked.

She seemed to need to be busy. He had thought a woman in her condition would be content to sleep or rest or simply sit and knit for most of the day. He decided it was either nervous energy or her way of avoiding the confrontation he'd promised her the night before.

She didn't ask questions or stand over his shoulder, so they rubbed along through the morning without incident. Once he glanced over to see her tucked into a corner of the sagging sofa reading a book on childbirth. Later she threw some things together in the kitchen and produced a thick, aromatic stew.

She said little. He knew she was waiting, biding her time until he pushed open the door he'd unlocked the night before. He, too, was waiting, biding his time. By midafternoon he decided she looked rested. Taking up his sketch pad and a piece of charcoal, he began to work while she sat across from him peeling apples.

"Why Denver?"

The only sign of her surprise was a quick jerk of the paring knife. She didn't look up or stop peeling. "Because I've never been there."

"Under the circumstances, wouldn't you be better off in some place that's familiar?"

"No."

"Why did you leave Dallas?"

She set the apple down and picked up another. "Because it was time."

"Where's the baby's father, Laura?"

"Dead." There wasn't even a shadow of emotion in her voice.

"Look at me."

Her hands stilled as she lifted her gaze, and he saw that that much, at least, was true.

"You don't have any family who could help you?"

"No."

"Didn't he?"

Her hand jerked again. This time the blade nicked her finger. The blood welled up as Gabe dropped his pad to take her hand. Once again she saw her face in the sweeping charcoal lines.

"I'll get you a bandage."

"It's only a scratch," she began, but he was already up and gone. When he returned he dabbed at the wound with antiseptic. Again Laura was baffled by the care he displayed. The sting came and went; his touch remained gentle.

He was kneeling in front of her, his brows drawn together as he studied the thin slice in her finger. "Keep this up and I'll think you're accident-prone."

"And I'll think you're the original Good Samaritan." She smiled when he looked up. "We'd both be wrong."

Gabe merely slipped a bandage over the cut and took his seat again. "Turn your head a little, to the left." When she complied, he picked up his pad and turned over a fresh sheet. "Why do they want the baby?"

Her head jerked around, but he continued to sketch.

"I'd like the profile, Laura." His voice was mild, but the demand in it was very clear. "Turn your head again, and try to keep your chin up. Yes, like that." He was silent as he formed her mouth with the charcoal. "The father's family wants the baby. I want to know why."

"I never said that."

"Yes, you did." He had to hurry if he was going to capture that flare of anger in her eyes. "Let's not beat that point into the ground. Just tell me why."

Her hands were gripped tightly together, but there was as much fear as fury in her voice. "I don't have to tell you anything."

"No." He felt a thrill of excitement—and, incredibly, one of desire—as he stroked the charcoal over the pad. The desire puzzled him. More, it worried him. Pushing it aside, he concentrated on prying answers from her. "But since I'm not going to let it drop, you may as well."

Because he knew how to look, and to see, he caught the subtle play of emotions over her face. Fear, fury, frustration. It was the fear that continued to pull him over the line.

"Do you think I'd bundle you and your baby off to them, whoever the hell they are? Use your head. I haven't got any reason to."

He'd thought he would shout at her. He'd have sworn he was on the verge of doing so. Then, in a move that surprised them both, he reached out to take her hand. He was more surprised than she to feel her fingers curl instinctively into his. When she looked at him, emotions he'd thought unavailable to him turned over in his chest.

"You asked me to help you last night."

Her eyes softened with gratitude, but her voice was firm. "You can't."

"Maybe I can't, and maybe I won't." But as much as it went against the grain of what he considered his character, he wanted to. "I'm not a Samaritan, Laura, good or otherwise, and I don't like to add someone else's problems to my own. But the fact is, you're here, and I don't like playing in the dark."

She was tired, tired of running, tired of hiding, tired of trying to cope entirely on her own. She needed someone. When his hand was covering hers and his eyes were calm and steady on hers, she could almost believe it was him she needed.

"The baby's father is dead," she began, picking her way carefully. She would tell him enough to satisfy him, she hoped, but not all. "His parents want the baby. They want... I don't know, to replace, to take back, something that they've lost. To... to ensure the lineage. I'm sorry for them, but the baby isn't their child." There was that look again, fierce, protective. A mother tiger shielding her cub. "The baby's mine."

"No one would argue with that. Why should you have to run?"

"They have a lot of money, a lot of power."

"So?"

"So?" Angry again, she pushed away. The contact that had been so soothing for both of them was broken. "It's easy to say that when you come from the same world. You've always had. You've never had to want and to wonder. No one takes from people like you, Gabe. They wouldn't dare. You don't know what it's like to have your life depend on the whims of others."

That she had was becoming painfully obvious. "Having money doesn't mean you can take whatever you want."

"Doesn't it?" She turned to him, her face set and cold. "You wanted a place to paint, somewhere you could be alone and be left alone. Did you have to think twice about how to arrange it? Did you have to plan or save or make compromises, or did you just write a check and move in?"

His eyes were narrowed as he rose to face her. "Buying a cabin is a far cry from taking a baby from its mother."

"Not to some. Property is property, after all."

"You're being ridiculous."

"And you're being naive."

His temper wavered, vying with amusement. "That's a first. Sit down, Laura, you make me nervous when you swing around."

"I'm not going to break," she muttered, but she eased into a chair. "I'm strong, I take care of myself. I had an examination just before I left Dallas, and the baby and I are fine. Better than fine. In a few weeks I'm going to check into a hospital in Denver and have my baby. Then we're going to disappear."

He thought about it. He almost believed the woman sitting across from him could accomplish it. Then he remembered how lost and frightened she'd been the night before. There was no use pointing out the strain she'd been under and its consequences for her. But he knew now what button to push.

"Do you think it's fair to the baby to keep running?"

"No, it's horribly, horribly unfair. But it would be worse to stop and let them take him."

"Why are you so damn sure they would, or could?"

"Because they told me. They explained what they thought was best for me and the child, and they offered to pay me." The venom came into her voice at that, black and bitter. "They offered to give me money for my baby, and when I refused they threatened to simply take him." She didn't want to relive that dreadful, terrifying scene. With an effort she cleared it from her mind.

He felt a swift and dark disgust for these people he didn't even know. He buried it with a shake of his head and tried to reason with her. "Laura, whatever they want, or intend, they couldn't just take what isn't theirs. No court would just take an infant from its mother without good cause."

"I can't win on my own." She closed her eyes for a moment because she wanted badly to lay her head down and weep out all the fear and anguish. "I can't fight them on their own ground, Gabe, and I won't put my child through the misery of custody suits and court battles, the publicity, the gossip and speculation. A child needs a home, and love and security. I'm going to see to it that mine has all of those things. Whatever I have to do, wherever I have to go."

"I won't argue with you about what's right for you and the baby, but sooner or later you're going to have to face this."

"When the time comes, I will."

He rose and paced over to the fire to light another cigarette. He should drop it, just leave it—her—alone and let her follow her own path. It was none of his business. Not his problem. He swore, because somehow, the moment she'd taken his arm to cross the road, she'd become his business.

"Got any money?"

"Some. Enough to pay a doctor, and a bit more."

He was asking for trouble. He knew it. But for the first time in almost a year he felt as though something really mattered. Sitting on the edge of the hearth, he blew out smoke and studied her.

"I want to paint you," he said abruptly. "I'll pay you the standard model's fee, plus room and board."

"I can't take your money."

"Why not? You seem to think I have too much for my own good, anyway."

Shame brought color flooding into her cheeks. "I didn't mean it—not like that."

He brushed her words aside. "Whatever you meant, the fact remains that I want to paint you. I work at my own pace, so you'll have to be patient. I'm not good at compromise, but owing to your condition I'm willing to make some concessions and stop when you're tired or uncomfortable."

It was tempting, very tempting. She tried to forget that she'd traded on her looks before and concentrate on what the extra money would mean to the baby. "I'd like to agree, but the fact is, your work is well-known. If the portrait was shown, they'd recognize me."

"True enough, but that doesn't mean I'd be obliged to tell anyone where we'd met or when. You have my word that no one will ever trace you through me."

She was silent for a moment, warring with herself. "Would you come here?"

Hesitating only a moment, he tossed his cigarette into the fire. He rose, walked over, then crouched in front of her chair. She, too, had learned how to read a face. "Your word?"

"Yes."

Some risks were worth taking. She held both hands out to his, putting her trust into them.

With the continuing fall of snow, it was a day without a sunrise, a sunset, a twilight. The day stayed dim from morning on, and then night closed in without fanfare. And the snow stopped.

Laura might not have noticed if she hadn't been standing by the window. The flakes didn't appear to have tapered off, but to have stopped as if someone had thrown a switch. There was a vague sense of disappointment, the same she remembered feeling as a young girl when a storm had ended. On impulse, she bundled herself in her boots and coat and stepped out onto the porch.

Though Gabe had shoveled it off twice during the day, the snow came almost to her knees. Her boots sank in and disappeared. She had the sensation of being swallowed up by a soft, benign cloud. She wrapped her arms around her chest and breathed in the thin, cold air.

There were no stars. There was no moon. The porch light tossed its glow only a few feet. All she could see was white. All she could hear was silence. To some the high blanket of snow might have been a prison, something to chafe against. To Laura it was a fortress.

She'd decided to trust someone other than herself again. Standing there, soaking up the pure dark, the pure quiet, she knew that the decision had been the right one.

He wasn't a gentle man, or even a contented man, but he was a kind one, and, she was certain, a man of his word. If they were using each other, her for sanctuary, him for art, it was a fair exchange. She needed to rest. God knew she needed whatever time she could steal to rest and recover.

She hadn't told him how tired she was, how much effort it took for her just to keep on her feet for most of the day. Physically the pregnancy had been an easy one. She was strong, she was healthy. Otherwise she would have crumpled long before this. But the last few months had drained every ounce of her emotional and mental reserves. The cabin, the mountains, the man, were going to give her time to build those reserves back up again.

She was going to need them.

He didn't understand what the Eagletons could do, what they could accomplish with their money and their power. She'd already seen what they were capable of. Hadn't they paid and maneuvered to have their son's mistakes glossed over? Hadn't they managed, with a few phone calls and few favors called in, to have his death, and the death of the woman with him, turned from the grisly waste it had been into a tragic accident?

There had never been any mention in the press about alcohol and adultery. As far as the public was concerned, Anthony Eagleton, heir to the Eagleton fortune, had died as a result of a slippery road and faulty steering, and not his criminally careless drunk driving. The woman who had died with him had been turned from his mistress into his secretary.

The divorce proceedings that Laura had started had been erased, shredded, negated. No shadow of scandal would fall over the memory of Anthony Eagleton or over the family name. She'd been pressured into playing the shocked and grieving widow.

She had been shocked. She had grieved. Not for what had been lost—not on a lonely stretch of road outside of Boston—but for what had been lost so soon after her wedding night.

There was no use looking back, Laura reminded herself. Now, especially now, she had to look forward. Whatever had happened between her and Tony, they had created a life. And that life was hers to protect and to cherish.

With the spring snow glistening and untouched as far as she could see, she could believe that everything would work out for the best.

"What are you thinking?"

Startled, she turned toward Gabe with a little laugh. "I didn't hear you."

"You weren't listening." He pulled the door closed behind him. "It's cold out here."

"It feels wonderful. How much is there, do you think?"

"Three and a half, maybe four feet."

"I've never seen so much snow before. I can't imagine it ever melting and letting the grass grow."

His hands were bare. He tucked them in the pockets of his jacket. "I came here in November and there was already snow. I've never seen it any other way."

She tried to imagine that, living in a place where the snow never melted. No, she thought, she would need the spring, the buds, the green, the promise. "How long will you stay?"

"I don't know. I haven't thought about it."

She turned to smile at him, though she felt a touch of envy at his being so unfettered. "All those paintings. You'll need to have a show."

"Sooner or later." He moved his shoulders, suddenly restless. San Francisco, his family, his memories, seemed very far away. "No hurry."

"Art needs to be seen and appreciated," she murmured, thinking out loud. "It shouldn't be hidden up here."

"And people should?"

"Do you mean me, or is that what you're doing, too? Hiding?"

"I'm working," he said evenly.

"A man like you could work anywhere, I think. You'd just elbow people aside and go to it."

He had to grin. "Maybe, but now and again I like to have some space. Once you make a name, people tend to look over your shoulder."

"Well, I, for one, am glad you came here, for whatever reason." She brushed the hair away from her face. "I should go back in, but I don't want to." She was smiling as she leaned back against the post.

His eyes narrowed. When he cupped her face in his hands, his fingers were cold and firm. "There's something about your eyes," he murmured, turning her face fully into the light. "They say everything a man wants a woman to say, and a great deal he doesn't. You have old eyes, Laura. Old, sad eyes."

She said nothing, not because her mind was empty, but because it was suddenly filled with so many things, so many thoughts, so many wishes. She hadn't thought she could feel anything like this again, and certainly not this longing for a man. Her skin warmed with it, even though his touch was cool, almost disinterested.

The sexual tug surprised her, even embarrassed her a little. But it was the emotional pull, the slow, hard drag of it, that kept her silent.

"I wonder what you've seen in your life."

As if of their own volition, his fingers stroked her cheek. They were long, slender, artistic, but hard and strong. Even so, he might merely have been familiarizing himself with the shape of her face, with the texture of her skin. An artist with his subject.

The longing leaped inside her, the foolish, impossible longing to be loved, held, desired, not for her face, not for the image a man could see, but for the woman inside.

"I'm getting tired," she said, managing to keep her voice steady. "I think I'll go to bed now."

He didn't move out of her way immediately. And his hand lingered. He couldn't have said what kept him there, staring at her, searching the eyes he found so fascinating. Then he stepped back quickly and shoved the door open for her.

"Good night, Gabe."

"Good night."

He stayed out in the cold, wondering what was wrong with him. For a moment, damn it, for a great deal longer than a moment, he'd found himself wanting her. Filled with self-disgust, he pulled out a cigarette. A man had to be sinking low to think about making love to a woman who was more than seven months along with another man's child.

But it was a long time before he could convince himself he'd imagined it.

Chapter Three

He wondered what she was thinking. She looked so serene, so quietly content. The pale pink sweater she wore fell into a soft cowl at her throat. Her hair shimmered to her shoulders. Again she wore no jewelry, nothing to draw attention away from her, nothing to draw attention to her.

Gabe rarely used models in his work, because even if they managed to hold the pose for as long as he demanded they began to look bored and restless. Laura, on the other hand, looked as though she could sit endlessly with that same soft smile on her face.

That was part of what he wanted to capture in the portrait. That inner patience, that...well, he supposed he could call it a gracious acceptance of time—what had come before, and what was up ahead. He'd never had much patience, not with people, not with his work, not with himself. It was a trait he could admire in her without having the urge to develop it himself.

Yet there was something more, something beyond the utterly feminine beauty and the Madonna-like calm. From time to time he saw a fierceness in her, a warriorlike determination. He could see that she was a woman who would do whatever was necessary to protect what was hers. Judging from her story, all that was hers was the child she carried.

She had more to tell, he mused as he ran the pencil over the pad. The bits and pieces she'd offered had only been given to keep him from asking more. He hadn't asked for more. It wasn't his usual style, once he'd decided an explanation was called for, to accept a partial one. He couldn't quite make himself push for the whole when even the portion she'd given him had plainly cost her so much.

There was still time. The radio continued to squawk about the roads that were closed and the snow that was yet to come. The Rockies could be treacherous in the spring. Gabe estimated it would be two weeks, perhaps three, before a trip could be managed with real safety.

It was odd, but he would have thought the enforced company would annoy him. Instead, he found himself pleased to have had his self-imposed solitude broken. It had been a long time since he'd done a portrait. Maybe too long. But he hadn't been able to face flesh and blood, not since Michael.

In the cabin, cut off from memories and reminders, he'd begun the healing process. In San Francisco he hadn't been able to pick up a brush. Grief had done more than make him weak. For a time it had made him . . . blank.

But here, secluded, solitary, he'd painted landscapes, still lifes, half-remembered dreams and seascapes from old sketches. It had been enough. Not until Laura had he felt the need to paint the human face again.

Once he'd believed in destiny, in a pattern of life that was meant to be even before birth. Michael's death had changed that. From that point, Gabe had had to blame something, someone. It had been easiest, and most painful, to blame himself. Now, sketching Laura, thinking over the odd set of circumstances that had brought her into his life, he began to wonder again.

And what, he asked himself yet again, was she thinking?

"Are you tired?"

"No." She answered, but she didn't move. He'd stationed a chair by the window, angling it so that she was facing him but still able to look out. The light fell over her, bringing no shadows. "I like to look at the snow. There are tracks in it now, and I wonder what animals might have passed by without us seeing. And I can see the mountains. They look so old and angry. Back east they're more tame, more good-natured."

He absently murmured his agreement as he studied his sketch. It was good, but it wasn't right, and he wanted to begin working on canvas soon. He set the pad aside and frowned at her. She stared back, patient and—if he wasn't reading her incorrectly—amused. "Do you have anything else to wear? Something off-the-shoulder, maybe?"

The amusement was even more evident now. "Sorry, my wardrobe's a bit limited at the moment."

He rose and began to pace, to the fire, to the window, back to the table. When he strode over to take her face in his hand and turn it this way and that, she sat obligingly. After three days of posing, she was used to it. She might have been an arrangement of flowers, Laura thought, or a bowl of fruit. It was as if that one moment of awareness on the snow-covered porch had never happened. She'd already convinced herself that she'd imagined that look in his eyes— and, more, her response to it.

He was the artist. She was the clay. And she'd been there before.

"You have a completely feminine face," he began, talking more to himself than to her. "Alluring and yet composed, and soft, even with the angular shape and those cheekbones. It's not threatening, and yet, it's utterly distracting. This—" his thumb brushed casually over her full lower lip "—says sex, even while your eyes promise love and devotion. And the fact that you're ripe—"

"Ripe?" She laughed, and the hands that had clenched in her lap relaxed again.

"Isn't that what pregnancy is? It only adds to the fascination. There's a promise and a fulfillment and—despite education and progress—a compelling mystery to a woman with child. Like an angel.''

''How?''

As he spoke, he began to fuss with her hair, drawing it back, piling it up, letting it fall again. ''We see angels as ethereal creatures, mystic, above human desires and flaws, but the fact is, they were human once.''

His words appealed to her, made her smile. ''Do you believe in angels?''

His hand was still in her hair, but he'd forgotten, totally forgotten, the practical reason for it. ''Life wouldn't be worth much if you didn't.'' She had the hair of an angel, shimmery-blond, cloud-soft. Feeling suddenly awkward, he drew his hand away and tucked it in the pocket of his baggy corduroys.

''Would you like to take a break?'' she asked him. Her hands were balled in her lap again.

''Yeah. Rest for an hour. I need to think this through.'' He stepped back automatically when she rose. When he wasn't working, he took great care not to come into physical contact with her. It was disturbing how much he wanted to touch her. ''Put your feet up.'' When she lifted a brow at that, he shifted uncomfortably. ''It recommended it in that book you leave lying around. I figured it wouldn't hurt for me to glance through it, under the circumstances.''

''You're very kind.''

''Self-preservation.'' Things happened to him when she smiled like that. Things he recognized but didn't want to acknowledge. ''The more I make sure you take care of yourself, the less chance there is of you going into labor before the roads are clear.''

''I've got more than a month,'' she reminded him. ''But I appreciate you worrying about me—about us.''

''Put your feet up,'' he repeated. ''I'll get you some milk.''

"But I—"

"You've only had one glass today." With an impatient gesture, he motioned her to the sofa before he walked into the kitchen.

With a little sigh of relief, Laura settled back against the cushions. Putting her feet up wasn't as easy as it once had been, but she managed to prop them on the edge of the coffee table. The heat from the fire radiated toward her, making her wish she could curl up in front of it. If she did, she thought wryly, it would take a crane to haul her back up again.

He was being so kind, Laura thought as she turned her head toward the sound of Gabe rummaging in the kitchen. He didn't like her to remind him of it, but he was. No one had ever treated her quite like this—as an equal, yet as someone to be protected. As a friend, she thought, without tallying a list of obligations, a list of debts that had to be paid. Whether he listed them or not, someday, when she was able, she'd find a way to pay him back. Someday.

She could see the future if she closed her eyes and thought calm thoughts. She'd have a little apartment somewhere in the city. Any city. There would be a room for the baby, something in sunny yellows and glossy whites, with fairy-tale prints on the walls. She'd have a rocking chair she could sit in with the baby during the long, quiet nights, when the rest of the world was asleep.

And she wouldn't be alone anymore.

Opening her eyes, she saw Gabe standing over her. She wanted, badly, to reach up, to take his hands and draw in some of the strength and confidence she felt radiating from him. She wanted, more, for him to run his thumb along her lip again, slowly, gently, as though she were a woman, rather than a thing to be painted.

Instead, she reached up to take the glass of milk he held. "After the baby's born and I finish nursing, I'm never going to drink a drop of milk again."

"This is the last of the fresh," he told her. "Tomorrow you go on powdered and canned."

"Oh, joy." Grimacing, she downed half the contents of the glass. "I pretend it's coffee, you know. Strong, black coffee." She sipped again. "Or, if I'm feeling reckless, champagne. French, in fluted crystal."

"It's too bad I don't have any wineglasses handy. It would help the illusion. Are you hungry?"

"It's a myth about eating for two, and if I gain much more weight I'll begin to moo." Content, she settled back again. "That painting of Paris... did you do it here?"

He glanced over at the work. So she'd been there, he thought. It was a moody, almost surreal study of the Bois de Boulogne. "Yes, from old sketches and memory. When were you there?"

"I didn't say I'd been to Paris."

"You wouldn't have recognized it otherwise." He took the empty glass out of her hand and set it aside. "The more secretive you are, Laura, the more it makes me want to dig."

"A year ago," she said stiffly. "I spent two weeks there."

"How did you like it?"

"Paris?" She ordered herself to relax. It had been a lifetime ago, almost long enough that she could imagine it had all happened to someone else. "It's a beautiful city, like an old, old woman who still knows how to flirt. The flowers were blooming, and the smells were incredible. It rained and rained, for three days, and you could sit and watch the black umbrellas hurrying by and the blossoms opening up."

Instinctively he put a hand over hers to calm the agitated movement of her fingers. "You weren't happy there."

"Paris in the spring?" She concentrated on making her hands go limp. "Only a fool wouldn't be happy there."

"The baby's father...was he with you there?"

"Why does it matter?"

It shouldn't have mattered. But now, whenever he looked at the painting, he would think of her. And he had to know. "Did you love him?"

Had she? Laura looked back at the fire, but the only answers were within herself. Had she loved Tony? Her lips curved a little. Yes, she had, she had loved the Tony she'd imagined him to be. "Very much. I loved him very much."

"How long have you been alone?"

"I'm not." She laid a hand on her stomach. When she felt the answering movement, her smile widened. Taking Gabe's hand, she pressed it against her. "Feel that? Incredible, isn't it? Someone's in there."

He felt the stirring beneath his hand, gentle at first, then with a punch that surprised him. Without thinking, he moved closer. "That felt like a left jab. Makes you feel as though it's fighting to get out." He knew the feeling, the impatience, the frustration at being trapped in one world while you longed for another. "How does it feel from the other side?"

"Alive." Laughing, she left her hand over his. "In Dallas they put a monitor on, and I could hear the baby's heartbeat. It was so fast, so impatient. Nothing in the world ever sounded so wonderful. And I think..."

But he was looking at her now, deeply, intently. Their hands were still joined, their bodies just brushing. Even as the life inside her quickened, so did her pulse. The warmth, the intimacy, of the moment washed over her, leaving her breathless and full of needs.

He wanted to hold her, badly. The urge to gather her close and just hold on was so sharp, so intense that he hurt. He dreamed of her every night when he struggled for sleep on the floor of the spare room. In his dreams they were curled in bed together, with her breath warm on his cheek and her hair tangled in his hands. And when he woke from the dreams he told himself he was mad. He told himself that again now and moved aside.

Though they were no longer touching, he could feel, as well as hear, her long, quiet sigh.

"I'd like to work some more, if you're up to it."

"Of course." She wanted to weep. That was natural, she told herself. Pregnant women wept easily. Their emotions ran on the surface, to be bruised and battered without effort, and often without cause.

"I've got something in mind. Hold on a minute."

She waited, still sitting, while he went into the spare room. Moments later he came back holding a navy blue shirt.

"Put this on. I think the contrast between the man's shirt and your face might be the answer."

"All right." Laura went into the bedroom and stripped off the big pink sweater. She started to draw an arm through the sleeve and then she caught his scent. It was there, clinging to the heavy cotton. Tough, and unapologetically sexual. Man. Unable to resist, she rubbed her cheek over it. The material was soft. The scent was not, but somehow even the scent of him made her feel safe. And yet, foolish as it seemed, it made her feel a dull, deep tremor of desire.

Wasn't it wrong to want as a woman, to want Gabe as a man, when she carried such a responsibility? But it didn't seem wrong when she felt so close to him. He had sorrows, too. She could see them, sense them. Perhaps it was that common ground, and their isolation, that made her feel as though she'd known him, cared about him, for so long.

With a sigh, she slipped into the shirt. What did she know about her own feelings? The first, the only, time she'd trusted them completely had brought misery. Whatever emotions Gabe stirred in her, she would be wise to keep gratitude in the forefront.

When she stepped back into the main cabin, he was going through his sketches, rejecting, considering, accepting. He glanced up and realized that his conception of Laura fell far, far short of the mark.

She looked like the angel he'd spoken of, illusory, golden, yet tied now to the earth. He preferred to think of her as an illusion rather than as a woman, one who stirred him.

"That's more of the look I want," he said, managing to keep his voice steady. "The color's good on you, and the straight-line masculine style is a nice contrast."

"You may not get it back anytime soon. It's wonderfully comfortable."

"Consider it a loan."

He walked over to the chair as she sat and shifted into the precise pose she'd been in before the break. Not for the first time, Gabe wondered if she'd modeled before. That was another question, for another time.

"Let's try something else." He shifted her, mere inches, muttering to himself. Laura nearly smiled. She was back to being a bowl of fruit.

"Damn, I wish we had some flowers. A rose. Just one rose."

"You could imagine one."

"I may." He tilted her head a fraction to the left before he stood back. "This feels right, so I'm going to draw it on canvas. I've wasted enough time on rough sketches."

"Three whole days."

"I've completed paintings in half that time when things clicked."

She could see it, him sitting on a tall stool at an easel, working feverishly, brows lowered, eyes narrowed, those long, narrow hands creating. "There are some in here you haven't finished at all."

"Mood changed." He was already making broad strokes on canvas with his pencil. "Do you finish everything you start?"

She thought about that. "I suppose not, but people are always saying you should."

"When something's not right, why drag it out to the bitter end?"

"Sometimes you promise," she murmured, thinking of her marriage vows.

Because he was watching her closely, he saw the swift look of regret. As always, though he tried to block it, her emotions touched a chord in him. "Sometimes promises can't be kept."

"No. But they should be," she said quietly. Then she fell silent.

He worked for nearly an hour, defining, refining, perfecting. She was giving him the mood he wanted. Pensive, patient, sensuous. He already knew, even before the first brush stroke, that this would be one of his best. Perhaps his very best. And he knew he would have to paint her again, in other moods, in other poses.

But that was for tomorrow. Today, now, he needed to capture the tone of her, the feel, the simplicity. That was pencil lines and curves. Black against white, and a few shades of gray. Tomorrow he would begin filling in, adding the color, the complexities. When he had finished he would have the whole of her on canvas, and he would know her fully, as no one had ever before or would ever again.

"Will you let me see it as you go along?"

"What?"

"The painting." Laura kept her head still but shifted her eyes from the window to him. "I know artists are supposed to be temperamental about showing their work before it's finished."

"I'm not temperamental." He lifted his gaze to hers, as if inviting her to disagree.

"Anyone could see that." Though she kept her expression sober, he could hear the amusement in her voice. "So will you let me see it?"

"Doesn't matter to me. As long as you realize that if you see something you don't like I won't change it."

This time she did laugh, more freely, more richly than before. His fingers tightened on the pencil. "You mean if I see something that wounds my vanity? You don't have to worry about that. I'm not vain."

"All beautiful women are vain. They're entitled."

"People are only vain if their looks matter to them."

This time he laughed, but cynically. He set down his pencil. "And yours don't matter to you?"

"I didn't do anything to earn them, did I? An accident of fate, or a stroke of luck. If I were terribly smart or talented somehow I'd probably be annoyed with my looks, because people look at them and nothing else." She shrugged, then settled with perfect ease into the pose again. "But since I'm neither of those, I've learned to accept that looking a certain way is . . . I don't know, a gift that makes up for a lack of other things."

"What would you trade your beauty for?"

"Any number of things. But then, a trade isn't earning, either, so it wouldn't count. Will you tell me something?"

"Probably." He took a rag out of his back pocket and dusted off his hands.

"Which are you more vain about, your looks or your work?"

He tossed the rag aside. It was odd that she could look so sad, so serious, and still make him laugh. "No one's ever accused me of being beautiful, so there's no contest." He started to turn the easel. When she began to rise, he motioned her back. "No, relax. Look from there and tell me what you think."

Laura settled back and studied. It was only a sketch, less detailed than many of the others he'd done. It was her face and torso, her right hand resting lightly just below her left shoulder. For some reason it seemed a protective pose, not defensive, but cautious.

He'd been right about the shirt, she realized. It made her seem more of a woman than any amount of lace or silks could have. Her hair was long and loose, falling in heavy, disordered curls that contradicted the pose. She hadn't expected to find any surprises in her face, but as she studied his conception of it, she shifted uncomfortably in her chair.

"I'm not as sad as you make me look."

"I've already warned you I wouldn't change anything."

"You're free to paint as you please. I'm simply telling you that you have a misconception."

There was a huffiness in her voice that amused him. He turned the easel around again but didn't bother to look at his work. "I don't think so."

"I'm hardly tragic."

"Tragic?" He rocked back on his heels as he studied her. "There's nothing tragic about the woman in the painting. *Valiant* is the word."

She smiled at that and pushed herself out of the chair. "I'm not valiant, either, but it's your painting."

"We agree on that."

"Gabe!"

She flung out a hand. The urgency in her voice had him crossing to her quickly and gripping her hand. "What is it?"

"Look, look out there." She turned to him, using her free hand to point.

Not urgency, Gabe realized. He was tempted to strangle her. Excitement. The excitement of seeing a solitary buck less than two yards from the window. It stood deep in snow, its head lifted, scenting the air. Arrogantly, and without a trace of fear, it stared at them through the glass.

"Oh, he's wonderful. I've never seen one so big before, or so close."

It was easy to share the pleasure. A deer, a fox, a hawk circling overhead . . . those were some of the things that had helped him over his own grief.

"A few weeks ago I hiked down to a stream about a mile south of here. I came across a whole family. I was downwind, and I managed three sketches before the doe spotted me."

"This whole place belongs to him. Can you imagine it? Acres and acres. He must know it, even enjoy it, or else he wouldn't look so sure of himself." She laughed again, and pressed her free hand to the frosted glass. "You know, it's as if we were exhibits and he'd come to take a quick look around the zoo."

The deer nosed down in the snow, perhaps looking for the grass that was buried far beneath, perhaps scenting another animal. He moved slowly, confident in his solitude. Around him the trees dripped with ice and snow.

Abruptly he raised his head, his crown of antlers plunging high in the air. In bounds and leaps he raced across the snow and disappeared into the woods beyond.

Laughing, Laura turned, then instantly forgot everything.

She hadn't realized they had moved so close together. Nor had he. Their hands were still linked. Beside them the sun streamed in, losing power as the afternoon moved toward evening. And the cabin, like the woods beyond, was absolutely silent.

He touched her. He hadn't known he would, but the moment his fingers grazed her cheek he knew he needed to. She didn't move away. Perhaps he would have accepted it if she had. He wanted to believe he would have accepted it. But she didn't move.

There were nerves. He felt them in the hand that trembled in his. He had them, too. Another new experience. How did he approach her, when he knew he had no business approaching her? How did he resist what common sense told him he had to resist?

Yet her skin was warm under his touch. Real. Not a portrait, but a woman. Whatever had happened in her life, whatever had made her into the woman she was, that was yesterday. This was now. Her eyes, wide and more than a little frightened, were on his. She didn't move. She waited.

He swore at himself even as he slowly, ever so slowly, lowered his lips to hers.

It was madness to allow it. It was more than madness to want it. But even before his lips touched hers she felt herself give in to him. As she gave, she braced herself, not knowing what to expect for herself, or for him.

It might have been the first. That was her one and only thought as his mouth closed over hers. Not just the first with him but the first with anyone. No one had ever kissed her like this. She had known passion, the quick, almost painful desire that came from heat and frenzy. She had known demands, some that she could answer, some that she could not. She had known the anger and the hunger a man could have for a woman, but she had never known, had never imagined, this kind of reverence.

And yet, even with that, there were hints of darker needs, needs held down by chains, that made the embrace more exciting, more involving, than any other. His hands were in her hair, searching, exploring, while his lips moved endlessly over hers. She felt the world tip and knew instinctively that he would be there to right it again.

He had to stop. He couldn't stop. One taste, just one taste, and he craved more. It seemed he'd been empty, without knowing it, and now—incredibly, swiftly, terrifyingly—he was filled.

Her hands, hesitant, somehow innocent, slipped over his arms to his shoulders. When she parted her lips, there was that same curious shyness in the invitation. He could smell the spring, though it was still buried beneath the snow, could smell it in her hair, on her skin. Even the woodsmoke that always tinted the air in the cabin couldn't overwhelm it. Logs shifted in the grate, and the wind that came up with evening began to moan against the window. And Laura, her mouth warm and giving under his, sighed.

He wanted to play out the fantasy, to draw her up into his arms and take her to bed. To lie with her, to slip his shirt from her and feel her skin against his own. To have her touch him, hold on to him. Trust him.

The war inside him raged on. She wasn't merely a woman, she was a woman who was carrying a child. And growing inside her was not merely a child, but the child of another man, one she had loved.

She wasn't his to love. He wasn't hers to trust. Still, she pulled at him, her secrets, her eyes, eyes that said much, much more than her words, and her beauty, which she didn't seem to understand went far beyond the shape and texture of her face.

So he had to stop, until he resolved within himself exactly what he wanted—and until she trusted him enough to tell him the whole truth.

He would have drawn her away from him, but she pressed her face into his shoulder. "Please don't say anything, just for a minute."

There were tears in her voice, and they left him more shaken than the kiss had. The tug-of-war increased, and finally he lifted a hand to stroke her hair. The baby turned, moving inside her, against him, and he wondered what in God's name he was going to do.

"I'm sorry." Her voice was under control again, but she didn't let go. How could she have known how badly she needed to be held, when there had been so few times in her life when anyone had bothered? "I don't mean to cling."

"You're not."

"Well." Drawing herself up straight, she stepped back. There were no tears, but her eyes glimmered with the effort it took to hold them in. "You were going to say that you didn't mean for that to happen, but it's all right."

"I didn't mean for that to happen," he said evenly. "But that's not an apology."

"Oh." A little nonplussed, she braced a hand on the back of the chair. "I suppose what I meant is that I don't want you to feel—I don't want you to think that I— Hell." With that, she gave in and sat. "I'm trying to say that I'm not upset that you kissed me and that I understand."

"Good." He felt better, much better than he'd thought he would. Casually he dragged over another chair and straddled it. "What do you understand, Laura?"

She'd thought he would let it go at that, take the easy way out. She struggled to say what she felt without saying too much. "That you felt a little sorry for me, and involved a bit, because of the situation, and the painting, too." Why couldn't she relax again? And why was he looking at her that way? "I don't want you to think that I misunderstood. I would hardly expect you to be..." The ground was getting shakier by the minute. She was ready to shut up entirely, but he quirked a brow and gestured with his hands, inviting her, almost challenging her, to finish.

"I realize you wouldn't be attracted to me—physically, that is—under the circumstances. And I don't want to think that I interpreted what just happened as anything other than a—a sort of kindness."

"That's funny." As if he were considering the idea, Gabe reached up and scratched his chin. "You don't look stupid.

I'm attracted to you, Laura, and there's a part of that attraction that's very, very physical. Making love with you may not be possible under the circumstances, but that doesn't mean that the desire to do so isn't there.''

She opened her mouth as if to speak, but ended up just lifting her hands and then letting them fall again.

''The fact that you're carrying a child is only part of the reason I can't make love with you. The other, though not as obvious, is just as important. I need the story, Laura, your story. All of it.''

''I can't.''

''Afraid?''

She shook her head. Her eyes glimmered, but her chin lifted. ''Ashamed.''

He would have expected almost any other reason than that. ''Why? Because you weren't married to the baby's father?''

''No. Please don't ask me.''

He wanted to argue, but he bit the words back. She was looking pale and tired and just too fragile. ''All right, for now. But think about this. I have feelings for you, and they're growing much faster than either of us might like. Right now I'm damned if I know what to do about it.''

When he rose, she reached up and touched his arm. ''Gabe, there's nothing to do. I can't tell you how much I wish it were otherwise.''

''Life's what you make it, angel.'' He touched her hair then stepped away. ''We need more wood.''

Laura sat in the empty cabin and wished more than she had ever wished for anything that she had made a better job of hers.

Chapter Four

More snow had fallen during the night. It was, compared to what had come before, hardly more than a dusting. The fresh inches lay in mounds and drifts over the rest, where the wind had blown them. In places the snow was as high as a man. Miniature mountains of it lay cozily against the windowpanes, shifting constantly in the wind.

Already the sun was melting the fresh fall, and if Laura listened she could hear the water sliding down the gutters from the roof like rain. It was a friendly sound, and it made her think of hot tea by a sizzling fire, a good book read on a lazy afternoon, a nap on the sofa in early evening.

But this was morning, only an hour or two past dawn. As usual, she had the cabin to herself.

Gabe was chopping wood. From the kitchen, where she was optimistically heating milk and a chocolate bar in a pan, she could hear the steady thud of the ax. She knew the woodbox was full, and the stack of logs outside the rear door was still high. Even if the snow lasted into June, they would still have an ample supply. Artist or not, he was a physical man, and she understood his need to do something manual and tiring.

It seemed so... normal, she thought. Her cooking in the kitchen, Gabe splitting logs, icicles growing long and shiny on the eaves outside the window. Their little world was so well tuned, so self-contained. It was like this every morning. She would rise to find him already outdoors, shoveling, chopping, hauling. She would make fresh coffee or warm what he'd left in the pot. The portable radio would bring her news from the outside, but it never seemed terribly important. After a little while he would come in, shake and stomp the snow off, then accept the cup of coffee she offered him. The routine would continue with him taking his place in behind the easel and Laura taking hers by the window.

Sometimes they would talk. Sometimes they would not.

Beneath the routine, she sensed some kind of hurry in him that she couldn't understand. Though he might paint for hours, his movements controlled and measured, he still seemed impatient to finish. The fact was, the portrait was coming along faster than she could ever have imagined. She was taking shape on canvas—or rather the woman he saw when he looked at her was taking shape. Laura couldn't understand why he had chosen to make her look so otherworldly, so dreamy. She was very much a part of the world. The child she carried grounded her to it.

But she'd learned not to complain, because he didn't listen.

He'd done other sketches, as well, some full-length, some just of her face. She told herself he was entitled, particularly if that was all the payment she could give him for the roof over her head. A few of the sketches made her uneasy, like the one he'd drawn when she'd fallen asleep on the sofa late one afternoon. She'd looked so...defenseless. And she'd felt defenseless when she'd realized that he'd watched her and drawn her while she was unaware of it.

Not that she was afraid of him. Laura poked halfheartedly at the mixture of powdered milk, water and chocolate. He'd been kinder to her than she'd had any right to expect. And, though he could be terse and brusque, he was the gentlest man she'd ever known.

Perhaps he was attracted to her. Men had often been attracted to her face. But whether he was or not he treated her with respect and care. She'd learned not to expect those things when there was attraction.

With a shrug, she poured the liquid into a mug. Now wasn't the time to focus on the feeling Gabe might or might not have. She was on her own. Fixing a mental image of creamy hot chocolate in her mind, Laura downed half the contents of the mug. She made a face, sighed, then lifted the mug again. In a matter of days she would be on her way to Denver again.

A sudden pain had her gripping the side of the counter for support. She held on, fighting back the instinctive need to call for Gabe. It was nothing, she told herself as it began to ease. Moving carefully, she started into the living room. Gabe's chopping stopped. It was in that silence that she heard the other sound. An engine? The panic came instantly, and almost as quickly was pushed down. They hadn't found her. It was ridiculous to even think it. But she walked quickly, quietly, to the front window to look out.

A snowmobile. The sight of it, shiny and toylike, might have amused and pleased her if she hadn't seen the uniformed state trooper on it. Preparing to stand her ground if it came to that, Laura moved to the door and opened it a crack.

Gabe had worked up a warm, healthy sweat. He appreciated being outdoors, appreciated the crisp air, the rhythm of his work. He couldn't say that it kept his mind off Laura. Nothing did. But it helped him put the situation into perspective.

She needed help. He was going to help her.

There were some who knew him who would have been more than a little surprised by his decision. It wasn't that anyone would have accused him of being unfeeling. The sensitivity in his paintings was proof of his capacity for emotion, passion, compassion. But few would have thought him capable of unconditional generosity.

It was Michael who had been generous.

Gabe had always been self-absorbed—or, more accurately, absorbed in his art, driven to depict life, with all its joys and pains. Michael had simply embraced life.

Now he was gone. Gabe brought the ax down, his breath whistling through his teeth and puffing white in the thin air. And Michael's leaving had left a hole so big, so great, that Gabe wasn't certain it could ever be filled.

He heard the engine when his ax was at the apex of his swing. Distracted, he let it fall so that the blade was buried in wood. Splinters popped out to join others on the trampled snow. With a quick glance toward the kitchen window, Gabe started around the cabin to meet the visitor.

He didn't make a conscious decision to protect the woman inside. He didn't have to. It was the most natural thing in the world.

"How ya doing?" The cop, his full cheeks reddened by wind and cold, shut off the engine and he nodded to Gabe.

"Well enough." He judged the trooper to be about twenty-five and half frozen. "How's the road?"

Giving a short laugh, the trooper stepped off the snowmobile. "Let's just say I hope you got no appointments to keep."

"Nothing pressing."

"Good thing." He offered a gloved hand. "Scott Beecham."

"Gabe Bradley."

"I heard somebody bought the old McCampbell place." With his hands on his hips, Beecham studied the cabin. "A hell of a winter to pick for moving in. We're swinging by to check on everybody on the ridge, seeing if they need supplies or if anyone's sick."

"I stocked up the day of the storm."

"Good for you." He gestured toward the Jeep. "At least you've got a fighting chance in a four-wheel drive.

Could've filled a used car lot with some of the vehicles towed in. We're checking around on a compact, an '84 Chevy that took a spin into the guardrail about a quarter mile from here. Abandoned. Driver might have wandered out and got lost in the blizzard."

"My wife," Gabe said. In the doorway, Laura opened her eyes wide. "She was worried that something had happened to me and got the idea of driving into town." Gabe grinned and drew out a cigarette. "Damn near ran into me. At the rate things were going, I figured it was best to leave the car where it was and get us back here. Haven't been able to get back out to check on the damage."

"Not as bad as some I've seen the last few days. Was she hurt?"

"No. Scared ten years off both of us, though."

"I'll bet. Afraid we're going to have to tow the vehicle in, Mr. Bradley." He glanced toward the house. His voice was casual, but Gabe sensed that he was alert. "Your wife, you say?"

"That's right."

"Name on the registration was Malone, Laura Malone."

"My wife's maiden name," Gabe said easily.

On impulse, Laura pushed open the door. "Gabe?"

Both men turned to look at her. The trooper pulled off his hat. Gabe merely scowled.

"I'm sorry to interrupt—" she smiled "—but I thought the officer might like some hot coffee."

The trooper replaced his hat. "That's mighty tempting, ma'am, and I appreciate it, but I have to get along. Sorry about your car."

"My own fault. Can you tell us when the road will be open?"

"Your husband ought to be able to manage a trip into town in a day or two," Beecham said. "I wouldn't recommend the drive for you, ma'am, for the time being."

"No." She smiled at him and hugged her elbows. "I don't think I'll be going anywhere for a little while yet."

"I'll just be on my way." Beecham straddled the snow-mobile again. "You got a shortwave, Mr. Bradley?"

"No."

"Might not be a bad idea to pick one up next time you're in town. More dependable than the phones. When's your baby due?"

Gabe just stared for a moment. The pronoun had stunned him. "Four or five weeks."

"You got yourself plenty of time, then." With a grin, Beecham started the engine. "This your first?"

"Yes," Gabe murmured. "It is."

"Nothing quite like it. Got myself two girls. Last one de-cided to be born on Thanksgiving. Hardly had two bites of pumpkin pie when I had to drive into the hospital. My wife still says it was my mother's sausage stuffing that started her off." He raised a hand and his voice. "Take care, Mrs. Bradley."

They watched, Gabe from the yard, Laura from the doorway, as the snowmobile scooted up the lane. And then they were alone.

Clearing his throat, Gabe started up the stairs. Laura said nothing, but she stepped out of the way and closed the door behind him. She waited until he was sitting on the low stone hearth, unlacing his boots.

"Thank you."

"For what?"

"You told the trooper that I was your wife."

Still frowning, he pried off a boot. "It seemed less com-plicated that way."

"For me," Laura agreed. "Not for you."

He shrugged his shoulders and then rose to go into the kitchen. "Any coffee?"

"Yes." She heard the glass pot chink against the mug, heard the liquid pour into the stoneware. He'd lied for her, protected her, and all she had done was take from him. "Gabe." Praying that her instincts and her conscience were right, she walked to the doorway.

"What the hell is this?" He had the pan she'd used to heat the milk in his hand.

For a moment the tension fled. "If you're desperate enough, it's hot chocolate."

"It looks like... Well, never mind what it looks like." He set it back on the stove. "That powdered stuff tastes filthy, doesn't it?"

"It's hard to argue with the truth."

"I'll try to make it into town tomorrow."

"If you do, could you..." Embarrassed, she let her words trail off.

"What do you want?"

"Nothing. It's stupid. Listen, could we sit down a minute?"

He took her hand before she could back away. "What do you want from town, Laura?"

"Marshmallows, to toast in the fireplace. I told you it was stupid," she murmured, and tried to tug her hand away.

He wanted, God, he wanted just to fold her into his arms. "Is that a craving or just a whim?"

"I don't know. It's just that I look at the fireplace and think about marshmallows." Because he wasn't laughing at her, it was easy to smile. "Sometimes I can almost smell them."

"Marshmallows. You don't want anything to go with them? Like horseradish?"

She made a face at him. "Another myth."

"You're spoiling all my preconceptions." He wasn't sure when he'd lifted her hand to his lips, but after the faintest taste of her skin he dropped it again. "And you're not wearing the shirt."

Though he was no longer touching it, her hand felt warm, warm and impossibly soft. "Oh." She took a long breath. He was thinking of the painting, not of her. He was the artist with his subject again. "I'll change."

"Fine." More than a little shaken by the extent of his desire for her, he turned back to the counter and his coffee.

The decision came quickly, or perhaps it had been made the moment she'd heard him lie for her, protect her. "Gabe, I know you want to work right away, but I'd like...I feel like I should...I want to tell you everything, if you still want to hear it."

He turned back, his eyes were utterly clear and intent. "Why?"

"Because it's wrong not to trust you." Again the breath seemed to sigh out of her. "And because I need someone. We need someone."

"Sit down," he said simply, leading her to the couch.

"I don't know where to start."

It would probably be easier for her to start further back, he thought as he tossed another log in the fire. "Where do you come from?" he asked when he joined her on the couch.

"I've lived a lot of places. New York, Pennsylvania, Maryland. My aunt had a little farm on the Eastern Shore. I lived with her the longest."

"Your parents?"

"My mother was very young when I was born. Unmarried. She...I went to live with my aunt until...until things became difficult for her, financially. There were foster homes after that. That isn't really the point."

"Isn't it?"

She took a steadying breath. "I don't want you to feel sorry for me. I'm not telling you this so that you'll feel sorry for me."

The pride was evident in the tilt of her head, in the tone of her voice—the same quiet pride he was trying to capture on canvas. His fingers itched for his sketchpad, even as they itched to touch her face. "All right, I won't."

With a nod, she continued. "From what I can gather, things were very hard on my mother. Even without the little I was told, it's easy enough to imagine. She was only a child. It's possible that she wanted to keep me, but it didn't work out. My aunt was older, but she had children of her own. I was essentially another mouth to feed, and when it became difficult to do so, I went into foster care."

"How old were you?"

"Six the first time. For some reason it just never seemed to work out. I would stay in one place for a year, in another for two. I hated not belonging, never being a real part of what everyone else had. When I was about twelve I went back with my aunt for a short time, but her husband had problems of his own, and it didn't last."

He caught something in her voice, something that made him tense. "What sort of problems?"

"They don't matter." She shook her head and started to rise, but Gabe put his hand firmly on hers.

"You started this, Laura, now finish it."

"He drank," she said quickly. "When he drank he got mean."

"Mean? Do you mean violent?"

"Yes. When he was sober, he was discontented and critical. Drunk, he was—could be—vicious." She rubbed a hand over her shoulder, as if she were soothing an old wound. "My aunt was his usual target, but he often went after the children."

"Did he hit you?"

"Unless I was quick enough to get out of his way." She managed a ghost of a smile. "And I learned to be quick. It sounds worse than it was."

He doubted it. "Go on."

"The social services took me away again and placed me in another home. It was like being put on hold. I remember when I was sixteen, counting the days until I'd be of age and able to at least fend for myself. Make...I don't know, make some of my own decisions. Then I was. I moved to Pennsylvania and got a job. I was working as a clerk in a department store in Philadelphia. I had a customer, a woman, who used to come in regularly. We got friendly, and one day she came in with a man. He was short and balding—looked like a bulldog. He nodded to the woman and told her she'd been absolutely right. Then he handed me a business card and told me to come to his studio the next day. Of course, I had no intention of going. I thought...that is, I'd gotten used to men..."

"I imagine you did," Gabe said dryly.

It still embarrassed her, but since he seemed to take it in stride she didn't dwell on it. "In any case, I set the card aside and would have forgotten about it, but one of the girls who worked with me picked it up later and went wild. She told me who he was. You might know the name. Geoffrey Wright."

Gabe lifted a brow. Wright was one of the most respected fashion photographers in the business—no, *the* most. Gabe might not know much about the fashion business, but a name like Geoffrey Wright's crossed boundaries. "It rings a bell."

"When I found out he was a professional, a well-known photographer, I decided to take a chance and go to see him. Everything happened at once. He was very gruff and had me in makeup and under the lights before I could babble an excuse. I was terribly embarrassed, but he didn't seem to notice. He barked out orders, telling me to stand, sit, lean, turn. He had a fur in his vault—a full-length sable. He took it out and tossed it around my shoulders. I thought I was dreaming. I must have said so aloud, because while he was shooting he laughed and told me that in a year I could wear sable to breakfast.''

Saying nothing, Gabe settled back. With his eyes narrowed, he could see her, enveloped in furs. There was a twist in his stomach as he thought about her becoming one of Wright's young and casually disposable mistresses.

''Within a month I had done a layout for *Mode* magazine. Then I did another for *Her*, and one for *Charm*. It was incredible. One day I was selling linens and the next I was having dinner with designers.''

''And Wright?''

''No one in my life had ever been as good to me as Geoffrey. Oh, I knew he saw me as a commodity half the time, but he set himself up as, I don't know, a watchdog. He had plans, he'd tell me. Not too much exposure too quickly. Then, in another two years, there wouldn't be a person in the Western world who wouldn't recognize my face. It sounded exciting. Most of my life I'd been essentially anonymous. He liked that, the fact that I'd come from nothing, from nowhere. I know some of his other models saw him as cold. He often was. But he was the closest thing I'd ever had to a father.''

''Is that how you saw him?''

''I suppose. And then, after all he'd done for me, after all the time he'd invested, I let him down.'' She started to rise again, and again Gabe stopped her.

''Where are you going?''

''I need some water.''

''Sit. I'll get it.''

She used the time to compose herself. Her story was only half done, and the worst part, the most painful part, was yet to come. He brought her a clear glass with ice swimming in it. Laura took two long sips, then continued.

"We went to Paris. It was like being Cinderella and being told midnight never had to come. We were scheduled to be there for a month, and because Geoffrey wanted a very French flavor to the pictures we went all over Paris for the shoot. We went to a party one night. It was one of the those gorgeous spring nights when all the women are beautiful and the men handsome. And I met Tony."

He caught the slight break in her voice, the shadow of pain in her eyes, and knew without being told that she was speaking now of her baby's father.

"He was so gallant, so charming. The prince to my Cinderella. For the next two weeks, whenever I wasn't working, I was with Tony. We went dancing, we ate in little cafés and walked in the parks. He was everything I'd thought I'd wanted and knew I could never have. He treated me as though I were something rare and valuable, like a diamond necklace. There was a time when I thought that was love."

She fell silent for a moment, brooding. That had been her mistake, her sin, her vanity. Even now, a year later, it cut at her.

"Geoffrey grumbled and talked about rich young pups sowing wild oats, but I wouldn't listen. I wanted to be loved, I wanted so terribly for someone to care, to want me. When Tony asked me to marry him, I didn't think twice."

"You married him?"

"Yes." She looked at him again. "I know I led you to believe that I hadn't married the baby's father. It seemed easiest."

"You don't wear a ring."

Color washed into her face. The shame of it. "I sold them."

"I see." There was no condemnation in the two words, but she felt it nonetheless.

"We stayed in Paris for our honeymoon. I wanted to go back to the States and meet his family, but he said we should stay where we were happy. It seemed right. Geoffrey was furious with me, lectured and shouted about me wasting myself. At the time I thought he meant my career, and I ignored him. It was only later that I realized he meant my life."

She jumped when a log fell apart in the fire. It was easier to continue if she looked at the flames, she discovered. "I thought I'd found everything I'd ever wanted. When I look back I realize that those weeks we spent in Paris were like a kind of magic, something that's not quite real but that you believe because you aren't clever enough to see the illusion. Then it was time to come home."

She linked her hands together and began to fidget. He had come to recognize it as a sign of inner turmoil. Though the urge was there, he didn't take them in his to calm her. "The night before we were to leave, Tony went out. He said he had some business to tie up. I waited for him, feeling a little sorry for myself that my new husband would leave me alone on our last night in Paris. Then, as it got later and later, I stopped feeling sorry for myself and started feeling frightened. By the time he got back, it was after three and I was angry and upset."

She fell silent again. Gabe pulled the afghan from the back of the couch and spread it over her lap. "You had a fight."

"Yes. He was very drunk and belligerent. I'd never seen him like that before, but I was to see him like that again. I asked him where he'd been and he said—essentially he told me it was none of my business. We started shouting at each other, and he told me he'd been with another woman. At first I thought he said that just to hurt me, but then I saw that it was true. I started to cry."

That was the worst of it, Laura thought. Looking back on the way she'd crumbled and wept. "That only made him angrier. He tossed things around the suite, like a little boy having a tantrum. He said things, but the gist of it was that I'd have to get used to the way he lived, and that I hardly had a right to be upset when I'd been Geoffrey's whore."

Her voice broke on the last word, so she lifted the glass and cooled her throat with the water. "That hurt the most," she managed. "Geoffrey was almost like a father to me, never, never anything else. And Tony knew, he knew that I'd never been with anyone before our wedding night. I was so angry then, I stood up and began to shout at him. I don't even know what I said, but he went into a rage. And he—"

Gabe saw her fingers tighten like wires on the soft folds of the afghan. Then he saw how she deliberately, and with great care, relaxed them again. With an effort, he kept his voice calm. "Did he hit you, Laura?"

She didn't answer, couldn't seem to push the next words out. Then he touched a hand to her cheek and turned her face to his. Her eyes were brimming over.

"It was so much worse than with my uncle, because I couldn't get away. He was so much stronger and faster. With my uncle, he'd simply struck out at anyone who didn't get out of the way in time. With Tony, there was something viciously deliberate in the way he tried to hurt me. Then he—" But she couldn't bring herself to speak of what had happened next.

It was a moment before she went on, and Gabe sat in silence as the rage built and built inside him until he thought he'd explode. He understood temper, he had a hair-trigger one of his own, but he could never understand, never forgive, anyone who inflicted pain on someone smaller, weaker.

"When it was over," she continued, calmer now, "he just went to sleep. I lay there, not knowing what to do. It's funny, but later, when I talked with other women who had

had some of the same experiences, I found out that it's fairly common to believe you had it coming somehow.

"The next morning, he wept and he apologized, promised that it would never happen again. That became the pattern for the time we were together."

"You stayed with him?"

The color came and went in her face, and part of that, too, was shame. "We were married, and I thought I could make it work. Then we went back to his parents' home. They hated me right from the start. Their son, the heir to the throne, had gone behind their back and married a commoner. We lived with them, and though there was talk about getting our own house, nothing was ever done about it. You could sit at the same table, hold a conversation with them, and be totally ignored. They were amazing. Tony got worse. He began to see other women, almost flaunting them. They knew what he was doing, and they knew what was happening to me. The cycle got uglier and uglier, until I knew I had to get out. I told him I wanted a divorce.

"That seemed to snap him out of it for a while. He made promises, swore he'd go into therapy, see a marriage counselor, anything I wanted. We even began to look at houses. I have to admit that I'd stopped loving him by this time, and that it was wrong, very wrong, for me to stay with him, to make promises myself. What I didn't realize was that his parents were pulling on the other end. They held the financial strings and were making it difficult for him to move out. Then I discovered I was pregnant."

She laid a hand over her belly, her fingers spread. "Tony was, well, at best ambivalent about the idea of having a child. His parents were thrilled. His mother immediately started redecorating a nursery. She bought antique cribs and cradles, silver spoons, Irish linen. Though it made me nervous, the way she was taking over, I thought that the baby might be the way to help us come together. But they weren't looking at me as the baby's mother, any more than they'd looked at me as Tony's wife. It was *their* grandchild, *their* legacy, *their* immortality. We stopped looking for houses, and Tony began to drink again. I left the night he came home drunk and hit me."

She drew a careful breath and continued to stare at the fire. "It wasn't just me he was hitting now, but the child. That made all the difference. In fact, it made it incredibly easy to walk out. I called Geoffrey, buried my pride and asked for a loan. He wired me two thousand dollars. I got an apartment of my own, found a job and started divorce proceedings. Ten days later, Tony was dead."

The pain came, dull and low. Laura shut her eyes and rode it out. "His mother came to see me, begged me to bury the divorce papers, to come to the funeral as Tony's widow. His reputation, his memory, were all that was important now. I did what she asked, because—because I could still remember those first days in Paris. After the funeral I went back to their house. They'd told me there were things we needed to talk about. That was when they told me what they wanted, what they intended to have. They said they would pay all my medical expenses, that I would have the best possible care. And that after the baby was born they would give me a hundred thousand dollars to step aside. When I refused, when I had the nerve to be angry at what they were suggesting, they explained that if I didn't cooperate they would simply take the baby. Tony's baby. They made it very clear that they had enough money and influence to win a custody suit. They would bring out the 'fact' that I had been Geoffrey's mistress, that I had taken money from him. They'd checked my background and would show that due to my upbringing I would be an unstable influence on a child. That they, as the child's grandparents, could provide a better environment. They gave me twenty-four hours to think it over. And I ran."

He didn't speak for several minutes. What she had told him had left a bitter taste in his mouth. He had asked for her story, had all but demanded it. Now that he had it, he wasn't at all sure he could handle it.

"Laura, no matter what you were told, how you were threatened, I don't believe they could take the child."

"That isn't enough? Don't you see? As long as there's a chance, I can't risk it. I'd never be able to fight them on their terms. I don't have the money, the connections."

"Who are they?" When she hesitated, he took her hand again. "You've trusted me with this much."

"Their name is Eagleton," she said. "Thomas and Lorraine Eagleton of Boston."

His brows drew together. He knew the name. Who didn't? But because of his family's position, it was more than a name, more than an image. "You were married to Anthony Eagleton?"

"Yes." She turned to him then. "You knew him, didn't you?"

"Not well. Barely. He was more—" More Michael's age, he'd started to say. "He was younger. I met him once or twice when he came to the Coast." And what he had seen hadn't impressed him enough to have him form any opinion. "I read that he had been killed in a car accident, and I suppose a wife was mentioned, but this past year has been a little difficult, and I didn't pay attention. My family has socialized with the Eagletons occasionally, but they aren't well acquainted."

"Then you know they're an old, well-established family with old, well-established money. They consider this child a part of their... holdings. They've had me followed all across the country. Every time I would settle in a place and begin to relax I'd discover that detectives were making inquiries about me. I can't—I won't—let them find me."

He rose, to pace, to light a cigarette, to try to organize his thoughts and, more, his feelings. "I'd like to ask you something."

She sighed tiredly. "All right."

"Once before, when I asked you if you were afraid, you said no, that you were ashamed. I want to know why."

"I didn't fight back, and I didn't try hard enough to fix what was wrong. I just let it happen to me. You have no idea how difficult it is to sit here and admit that I let myself be used, that I let myself be beaten, that I let myself be driven down so low that I accepted it all."

"Do you still feel that way?"

"No." Her chin lifted. "No one's ever going to take control of my life again."

"Good." He sat on the hearth. The smoke from his cigarette disappeared up the draft. "I think you've had a hell of a time, angel, worse than anyone deserves. Whether you brought some of it on yourself, as you choose to think, or if it was just a matter of circumstances, doesn't really matter at this point. It's over."

"It's not as easy as that, Gabe. I don't just have myself to worry about now."

"How far are you willing to go to fight them?"

"I've told you I can't—"

He interrupted her with a wave of his hand. "If you had the means. How far?"

"All the way. As far and as long as it takes. But that isn't the point, because I don't have the means."

He drew on his cigarette, studied it with apparent interest, then tossed it into the fire. "You would, if you were married to me."

Chapter Five

She said nothing, could say nothing. He sat on the hearth, his legs folded up, his eyes very cool, very calm, on her face. Part of the enormity of his talent was his ability to focus on an expression and draw the underlying emotions out of it. Perhaps because he did it so well, he also knew how to mask emotions when they were his own.

She could hear the logs sizzling behind him. The mid-morning sunlight sparkled through the frost on the win-dowpanes and landed at his feet. He seemed totally at ease, as though he'd just suggested that they have soup for lunch. If her life had depended upon it, Laura couldn't have said whether it meant any more to him than that.

Using the table for leverage, she rose.

"I'm tired. I'm going in to lie down."

"All right. We can talk about this later."

She whirled around, and it wasn't anguish or fear he saw on her face now, it was fury, livid and clear. "How could you sit there and say something like that to me after every-thing I've told you?"

"You might consider that I said it because of everything you've told me."

"Oh, the Good Samaritan again." She detested the bit-terness in her voice, but she could do nothing to stop it. "The white knight, riding in full of chivalry and good in-tentions to save the bumbling, inept female. Do you think I should fall on my knees and be grateful? That I would blindly let myself be taken over again, fall back into the same pitiful, destructive pattern a second time, because a man offers me a way out?"

He thought about controlling his temper, then rose, deciding to let her see it. "I have no desire to control you, and I'll be damned if you're going to stand there and compare me with some weak-minded alcoholic wife-beater."

"What then—the knight on a white charger, selflessly rescuing damsels in distress?"

He laughed at that, but his anger was still on the edge. "No one's ever accused me of that. I'm very selfish, which is another reason for my suggestion. I'm moody—you've been around me long enough to know that. I have a temper and I can get angry. But I don't hit women, and I don't use them."

With an effort, she pulled her emotions back in and forced them to settle. "I didn't mean to imply that you did, or to compare you with someone else. It's the situation that's comparable."

"One has nothing to do with the other. The fact that I have money only works to your advantage."

"I didn't marry Tony for his money."

"No." His tone softened. "No, I'm sure you didn't. But in this case I'm willing to accept that you marry me for mine."

"Why?"

Something flickered in his eyes and was gone before she could read it. "That might have been the wisest question to ask first."

"Maybe you're right." She already regretted the outburst of temper and harsh words, as she invariably did. "I'm asking it now."

With a nod, he roamed the room, stopping before the nearly completed portrait. He stared at it, as he had stared at it countless times before, trying to understand, to define, not only Laura, but himself.

"I feel something for you. I'm not sure what it is, but it's very strong. Stronger than anything I've felt before." He lifted a finger to the face on canvas. He wished he could explain himself completely, to himself, to her, but he'd always expressed himself best through painting. "I'm attracted to you, Laura, and I've discovered recently that I've been alone long enough."

"That might be enough, almost enough, for marriage, but not for me, not to me. Not with what you'd be taking on."

"I have some debts to pay," he murmured, then turned to her again. "Helping you, and the child, might just clear the slate."

Whatever anger she'd felt evaporated. It only took the kindness and the grief in his eyes. "You've already helped us, more than I can ever repay."

"I don't want payment." The impatience, the edge, was back in his voice. "What I want is you. How many ways do you want me to say it?"

"I don't think I want you to say it." The nerves began to eat at her again, and she twisted her fingers together. He meant it. She had no doubt that he meant what he said. The prospect of being wanted by him both thrilled and terrified her. "Don't you see, I've already made one terrible mistake."

He crossed to her, gently drawing her hands apart and into his. "You're not indifferent to me?"

"No, but—"

"You're not afraid of me?"

Some of the tension seeped out of her. "No."

"Then let me help you."

"I'm going to have another man's child."

"No." He took her face in his hands because he wanted her eyes on his. "Marry me, and the child is ours. Privately, publicly, totally."

The tears came back. "They'll come."

"Let them. They won't touch you again, and they won't take the baby."

Safety. Could what had always eluded her really be only a promise away? She opened her mouth, knowing that agreement was on her tongue. Then her heart turned over in her chest and she lifted a hand to his cheek. "How could I do this to you?"

For an answer, he put his lips to hers. The need was there, she couldn't deny it, couldn't pretend it away. She tasted it as his mouth drew from hers. She felt it when his hand skimmed through her hair to brace, both possessive and supportive, at the back of her neck. Instinctively, wanting to give, she lifted her other hand to his face. They rested there, comforting.

She wasn't the only one who had demons, Laura thought. She wasn't the only one who needed love and understanding. Because he was strong, it was easy to forget that he, too, might have pain. Seeking to soothe, she drew him closer into her arms.

He could have sunk into her, into the softness, the generosity. This was what he wanted to capture on canvas, her warmth, her spirit. And this was what he was forced to admit he would never have the skill to translate. This part of her beauty, this most essential part, could never be painted. But it could be cherished.

"You need me," he murmured as he drew her away. "And I need you."

She nodded, then rested her head on his shoulder, because that seemed to say it all.

Due to fresh flurries, it was three days before Gabe risked a trip into town. Laura watched him as he downed a final cup of coffee before pulling on his coat.

"I'll be as quick as I can."

"I'd rather you took your time and paid attention to the roads."

"The Jeep drives like a tank." He accepted the gloves she held out to him but didn't put them on. "I don't like leaving you alone."

"Gabe, I've been taking care of myself for a long time."

"Things have changed. My lawyers have probably sent the marriage license."

Immediately she began to fuss with the breakfast dishes. "That would be quick work."

"They get paid to work fast, and it's been three days since I contacted them. If I can arrange it, I'd like to bring a justice of the peace back here with me."

A cup slipped out of her hand and plopped into the soapy water. "Today?"

"You haven't changed your mind?"

"No, but—"

"I want my name on the birth certificate." He had a moment of panic, vague and disturbing, at her hesitation. "It would be less complicated if we were married before the baby's born."

"Yes, that makes sense." It seemed so rushed. She plunged her hands into the water and began to wash. Her first wedding had been rushed, too, a whirlwind of flowers and champagne and white silk.

"I realize you might prefer something a little more festive, but under the circumstances—"

"No." She turned and managed a smile. "No, I don't care about that. If you can arrange it for today, here, that's fine."

"All right, then. Laura, I'd feel better if you rested until I got back. You didn't sleep well."

She turned back again. No, she hadn't slept well. The nightmare had come back, and she hadn't rested until Gabe had come in and finally slipped into bed with her. "I won't overdo."

"I don't think it would tax your strength for you to kiss me goodbye."

That made her smile. She turned, her hands still dripping, to lift her lips to his.

"Not even married yet and you're already kissing me as though we've been together twenty years." He changed the mood simply by nipping her lip. In seconds she was clinging to him, and there was nothing casual about the embrace.

"Better," he murmured. "Now go lie down. I'll be back in less than two hours."

"Be careful."

He closed the door. In moments she heard the sound of the Jeep's engine chugging to life. Moving into the living room, she watched Gabe drive away.

Strangely enough, even as the quiet settled over the cabin, she didn't feel alone. She felt nervous, she admitted with a little laugh. Brides were entitled to nerves. If Gabe had his way—and she'd come to believe that he nearly always did—they would be married that afternoon.

And her life, Laura realized, would change yet again.

This time it would be better. She would make it better.

As the ache in her lower back grew worse, she pressed her hand against it. Blaming the discomfort she'd been feeling all morning on the mattress and a restless night, she walked over to the portrait.

He'd finished it the day before. She knew, because he'd explained it to her, that the paint would take a few days to set and dry completely, so she didn't touch it. She sat on the stool Gabe sometimes used and studied her own face.

So this was how he saw her, she thought. Her skin was pale, with only a faint shadow of color along her cheekbones. It was partly that whiteness, that translucence, that made her appear like the angel he sometimes called her. She looked as though she were caught in a daydream, one of the many she'd indulged in during the hours Gabe had painted. As she had told him—as she had complained—there was too much vulnerability. It was in her eyes, around her mouth. There was something strong and independent about the pose, about the way her head was tilted, but that lost, sad look in her eyes seemed to negate the strength.

She was reading too much into it, Laura decided as the pain dug, deep and dull, into her back. Rubbing at it, she rose to look around the cabin.

She would be married here, in a matter of hours. There would be no crowd of well-wishers, no pianist playing romantic songs, no trail of rose petals. Yet, with or without the trimmings, she would be a bride. She might not be able to make it look festive, but at least she could tidy up.

The pain in her back drove her to lie down. Two hours later she heard the Jeep coming down the lane. For a moment longer she lay there, working to block out the discomfort. Later, she told herself, she would soak the ache away in a hot tub. She walked into the living room just as Gabe ushered an elderly couple into the cabin.

"Laura, this is Mr. and Mrs. Witherby. Mr. Witherby is a justice of the peace."

"Hello. It's so nice of you to come all this way."

"Part of the job," Mr. Witherby said, adjusting his fogging glasses. "'Sides that, your young man here wasn't going to take no for an answer."

"Don't you worry about this old man here." Mrs. Witherby patted her husband's arm and studied Laura. "He loves to complain."

"Can I get you something, some coffee?"

"Don't you fuss. Mr. Bradley's got a carload of supplies. You just sit down and let him take care of it." She had already walked over to lead Laura to the couch with her frail hands. "Man's nervous as a goose at Christmas," she confided. "Let him keep busy for a spell."

Though she couldn't imagine Gabe being nervous about anything, she thought the Witherbys would expect such emotion from a man about to marry. Laura listened to Gabe rattling bags and cans in the kitchen. "Maybe I should help him."

"Now, you sit right here." Mrs. Witherby motioned to her husband to sit, as well. "A woman's entitled to be waited on when she's carrying. The good Lord knows you won't have much time to sit once that baby's born."

Grateful, Laura shifted to ease the throbbing in her back. "You have children?"

"Had six of them. Now we've got twenty-two grandchildren and five great-grandchildren."

"And another on the way," Mr. Witherby stated, pulling out a pipe.

"You can just put that smelly thing away," his wife told him. "You aren't smoking up this room with this lady expecting."

"I wasn't going to light it," he said, and began to chew on the stem.

Satisfied that her husband had been put in his place, Mrs. Witherby turned back to Laura. "That's a pretty picture there." She indicated a sprawling landscape that might very well sell for an amount in six figures. "Your man's an artist fellow?"

Her man. Laura experienced a twinge of panic and a glow of pleasure at the phrase. "Yes, Gabe's an artist."

"I like pictures," she said comfortably. "Got me one of the seashore over my sofa."

Gabe walked back in carrying an armful of flowers. Feeling awkward, he cleared his throat. "They sold them at the market."

"And he bought them out, too," Mrs. Witherby cackled. Then, with a few wheezes, she heaved herself off the couch. "You got a vase? She can't be carrying all of them."

"No, at least . . . I don't know."

"Men." She sighed and then winked at Laura. "Give them to me and let me take care of it. You can do something useful, like putting more wood on that fire. Wouldn't want your lady to catch a chill."

"Yes, ma'am."

If he'd ever felt more of a fool, he couldn't remember when. Wanting to keep his hands busy, he moved to the fire.

"Don't let her browbeat you, boy," Mr. Witherby advised him from the comfort of his chair. "She's already spent fifty-two years nagging me."

"Somebody had to," Mrs. Witherby called out from the kitchen, and he chuckled.

"Sure you two know what you're getting into?"

Gabe dusted his hands on the thighs of his jeans and grinned. "No."

"That's the spirit." Witherby laughed and rested his head against the back of the chair. "Essie, get that bag of bones you call a body moving, will you? These two people want to get married while they're still young."

"Keep your tongue in your mouth," she muttered. "Already lost his teeth." She came in carrying a watering can filled with flowers. She set it in the middle of the coffee table, nodded her approval, then handed Laura a single white carnation.

"Thank you. They're lovely." She started to rise and nearly winced at the stab of pain in her back. Then Gabe was there to take her hand and draw her to his side.

They stood in front of the fire with wood crackling and the scent of the flowers merging with that of the smoke. The words were simple and very old. Despite the countless weddings she'd been to, Mrs. Witherby dabbed at her eyes.

To love. To honor. To cherish.

For richer. For poorer.

Forsaking all others.

The ring he slipped onto her finger was very plain, just a gold band that was a size too large. Looking at it, Laura felt something grow inside her. It was warm and sweet and tremulous. Curling her hand into his, she repeated the words, and meant them, from her heart.

Let no man put asunder.

"You may kiss the bride," Witherby told him, but Gabe didn't hear.

It was done. It was irrevocable. And until that moment he hadn't been completely aware of how much it would mean to him.

With her hand still caught in his, he kissed her and sealed the promise.

"Congratulations." Mrs. Witherby brushed her dry lips over Gabe's cheek, then Laura's. "Now you sit down, Mrs. Bradley, and I'm going to fix you a nice cup of tea before we drag your husband off again."

"Thank you, but we don't have any tea."

"I bought some," Gabe put in.

"That and everything else he could lay his hands on. Come on, Ethan, give me a hand."

"You ought to be able to fix a cup of tea by yourself."

Mrs. Witherby rolled her eyes. "You'd think the old goat would have a little more romance, seeing as he's married more'n five hundred couples in his time. In the kitchen, Ethan, and give these young people five minutes alone."

He grumbled about wanting his supper, but he followed her.

"They're wonderful," Laura murmured.

"I don't think I'd have gotten him away from his TV if she hadn't shoved him out the door."

Silence followed, awkward. "It was nice of you to think of flowers . . . and the ring."

He lifted her hand and studied it. "They don't have a jewelry store in Lonesome Ridge. They sell these at the hardware in a little case next to sixpenny nails. It may just turn your finger green."

She laughed and knew she'd treasure it even more now. "You may not believe it, but you may have saved my life by buying that tea."

"I got some marshmallows, too."

She hated it, despised herself for not being able to control it, but she started to cry. "I'm sorry. I can't seem to do anything about this."

Discomfort surged through him. He was feeling edgy himself, and tears did nothing to help matters. "Look, I know it wasn't exactly the wedding of the century. We can have some sort of party or reception back in San Francisco."

"No, no, that's not it." Though she urged her hands over her face, the tears kept coming. "It was lovely and sweet and I don't know how to thank you."

"Not crying would be a good start." He had a bandanna in his pocket, one that he used more often than not as a paint rag. He drew it out and offered it to her. "Laura, we're legally married. That means you don't have to be grateful for every bunch of daisies I hand you."

She sniffled into the cloth and tried to smile. "I think it was the marshmallows that did it."

"Keep this up and you won't get any more."

"I want you to know . . ." She dried her face and managed to compose herself. "I want you to know that I'm going to do everything I can to make you happy, to make you comfortable, so that you never regret what you did today."

"I'm going to regret it," he said suddenly impatient, "if you keep making it sound as though I gave someone else the last life jacket as the ship was sinking. I married you because I wanted to, not to be noble.''

''Yes, but I—''

''Shut up, Laura.'' To make certain she did, he closed his mouth over hers. And for the first time she felt the true strength of his passion and need and desire. With a little murmur of surprise, she drew him closer.

This was what he had needed, all he had needed, to settle him. Yet even as the first layer of tension dissolved, a new layer, one built on desire, formed.

''Before too much longer,'' he said against her mouth, ''we're going to finish this. I want to make love with you, Laura. And after I do you won't have the strength to thank me.''

Before she could think of a response, Mrs. Witherby came in with her tea. ''Now let the poor thing rest and drink this while it's hot.'' She set the cup on the table in front of Laura. ''I hate to drag you out on your wedding day, Mr. Bradley, but the sooner you drive us back to town, the sooner you can get back and fix your wife that nice steak you bought for supper.''

She moved over to gather up her coat. On impulse, Laura drew one of the flowers from the watering can and took it to her. ''I'm never going to forget you, Mrs. Witherby.''

''There now.'' Touched, she sniffed at the flower. ''You just take care of yourself and that baby of yours. Shake a leg, Ethan.''

''I should only be an hour,'' Gabe told her. ''The roads aren't too bad. I really think you should rest, Laura. You look exhausted.''

''I'm supposed to look glowing, but I promise I won't lift anything heavier than a teacup until you get back.''

This time she watched the Jeep drive away, running her finger over and over her wedding ring. It took so little, she thought, to change so much. She bent, trying to ease the ache in her back, then she crossed the room to finish her tea.

Her back had never ached like this, not even after she'd worked a full day on her aunt's farm. The pain was constant and deep. She tried stretching out, then curling up, then stretching out again. Impatient with herself, she tried to ignore it, concentrating instead on roasting marshmallows and warming tea.

She'd been alone less than ten minutes when the first contraction hit.

It wasn't the vague warning pain she'd read about. It was sharp and long. Caught off guard, she had no time to breathe her way over it. Instead, she tensed, fought against it, then collapsed against the cushions when it faded.

It couldn't be labor. Her forehead broke out in sweat as she tried to dismiss the idea. It was too early, a month too early, and it had come on so suddenly. False labor, she assured herself. Brought on by nerves and by the excitement of the day.

But the back pain. Struggling to keep calm, she pushed herself into a sitting position. Was it possible she'd been having back labor all morning?

No, it had to be false labor. It had to be.

But when the second contraction hit she began to time them.

She was in bed when Gabe returned, but she couldn't call out to him, because she was riding out the latest contraction. The fear that had gripped her in a stranglehold for the past hour faded a bit. He was here, and somehow that meant that everything would be all right. She heard him toss a log on the fire, took a last cleansing breath as the pain passed and called out.

The urgency in her voice had him across the room in three strides. At the bedroom door he paused, and his heart jumped into his throat.

She was propped against the pillows, half lying, half sitting. Her face was bathed in sweat. Her eyes, always dark, were sheened with moisture and nearly black.

"I have to go back on our deal," she managed, struggling with a smile because she saw the same blank fear she felt reflected on his face. "The baby's decided to come a little early."

He didn't ask if she was sure or fumble with reasons why it wasn't a good idea. He wanted to, but he found himself beside the bed, with her hand gripped in his. "Take it easy. Just hold on and I'll phone for a doctor."

"Gabe, the phone's out." Nerves skipped in and out of her voice. "I tried it when I realized this was happening so fast."

"Okay." Fighting for calm, he brushed the damp hair away from her face. "There was an accident on the way into town. Lines must have gone down. I'll get some extra blankets and I'll take you in."

She pressed her lips together. "Gabe, it's too late. I couldn't make the trip." She tried to swallow, but fear had dried up the moisture in her mouth and throat. "I've been in labor for hours, all morning, and I didn't know it. It was back labor, and I didn't pay attention. With everything that was going on, I thought it was nerves and the restless night I'd had."

"Hours," he murmured, and eased himself down on the edge of the bed. His mind went blank, but then her fingers tightened on his. "How far apart are the pains?"

"Five minutes. I've been—" She let her head fall back and began to breathe in short, deep gasps. Gabe slipped his hand over her and felt the hardening of her abdomen.

He'd glanced through the birth and baby books she'd brought with her. To pass the time, he'd told himself, but there had been something deep inside him that had been compelled to understand what she was going through. Perhaps it was instinct that had had him absorbing the advice, the details, the instructions. Now, seeing her in pain, everything he'd read seemed to slip away from him.

When the contraction passed, her face was shiny with fresh sweat. "Getting closer," she whispered. "There's not much time." Though she bit down on her lips, a sob escaped her. "I can't lose the baby."

"The baby's going to be fine, and so are you." He squeezed her hand once reassuringly. They would need towels, lots of them. String and scissors had to be sterilized. It was really very simple when you thought about it. He only hoped it was as simple when you put it into practice.

"Just hang on. I have to get some things." He saw the doubt flash in her eyes, and he leaned over her. "I'm not going to leave you. I'm going to take care of you, Laura. Trust me."

She nodded, and with her head slumped back on the pillow, she closed her eyes.

When he came back, her eyes were focused on the ceiling and she was panting. After setting fresh towels on the foot of the bed, he spread another blanket over her. "Are you cold?"

She shook her head. "The baby will need to be kept warm. He's not full-term."

"I've built up the fire, and there are plenty of blankets." Gently he wiped her face with a cool, damp cloth. "You've talked to doctors, you've read the books. You know what to expect."

She looked up at him, trying to swallow past a dry throat. Yes, she knew what to expect, but reading about it, imagining it, was a far cry from the experience.

"They lied." Her mouth moved into a weak smile when his brows drew together. "They try to tell you it doesn't hurt so much if you ride out the pain."

He brought her hand to his lips and held it there. "Yell all you want. Scream the roof down. Nobody's going to hear."

"I'm not screaming this baby into the world." Then she gasped, and her fingers dug into his. "I can't—"

"Yes, you can. Pant. Pant, Laura. Squeeze my hand. Harder. Concentrate on that." He kept his eyes locked on hers while she pushed air out. "You're doing fine, better than fine." When her body went lax, he moved to the foot of the bed. "The pains are closer?" As he spoke, he knelt on the mattress and shifted the blanket.

"Almost on top of each other."

"That means it's almost over. Hold on to that."

She tried to moisten her dry lips, but her tongue was thick. "If anything happens to me, promise you'll—"

"Nothing's going to happen." He bit off the words. Their eyes met again, hers glazed with pain, his dark with purpose. "Damn it, I'm not going to lose either of you now, understand? The three of us are going to pull this off. Now, you've got work to do, angel."

Each time the pains hit her, he shuddered with it. Time seemed to drag as she struggled through them, then race again as she rested. Gabe moved back and forth, to arrange her pillows, to wipe her face, then knelt again to check the progress of birth.

He could hear the fire roaring in the next room, but he still worried that the cabin would be too cold. Then he worried about the heat, because Laura's laboring body was like a furnace.

He hadn't known birth could be so hard on a woman. He knew she was close to total exhaustion, but she managed to pull herself through time after time, recharging somehow during the all-too-brief moments between contractions. Pain seemed to tear through her, impossibly hard, impossibly ruthless. His own shirt was soaked with sweat, and he swore constantly, silently, as he urged her to breathe, to pant, to concentrate. All his ambitions, his joys, his griefs, whittled down to focus on that one room, that one moment, that one woman.

It seemed to him that she should weaken, with her body being battered by the new life fighting to be born. But as the moments passed she seemed to draw on new reserves of strength. There was something fierce and valiant about her face as she pushed herself forward and braced for whatever happened next.

"Do you have a name picked out?" he asked, hoping to distract her.

"I made lists. Sometimes at night I'd try to imagine what the baby would look like and try to— Oh, God."

"Hold on. Breathe, angel. Breathe through it."

"I can't. I have to push."

"Not yet, not yet. Soon." From his position at the foot of the bed, he ran his hands over her. "Pant, Laura."

Her concentration kept slipping in and out. If she stared into his eyes, if she pulled the strength from them, she would make it. "I can't hold off much longer."

"You don't have to. I can see the head." There was wonder in his voice when he looked back at her. "I can see it. Push with the next one."

Giddy, straining with the effort, she bore down. She heard the long, deep-throated moan, but she didn't know it was her own voice. Gabe shouted at her, and in response she automatically began to pant again.

"That's good, that's wonderful." He barely recognized his own voice, or his own hands. Both were shaking. "I have the head. Your baby's beautiful. The shoulders come next."

She braced herself, desperate to see. "Oh, God." Tears mixed with sweat as she steepled her hands over her mouth. "It's so little."

"And strong as an ox. You have to push the shoulders out." Sweat dripped off his forehead as he cupped the baby's head in his hand and leaned over it. "Come on, Laura, let's have a look at the rest of it."

Her fingers dug into the blankets, and her head fell back. And she gave birth. Over her own gasping breaths she heard the first cry.

"A boy." Gabe's eyes were wet as he held the squirming new life in his hands. "You have a son."

As the tears rolled, she began to laugh. The pain and the terror were forgotten. "A boy. A little boy."

"With a loud mouth, ten fingers and ten toes." He reached for her hand and gripped it hard. "He's perfect, angel."

Their fingers linked over the baby, and the cabin echoed with the high, indignant wails of the newborn.

She couldn't rest. Laura knew Gabe wanted her to sleep, but she couldn't shut her eyes. The baby, nearly an hour old now, was wrapped in blankets and tucked in the curve of her arm. He was sleeping, she thought, but she couldn't stop herself from tracing a fingertip over his face.

So tiny. Five pounds, seven ounces, on the vegetable scale that Gabe had unearthed and scrubbed down. Seventeen and a half inches tall, and with only a bit of pale blond peach fuzz covering his head. She couldn't stop looking at him.

"He's not going to disappear, you know."

Laura glanced up at the doorway and smiled. Fatigue had left her skin almost pale enough to see through. Triumph had given her eyes a rich glow. "I know." She held out a hand in invitation. "I'm glad you came in," she said as he sat on the bed. "I know you must be exhausted, but I'd like you to stay a minute."

"You did all the work," he murmured, running a finger down the baby's cheek.

"That's not true, and that's the first thing I want to say. We wouldn't have made it without you."

"Of course you would have. I was basically a cheerleader."

"No." Her hand tightened on his, demanding that he look at her. "You were as responsible for his life as I was. I know what you said about having your name on the birth certificate, about helping us, but I want you to know it's more than that. You brought him into the world. There's nothing I can ever do or say that could be enough. Don't look like that." She gave a quiet laugh and settled back among the pillows. "I know you hate to be thanked, and that's not what I'm doing."

"Isn't it?"

"No." She shifted the baby from her arm to his. It was a gesture that said more, much more, than the words that followed it. "I'm telling you that you got more than a wife today."

The baby went on sleeping peacefully, cupped between them.

He didn't know what to say. He touched the tiny hand and watched it curl reflexively. As an artist he'd thought he understood the full range of beauty. Until today.

"I've been reading about preemies," he began. "His weight is good, and from what the book says a baby born after the thirty-fourth week is in pretty good shape, but I want to get you both into a hospital. Will you be strong enough to travel into Colorado Springs tomorrow?''

"Yes. We'll both be strong enough."

"We'll leave in the morning, then. Do you think you could eat now?"

"Only a horse."

He grinned, but he couldn't quite bring himself to give her back the baby. "You may have to settle for beefsteak. Isn't he hungry?"

"I imagine he'll let us know."

Just as Laura had been, he was compelled to trace the shape of the child's face. "What about that name? We can't keep calling him *he*."

"No, we can't." Laura stroked the soft down on his head. "I was wondering if you'd like to pick his name."

"Me?"

"Yes, you must have a favorite, or a name of someone who's important to you. I'd like you to choose."

"Michael," he murmured, looking down at the sleeping infant.

Chapter Six

San Francisco. It was true that Laura had always wanted to see it, but she had never expected to arrive there with a two-week-old son and a husband. And she had never expected to be shown into a tall, gracious house near the Bay.

Gabe's house. Hers, too, she thought as she rubbed her thumb nervously over her wedding ring. It was foolish to be jumpy because the house was beautiful and big. It was ridiculous to feel small and insecure because you could taste the wealth and the prominence just by breathing the air.

But she did.

She stepped into the tiled foyer and wished desperately for the comfort of the tiny cabin. It had begun to snow again the day they'd left Colorado, and though the mild spring breeze and the tiny buds here were wonderful, she found herself wishing for the cold and ferocity of the mountains.

"It's lovely," she managed, glancing up at the gentle curve of the stairs.

"It was my grandmother's." Gabe set down the luggage and took in the familiar surroundings. It was a house he'd always appreciated for its beauty and its balance. "She held on to it after her marriage. Shall I show you around, or would you rather rest?"

She nearly winced. It was as though he were talking to a guest. "If I rested as much as you'd like, I'd sleep my way through the rest of the year."

"Then why don't I show you the upstairs." He knew he sounded polite, overly polite, but he'd been edgy ever since they'd stepped off the plane. The farther away from Colorado they'd gotten, the farther Laura had withdrawn from him. It was nothing he could put his finger on, but it was there.

Hefting two cases, he started up the stairs. He was bringing his wife, and his son, home. And he didn't know quite what to say to either of them. "I've used this bedroom." He strode in and set the cases at the foot of a big oak bed. "If there's another you'd prefer, we can arrange it."

She nodded, thinking that though they'd shared a motel room while the baby had been in the hospital they had only shared a bed in the cabin, the night before Michael had been born. It would be different here. Everything would be different here.

"It's a beautiful room."

Her voice was a little stiff, but she smiled, trying to soften it. The room was lovely, with its high ceilings and the glossy antiques. There was a terrace, and through the glass doors she could see a garden below, with green leaves already formed. The floors were dark with age and gleaming, just as the Oriental rug was faded with age and rich with heritage.

"The bath's through there," Gabe told her as she ran a finger down the carving in an old chifforobe. "My studio's at the end of the hall. The light's best there, but there's a room next to this that might do as a nursery."

When they spoke of the baby, things always relaxed between them. "I'd love to see it. After all those days in the incubator, Michael deserves a room of his own."

She followed Gabe out and into the next room. It was decorated in blues and grays with a stately four-poster and a many-cushioned window seat. As with the other rooms she'd seen, paintings hung on the wall, some of them Gabe's, others by artists he respected.

"It's beautiful, but what would you do with all these things?"

"They can be stored." He dismissed the furnishings with a shrug. "Michael can stay in our room until his is finished."

"You don't mind? He's bound to wake during the night for weeks yet."

"I could stick the pair of you in a hotel until it's convenient."

She started to speak, but then she recognized the look in his eyes. "Sorry. I can't get used to it."

"Get used to it." He moved over to cup her face in his hand. Whenever he did that, she was almost ready to believe that dreams came true. "I may not have the equipment to feed him, but I figure I can learn to change a diaper." He stroked a thumb under her jawline. "I've been told I'm clever with my hands."

The heat rushed into her face. She was torn between stepping into his arms and backing away. The baby woke and decided her. "Speaking of feeding..."

"Why don't you use the bedroom, where you can be comfortable? I have some calls to make."

She knew what was coming. "Your family?"

"They're going to want to meet you. Are you up to it this evening?"

She wanted to snap that she wasn't an invalid, but she knew he wasn't speaking of her physical health. "Yes, of course."

"Fine. I'll make arrangements about the nursery. Did you have any colors in mind?"

"Well, I..." She expected to paint the room herself. She'd wanted to. Things were different now, she reminded herself. The cabin had easily become theirs, but the house was his. "I'd like yellow," she told him. "With white trim."

She sat in a chair by the window while Michael suckled hungrily. It was so good to have him with her all the time instead of having to go to the hospital to feed him, touch him, watch him. It had been so hard to leave him there and go back to a hotel room and wait until she could go back and see him again.

Smiling, she looked down at him. His eyes were closed, and his hand was pressed against her breast.

He was already gaining weight. Healthy, the doctor in Colorado Springs had said. Sound as a dollar. And the tag on his little wristband had read Michael Monroe Bradley.

Who was Michael? she wondered. Gabe's Michael. She hadn't asked, but knew that the name, the person, was important.

"You're Michael now," she murmured as the baby began to doze at her breast.

Later she laid him on the bed, surrounding him with pillows though she knew he couldn't roll yet. Going to her suitcase, she took out her hairbrush. It was silly, of course, to feel compelled to leave some mark of herself on the room. But she set the brush on Gabe's bureau before she left.

She found him downstairs, in a dark-paneled library with soft gray carpet. Because he was on the phone, she started to back out, but he waved her in and continued to talk.

"The paintings should be here by the end of the week. Yes, I'm back in harness again. I haven't decided. You take a look first. No, I'm going to be tied up here for a few days, thanks anyway. I'll let you know." He hung up, then glanced at Laura. "Michael?"

"He's asleep. I know there hasn't been time, but he's going to need his own bed. I thought I could run out and buy something if you could watch him for a little while."

"Don't worry about it. My parents are coming over soon."

"Oh."

He sat on the edge of the desk and frowned at her. "They're not monsters, Laura."

"Of course not, it's just that . . . It seems we're so out in the open," she blurted out. "The more people who know about Michael, the more dangerous it is."

"You can't keep him in a glass bubble. I thought you trusted me."

"I did. I do," she amended quickly, but not quickly enough.

"Did," Gabe repeated. It wasn't anger he felt so much as pressing regret. "You made a decision, Laura. On the day he was born, you gave him to me. Are you taking him back?"

"No. But things are different here. The cabin was—"

"An excellent place to hide. For both of us. Now it's time to deal with what happens next."

"What does happen?"

He picked up a paperweight, an amber ball with darker gold streaks in the center. He set it down again, then crossed to her. She'd shed weight quickly. Her stomach was close to flat, her breasts were high and full, her hips were impossibly narrow. He wondered how it would feel to hold her now, now that the waiting was over.

"We might start with this."

He kissed her, gently at first, until he felt her first nerves fade into warmth. That was what he'd been desperate for, that promise, that comfort. When he gathered her close, she fitted against him as he'd once imagined she would. Her hair, bound up, was easily set free with a sweep of his hand. She made a small sound—a murmur of surprise or acceptance—and then her arms went around him.

And the kiss was no longer gentle.

Passion, barely restrained, and hunger, far from sated, rippled from him into her. An ache, long buried, grew in her until she was straining against him, whispering his name.

Then his lips were roaming over her face, raking over her throat, searing her skin, then cooling it, then searing it again, while his hands stroked and explored with a new freedom.

Too soon. Some sane part of him knew it was too soon for anything more than a touch, a taste. But the more he indulged in her, the more his impatience grew. Taking her by the shoulders, he drew her away and fought to catch his breath.

"You may not trust me as you once did, angel, but trust this. I want you."

Giving in to the need, she held on to him, pressing her face into his shoulder. "Gabe, is it so wrong of me to wish it was just the three of us?"

"Not wrong." He stared over the top of her head as he stroked her hair. "Just not possible, and less than fair to Michael."

"You're right." Drawing a breath, she stepped back. "I want to go check on him."

Shaken by the emotions he pulled out of her, she started back up the stairs. Halfway up, she stopped, stunned.

She was in love with him. It wasn't the love she'd come to accept, the kind that came from gratitude and dependence. It wasn't even the strong, beautiful bond that had been forged when they'd brought Michael into the world. It was more basic than that, the most elemental love of woman for man. And it was terrifying.

She had loved once before, briefly, painfully. That love had kept her chained down. All her life she'd been a victim, and her marriage had both accented that and ultimately freed her. She'd learned through necessity how to be strong, how to take the right steps.

She couldn't be that woman again, she thought as her fingers gripped the banister. She wouldn't. That was what had bothered her most about the house, about the things in it. She had stepped into a house like this before, a house in which she had been out of place and continually helpless.

Not again, she told herself, and shut her eyes. Never again.

Whatever she felt for Gabe, she wouldn't allow it to change her back into that kind of woman. She had a child to protect.

The doorbell rang. Laura sent one swift look over her shoulder, then fled up the stairs.

When Gabe opened the door, he was immediately enveloped in soft fur and strong perfume. It was his mother, a woman of unwavering beauty and unwavering opinions. She didn't believe in brushing cheeks, she believed in squeezing, hard and long.

"I've missed you. I didn't know what it would take to drag you off that mountain, but I didn't think it would be a wife and a baby."

"Hello, Mother." He smiled at her, giving her a quick sweeping look that took in her stubbornly blond hair and her smooth cheeks. She had Michael's eyes. They were a darker green than his own, with touches of gray. Seeing them brought a pang and a pleasure. "You look wonderful."

"So do you, except for the fact that you've lost about ten pounds and can't afford to. Well, where are they?" With that, Amanda Bradley marched inside.

"Give the boy a chance, Mandy." Gabe exchanged bear hugs with his father, a tall, spare man with a hangdog expression and a razor-sharp mind. "Glad you're back. Now she'll take to rattling your cage instead of mine."

"I can handle you both." She was already slipping off her gloves with short, quick little motions. "We brought a bottle of champagne over. I thought since we missed the wedding, the birth and everything else, we should at least toast the homecoming. For heaven's sake, Gabe, don't just stand there, I'm dying to see them."

"Laura went up to check the baby. Why don't we go in and sit down?"

"This way, Mandy," Cliff Bradley said, taking his wife's arm when she started to object.

"Very well, then. You can hold me off for five minutes by telling me how your work's been going."

"Well." He watched his parents sit but couldn't relax enough to follow suit. "I've already called Marion. The paintings I finished in Colorado should be delivered to her gallery by the end of the week."

"That's wonderful. I can't wait to see them."

His hands were in his pockets as he moved around the room with a restlessness both of his parents recognized. "There's one piece in particular I'm fond of. I plan to hang it in here, over the fire."

Amanda lifted a brow and glanced at the empty space above the mantel. Gabe had always claimed that nothing suited that spot. "It must be very special."

"You'll have to judge for yourself." He drew out a cigarette, then set it down when Laura moved into the doorway.

She said nothing for a moment, just studied the couple on the couch. His parents. His mother was lovely, her smooth skin almost unlined, her hair swept back to accent her aristocratic features and fine bones. There were emeralds at her ears and at her throat. She wore a rose silk suit with a fox stole carelessly thrown over her shoulders.

His father was tall and lean, like Gabe. Laura saw a diamond wink at his pinky. He looked sad and quiet, but she saw his eyes sharpen as he studied her.

"This is my wife, Laura, and our son."

Braced for whatever was to come, holding the baby protectively against her breasts, she stepped into the room.

Amanda rose first, only because she always seemed to move quicker than anyone else.

"It's so nice to meet you at last." Amanda had reservations, a chestful of them, but she offered a polite smile. "Gabe didn't mention how lovely you were."

"Thank you." She felt a little trip-hammer of fear in her throat. Laura knew formidable when she saw it. Instinctively she lifted her chin. "I'm glad you could come. Both of you."

Amanda noted the little gesture of pride and defiance and approved. "We wanted to meet you at the airport, but Gabe put us off."

"Rightly so," Cliff added in his soothing take-your-time voice. "If I'd been able to, I'd have held Mandy off another day."

"Nonsense. I want to see my grandchild. May I?"

Laura's arms had tightened automatically. Then she looked at Gabe and relaxed her hold. "Of course." With care and caution, she shifted the slight weight into Amanda's arms.

"Oh, how beautiful." The cool, sophisticated voice wavered. "How precious." The scents, the baby scents of talc and mild soap and fragile skin, made her sigh. "Gabe said he was premature. No problems?"

"No, he's fine."

As if to prove it, Michael opened his eyes and stared out owlishly.

"There, he looked right at me." With emeralds glowing on her skin, Amanda grinned foolishly and cooed. "Looked right at your gran, didn't you?"

"He looked at me." Cliff leaned closer to chuck the baby under the chin.

"Nonsense. Why should he want to look at you? Do something useful, Cliff, like opening the champagne." She clucked and cooed at the baby while Laura stood twisting her hands. "I hope you don't object to the wine. I didn't ask if you were nursing."

"Yes, I am, but I don't think a sip would hurt either of us."

Approving a second time, Amanda started for the couch. Laura took an instinctive step forward, then made herself stop. This wasn't Lorraine Eagleton, and she wasn't the same woman who had once cowered. But as hard as she tried to dispel the image, she saw herself standing just outside the family circle.

"I'd get glasses," she said lamely, "but I don't know where they are."

Saying nothing, Gabe went to a cabinet and drew out four champagne flutes.

Cliff took Laura's arm. "Why don't you sit down, dear? You must be tired after traveling."

"You sound like Gabe." Laura found herself smiling as she eased into a chair.

Glasses were passed. Amanda lifted hers. "We'll drink to— For goodness' sake, I don't know the child's name."

"It's Michael," Laura offered. She saw the grief flash into Amanda's eyes before she closed them. When she opened them again, they were wet and brilliant.

"To Michael," she murmured, and after a sip she leaned down to kiss the baby's cheek. Looking up, she smiled at Gabe. "Your father and I have something in the car for the baby. Would you get it?"

Though they didn't touch, and the glance lasted only a moment, Laura saw something pass between them. "I'll just be a minute."

"We won't eat her, for heaven's sake," Amanda muttered as her son left the room.

With a laugh, Cliff rubbed her shoulder. There was something familiar about the gesture. It was Gabe's, Laura realized. The same casual intimacy.

"Have you been to San Francisco before?" he asked Laura, snapping her back to the present.

"No, I— No. I'd like to offer you something, but I don't know what we have." Or even where the kitchen is, she thought miserably.

"Don't worry about it." Cliff draped his arm comfortably over the back of the chair. "We don't deserve anything after barging in on your first day home."

"Families don't barge," Amanda put in.

"Ours does." Grinning, he leaned over and chucked the baby under the chin again. "Smiled at me."

"Grimaced, you mean." With a laugh of her own, Amanda kissed her husband's cheek. "Granddad."

"I take it the cradle's for Michael and the roses are for me." Gabe strode in, carrying a dark pine cradle heaped with frilly sheets and topped with a spray of pink roses.

"Oh, the flowers. I completely forgot. And no, they're certainly not for you, but for Laura." Amanda handed the baby to her husband and rose. Though she moved to rise, Laura saw Cliff tuck the baby easily in the crook of his arm. "We'll need some water for these," Amanda decided. "No, no, I'll get it myself."

No one argued with her as she marched out of the room, carrying the flowers.

"It's very lovely," Laura began, bending from the chair to run a finger along the smooth wood of the cradle. "We were just talking about the baby needing a bed of his own."

"The Bradley bed," Cliff stated. "Fix those sheets, Gabe, and let's see how he takes to it."

"This cradle's a family tradition." Obediently Gabe lifted out the extra sheets and smoothed on white linen. "My great-grandfather built it, and all the Bradley children have had their turn rocking in it." He took the baby from his father. "Let's see how you fit, old man."

Laura watched Gabe set the baby down and give the cradle a gentle push. Something seemed to break inside her. "Gabe, I can't."

Crouched at her feet beside the cradle, he looked up. There was a dare in his eyes, a challenge, and, she was certain, a buried anger. "Can't what?"

"It isn't right, it isn't fair." She drew the baby from the cradle into her arms. "They have to know." She might have fled right then and there, but Amanda came back into the room holding a crystal vase filled with roses. Sensing tension, and intrigued by it, she continued in.

"Where would you like these, Laura?"

"I don't know, I can't— Gabe, please."

"I think they'll look nice by the window," she said mildly, then moved over to arrange them to her satisfaction. "Now, then, don't you three gentlemen think you could find something to occupy yourselves while Laura and I have a little talk?"

Panic leaping within, Laura looked from one to the other, then back at her husband. "Gabe, you have to tell them."

He took the baby and settled him on his shoulder. His eyes, very clear and still sparking with anger, met hers. "I already have." Then he left her alone with his mother.

Amanda settled herself on the sofa again. She crossed her legs and smoothed her skirts. "A pity there isn't a fire. It's still cool for this time of year."

"We haven't had a chance—"

"Oh, dear, don't mind me." She waved a hand vaguely at a chair. "Wouldn't you rather sit?" When Laura did so without a word, she lifted a brow. "Are you always so amenable? I should certainly hope not, as I liked you better when you stuck your chin out at me."

Laura folded her hands in her lap. "I don't know what to say. I hadn't realized Gabe had explained things to you. The way you were acting..." She let her words trail off. Then, when Amanda continued to wait patiently, she tried again. "I thought you believed that Michael was, well, biologically Gabe's."

"Should that make such a big difference?"

She was calm again, at least outwardly, and able to meet Amanda's eyes levelly. "I would have expected it to, especially with a family like yours."

Amanda drew her brows together as she thought that through. "Shall I tell you that I'm acquainted with Lorraine Eagleton?" She saw the instant, overwhelming fear and backed up. She wasn't often a tactful woman, but she wasn't cruel. "We'll save talk of her for another time. Right now, I think I should explain myself instead. I'm a pushy woman, Laura, but I don't mind being pushed back."

"I'm not very good at that."

"Then you'll have to learn, won't you? We may be friends, or we may not, I can't tell so soon, but I love my son. When he left all those months ago, I wasn't sure I'd ever have him back. You, for whatever reason, brought him back, and for that I'm grateful."

"He would have come when he was ready."

"But he might not have come back whole. Let's leave that." Again, the vague gesture. "And get to the point. Your son. Gabe considers the child his. Do you?"

"Yes."

"No hesitation there, I see." Amanda smiled at her, and Laura was reminded of Gabe. "If Gabe considers Michael his son, and you consider Michael his son, why should Cliff and I feel differently?"

"Bloodlines."

"Let's leave the Eagletons out of this for the time being," Amanda said. Laura merely stared, surprised that the mark had been hit so directly. "If Gabe had been unable to have children and had adopted one, I would love it and think of it as my grandchild. So, don't you think you should get past this nonsense and accept it?''

"You make it sound very simple."

"It sounds to me as though your life's been complicated enough." Amanda picked up the glass of champagne she'd discarded before. "Do you have any objections to our being Michael's grandparents?"

"I don't know."

"An honest woman." Amanda sipped.

"Do you have any objections to me being Gabe's wife?"

With the slightest of smiles, Amanda raised her glass to Laura. "I don't know. So I suppose we'll both have to wait and see. In the meantime, I'd hate to think that I'd be discouraged from seeing Gabe or Michael because we haven't made up our minds about each other."

"No, of course not. I wouldn't do that. Mrs. Bradley, no one's ever been as kind or as generous with me as Gabe. I swear to you I won't do anything to hurt him."

"Do you love him?"

Uneasy, Laura cast a look toward the doorway. "We haven't . . . Gabe and I haven't talked about that. I needed help, and I think he needed to give it."

Pursing her lips, Amanda studied her glass. "I don't believe that's what I asked you."

The chin came up again. "That's something I should discuss with Gabe before anyone else."

"You're tougher than you look. Thank God for that." Finishing off the sparkling beverage, she set down the empty glass. "I might just like you at that, Laura. Or, of course, we might end up detesting each other. But whatever is between the two of us doesn't change the fact that Gabe has committed himself to you and the child. You're family." She sat back, lifting both brows, but inside she felt a faint twist of sympathy. "From the look on your face, that doesn't thrill the life out of you."

"I'm sorry. I'm not used to being in a family."

"You've had a very rough time, haven't you?" There was compassion there, but not so much that it made Laura uncomfortable. Mentally Amanda made a note to do a little digging on the Eagletons.

"I'm trying to put that behind me."

"I hope you succeed. Some things in the past need to be remembered. Others are best forgotten."

"Mrs. Bradley, may I ask you something?"

"Yes. On the condition that after this question call me Amanda or Mandy or anything—except, please God, Mother Bradley."

"All right. Who was Michael named for?"

Amanda's gaze drifted to the empty cradle and lingered there. There was a softening, a saddening, in her face that compelled Laura to touch her hand. "My son, Gabe's younger brother. He died just over a year ago." With a long sigh, she rose. "It's time we left you to settle in."

"Thank you for coming." She hesitated because she was never quite sure what people expected. Then listening to her heart, she kissed Amanda's cheek. "Thank you for the cradle. It means a great deal to me."

"And to me." She brushed her hand over it before she left the room. "Clifton, aren't you the one who said we shouldn't stay more than a half hour?"

His voice carried, muffled, from upstairs. Clucking her tongue, Amanda pulled on her gloves. "Always poking around in Gabe's studio. The poor dear doesn't know a Monet from a Picasso, but he loves to look over Gabe's work."

"He did some beautiful things in Colorado. You must be so proud of him."

"More every day." She heard her husband coming and glanced upstairs. "Do let me know if you want any help setting up the nursery or finding a good pediatrician. I also expect you'll understand if I buy out the baby boutiques.''

"I don't—"

"Not understand, then, but you'll have to tolerate. Kiss your new daughter-in-law goodbye, Cliff.''

"You don't have to tell me that.'' Rather than the formal, meaningless kiss she was expecting, Laura received a hearty hug that left her dazed and smiling. "Welcome to the Bradleys, Laura.''

"Thank you.'' She had an urge to hug him back, to just throw her arms around his neck and breath in that nice, spicy after-shave she'd caught on his throat. Feeling foolish, she folded her hands instead. "I hope you'll come back, maybe next week for dinner, when I've had a chance to find things.''

"Cooks, too?'' He pinched Laura's cheek. "Nice work, Gabe.''

When they were gone, she stood in the foyer, rubbing a finger over her cheek. "They're very nice.''

"Yes, I've always thought so.''

The sting was still in his voice, so she steadied herself and looked at him. "I owe you an apology.''

"Forget it.'' He started to stride back into the library, then stopped and turned around. He'd be damned if he'd forget it. "Did you think I would lie to them about Michael? That I would have to?''

She accepted his anger without flinching. "Yes.''

He opened his mouth, rage boiling on his tongue. Her answer had him shutting it again. "Well, you shoot straight from the hip.''

"I did think so, and I'm glad I was wrong. Your mother was very kind to me, and your father...''

"What about my father?''

He hugged me, she wanted to say, but she didn't believe he could possibly understand how much that had affected her. "He's so much like you. I'll try not to disappoint them, or you."

"You'd do better not to disappoint yourself." Gabe dragged a hand through his hair. It fell in a tumble of dark blond disorder, the way she liked it best. "Damn it, Laura, you're not on trial here. You're my wife, this is your home, and for better or worse the Bradleys are your family."

She set her teeth. "You'll have to give me time to get used to it," she said evenly. "The only families I've ever known barely tolerated me. I'm through with that." She swung away to start up the stairs, then called over her shoulder, "And I'm painting Michael's nursery myself."

Not certain whether to laugh or swear, Gabe stood at the foot of the stairs and stared after her.

Chapter Seven

Laura brushed the glossy white enamel paint over the baseboard. In her other hand she held a stiff piece of cardboard as a guard against smearing any of the white over the yellow walls she'd already finished.

On the floor in the far corner was a portable radio that was tuned to a station that played bouncy rock. She'd kept the volume low so that she could hear Michael when he woke. It was the same radio Gabe had kept on the kitchen counter in the cabin.

She wasn't sure which pleased her more, the way the nursery was progressing or the ease with which she could bend and crouch. She'd even been able to use part of her hospital fund to buy a couple of pairs of slacks in her old size. They might still be a tad snug in the waist, but she was optimistic.

She wished the rest of her life would fall into order as easily.

He was still angry with her. With a shrug, Laura dipped her brush into the paint can again. Gabe had a temper, he had moods. He had certainly never attempted to deny or hide that. And the truth was, she'd been wrong not to trust him to do the right thing. So she'd apologized. She couldn't let his continuing coolness bother her. But, of course, it did.

They were strangers here, in a way that they had never been strangers in the little cabin in Colorado. It wasn't the house, though a part of her still blamed the size and the glamour of it. Before, the simple mechanics of space had required them to share, to grow close, to depend on each other. Being depended on had become important to Laura, even if it had only been to provide a cup of coffee at the right time. Now, beyond her responsibilities to Michael, there was little for her to do. She and Gabe could spend hours under the same roof and hardly know each other existed.

But it wasn't walls and floors and windows that made the difference. It was quite simply the difference—the difference between them. She was still Laura Malone, from the wrong side of the tracks, the same person who had been moved and shuffled from house to house, without ever being given the chance to really live there. The same person who had been handed from family to family without ever being given the chance to really belong.

And he was... Her laugh was a bit wistful. He was Gabriel Bradley, a man who had known his place from the moment he'd been born. A man who would never wonder if he'd have the same place tomorrow.

That was what she wanted for Michael, only that. The money, the name, the big, sprawling house with the stained-glass windows and the graceful terraces, didn't matter. Belonging did. Because she wanted it, was determined to have it for her son, she was willing to wait to belong herself. To Gabe.

The only time they were able to pull together was when Michael was involved. Her lips curved then. He loved the baby. There could be no doubt about that. It wasn't pity or obligation that had him crouching beside the cradle or walking the floor at three in the morning. He was a man capable of great love, and he had given it unhesitatingly to Michael. Gabe was attentive, interested, gentle and involved. When it came to Michael.

It was only with her, when they had to deal with each other one on one, that things became strained.

They didn't touch. Though they lived in the same house, slept in the same bed, they didn't touch, except in the most casual and impersonal of ways. As a family they had gone out to choose all the things Michael would need—the crib and other nursery furniture, blankets, a windup swing that played a lullaby, soft stuffed animals that Michael would undoubtedly ignore for months. It had been easy, even delightful, to discuss high chairs and playpens and decide together what would suit. Laura had never expected to be able to give her son so much or to be able to share in that giving.

But when they'd come home the strain had returned.

She was being a fool, Laura told herself. She'd been given a home, protection and care, and, most of all, a kind and loving father for her son. Wishing for more was what had always led her to disappointment before.

But she wished he would smile at her again—at her, not at Michael's mother, not at the subject of his painting.

Perhaps it was best that they remained as they were, polite friends with a common interest. She wasn't entirely sure how she would manage when the time came for him to turn to her as a woman. The time would come, his desire was there, and he was too physical a man to share the bed with her without fully sharing it much longer.

Her experience with lovemaking had taught her that man demanded and woman submitted. He wouldn't have to love her, or even hold her in affection, to need her. God, no one knew better how little affection, how little caring, there could be in a marriage bed. A man like Gabe would have many demands, and loving him as she did she would give. And the cycle she'd finally managed to break would begin again.

Gabe watched her from the doorway. Something was wrong, very wrong. He could see the turmoil on her face, could see it in the set of her shoulders. It seemed that the longer they were here the less she relaxed. She pretended well, but it was only pretense.

It infuriated him, and the harder he held on to his temper the more infuriated he became. He hadn't so much as raised his voice to her since their first day in the house, and yet she seemed continually braced for an outburst.

He'd given her as much room as was humanly possible, and it was killing him. Sleeping with her, having her turn to him during the night, her skin separated from his only by the fragile cotton of a nightgown, had given new meaning to insomnia.

He'd taken to working during the middle of the night and spending his free time in the studio or at the gallery, anywhere he wouldn't be tempted to take what·was his only legally.

How could he take when she was still so delicate, physically, emotionally? However selfish he'd always been, or considered himself, he couldn't justify gratifying himself at her expense—or frightening her by letting her see just how desperately, how violently, he wanted her.

Yet there was passion in her, the dark, explosive kind. He'd seen that, and other things, in her eyes. She needed him, as much as he needed her. He wasn't sure either of them understood where their need might take them.

He could be patient. He was aware that her body needed time to heal, and he could give her that. But he wasn't sure he could give her the time it might take for her mind to heal.

He wanted to cross to her, to sit down beside her and stroke his hand over her hair. He wanted to reassure her. But he had no idea what words to use. Instead, he tucked his hands into his pockets.

"Still at it?"

Laura started, splattering paint on her hand. She sat back on her heels. "I didn't hear you come in."

"Don't get up," he told her. "You make quite a picture." He stepped into the room, glancing at the sunny walls before looking down at her. She wore an old pair of jeans, obviously his, he could see the clothesline she'd used to secure the waist. One of his shirts was tented over her, its hem torn at her hip.

"Mine?"

"I thought it would be all right." She picked up a rag to wipe the paint from her hand. "I could tell from the splatters on them they'd already been worked in."

"Perhaps you don't know the difference between painting and—" he gestured toward the wall "—painting."

She'd nearly fumbled out an apology before she realized he was joking. So the mood had passed. Perhaps they were friends again. "Not at all. I thought your pants would give me artistic inspiration."

"You could have come to the source."

She set the brush on top of the open paint can. Relief poured through her. Though he didn't know, Gabe had found exactly the right words to reassure her. "I would never have suggested that the celebrated Gabriel Bradley turn his genius to a lowly baseboard."

It seemed so easy when she was like this, relaxed, with a hint of amusement in her eyes. "Obviously afraid I'd show you up."

She smiled, a bit hesitantly. He hadn't looked at her in quite that way for days. Then she was scrambling back up on her knees as he joined her on the floor. "Oh, Gabe, don't. You'll get paint all over you, and you look so nice."

He had the brush in his hand. "Do I?"

"Yes." She tried to take it away from him, but he didn't give way. "You always look so dashing when you go to the gallery."

"Oh, God." The instant disgust on his face made her laugh.

"Well, you do." She checked the urge to brush at the hair on his forehead. "It's quite different from the rugged-outdoorsman look you had in Colorado, though that was nice, too."

He wasn't certain whether to smile or sneer. "Rugged outdoorsman?"

"That's right. The cords and the flannel, the untidy hair and the carelessly unshaven face. I think Geoffrey would have loved to photograph you with an ax...." She was staring at him, seeing him as he'd been and as he was. Abruptly she became aware that her hand was still covering his on the handle of the brush. Drawing it away, she struggled to remember her point. "You're not dressed for work now, and I was in the fashion business long enough to recognize quality. Those pants are linen, and you'll ruin them."

He was well aware of the sudden tension in her fingers and the look that had come into her eyes, but he only lifted a brow. "Are you saying I'm sloppy?"

"Only when you paint."

"Pot calling the kettle," he murmured, ignoring the way she jumped when he ran a finger down her cheek. He held it up to prove his point.

Laura wrinkled her nose at the smear of white paint on his fingertip—and tried to ignore the heat on her skin where his finger had brushed. "I'm not an artist." With a rag in one hand, she took his wrist in the other to clean the paint from his fingertip.

Such beautiful hands, she thought. She could imagine how it would feel to have them move over her, slowly, gently. To have them stroke and caress the way a man's might if he cared deeply about the woman beneath the skin he was touching. Her imagination had her moistening her lips as she lifted her gaze to his.

They knelt knee to knee on the drop cloth, with his hand caught in hers. It amazed her when she felt his pulse begin to thud. In his eyes she saw what he hadn't allowed her to see for days. Desire, pure and simple. Unnerved by it, drawn to it, she leaned toward him. The rag slipped out of her hand.

And the baby cried out.

They both jerked, like children caught raiding the cookie jar.

"He'll be hungry, and wet, too, I imagine," she said as she started to rise. Gabe shifted his hand until it captured hers.

"I'd like you to come back here after you've tended to him."

Longing and anxiety tangled, confusing her. "All right. Don't worry about the mess. I'll finish up later."

She was more than an hour with Michael, and she was a bit disappointed that Gabe didn't come in, as he often did, to hold the baby or play with him before he slept again. Those were the best times, those simple family times. Tucking the blankets around her son, she reminded herself that she couldn't expect Gabe to devote every free minute to her and the child.

Satisfied that the baby was dry and content, she left him to go into the adjoining bath and freshen up. After she'd washed the paint from her face, she studied herself in the mirrored wall across from the step-down tub. She didn't look seductive in baggy, masculine clothes, with her hair tugged back in a ponytail. Regardless of that, for an instant in the nursery, Gabe had been seduced.

Was that what she wanted?

How could she know what she wanted? She pressed her fingers to her eyes and tried to sort out her feelings. Confusion, and little else. One moment she imagined what it would be like, being with Gabe, making love with him. The next moment she was remembering the way it had been before, when love had had little to do with it.

It was wrong to continually let memories intrude. She told herself she was too sensible for that. Or wanted to be. She'd been in therapy, she'd talked to counselors and other women who had been in situations all too similar to her own. Because she'd had to stay on the move, she hadn't been able to remain with any one group for long, but they had helped her. Just learning that she wasn't alone in what had happened to her, seeing and talking with others who had turned their lives around again, had given her the strength to go on.

She knew—intellectually she knew—that what had happened to her was the result of a man's illness and her own insecurity. But it was one thing to know it and another to accept it and go on, to risk another relationship.

She wanted to be normal, was determined to be. That had been the communal cry from all the sessions in all the towns. Along with the fear and the anger and the self-disgust, there had been a desperate mutual need to be normal women again.

But that step, that enormous, frightening step from past to future, was so difficult to take. Only she could do it, Laura told herself as she continued to stare into her own eyes. With Gabe, and her feelings for him, she had a chance. If she was willing to take it.

How could she know how close they could be, how much they could mean to each other, if she didn't allow herself to want the intimacy?

Catching her lower lip between her teeth, she turned to study the lush bath. It was nearly as large as many of the rooms she'd lived in during her life. White on white on white, it gleamed and glistened and invited indulgence. She could sink into hot, deep water in the tub and soak until her skin was soft and pink. She still had most of a bottle of perfume, French and suggestive, that Geoffrey had bought her in Paris. She could dab it on her damp skin so that the scent seeped into her pores. Then she could...what?

She had nothing lovely or feminine to wear. The only clothes she hadn't taken to thrift shops or secondhand stores during her cross-country flight were maternity clothes. The two pairs of slacks and the cotton blouses didn't count.

In any case, what would it matter if she had a closetful of lace negligees? She wouldn't know what to do or say. It had been so long since she'd thought of herself strictly as a woman. Perhaps she never had. And surely it was better to try to reestablish that early friendship with Gabe before they attempted intimacy.

If that was what he wanted. What she wanted.

Turning away from the mirror, she went to find him.

She couldn't have been more surprised when she walked into the nursery and found the painting finished, the cans sealed and the brushes cleaned. As she stared, Gabe folded the drop cloth.

"You finished it," she managed.

"I seem to have struggled through without doing any damage."

"It's beautiful. The way I'd always imagined." She stepped into the empty room and began arranging furniture in her head. "There should be curtains, white ones, though I suppose dotted swiss is too feminine for a boy."

"I couldn't say, but it sounds like it. It's warm enough, so I've left the windows open." He tossed the drop cloth over a stepladder. "I don't want to put Michael in here until the smell of the paint's gone."

"No," she agreed absently, wondering if the crib should go between the two windows.

"Now that this is out of the way, I have something for you. A belated Mother's Day present."

"Oh, but you gave me the flowers already."

He took a small box out of his pocket. "There wasn't the time or the opportunity for much else then. We were living out of a suitcase and spending all of our time at the hospital. Besides, the flowers were from Michael. This is from me."

That made it different. Intimate. Again she found herself drawn to him, and again she found herself pulled away. "You don't have to give me anything."

The familiar impatience shimmered. He barely suppressed it. "You're going to have to learn how to take a gift more graciously."

He was right. And it was wrong of her to continue to compare, but Tony had been so casual, so lavish, in his gifts. And they had meant so little. "Thank you." She took the box, opened it and stared.

The ring looked like a circle of fire, with its channel-linked diamonds flashing against its gold band and nestled in velvet. Instinctively she ran a fingertip over it and was foolishly amazed that it was cool to the touch.

"It's beautiful. Absolutely beautiful. But—"

"There had to be one."

"It's just that it's a wedding ring, and I already have one."

He took her left hand to examine it. "I'm surprised your finger hasn't fallen off from wearing this thing."

"There's nothing wrong with it," she said, and nearly snatched her hand away.

"So sentimental, angel?" Though his voice had gentled, his hand was firm on hers. Now, perhaps, he would be able to dig a bit deeper into what she was feeling for him, about him. "Are you so attached to a little circle of metal?"

"It was good enough for us before. I don't need anything else."

"It was a temporary measure. I'm not asking you to toss it out the window, but be a little practical. If you weren't always curling your finger up, it would fall right off."

"I could have it sized."

"Suit yourself." He slipped it from her finger, then replaced it with the diamond circle. "Just consider that you have two wedding rings." When he offered her the plain band, Laura curled it into her fist. "The new one holds the same intentions."

"It is beautiful." Still, she pushed the old ring onto the index finger of her right hand, where it fit more snugly. "Thank you, Gabe."

"We did better than that before."

She didn't have to be reminded. Yet the memories flooded back when he slipped his arms around her. Emotions poured through with those memories the moment his mouth was on hers. His lips were firm and warm and hinted, just hinted, at his impatience as they slanted across hers. Though his arms remained gentle around her, his touch light and testing, she sensed a volcano in him, simmering and smoking.

As if to soothe, she leaned into him and lifted a hand to his cheek. Understanding. Acceptance.

Her touch triggered the need crawling inside him, and his arms tightened and his mouth crushed down on hers. She responded with a moan that he barely heard, with a shudder that he barely felt. Tense, hungry, he fell victim to her as much as to his own demands.

He had wanted before, casually and desperately and all the degrees in between. Why, then, did this seem like a completely new experience? He had held women before, known their softness, tasted their sweetness. But he had never known a softness, never experienced a sweetness, like Laura's.

He took his mouth on a slow, seeking journey over her face, along her jawline, down her throat, drinking in, then devouring. His hands, long and limber, slipped under her full shirt, then roamed upward. At first the slender line of her back was enough, the smooth skin and the quick tremors all he required. Then the need to touch, to possess, grew sharper. As his mouth came back to hers, he slid his hand around to cup, then claim, her breast.

The first touch made her catch her breath, pulling air in quickly, then letting it out again in a long, unsteady sigh. How could she have known, even blinded by love and longings, how desperately she'd need to have his hands on her? This was what she wanted, to be his in every way, in all ways. The confusion, the doubts, the fears, drained away. No memories intruded when he held her like this. No whispers of the past taunted her. There was only him, and the promise of a new life and an enduring love.

Her knees were trembling so she braced her body against his, arching in an invitation so instinctive that only he recognized it.

The room smelled of paint and was bright with the sun that streamed through the uncurtained windows. It was empty and quiet. He could fantasize about pulling her to the floor, tugging at her clothes until they were skin-to-skin on the polished hardwood. He could imagine taking her in the sun-washed room until they were both exhausted and replete.

With another woman he might have done so without giving a thought to where or when, and little more to how. But not with Laura.

Churning, he drew her away from him. Her eyes were clouded. Her mouth was soft and full. With a restraint he hadn't known he possessed, Gabe swore only in his mind.

"I have work to do."

She was floating, drifting on a mist so fine it could only be felt, not seen. At his words, she began the quick, confused journey back to earth. "What?"

"I have work to do," he repeated, stepping carefully away from her. He detested himself for taking things so far when he knew she was physically unable to cope with his demands. "I'll be in the studio if you need me."

If she needed him? Laura thought dimly as his footsteps echoed down the hall. Hadn't she just shown him how much she needed him? It wasn't possible that he hadn't felt it, that he hadn't understood it. With an oath, she turned and walked to the window. There she huddled on the small, hard seat and stared down at the garden, which was just beginning to bloom.

What was there about her, she wondered, that made men look at her as a thing to be taken or rejected at will? Did she appear so weak, so malleable? She curled her hands into fists as frustration spread through her. She wasn't weak, not any longer, and a long time, in some ways a lifetime, had passed since she had been malleable. She wasn't a young girl caught up in fairy-tale lies now, she a woman, a mother, with responsibilities and ambitions.

Perhaps she loved, and perhaps this time would be as unwise a love as before. But she wouldn't be used, she wouldn't be ignored, and she wouldn't be molded.

Talk was cheap, Laura thought as she propped her chin on her knees. Doing something about it was a little costlier. She should go in to Gabe now and make herself clear. She cast a look at the door, then turned back to the window. She didn't have the courage.

That had always been her problem. She could say what she would or would not do, but when it came down to acting on it she found passivity easier than action. There had been a time in her life when she'd believed that the passive way was best for her. That had been until her marriage to Tony had fallen viciously apart. She'd done something then, Laura reminded herself, or had begun to do something, then had allowed herself to be pressured and persuaded to erase it.

It had been like that all her life. As a child she hadn't had a choice. She'd been told to live here or live there, and she had. Each house had had its own sets of rules and values, and she'd had to conform. Like one of those rubber dolls, she thought now, that you could bend and twist into any position you liked.

Too much of the child had remained with the woman, until the woman had been with child.

The only positive action she felt she'd ever taken in her life had been to protect the baby. And she had done it, Laura reminded herself. It had been terrifying and hard, but she hadn't backed down. Didn't that mean that buried beneath years of quiet compliance was the strength she'd always wanted to have? She had to believe that and, if she did, to act on it.

Loving Gabe didn't mean, couldn't mean, that she would sit quietly by while he made decisions for her. It was time to take a stand.

Rising, she walked out of the empty nursery and started down the hall. With each step her resolve wavered and had to be shored up again. At the door to his studio, she hesitated again, rubbing the heel of her hand on her chest, where the ache of uncertainty lodged. Taking one last breath, she opened the door and walked in.

He was by the long bank of windows, a brush in his hand, working on one of the paintings that had been stacked half-finished against the wall of the cabin. She remembered it. It was a snow scene, very stark and lonely and somehow appealing. The whites and cold blues and silvers gave a sense of challenge.

Laura was glad of it. A sense of challenge was precisely what she needed.

He hadn't heard her come in, so intent was he on his work. There was no sweeping strokes or bold slashes now, only a delicacy. He was adding details so minute, so exact, that she could almost hear the winter wind.

"Gabe?" It was amazing how much courage it could take to say a name.

He stopped immediately, and when he turned the annoyance on his face was very apparent. Interruptions were never tolerated here. Living alone, he hadn't had to tolerate them.

"What is it?" He clipped the words off, and he didn't set down his brush or move from the painting. It was obvious that he intended to continue exactly where he'd left off the moment he'd nudged her out of his way.

"I need to talk to you."

"Can't it wait?"

She nearly said yes, but then she brought herself up short. "No." She left the door open in case the baby should cry out and walked to the center of the room. Her stomach twisted, knotted. Her chin came up. "Or, if it can, I don't want it to."

He lifted a brow. He'd heard that tone in her voice only a handful of times in the weeks they'd been together. "All right, but make it fast, will you? I want to finish this."

Her temper flared too quickly to surprise her. "Fine, then, I'll sum it up in one sentence. If I'm going to be your wife, I want you to treat me like one."

"I beg your pardon?"

She was too angry to see that he was stunned, and too angry to recognize her own shock at her words. "No, you don't. You've never begged anyone's pardon in your life. You don't have to. You do exactly what suits you. If that means being kind, you can be the kindest man I've ever known. If it means being arrogant, you take that just as far."

With deliberate care, he set his brush down. "If there's a point to this, Laura, I'm missing it."

"Do you want me or don't you?"

He only stared at her. If she continued to stand in the pool of light, her eyes dark and defiant, her cheeks flushed with color, he might beg. "That's the point?" he said steadily.

"You tell me you want me, then you ignore me. You kiss me, then you walk away." She dragged a hand through her hair. When her fingers tangled with the ribbon that held it back, she tugged it out in annoyance. Pale and fragile, her hair fell around her shoulders. "I realize the main reason we're married is because of Michael, but I want to know where I stand. Am I to be a guest here who's alternately indulged and ignored, or am I to be your wife?"

"You are my wife." With his own temper rising, he pushed himself off his stool. "And it's not a matter of me ignoring you. I've simply got a lot of work to catch up on."

"You don't work twenty-four hours a day. At night—" Her courage began to fail. She thrust out the rest of the words. "Why won't you make love with me?"

It was fortunate that he'd set his brush down, or else he might have snapped it in half. "Do you expect performance on demand, Laura?"

Embarrassed color flooded her cheeks. That had once been expected of her, and it shamed her more than she could say to think she'd demanded it. "No. I didn't mean it to sound that way. I only thought it was best that you know how I felt." She took a step back, then turned to go. "I'll let you get back to work."

"Laura." He preferred, much preferred, her anger to the humiliation he'd seen. And caused. "Wait." He started after her when she whirled around.

"Don't apologize."

"All right." There was still fire in her, he saw, and he wasn't entirely sure he should be relieved. "I'll just give you a more honest explanation."

"It isn't necessary." She started toward the door again, but he grabbed her arm and yanked her around. He saw it and cursed at it—the instant fear that leaped into her eyes.

"Damn it, don't look at me like that. Don't ever look at me like that." Without his realizing it, his fingers had tightened on her arm. When she winced, he released her, dropping his hands to his side. "I can't make myself over for you, Laura. I'll yell when I need to yell and fight when I need to fight, but I told you once before, and I'll say it again. I don't hit women."

The fear had risen, a bitter bile in her throat. It was detestable. She waited for it to pass before she spoke. "I don't expect you to, but I can't make myself over for you, either. Even if I could, I don't know what you want. I know I should be grateful to you."

"The hell with that."

"I should be grateful," she continued, calm again. "And I am, but I've found out something about myself this past year. I'll never be anyone's doormat ever again. Not even yours."

"Do you think that's what I want?"

"I can't know what you want, Gabe, until you know yourself." She'd gone this far, Laura told herself, and she would finish. "Right from the beginning you expected me to trust you. But after everything we've been through you still haven't been able to make yourself trust me. If we're ever going to be able to make this marriage work you're going to have to stop looking at me as a good deed and start seeing me as a person."

"You have no idea how I see you."

"No, I probably don't." She managed a smile. "Maybe when I do it'll be easier for both of us." She heard the baby crying and glanced down the hall. "He doesn't seem to be able to settle today."

"I'll get him in a minute. He can't be hungry again. Wait." If she could be honest, he told himself, then so could he. He put a hand on her arm to hold her there. "It's easy enough to clear up one misunderstanding. I haven't made love with you, not because I haven't wanted to, but because it's too soon."

"Too soon?"

"For you."

She started to shake her head. Then his meaning became clear. "Gabe, Michael's over four weeks old."

"I know how old he is. I was there." He held up a hand before she could speak. "Damn it, Laura, I saw what you went through. How hard it was on you. However I feel, it simply isn't possible for me to act on it until I know you're fully recovered."

"I had a baby, not a terminal illness." She let out a huff of breath, but she found it wasn't annoyance or even amusement she felt. It was pleasure, the rare and wonderful pleasure of being cared for. "I feel fine. I am fine. In fact, I've probably never been better in my life."

"Regardless of how you feel, you've just had a baby. From what I've read—"

"You've read about this, too?"

That infuriated him—that wide-eyed wonder and the trace of humor in her eyes. "I don't intend to touch you," he said stiffly, "until I'm sure you're fully recovered."

"What do you want, a doctor's certificate?"

"More or less." He started to touch her cheek, then thought better of it. "I'll see to Michael."

He left her standing in the hall, unsure whether she was angry or amused or delighted. All that she was sure of was that she was feeling, and her feelings were all for Gabe.

Chapter Eight

I can't believe how fast he's growing." Feeling very grandmotherly but sporting a sleek new hairstyle, Amanda sat in the bentwood rocker in Michael's new nursery and cuddled the baby.

"He's making up for being premature." Still not quite certain how she felt about her mother-in-law, Laura continued to fold tiny clothes that were fresh from the laundry. "We had our checkup today, and the doctor said Michael was healthy as a horse." She pressed a sleeper to her cheek. It was soft, almost as soft as her son's skin. "I wanted to thank you for recommending Dr. Sloane. She's wonderful."

"Good. But I don't need a pediatrician to tell me this child's healthy. Look at this grip." Amanda chuckled as Michael curled his fingers around hers, but she stopped short of allowing him to suck on her sapphire ring. "He has your eyes, you know."

"Does he?" Delighted, Laura moved to stand over them. The baby smelled of talc—Amanda of Paris. "It's too early to tell, I know, but I'd hoped he did."

"No doubt about it." Amanda continued to rock as she studied her daughter-in-law. "And what about *your* checkup? How are you?"

"I'm fine." Laura thought about the slip of paper she'd tucked into the top drawer of her dresser.

"Looking a bit tired to me." There wasn't any sympathy in the voice; it was brusque and matter-of-fact. "Haven't you done anything about getting some help?"

Laura's spine straightened automatically. "I don't need any help."

"That's absurd, of course. With a house this size, a demanding husband and a new baby, you can use all the help you can get, but suit yourself." Michael began to coo, pleasing Amanda. "Talk to Gran, sweetheart. Tell Gran just how it is." The baby responded with more gurgles. "Listen to that. Before long you'll have plenty to say for yourself. Just make sure 'My gran's beautiful' is one of the first. There's a sweet boy." She dropped a kiss on his brow before looking up at Laura. "I'd say a change is in order here, and I'm more than happy to leave that to you." With what she considered a grandmother's privilege, Amanda handed the wet baby to Laura. She continued to sit as Laura took Michael to the changing table.

There was a great deal she'd have liked to say. Amanda was accustomed to voicing her opinions loud and clear—and, if necessary, beating anyone within reach over the head with it. It chafed a bit to hold back, but she'd learned enough in the past few weeks about the Eagletons and about Laura's life with them. Treading carefully, she tried a new tactic.

"Gabe's spending a lot of time at the gallery."

"Yes. I think he's nearly decided to go ahead with a new showing." Almost drowning in love, Laura leaned over to nuzzle Michael's neck.

"Have you been there?"

"The gallery? No, I haven't."

Amanda tapped a rounded, coral-tipped nail on the arm of the rocker. "I'd think you'd be interested in Gabe's work."

"Of course I am." She held Michael over her head, and he began to bubble and smile. "I just haven't thought it wise to take Michael in and interrupt."

It was on the tip of Amanda's tongue to remind Laura that Michael had grandparents who would delight in having him to themselves for a few hours. Again she bit the words back. "I'm sure Gabe wouldn't mind. He's devoted to the boy."

"Yes, he is." Laura retied the ribbons on Michael's pale blue booties. "But I also know he needs some time to organize his work, his career." She handed her son a small cloth bunny, and he stuck it happily in his mouth. "Do you know why Gabe is hesitating about a showing?"

"Have you asked him?"

"No, I—I didn't want to pressure him about it."

"A little pressure might be just what he needs."

Frowning, Laura turned. "Why?"

"It has to do with Michael, my son Michael. I'd prefer it if you asked Gabe the rest."

"They were close?"

"Yes." She smiled. She'd learned it hurt less to remember than to try to forget. "They were very close, though they were very different. He was devastated when Michael was killed. I believe the time in the mountains helped Gabe get back his art. And I believe you and the baby helped him get back his heart."

"If that's true, I'm glad. He's helped me more than I can ever repay."

Amanda gave Laura an even look. "Payments aren't necessary between a husband and wife."

"Perhaps not."

"Are you happy?"

Stalling, Laura laid the baby in the crib and wound the musical mobile so that he could shake his fists and kick at it. "Of course I am. Why wouldn't I be?"

"That was my next question."

"I'm very happy." She went back to folding and storing baby clothes. "It was nice of you to visit, Amanda. I know how busy your schedule is."

"Don't think you can politely show me out the door before I'm ready to go."

Laura turned and saw the faint, amused smile on Amanda's lips. Bad manners were enough out of character for her to make her flush. "I'm sorry."

"Don't be. I don't expect for you to be comfortable with me yet. I'm not entirely sure I'm comfortable with you, either."

A bit more relaxed, Laura smiled back. "I'm sure you're always comfortable. I envy that about you. And I am sorry."

Amanda brushed aside the apology and rose to roam the room. She liked what her daughter-in-law had done here. It was a bright, cheerful place, not overly fussy, and just traditional enough to make her remember the nursery she had set up herself so many years before. There were the scents of powder and fresh linen.

A loving place, she thought. She knew she wouldn't have wanted any more for her son. It was very obvious to her that Laura had untapped stores of love.

"This is a charming room. I think so every time I step into it." Amanda patted the head of the four-foot lavender teddy bear. "But you can't hide here forever."

"I don't know what you mean." But she did.

"You said you'd never been to San Francisco, and now you're here. Have you gone to a museum, to the theater? Have you strolled down to Fisherman's Wharf, ridden a streetcar, explored Chinatown, any of the things a newcomer would surely do?"

Defensive now, Laura spoke coolly. "No, I haven't. But it's only been a few weeks."

It was time, Amanda decided, to stop circling and get to the point. "Let's deal woman-to-woman a moment, Laura. Forget the fact that I'm Gabe's mother. We're alone. Whatever is said here doesn't have to go any further."

Laura's palms were starting to sweat. She brushed them dry on the thighs of her slacks. "I don't know what you want me to say."

"Whatever needs to be said." When Laura remained silent, Amanda nodded. "All right, I'll begin. You've had some miserable spots in your life, some of them tragic. Gabe gave us the bare essentials, but I learned a good deal more by knowing who and what to ask." Amanda sat down again and crossed her legs. She didn't miss the flash in Laura's eyes. "Wait until I've finished. Then you can be as offended as you like."

"I'm not offended," Laura said stiffly. "But I don't see the purpose in discussing what used to be."

"Until you look what used to be square in the face, you won't be able to go on with what might be." She tried to keep her voice brisk, but even her solid composure wavered. "I know that Tony Eagleton abused you, and that his parents overlooked what was monstrous, even criminal, behavior. My heart breaks for you."

"Please." Her voice was strangled as she shook her head. "Don't."

"No sympathy allowed, Laura, even woman-to-woman?"

Again she shook her head, afraid to accept it and, more, to need it. "I can't bear to think back on it. And I can't stand pity."

"Sympathy and pity are entirely different things."

"All that's behind me. I'm a different person than I was then."

"I have no way of agreeing, as I didn't know you before. But I can say that anyone who stood on her own all these months must have great reserves of strength and determination. Isn't it time you used them, and fought back?"

"I have fought back."

"You've taken sanctuary, a much-needed one. I won't argue that running as you did took courage and stamina. But there comes a time to take a stand."

Hadn't she said that to herself time and time again? Hadn't she hated herself for only saying it? She looked at her son, who gurgled and reached for the colorful birds circling over his head.

"And what? Go to court, to the press, drag the whole ugly mess out for everyone to gawk at?"

"If necessary." Her voice took on a tone of pride that carried to all corners of the room. "The Bradleys aren't afraid of scandal."

"I'm not a—"

"But you are," Amanda told her. "You're a Bradley, and so is that child. It's Michael I'm thinking of in the long run, but I'm also thinking of you. What difference does it make what anyone thinks, what anyone knows? You have nothing to be ashamed of."

"I let it happen," Laura said, with a kind of dull fury. "I'll always be ashamed of that."

"My dear child." Unable to prevent herself, Amanda rose to put her arms around Laura. After the first shock, Laura felt herself being drawn in. Perhaps it was because the comfort came from a woman, but it broke down her defences as nothing else ever had.

Amanda let her weep, even wept with her. The fact that she did, that she could, was more soothing than any words could have been. Cheek-to-cheek, woman-to-woman, they held each other until the storm passed. The bond that Laura had never expected to know was forged in tears. With her arm still around Laura, Amanda led her to the gaily striped daybed.

"That's been coming on for a while, I'd say," Amanda murmured. She drew a lace-edged handkerchief out of her breast pocket and unashamedly wiped her eyes.

"I don't know." Laura used the back of her wrist to smear away already-drying tears. "I suppose. Crying isn't something I should need, not anymore. It's only when I look back and remember."

"Now listen to me," Amanda said. All the softness had been erased from her voice. "You were young and alone, and you have nothing, nothing, to be ashamed of. One day you'll realize that for yourself, but for now it might be enough to know you're not alone anymore."

"Sometimes I'm so angry, just so angry that I was used as a convenience, or a punching bag, or a status symbol." It was amazing to her that fury could bring calm and wipe out pain. "When I am I know that no matter what it costs I'll never go back to that."

"Then stay angry."

"But...the anger for me, that's personal." She looked across the room at the crib. "It's when I think of Michael and I know they're going to try to take him...then I'm afraid."

"They don't just have to go through you now, do they?"

Laura looked back. Amanda's face was set. Her eyes glittered. So this was where Gabe got his warrior look, Laura thought, and felt a new kind of love stir. It was the most natural thing in the world for Laura to reach out and take her hand. "No, they don't."

They both heard the door open and close on the first floor. Immediately Laura began to brush her hands over her face. "That must be Gabe, home from the gallery. I don't want him to see me like this."

"I'll go down and keep him occupied." On impulse, she glanced at her watch. "Do you have plans for this afternoon?"

"No. Just to—"

"Good. Come down when your tidied up."

Ten minutes later, Laura came down to find Gabe cornered in the living room, scowling into a glass of club soda.

"Then it's all settled." Amanda fluffed a hand through her hair, well satisfied. "Laura. Good. Are you ready?"

"Ready?"

"Yes. I've explained to Gabe that we're going shopping. He's absolutely delighted with the reception I've planned for the two of you next week." The reception she'd only begun to plan on her way downstairs.

"Resigned," he corrected, but he had to smile at his mother. The smile faded when he glanced over at Laura. "What's wrong?"

"Nothing." It had been foolish to think that a quick wash and fresh makeup could hide anything from him. "Your mother and I were getting sentimental over Michael."

"What your wife needs is an afternoon out." Amanda rose, then leaned over to kiss Gabe. "I'd scold you for keeping her locked up this way, but I love you too much."

"I never—"

"Never once nudged her out of the house," his mother finished for him. "So it's up to me. Get your purse, dear. We have to find you something wonderful for the reception. Gabe, I imagine Laura needs your credit cards."

"My— Oh." Feeling like a tree blowing in a strong wind, he reached for his wallet.

"These should do." Amanda plucked two of them and handed them to Laura. "Ready?"

"Well, I . . . Yes," she said on impulse. "Michael's just been fed and changed. You shouldn't have any trouble."

"I can handle things," he told her, feeling more than a little put out. In the first place, he'd have taken her shopping himself if she'd asked. And in the second, though he didn't want to admit it, he wasn't totally sure of himself alone with the baby.

Reading her son perfectly, Amanda kissed him again. "Behave and we may bring you back a present."

He couldn't suppress the grin. "Out," he ordered. Then he caught Laura in turn and kissed her with the same light affection. It surprised him when she returned the embrace so ardently.

"Don't let her talk you into anything with bows," he murmured. "They wouldn't suit you. You should try to find something to match your eyes."

"If you don't let the girl go, we won't buy anything at all," Amanda said dryly, but she was pleased and a bit misty-eyed to see that her son was indeed in love with his wife.

It wasn't anyone's fault that Michael chose that particular afternoon to demand all the time and attention an infant could possibly demand. Gabe walked, rocked, changed, coddled and all but stood on his head. For his part, Michael gurgled, stared owlishly—and wept piteously whenever he was set down. He did everything but sleep.

In the end, Gabe gave up any idea of working for the rest of the day and carted Michael around with him. With the baby nestled in the crook of his arm, he ate a chicken leg and scanned the newspaper. Since no one was around to chuckle at him behind their hands, he discussed world politics and the major-league box scores with Michael while the baby shook a rattle and blew bubbles.

They took a walk in the garden once Gabe located one of the small knit hats Laura had bought to protect Michael from spring breezes. It gave him enormous pleasure to watch the baby's cheeks turn pink and his eyes look around, alert and interested.

He had Laura's eyes, Gabe thought as he studied them. The same shape, the same color, but without the shadows that made hers both sad and fascinating. Michael's eyes were clear and innocent of sorrow.

Michael whimpered at first, then decided to accept his fate, when Gabe slipped him into the little baby swing. After tucking his blankets in around him, Gabe sat cross-legged in front of him and began to stretch.

The daffodils were up in a glory of white and yellow trumpets. Baby irises poked through, purple and exotic. Lilacs, though still shy of their full bloom, offered their scent. For the first time since his own tragedy, Gabe felt at peace. In the mountains, all through the winter, he'd begun to heal. But here, at home, with spring all around, he could finally see and accept that life did go on.

The baby continued to rock, pink-cheeked and bright-eyed, his hands lifting and falling to the rhythm. His little face was already filling out, taking on his own personal look and shape. Gone was the terrifying fragility of the newborn. He was, Gabe supposed, already growing up.

"I love you, Michael."

And when he spoke he spoke both to the one who was gone and to the one who rocked contentedly in front of him.

She hadn't meant to be gone so long, but the chaotic few hours breezing through the shops had brought back the way she had felt during that brief period when she'd been on her own and eager to test life.

There had been a moment or two of guilt over using Gabe's credit cards so freely. Then it had been almost too easy, with Amanda lending support, to justify the purchases. She was Laura Bradley now.

She had an eye for color and line that came naturally and had been sharpened by her time as a model, so what she had chosen was neither extravagant nor fussy. It had given Laura a great deal of satisfaction to see Amanda nod with approval over her selections.

It was a step, Laura told herself as she carried her bags and boxes through the front door. It might be a step only a woman would understand, but it was definitely a step. She was taking her life in hand again, if only by acknowledging that she needed clothes—clothes that suited her own taste and style—to live it. She was humming when she walked upstairs.

It was there that she found them together, Gabe sprawled over the bed, with Michael snuggled in the curve of his arm. Her husband was sound asleep. Her son had kicked free of his light blanket and was shaking a rattle at the ceiling.

Quietly she set down her bags and crossed to them. It was a purely male scene, the man stretched across the bed, shoes still on, a spy thriller lying facedown on the coverlet, a glass of something that had once been cold leaving a ring on the antique nightstand.

The child, as if he understood that he was a part of this man's world, lay quietly and thought his own thoughts.

She wished she had even a portion of Gabe's skill. If she had, she would have drawn them together like this. Then the scene, the sweetness of it, would never be lost. For a while she sat on the edge of the bed and watched them.

It was so intimate, she thought, watching a man while he slept. She wanted to brush at the dark blond hair on his forehead, to trace the roughly hewn lines of his face, but she was afraid it would disturb him. Then the vulnerability would be gone, and this look at the private side of him would be over.

He was a beautiful man, though he didn't like to hear it. The compassion in him, which he often coated over with sarcasm or temper, ran deep. When she looked at him now, freely, without his being aware, she could see every reason why she'd fallen in love with him.

When Michael began to fret, she murmured and leaned over him, trying to pick him up without waking Gabe. At the first movement, Gabe's eyes opened. They were drowsy and very close to hers.

"I'm sorry. I didn't want to wake you."

He said nothing. Going with a dream she couldn't see but was very much a part of, he cupped a hand at the back of her head and drew her lips to his. There was a tenderness there that she hadn't felt for a very long time, an offering, a promise.

It was a promise she wanted, if only he would give it. It was a promise she would believe in.

Michael, scenting his mother, decided it was time to eat.

Unsettled and wishing they'd had just a moment more, Laura eased back. When Michael began to root at her breast, she undid two buttons and let him have his way.

"Did he wear you out?"

"We were taking a short break." It never failed to fascinate him how perfectly beautiful she looked when she was nursing the baby. He'd already sketched her like this, but that was for himself. "I didn't realize how much energy you need to handle someone so small."

"It gets worse. When we were shopping I saw a woman with a toddler. She never stopped running. Your mother tells me she used to collapse every afternoon when you'd finally worn down enough to take a nap."

"Lies." He shoved a couple of pillows behind his back and settled comfortably. "I was a perfectly behaved child."

"Then it was some other child who drew with crayon all over the silk wallpaper."

"Artistic expression. I was a prodigy."

"No doubt."

He just lifted a brow. Then he spotted her bags across the room. "I was going to ask if you had a good time with my mother, but the answer's obvious."

She caught herself on the verge of an apology. That had to stop, she reminded herself. "It was wonderful to buy shoes and actually see them when I stood up, and a dress that had a waist in it."

"I suppose that's difficult for a woman, losing her figure during pregnancy."

"I loved every minute of it. The first time I couldn't hook a pair of slacks I was ecstatic." She started to go on, then stopped. That was something he would never be a part of, she realized. The first joys and fears, the first movements. Looking down at Michael, she wished with all her heart that he was Gabe's child in every way. "Still, I'm happy now not to look like an aircraft carrier."

"It was more like a dirigible."

"You give the most charming compliments."

He waited until she shifted Michael to her other breast. There was an urge inside of him to trace his finger there, just above where the baby suckled. It wasn't sexual, or even romantic, it was more a wondering. Instead, he tucked his hands behind his head.

"I tossed some leftovers together. I've no idea if they're edible."

Again there was the urge to apologize. Determined, Laura merely smiled. "I'm hungry enough for marginally edible."

"Good." Now he he did lean forward, but only to trace a fingertip over Michael's head. "Come on down when he's settled. After this afternoon, I have a feeling he'll go out like a light when his belly's full."

"I won't be long." She waited until she was alone, then closed her eyes, hoping she had the courage to carry out her plans for the rest of the evening.

She hadn't been just a woman in so long. Laura stood in front of the mirrored wall, fogged now from the steam of her bath. She looked like a woman. Her nightgown was the palest blue, nearly white. She'd chosen it because it had reminded her of the way the snow had looked on the mountains in Colorado. It fell down her body from thin straps and a lacy bodice. She ran her hand down it experimentally. The material was very thin and very soft.

Should she wear her hair up, or wear it down? Did it matter?

What would it be like to be Gabe's wife...really his wife? She pressed a hand to her stomach, waiting for the nerves to ebb. Memories threatened to surface, and she fought them back. Tonight she would take Amanda's advice. She would think not of what had been, but of what could be.

She loved him so much, but she didn't know how to tell him. Words were so difficult, so irrevocable. Worse, she was afraid that he would take her love with the same discomfort and disregard as he did her gratitude. But tonight...she hoped tonight she could begin to show him.

He was stripping off his shirt when she opened the door to the adjoining bedroom. For a moment the light coming from behind her fell over her hair and ran through the thin fabric of her gown. All movement stopped as though it were a play, just as the curtain rose. He felt the heat and the tightening in his stomach.

Then she switched off the bathroom light. He pulled off his shirt.

"I checked on Michael." Gabe was surprised he could speak at all, but the words sounded normal enough. "He's sleeping. I thought I might work for an hour or two."

"Oh." She caught herself before she could twist her hands together. She was a grown woman. A grown woman should know how to seduce her husband. "I know you lost time this afternoon when I went out."

"I liked taking care of him." She was so slim, so beautifully frail, with her milky white skin and that blue-white gown. The angel again, with a fall of blond curls instead of a halo.

"You're a wonderful father, Gabe." She took a step toward him. She was already beginning to tremble.

"Michael makes it easy."

Should she have known it would be so difficult to simply cross a room? "Do I make it hard, to be a husband?"

"No." He lifted the back of his hand to her cheek. Her eyes were shades upon shades darker than the flow of silk she wore. He drew back, surprised by his own nerves. "You must be tired."

She bit off a sigh as she turned away. "It's obvious I'm not very good at this. Since seducing you isn't working, we'll try the more practical approach."

"Is that what you were doing?" He wanted to be amused, but his muscles were tight with tension. "Seducing me?"

"Badly." Opening her drawer, she drew out a small slip of paper. "This is my doctor's report. It says that I'm a normal, healthy woman. Would you care to read it?"

This time his lips twitched. "Covered all the bases, did you?"

"You said you wanted me." The paper crumpled in her hand. "I thought you meant it."

He had her arms before she could retreat. Her eyes were dry, but he could see, just by looking, her fractured pride. The burden he already felt grew heavier. What they had was still so tenuous. If he made a mistake it might vanish completely.

"I meant it, Laura, started meaning it from the first day you were with me. It hasn't been easy, being with you, needing you, and not being able to touch."

Gingerly she laid a hand on his chest and felt his muscles tighten. "There's no reason you can't now."

He slid his hands up to her shoulders so that his fingers brushed over the thin straps of her gown. If it was a mistake, he had no choice but to make it. "No physical one any longer. When I take you to bed, there can only be the two of us. No ghosts. No memories." When she dropped her gaze, he drew her closer, challenging her to lift it again. "You won't think of anyone but me."

Whether it was a threat or a promise, he lowered his mouth to hers. Her hands fluttered, then were trapped between their bodies.

It was only the press of lips upon lips, but her blood began to pound. The stirring he could cause so easily started in her stomach and spread, long before his hands moved over her, long before her lips parted.

Her hands were imprisoned, but she didn't feel vulnerable. His mouth wasn't gentle, but she didn't feel afraid. As the kiss deepened, as the intimacy grew, she didn't think of anyone but him.

She tasted as she had the very first time, ripe and fresh. With his tongue he plundered her mouth, greedy for the flavor of her. There would be no turning back now, not when she was caught close in his arms and the lights were dim. He could hear her shuddering breath, and the steady ticking of the pendulum clock in the hallway. It was dark, it was quiet, they were alone. And tonight he would take a wife.

Her heart thudded against his bare chest, adding excitement. He ran his hands over her, feeling the smoothness of her skin, the slickness of her gown, feeling every tremble and every sigh his touch incited.

Greedy, he nipped his teeth into her lip as his hands moved lower. Passion sprung out, from him, from her, mixing together in a sudden, breath-stopping fury. Then he felt her body give against his in the ultimate gift of trust. The emotions that rose up in him tempered his desire. Tenderness, achingly sweet, more precious than diamonds, took its place.

Her hands were free. The paper still crumpled in her palm
fluttered to the floor as she slipped her arms around him.
Tentatively still. Her bones seemed to liquefy, degree by degree, until she wondered why she didn't simply slide out of
his hands. Her mind, which had been swirling with needs,
clouded with a pleasure that was softer, truer, than any she
had ever imagined.

She stroked her hands over his back, feeling the muscle,
the power. Wonder filled her at the discovery that anyone
with such strength could be so gentle. His lips brushed over
hers, testing, almost teasing, inviting her to set the pace. Or
perhaps he was challenging her.

Hunger leaped inside her until she was locked against
him, her mouth seeking, avid, impatient. Then she was
swept up into his arms. In the dim light she saw his eyes,
only his eyes, their clear green darkened by need. Hers remained open and on his as he lowered her onto the bed.

She expected speed, a frenzy of greed and a drive for
gratification. She wouldn't have thought less of him for it.
Her love wouldn't have diminished. Against hers, his body
was taut and straining. Circling her arms around him, she
prepared to give him whatever he required.

But it wasn't speed he sought. And the greed was not only
to take, but also to give.

When he ranged kisses over her throat, lingering, nib-
bling, she, too, went taut. She could only whisper his name
as he continued the slow journey over her shoulders and
down to the curve of her breasts, then up again, in teasing
circles. Instinctively she turned her head, seeking his mouth,
his jaw, his temple, as her body turned hot and cold with
pleasure.

He needed to take care, for her. At the first touch, he'd
been terrified. She had been with another man, she had had
a child, but he knew the extent of her innocence. He'd seen
it, hour after hour, when he'd painted her. He'd felt it each

and every time he'd drawn her against him. If he was going to take that innocence, he was going to give her beauty in return.

She was so... responsive. Her body seemed to ebb and flow at the touch of his hands. Wherever he tasted, her skin grew warm. Yet even as she gave, and offered, there was a shyness about her, the slightest of hesitations. He wanted to take her beyond that.

Slowly, with movements that were little more than a whisper along her skin, he drew the gown downward, following the trail of lace with his lips. At her first moan, his blood swam. He hadn't known that a sound, only a sound, could be so alluring. With light, openmouthed kisses he sensitized her skin until she began to shiver beneath him. In the lamplight she was exquisite, her skin like marble, her hair like silver. Her eyes were full of needs and uncertainties.

As he had once used his skill, his insight, to draw her emotions on canvas, he used it now to set them free.

She had never known there could be such sensitivity between a man and a woman. Even through the clouds of pleasure and the steadily rising tide of desire, she sensed his patience. She had never been so driven to touch a man before. With her fingertips and her palms, with her lips and her tongue, she discovered him. The urge came, strong, just to hold him, to wrap tight around him and hold on.

Then, without warning, he was taking her up, making her arch and gasp in shock and indescribable delight. Her mind and body were drained of everything but sensation. For an instant there was a terror of being totally out of control. His name burst out of her as she was carried away by a climax so strong, so intense, that she was left limp and dazed in the aftermath.

"Please, I can't... I've never..."

"I know." Strangely humbled, he lowered his lips to hers. He had wanted to give, had been driven to, but he hadn't known that in giving, so much would be returned to him. "Just relax. There's no hurry."

"But you haven't—"

He laughed against her throat. "I intend to. There's time. I want to touch you," he murmured, and began the slow, seductive journey again.

It wasn't possible. She would have said it couldn't be possible for her body to leap back in response to so gentle, so light, a touch. Yet within moments she was trembling again, aching again, wanting again. His tongue skimmed over her stomach, dipped to the curve of her thigh, until she was writhing, a victim now of her own desire and of the taste of heaven he'd already given her.

Then, impossibly, incredibly, she was tossed up and over again. This time, when she gasped and faltered, he slid into her.

Her moan merged with his.

Damp flesh pressed against damp flesh as they moved together. She'd never felt so strong, so utterly free, as she did now, joined as closely as was conceivable with Gabe.

She was everything he'd ever wanted, everything he'd ever dreamed of. Indeed, it was like a dream now, with the bursts and shudders of pleasure ripping through him. With his face pressed against her throat, he could smell her lightly provocative fragrance, mixed with the pungent, earthy scent of passion. He would go to the grave remembering that dizzying combination.

Her breath was fast and frenzied in his ear. Her body was just as fast and frenzied beneath his. He could feel her nails as she dug heedlessly into his back.

He would remember all of it.

Then he remembered nothing, and he let himself go.

Chapter Nine

There had been a time, a brief time, when Laura had dressed in elegant clothes and gone to elegant parties. She had met people whose names were printed in slick magazines and flashed in bold headlines in tabloids. She'd danced with celebrities and dined with princes of fashion. However much it had seemed like a dream, it had been real.

It was true enough that she had enjoyed her time modeling for Geoffrey. The work might have been hard, but she'd been young enough, untried enough, to have been dazzled by the glamour—even after ten hours on her feet.

He had taught her how to stand, how to walk, even how to look interested when fatigue was all but pouring out of her ears. He'd shown her how to use makeup to enhance subtly or strikingly, how to use her hair to express a mood.

All the things he'd taught her had helped her maintain an image during public events with the Eagletons. She'd been able to appear sophisticated and untroubled. At times, appearances were a great comfort.

She wasn't afraid she would embarrass herself or Gabe at the reception his parents were giving at their Nob Hill estate. But she wasn't certain she wanted to step back into that life again, either.

How might things have been if Gabe had been an ordinary man, a man of ordinary means? They might have found a little house with a little backyard and been swallowed up by anonymity. A part of her yearned for that, for the simplicity of it.

But that was wrong. Laura fastened the earrings she'd bought the week before, starbursts of blue stones. If Gabe had come from a different family and a different life, he wouldn't be the man she loved. The man she was almost ready to believe was beginning to love her.

There was nothing about him she wanted to change, not his looks, not his manner. She might wish occasionally that he would share with her a bit more of his thoughts and feelings, but she continued to hope that someday he would.

She wanted to be a full part of his life—lover, wife and partner. So far, she had come to be the first two.

When the door opened, she turned.

"If you're about ready, we'll—"

And he stopped and stared. This was the woman she'd only told him about, the one who had graced the covers of magazines and modeled silks and sables. Long-limbed and slender, she stood in front of the beveled mirror in a dress of midnight blue. It was very simple, leaving her shoulders and throat bare, then caught like a wish at her breasts to fall ruler-straight to her feet.

She'd wound her hair up, swept it back, so that only a few wheat-colored curls escaped to tease her temples.

She was beautiful, gloriously so, yet even as he was drawn to her, he felt as though he were looking at a stranger.

"You look wonderful." But he kept his hand on the knob and the room between them. "I'll have to paint you like this." *Beauty on Ice*, he thought, cool, aloof and unapproachable.

"I took your advice on the color." She picked up her purse, then clasped and unclasped it as she wondered why he was looking at her as though he'd never seen her before. "And I avoided bows."

"So I see." She should have sapphires, a collar of them, around her throat. "It's still a bit cool. Do you have a wrap?"

"Yes." Irked by his tone, she walked to the bed and snatched up a wide silk scarf in a riot of jewellike colors. It was then that he noticed that the back of the skirt was slit to the thigh.

"I imagine you'll create quite a stir in that little number."

She cringed inwardly, but, falling back on appearances, she managed to keep her face calm. "If you don't like the dress, why don't you just say so?" She swirled the scarf over her shoulders. "It's too late to change, but believe me, I won't wear it again."

"Just a minute." He grabbed her hand as she stared through the doorway. He could feel the smooth gold of her plain wedding ring on the index finger of her right hand. She was still his Laura, he thought as he linked his fingers with hers. He'd only had to look in her eyes to see it.

"I have to get Michael ready," she mumbled, and tried again to move past him.

"Do you expect an apology because I'm human enough to be jealous?"

Her face went still, her eyes blank,. "I'm not wearing it to attract other men. I bought it because I liked it and I thought it suited me."

He brought a hand to her face and swore roundly when he jerked. "Look at me. No, damn it, not at him, at me." Her eyes lashed back up to him. "Remember who I am, Laura. And remember this—I won't tolerate having my every mood, my every word, compared with someone else's."

"I'm not trying to do that."

"Maybe you're not trying to, but you do."

"You expect me to turn my life around overnight. I can't."

"No." He ran his thumb over the ring again. "I don't suppose you can. But you can remember that I'm part of your new life, not your old one."

"You're nothing like him." It was becoming easier to let her hand relax in his. "I know that. I guess sometimes it's easier to expect the worst than to hope for the best."

"I can't promise you the best."

No, he wouldn't make promises he couldn't keep. That was the beauty of him. "You could hold me. That's as close as I need to get."

When his arms came around her, he pressed her cheek against the shoulder of his black evening jacket. It smelled of him, and that made the last twists of tension dissolve.

"I suppose I was jealous, too."

"Oh?"

She smiled as she drew back enough to look into his face. "You look so good tonight."

"Really?" There was both discomfort and amusement in his tone.

"I've never seen you in evening clothes." She ran her finger down the dark lapel, which rested against a crisp white shirt. "Sort of like Heathcliff in a tux."

He laughed and cupped her face in his hands. "What a mind you have, angel. There's no hero in here."

"You're wrong." Her eyes were very solemn, very serious. "You're mine." He shrugged, but she kept him close. "Please, just this once, let me say it without you brushing it aside."

He just flicked a finger down her nose. "Don't expect me to walk around in armor too long. Let's get the baby. My mother knows how to make you miserable if you're late."

He wasn't a hero. He certainly wasn't comfortable being seen as one. Gabe was much more at ease discussing his work or speculating on the Giants' chances during the rest of the baseball season. He preferred arguments to good deeds.

When someone saw you as heroic, you invariably let them down. They expected you to have the right answers, the key to the lock, the light in the dark.

Michael had seen him as a hero. And, of course, he had let his brother down.

Michael had loved parties like this, Gabe thought as he sipped at the champagne that seemed to flow endlessly. He had loved the laughter, the people and the gossip. Michael had been unashamedly fond of rumors and whispers.

People had loved him moments after meeting him. He had been outgoing, funny, and as warm with strangers as with friends. It was Michael who had been the hero, doing favors without tallying the score, always willing to help or simply to be enthusiastic about a project.

Yet he'd had that streak of temper and toughness that had balanced him, prevented him from being overly... overly good, Gabe supposed.

God, he missed him still, at times unbearably.

There were people here who had known Michael, who had raised a glass with him or swapped stories with him. Perhaps that was what made it seem worse tonight, being in their parents' home, where they had grown up and shared so much and knowing that Michael would never walk into that room again.

Somehow you went on. One part of your life closed up, and another opened. Gabe looked across the room to where Laura stood talking to his father.

Sometime between the moment she'd rolled down the window of a wrecked car and the moment she'd placed a newborn child in his arms he'd fallen in love with her. It had come not with trumpets and flares but with quiet, soothing murmurs.

If there were such things as angels, one had sent Laura to him when he'd needed her most.

She was grateful to him, and open enough to give him love and affection in return for what he had given her. There were days when he believed that would be enough, for today, and for the tomorrows they would have together.

Then there were the other times.

He wanted to grab her, to demand again and again that she look at him, see who he was, what he felt. That she forget what had happened before and trust in what was happening now. He wanted to erase, the way he might have blanked out a canvas, what had gone on before, all the things that had put shadows in her eyes, all the things that made her hesitate just that split second before she smiled.

But he knew better than most that when you painted over part of someone's life you stole something. Bad experience or good, what had happened to Laura had made her what she was, the woman he loved.

But loving as he did, and being a selfish man, he wanted to be loved back, completely, without the strings of gratitude or the shadows of vulnerability. Wanting wouldn't make it so, but time might. He could give her a little more of that.

Someone laughed across the room. Glasses chinked. There was a scent of wine, flowers and women's fragrances. The night had cooperated with a full moon, and its glow shimmered just outside the open terrace doors. The room was ablaze with lamplight. Wanting a few moments away from the crowd and the noise, he slipped upstairs to check on his son.

"The boy looks more like you every time I see him," Cliff was saying.

"Do you think so?" The thought had Laura lighting up. Perhaps she was vain after all.

"Absolutely. Though no one would believe you were a new mother, the way you're looking tonight." He patted her cheek in the way that always made her feel shy and delighted. "My Gabe has excellent taste."

"Shame on you, Cliff, flirting with a beautiful woman when your wife's not looking."

"Marion." Cliff bent down from his rangy height to give the newcomer a kiss. "Late as always."

"Amanda's already scolded me." She turned, sipping at her champagne, to give Laura a thorough study. "So this is the mysterious Laura."

"My new daughter." Cliff gave Laura a quick squeeze around the shoulders. "An old friend, Marion Trussalt. The Trussalt Gallery handles Gabe's paintings."

"Yes, I know. It's nice to meet you." She wasn't a beautiful woman, Laura thought, but she was oddly striking, with her sleek cap of black hair and her dark eyes. She wore a flowing rainbow-colored sheath that managed to be both arty and sophisticated.

"Yes, it is, since we have Gabe in common." Marion tapped a finger on the rim of her glass and smiled, but her eyes didn't warm. Laura recognized carefully polished disdain when she saw it. "You have his heart, and I his soul, you might say."

"Then it would seem we both want the best for him."

"Oh." Marion raised her glass. "Absolutely. Cliff, Amanda told me to remind you that hosts are supposed to mingle."

He grimaced. "Slave driver. Laura, be sure to work your way over to the buffet. You're getting too thin already." With that he went to do his duty.

"Yes, you're amazingly slender for someone who had a child—what was it? A month ago?"

"Almost two." Laura shifted her glass of sparkling water to her other hand. She didn't deal well with subtle attacks.

"Time flies." Marion touched her tongue to her upper lip. "It's odd that in all that time you haven't stirred yourself to come down to the gallery."

"You're right. I'll have to come down and see Gabe's work in a proper setting." She steadied herself. Under no circumstances was she going to allow herself to be intimidated or to fall into the trap of reading between the lines. If Gabe had ever had any kind of romantic involvement with Marion, it had ended. "He relies on you, I know. And I hope you'll be able to persuade him to go through with a new showing."

"I haven't decided that's really a good idea for the time being." Marion turned to smile at someone across the room who had called her name.

"Why? The paintings are wonderful."

"That isn't the only issue." She turned back to give Laura a quick, glittering look. She hadn't been Gabe's lover, nor had there every been any urge on either side to make it so. Her feelings for Gabriel Bradley went far beyond the physical. Gabe was an artist, a great one, and she had been—and intended to go on being—the catalyst for his success.

If he had married within his circle, or chosen someone who could have enhanced or furthered his career, she would have been pleased. But for him to have wasted himself, and her ambitions, on a beautiful face and a smeared reputation was more than Marion could bear.

"Did I mention that I knew your first husband?"

If she had thrown her drink into Laura's face she would have been no less shocked. The cocoon that she had been able to draw around herself and Michael suffered its first crack.

"No. If you'll excuse me—"

"A fascinating man, I always thought. Certainly young, and a bit wild, but fascinating. A tragedy that he died so young, before he ever saw his child." She tilted her glass back until only a sheen of bubbles remained.

"Michael," Laura said evenly, "is Gabe's child."

"So I'm told." She smiled again. "There were the oddest rumors just before and just after Tony died. Some said that he was on the verge of divorcing you, that he'd already removed you from the family home because you were, well, indiscreet." With a shrug, Marion set her glass aside. "But that's all in the past now. Tell me, how are the Eagletons? I haven't spoke with Lorraine for ages."

She was going to be ill, violently and humiliatingly ill, unless she succeeded in fighting back her rolling nausea. "Why are you doing this?" she whispered. "Why should you care?"

"Oh, my dear, I care about anything that has to do with Gabe. I intend to see him reach the very top, and I don't intend to watch him be dragged down. That's a lovely dress," she added. Then she saw Amanda approaching and slipped away.

"Laura, are you all right? You're white as a sheet. Come, let me find you a chair."

"No, I need some air." Turning, she fled through the open glass doors and onto the smooth stone terrace beyond.

"Here, now." Coming up behind her, Amanda took her arm and steered her to a chair. "Sit a minute before Gabe comes along. He'll take one look at you and pounce on me for insisting you come out and socialize too soon."

"It's nothing to do with that."

"And something to do with Marion." Amanda took the water glass out of Laura's tightening grip. "If she led you to believe that there was something—personal—between herself and Gabe, I can only say its totally untrue."

"That wouldn't matter."

With a little laugh, Amanda cast a look back inside. "If you mean that, then you're a better woman than I. I've known one of my husband's former . . . interests for over thirty-five years. I'd still like to spit in her eye."

With a laugh of her own, Laura drew in the softly scented evening. "I know Gabe's faithful to me."

"And so you should. You should also know that Marion and Gabe were never lovers." She moved her shoulders a bit. "I can't say that I know about all of my son's affairs, but I do know that he and Marion only have art in common. Now, what did she say to upset you?"

"It was nothing." Laura brushed her fingers over her temples, as if to soothe away an ache. "Really, it was my own fault, overreacting. She only mentioned that she'd met my first husband."

"I see." Annoyed, Amanda turned her sharp-eyed glance into the drawing room again. "Well, I have to say I find it very insensitive to bring up the subject at your wedding reception. One would have thought a woman like Marion would have more taste."

"It's over and it's best forgotten." Straightening her shoulders, Laura prepared to go back in. "I'd appreciate it if you wouldn't mention any of this to Gabe. There's no reason to annoy him."

"No, I agree. I'll speak with Marion myself."

"No." Laura picked up her glass again and sipped slowly. "If there's anything that needs to be said, I'll say it myself."

Amanda's smile spread and she said easily, "If that's what you'd like."

"Yes. Amanda . . ." A decision made quickly, she thought, was sometimes the best. "Could I leave Michael with you one day next week? I'd like to go into the gallery and see Gabe's paintings."

* * *

Laura woke up out of breath and shivering. She struggled her way out of the nightmare to find herself in Gabe's arms.

"Just relax. You're all right."

She drew in a big gulp of air, then let it out slowly. "Sorry," she muttered, dragging a hand through her hair.

"Want anything? Some water?"

"No." As the fear passed, annoyance took its place. The glowing dial of the alarm clock read 4:15. They'd been in bed for only three hours, and now she was wide-awake and restless.

With his arm still around her, Gabe lay back on his pillow. "You haven't had a nightmare since Michael was born. Did something happen at the party tonight?"

She thought of Marion and gritted her teeth. "Why do you ask?"

"I noticed that you seemed upset, and my mother annoyed."

"Did you think that I had an argument with your mother?" That made her smile and settle more comfortably against him. "No, in fact we get along very well."

"You sound surprised."

"I didn't expect to make friends with her. I kept waiting for her to bring out her broom and pointed hat."

He laughed and kissed her shoulder. "Just try criticizing my work."

"I wouldn't dare." Unconsciously she began to stroke her fingers through his hair. When she was here, like this, she believed she could handle anything that threatened her new family. "She showed me the mural in the parlor. The one with all the mythical creatures."

"I was twenty, and romantic." And he'd asked his mother a dozen times to have it painted over.

"I like it."

"No wonder you get along with her."

"I did like it." She shifted so that she could rest her arms on his chest. There was only a little moonlight, but she could see him. She didn't realize that it was her first completely unstudied move toward him, but he did. "What's wrong with unicorns and centaurs and fairies?"

"They have their place, I suppose." But all he was currently interested in was making love with her.

"Good. Then don't you think the side wall in Michael's room is the perfect place for a mural?"

He tugged at a curl that fell over her cheek. "Are you offering me a commission?"

"Well, I've seen a few samples of your work, and it's not bad."

He tugged harder. "Not bad?"

"Shows promise." With a quick laugh, she ducked before he could pull her hair again. "Why don't you submit some sample sketches for consideration?"

"And my fee?"

He was smiling; her skin was warming. Laura began to think the nightmare had been a blessing in disguise. "Negotiable."

"Tell you what. I'll do the mural on one condition."

"Which is?"

"That you let me paint you again, nude."

Her eyes widened. Then she laughed, sure he was joking. "You should at least let me wear a beret."

"You've been watching too many old movies, but you can wear a beret if you like—just nothing else."

"I couldn't."

"All right, then, scratch the beret."

"Gabe, you're not serious."

"Of course I am." To prove it, and to please himself, he ran a hand over her. "You have a beautiful body... long dancer's limbs, smooth white skin, a narrow waist."

"Gabe." She spoke to stop not his roaming hands but his conversation. She stopped neither.

"I've wanted to paint you nude since the first time we made love. I can still see the way you looked when I drew the nightgown away. Capturing that femininity, that subtle sexuality, would be a triumph."

She laid her cheek on his heart. "I'd be embarrassed."

"Why? I know what you look like. Every inch of you." He cupped her breasts, scraping his thumbs lightly over her nipples. Her instant response rippled through him.

"No one else does." Her voice was husky now. Hardly realizing it, she began to run her hands over him. The journey was long, lazy, thorough.

There was something incredibly exciting about the idea. No one else knew the secrets of her body, the dips and curves. No one else knew how a touch here, a stroke there, could make her shyness melt into passion. He did want to capture that on canvas, the beauty of her, the sweetness of her inhibitions. The fire of passion just discovered. But he could wait.

"I suppose I could just hire a model."

Her head came up at that. "You—" The jealousy rose, so swift and powerful that it left her momentarily speechless.

"It's art, angel," he said, amused and not at all displeased. "Not a centerfold."

"You're trying to blackmail me."

"You're very sharp."

Her eyes narrowed. In deliberate seduction that surprised them both, she shifted so that her body rubbed tantalizingly over his. "Only if I get to choose the model."

His pulse was thudding. As she lowered her head to brush kisses over his chest, he closed his eyes. "Laura."

"No, Mrs. Drumberry. I met her tonight."

He opened his eyes. But when she used her teeth to tug on his nipple he arched beneath her. "Mabel Drumberry is a hundred and five."

"Exactly." She chuckled but continued her explorations, with a growing sense of power and discovery. "I wouldn't trust you closed up in your studio with some sexy young redhead with lush curves."

He started to laugh, but the sound became a moan as her hand ranged lower. "Don't you think I can resist a sexy young redhead?"

"Of course, but she wouldn't be able to resist you." She rubbed her cheek along his jawline, which was already roughened with morning stubble. "You're so beautiful, Gabe. If I could paint, I'd show you."

"What you're doing is driving me crazy."

"I hope so," she murmured, and lowered her mouth to his.

She'd never had the confidence to take charge, had never been sure enough of her skill or her appeal. Now it seemed right and wonderfully fulfilling to tease and taunt her man in passion.

His hands were in her hair, his fingers tangled and tense, as she dipped her tongue into his mouth and explored. Her moves were instinctive rather than experienced, and all the more seductive for it.

The power came to her not in a wild burst but with quiet certainty. She could be his partner here, his full partner. It was easy to show love, almost as easy as it was to feel it.

As she discovered him, she discovered herself. She wasn't as patient as he, not here. Strangely, in the daylight, the opposite was true. She saw him as a man who needed to move quickly, decisively, and if mistakes were made because of hurry they could be corrected or just as easily ignored. She was more cautious, more prone to think through alternatives before acting.

But in bed, in the role of the seductress, she found little patience in herself.

She was wild and wanton. Gabe found himself reaching for her, then being rocked helplessly by the sensations she brought to him. It was like having different woman in bed, one who felt like Laura, smelled like Laura, one he wanted as desperately as he wanted Laura.

When her mouth came down on his, it was Laura's taste, yet somehow darker, riper. And her body was like a furnace as she moved over him.

He tried to remember that this was his wife, his shy and still-innocent wife, who required infinite care and gentleness. He had yet to release his full range of passion with her. With Laura he had taken his time, used every drop of his sensitivity.

Now she was stripping him down to the nerve ends.

She could feel the power, and it was glorious. Despite her excitement, her mind was clear as a bell. She could make him weak, she could make him desperate. She could make him tremble. Breathlessly she pressed her lips to pulse points that she found by instinct. His heart was racing. For her. She could feel his body shudder at her touch. When he groaned, it was her own name she heard.

She heard herself laugh, and there was something sultry in the sound. A feminine triumph. The clock in the hallway struck five, and the echo went on and on in her head.

Then his arms were locked around her and the sound that was coming from his throat was long and primitive. His control snapped like a rubber band stretched too far. Needs only half satisfied, so long held in check, flooded free. His mouth covered hers, bruisingly. But it wasn't a skip of fear she felt. It was a leap of victory.

Trapped in madness, they rolled across the bed, seeking, taking, demanding, with a kind of greed that made the mouth go dry and the soul shudder. The modest gown she wore was torn aside, seams ripping, lace shredding. His hands were everywhere, and they were far from gentle.

There was no shame. There was no shyness. This was freedom, a different kind from what he had already shown her. As desperate as he, she opened for him. When he plunged into her, the shock vibrated, wave after wave.

Fast and furious, they locked into their own rhythm, each driving the other.

Endless pleasure, sharp and edgy. Insatiable need spreading like wildfire. As she gave herself to him, as she asked and received more, Laura realized that, for the lucky, time could indeed stop.

Chapter Ten

When the sky darkened, Laura was in the garden. It had become her habit to spend her mornings there while the baby slept or sat rocking in his swing in the sunlight. Since her arrival in Gabe's home, she'd found little to do indoors. The house almost took care of itself and, as she had once told him, Gabe was only sloppy when he painted.

More than that, there were too many rooms, too much space that she didn't yet feel a part of. In the nursery, which she'd decorated herself and where, through necessity, she spent many hours during the day and night, she felt at home. The rest of the house, with its heirlooms and its beautiful old rugs, its polished wood and its faded wallpaper, remained aloof to her.

But as spring had taken hold she had discovered an affinity and a talent for gardening, as well as a need for space and air. She liked the sunlight and the smells and the feel of the earth under her hands. She devoured books on plants, much as she had on childbirth, so that she could become familiar with flowers and shrubs and the care they required.

The tulips were beginning to bloom, and the azaleas were already ripe with blossoms. Someone else had planted them, but Laura had no trouble taking them to heart as her own. They flowered afresh every year. Nor did she feel awkward adding her own touches with moss roses and snapdragons.

Already she was planning to plant new bulbs in the fall, daylilies, windflowers, poppies. Then, over the winter, she would root her own spring flowers from seed, starting them in little peat pots that she would set in the sun room on the east side of the house.

"I'll teach you how to plant them next year," she told Michael. She could already imagine him toddling around the garden on short, sturdy legs, patting at the dirt, trying to snatch butterflies off blossoms.

He would laugh. There would be so much for him to laugh about. She would be able to catch him up in her arms and swing him around so that his eyes, which were still as stubbornly blue as hers, glowed and his laughter bounced on the air. Then Gabe would stick his head out of his studio window and demand to know what all the ruckus was about.

But he wouldn't really be annoyed. He'd come down, saying that if there was going to be so much noise he might as well forget about working for the morning. He'd sit on the ground with Michael in his lap and they'd laugh together about nothing anyone else would understand.

Sitting back on her heels, Laura wiped her brow with the back of a gloved hand. Dreaming had always been her escape, her defense, her survival. Now it didn't seem like any of those things, because she was beginning to believe dreams could come true.

"I love your daddy," she told Michael, as she told him at least once every day. "I love him so much that it makes me believe in happy endings."

When the shadow fell over her, Laura glanced up and saw the first dark clouds roll over the sun. She was tempted to ignore them, and she might have if she hadn't known it took more than a quick minute to gather up all her gardening tools, Michael's supplies and the baby himself.

"Well, the rain's good for the flowers, isn't it, sweetie?" She stored the tools and bags of peat moss and fertilizers in the small shed near the back door, then drew Michael out of the swing. With the acquired coordination of motherhood, she carried the baby, his little cache of toys and the folded swing indoors.

She'd barely started upstairs when the first crack of thunder had both her and Michael jumping. As he began to wail, she fought back her own longstanding fear of storms and soothed him.

He calmed down much more quickly than she as she walked and rocked and murmured reassurances. Though the rain held off, she could watch the fury raging in the sky through Michael's windows. Lightning slashed, turning the light from gray to mauve, then back to gray, in the blink of an eye.

Eventually he began to doze, but she continued to hold him, as much for her own comfort as his.

"Silly, isn't it?" she murmured. "A grown woman more afraid of thunder than a tiny baby." As the rain began to lash at the house, she made herself set the sleeping child in his crib so that she could close the windows.

At least that would keep her busy, Laura told herself as she moved from room to room to shut the windows against the pelting rain. Still, each time thunder boomed she jerked back. It wasn't until she started back into the nursery, telling herself she'd curl up on the daybed and read until the storm passed, that she remembered Gabe's studio. Thinking only of his work, she rushed down the hall.

She was grateful that the storm hadn't knocked out the power. The lights flared on at a touch. It seemed that her luck had held. The floor was wet by the ribbon of windows, but none of his paintings were stored there. Laura hurried down the line, shutting each one until the rain was muffled by the glass.

She started to do the practical thing and go for a mop, but then it struck her that this was the first time she had been in Gabe's studio alone. He'd never asked her not to go in, but the lack of privacy she'd lived with most of her life had made her fastidious about respecting that of others. Now, though, with the lights bright overhead and the thunder rolling in the distance, she felt comfortable there, as she did in the nursery. As she had in the cabin in the mountains.

The room smelled of him, she realized. It held that mixture of paint and turpentine, with the powdery addition of chalk, that often clung to his clothes and his hands. It was a scent that invariably put her at ease, even though it was also a scent that invariably aroused her. Like the man, she thought, the scent drew her emotions. She could love him and be comforted by him, just as she could be excited and confused by him.

What did he want from her? she wondered. And why? She thought she understood part of it. He wanted the solidity of family, an end to his own loneliness and passion in bed. He'd chosen her for those things because she'd been as anxious to give them as he was to take them.

It could be enough, or nearly enough. Her problem was, and continued to be, a quiet longing for more.

Shaking off the mood, she tried to picture him there in that room, alone, working, envisioning.

So much had been done here, she thought, so many hours creating, perfecting, experimenting. What made one man different from another in the way he saw and expressed what he saw? Crossing to his easel, she studied his work in progress.

A painting of Michael. The deep and simple pleasure of it had her hugging herself. There was a rough sketch tacked to the easel, and the portrait on canvas was just beginning to take shape. She could see that even since the sketch, which he'd drawn perhaps a week before, Michael had changed and grown. But because of this she would always be able to look back and see him exactly as he'd been in that one precious moment of time.

With her arms still crossed over her breasts, she turned to
study the room. It was different without Gabe in it.
Less...dramatic, she thought. Then she laughed a little,
knowing he would hate that description.

Without him it was a wide, airy room, largely empty. On
the floor were dried drops and smears of paint that could
have been there for a week or a year. A small pedestal sink
was built into one corner. She saw a towel tossed carelessly
over its lip. There were shelves and a worktable with equipment scattered on them. Paints and bottles, jars crammed
with brushes, pallet knives, hunks of charcoal and balled-up
rags. Unframed canvases were stacked against the walls,
much as they had been in Colorado. He hadn't hung anything here.

She wondered why she hadn't thought before to ask Gabe
if he had anything she might hang in Michael's room. The
posters she'd chosen were colorful, but one of Gabe's
paintings would mean more. With that in mind, she knelt
down and began to go through canvases.

How easily he drew out emotion. One of his pastel landscapes would make you dreamy. Next an edgy, too-realistic
view of a slum would make you shudder. There were por-
traits, too—an impossibly old man leaning on a cane at a
bus stop, three young girls giggling outside a boutique.
There was a spectacular nude study of a brunette sprawled
on white satin. Instead of jealousy, it raised a feeling of awe
in Laura.

She went through more than a dozen, wondering why
he'd stacked them so carelessly. Many were unframed, and
all were facing the wall. Each one she held left her more
astonished that she could be married to a man who could do
so much with color and brush. More, each painting gave her
a closer look at who he was. She could sense the mood that
had held him as he'd worked. Rage for this, humor for that.

Sorrow, impatience, desire, delight. Whatever he could feel he could paint.

These didn't belong here, she thought, frustrated that h would close them up in a room where no one could see then or appreciate them or be touched by them. His signature wa dashed in each corner, with the year just below. Everythin; she found had been painted no more than two years before and no less than one year.

She turned the last canvas over and was caught immedi ately. It was another portrait, and this one had been painte with love.

The subject, a young man of no more than thirty, wa grinning, a bit recklessly, as though he had all the time in th world to accomplish what he wanted to do. His hair wa blond, a few shades lighter than Gabe's, and brushed bac from a lean, good-looking face. It was a casual study, full length, with the subject sprawled in a chair, legs spread ou and crossed at the ankle. But, despite the relaxing pose there was a sense of movement and energy.

She recognized the chair. It sat in the parlor of the Brad ley mansion on Nob Hill. And she recognized the subject b the shape of the face, which was so much like her hus band's. This was Gabe's brother. This was Michael.

For a long time she sat there, holding the painting in he lap, no longer hearing the storm. The lights flickered once but she didn't notice.

It was possible, she discovered, to grieve for someone yo hadn't even known, to feel the loss and the regret. Tha Gabe had loved his brother deeply was obvious in eac brush stroke. Not only loved, she thought, but respecte Now more than ever she wished he trusted her enough t speak of this Michael, his life and his death. In the sketch the baby Gabe had tacked on the easel she had seen th same kind of unconditional love.

If he was using the baby to help him get over the loss of his brother, should she begrudge him that? It didn't mean he loved their Michael any less. Still, it made her sad to think of it. Until he talked to her, opened up his emotions to her as he did in his work, she would never really be his wife and Michael would never really be his son.

Gently she turned the canvas back to the wall and replaced the others.

When the rain stopped, Laura decided to call Amanda and follow through with her decision to visit the gallery. If she wanted Gabe to take another step toward her, she would have to take another toward him. She'd avoided going to the gallery, not for all the reasons she had given, but because she hadn't felt comfortable in her role as wife to the public person, the well-known artist. Insecurity, she knew, could only be overcome by taking a confident step forward, even if that step took all the courage you could muster.

She'd grown, Laura told herself. In the past year she'd learned not just to be strong but to be as strong as she needed to be. She might not have reached the peak, but she was no longer scrambling for a foothold at the bottom of the hill.

It was as easy as asking. After her thanks were brushed aside Laura hung up the phone and glanced at her watch. If Michael stuck to his usual schedule, he would wake within the hour and demand to be fed. She could take him to Amanda—the first big step—then drive to the gallery. She glanced down at the dirt—stained knees of her jeans. First she had to change.

The doorbell caught her halfway up the stairs. Feeling too optimistic to be annoyed by the interruption, she went to answer it.

And the world crashed silently at her feet.

"Laura." Lorraine Eagleton gave a brisk nod, then strode into the hall. She stood and glanced idly around as she drew off her gloves. "My, my, you've certainly landed on your feet, haven't you?" She tucked her gloves tidily in a buff colored alligator bag. "Where is the child?"

She couldn't speak. Both words and air were trapped in her lungs, crowding there so that her chest ached. Her hand, still gripping the doorknob, was ice-cold, though the panicked rhythm of her heart vibrated in each fingertip. She had a sudden, horrible flash of the last time she had seen this woman face-to-face. As if they had just been spoken, she remembered the threats, the demand and the humiliation. She found her voice.

"Michael's asleep."

"Just as well. We have business to discuss."

The rain had cooled the air and left its taste in it. Watery sunlight crept through the door, which Laura still hadn't closed. Birds were beginning to chirp optimistically again. Normal things. Such normal things. Life, she reminded herself, didn't bother to stop for personal crises.

Though she couldn't make her fingers relax on the doorknob, she did keep her eyes and her voice level. "You're in my home now, Mrs. Eagleton."

"Women like you always manage to find rich, gullible husbands." She arched a brow, pleased that Laura was still standing by the door, tense and pale. "That doesn't change who you are, what you are. Nor will your being clever enough to get Gabriel Bradley to marry you stop me from taking what's mine."

"I have nothing that belongs to you. I'd like you to leave."

"I'm sure you would," Lorraine said, smiling. She was a tall, striking woman with dark, sculpted hair and an unlined face. "Believe me, I have neither the desire nor the intention to stay long. I intend to have the child."

Laura had a vision of herself standing in the mist, holding an empty blanket. "No."

Lorraine brushed the refusal aside as she might have brushed a speck of lint from her lapel. "I'll simply get a court order."

The cold fear was replaced by heat, and she managed to move then, though it was only to stiffen. "Then do it. Until you do, leave us alone."

Still the same, Lorraine thought as she watched Laura's face. She spit a bit now when she was backed into a corner, but she was still easily maneuvered. It infuriated her now, as it always had, that her son had settled for so little when he could have had so much. Even in fury she never raised her voice. Lorraine had always considered derision a better weapon than volume.

"You should have taken the offer my husband and I made to you. It was generous, and it won't be made again."

"You can't buy my baby, any more than you can buy back Tony."

Pain flashed across Lorraine's face, pain that was real enough, sharp enough, to make Laura form words of sympathy. They could talk, had to be able to talk now, as one mother to another. "Mrs. Eagleton—"

"I won't speak of my son with you," Lorraine said, and the pain vanished into bitterness. "If you had been what he needed, he'd still be alive. I'll never forgive you for that."

There had been a time when she would have crumbled at those words, ready to take the blame. But Lorraine had been wrong. Laura was no longer the same. "Do you want to take my baby to punish me or to bind your wounds? Either reason is wrong. You have to know that."

"I know I can and will prove that you're unfit to care for the child. I'll produce documentation that you made yourself available to other men before and after your marriage to my son."

"You know that's not true."

Lorraine continued as if Laura hadn't spoken. "Added to that will be the record of your unstable family background. If the child proves to be Tony's, there'll be a custody hearing, and the outcome is without question."

"You won't take Michael, not with money, not with lies." Her voice rose, and she fought to bring it back down. Losing her temper would get her nowhere. Laura knew all too well how easily Lorraine could bat aside emotion with one cold, withering look. She believed, she had to believe, there was still a way of reasoning with her. "If you ever loved Tony, then you'll know just how far I'll go to keep my son."

"And you should know just how far I'll go to see to it that you have no part in raising an Eagleton."

"That's all he is to you, a name, just a symbol of immortality." Despite her efforts, her voice was growing desperate and her knees were beginning to shake. "He's just a baby. You don't love him."

"Feelings have nothing to do with it. I'm staying at the Fairmont. You have two days to decide whether or not you want a public scandal." Lorraine drew out her gloves again. The terror on Laura's face assured her that there was no risk of that. "I'm sure the Bradleys would be displeased, at the least, to learn of your past indiscretions. Therefore, I have no doubt you'll be sensible, Laura, and not risk what you've so conveniently acquired." She walked out the door and down the steps to where a gray limo waited.

Without waiting for it to drive away, Laura slammed the door and bolted it. She was panting as though she'd been running. And it was running that occurred to her first. Dashing up the stairs, she raced into the nursery and began to toss Michael's things into his carryall.

They'd travel light. She'd only pack what was absolutely necessary. Before sundown they could be miles away. Headed north, she thought quickly. Maybe into Canada.

There was still enough money left to help them get away, to buy them enough time to disappear. A rattle slipped out of her hand and landed with a clatter. Giving in to despair, she sunk onto the daybed and buried her face in her hands.

They couldn't run. Even if they had enough funds to keep them for a lifetime, they couldn't run. It was wrong, wrong for Michael, for Gabe, even for herself. They had a life here, the kind she'd always wanted, the kind she needed to give her son.

But what could she do to protect it?

Take a stand. Ride out the attack. Not cave in. But caving in was what she'd always done best. Lifting her head, she waited until her breathing had calmed. That was the old Laura's thinking, and that was exactly what Lorraine was counting on. The Eagletons knew how easily manipulated she had been. They expected her to run, and they would use that impulsive, erratic behavior to take her baby. They thought that if she was too tired to run she would sacrifice her child to protect her position with the Bradleys.

But they didn't know her. They had never taken the time or effort to really know her. She wouldn't cave in. She wouldn't run with her son. She was damn well going to fight for him.

The anger came then, and it felt wonderful. Anger was a hot, animate emotion, so unlike the icy numbness of fear. She'd stay angry, as Amanda had advised, because angry she would not only fight but fight rough and dirty. The Eagletons were in for a surprise.

By the time she reached the gallery she was in control again. Michael was safe with Amanda, and Laura was taking the first step of the route she'd already mapped out to see that he stayed safe.

The Trussalt Gallery was in a gracefully refurbished old building. Flowers, neatly trimmed and still wet from the re-

cent rain, were grouped near the main entrance. Laura could
smell roses and damp leaves as she pulled the door open.

Inside, skylights offered an open view of the still-cloudy
sky, but the gallery itself was brilliant with recessed and
track lighting. It was as quiet as a church. Indeed, as Laura
paused to look, she could see that this was a place designed
for the worship of art. Sculptures in marble and wood, in
iron and bronze, were placed lovingly. Rather than com-
peting with each other, they harmonized. As did the paintings aligned stylishly on the walls.

She recognized one of Gabe's, a particularly solemn view
of a garden going to seed. It wasn't pretty; it certainly wasn't
joyful. Looking at it, she thought of the mural he'd painted
for his mother. The same man who believed enough in fantasies to bring them to life also saw reality, perhaps a bit too
clearly. They had that in common, as well.

There were only a few patrons here on this rainy week-
day afternoon. They had time to browse, Laura reminded
herself. She didn't. Spotting a guard, she moved toward
him.

"Excuse me, I'm looking for Gabriel Bradley."

"I'm sorry, miss. He wouldn't be available. If you have
a question about one of his paintings, you may want to see
Ms. Trussalt."

"No. You see, I'm—"

"Laura." Marion breezed out of an alcove. She was
wearing pastels today, a long, slim skirt in baby blue that
reached to her ankles, with a hip-skimming sweater in soft
pink. The quiet colors only accentuated her exotic looks.
"So you decided to pay us a visit after all."

"I'd like to see Gabe."

"What a pity." Without so much as a glance, Marion
motioned the guard aside. "He's not here at the moment."

Laura curled her fingers tighter around the clasp of her purse. Intimidation from this quarter meant less than nothing now. "Do you expect him back?"

"As a matter of fact, he should be back before too long. We're booked for drinks in, oh—" she glanced at her watch "—half an hour."

Both the glance and the tone were designed to dismiss her, but Laura was far beyond worrying about games. "Then I'll wait."

"You're welcome to, of course, but I'm afraid Gabe and I have business to discuss. So boring for you."

Weariness was a dull throb at the base of her skull. She had no desire to cross swords now. Her energy had to remain focused for a much more vital fight. "I appreciate your concern, but nothing about Gabe's art is boring for me."

"Spoken like a little Trojan." Marion tilted her head. There was a smile that had nothing to do with friendship in her eyes. "You're looking a bit pale. Trouble in paradise?"

And she knew. As clearly as if Marion had said it out loud, she knew how Lorraine had found her. "Nothing that can't be dealt with. Why did you call her, Marion?"

The smile remained in place, cool and confident. "I beg your pardon?"

"She was already paying good money for detectives. I only had a week or two longer at most."

Marion considered a moment, then turned to fuss with the alignment of a painting. "I've always thought time was better saved than wasted. The sooner Lorraine deals with you, the sooner I can get Gabe back on track. Let me show you something."

Marion moved across the gallery in a separate room, where the walls and floors were white. A sweeping spiral staircase, again in white, rose up in one corner. Above, balconies ran in a circle. A trio of ornamental trees grew under the staircase, fronted by a towering ebony sculpture of a man and a woman in a passionate, yet somehow despairing, embrace.

But it was the portrait that caught her attention, that drew it and demanded it. It was her own face that looked serenely back at Laura, from the portrait Gabe had painted during those long, quiet days in Colorado.

"Yes, it's stunning." Marion rubbed a finger over her lip as she studied it. She'd been tempted to take a knife to the canvas when Gabe had first unpacked it, but the temptation had faded quickly. She was too much a patron of the arts to let personal feelings interfere. "It's one of his best and most romantic pieces. It's been hanging only three weeks and I've already had six serious offers for it."

"I've already seen the painting, Marion."

"Yes, but I doubt you understand it. He calls it *Gabriel's Angel*. That should tell you something."

"*Gabriel's Angel*," Laura repeated in a murmur. The warmth spread through her as she took a step closer. "What should that tell me?"

"That he, like Pygmalion, fell a bit in love with his subject. That's expected now and again, even encouraged, as it often inspires great work such as this." She tapped a finger against the frame. "But Gabe's much too practical a man to string out the fantasy for long. The portrait's finished, Laura. He doesn't need you any longer."

Laura turned her head so that she could look directly at Marion. What was being said had run through her mind countless times. She told Marion what she had already told herself. "Then he'll have to tell me that."

"He's an honorable man. That's part of his charm. But once things come to a head, once he realizes his mistake, he'll cut his losses. A man only believes in an image," she said, with a gesture toward the portrait, "as long as the image is unsmeared. From what Lorraine tells me, you don't have much time.''

Laura fought back the urge to turn and run. Oddly, she discovered it didn't take as much effort this time. ''If you believe that, why are you taking so much trouble to move me along?''

''No trouble.'' She smiled again and let her hand fall away from the painting. ''I consider it part of my job to encourage Gabe to concentrate on his career and avoid the kind of controversies that can only detract from it. As I've already explained, his involvement with you isn't acceptable. He'll realize that soon enough himself.''

No wonder she had called Lorraine, Laura thought. They were two of a kind. ''You're forgetting something, Marion. Michael. No matter what Gabe feels or doesn't feel for me, he loves Michael.''

''It takes a particularly pitiful woman to use a child.''

''You're right.'' Laura met her eyes levelly. ''You couldn't be more right.'' When Laura saw that retort had hit home, she continued calmly, ''I'll wait here for Gabe. I'd appreciate it if you'd tell him when he gets back.''

''So you can run and hide behind him?''

''I can't see that Laura's reasons for coming to see me are your concern.''

Gabe spoke from the entranceway. Both women turned toward him. He could read fury on Marion's face and distress on Laura's. Even as he watched, both women composed themselves in their own way. Marion lifted her brow and smiled. Laura folded her hands and raised her chin.

''Darling. You know it's part of my job to protect my artists from panicky spouses and lovers.'' Crossing to him, Marion laid a hand on his arm. ''We're going to be meeting with the Bridgetons in a few minutes about the three paintings. I don't want you distracted and out of sorts.''

He spared her only the briefest of glances, but in it Marion saw that he had heard too much. "I'll worry about my moods. If you'll excuse us now?"

"The Bridgetons—"

"Can buy the paintings or go to hell. Leave us alone, Marion."

She aimed a vicious glare at Laura, then stormed out of the room. Her heels echoed on the tile. "I'm sorry," Laura said after a long breath. "I didn't come here to make waves."

"Why, then? From the look of you, you didn't come to spend an afternoon in art appreciation." Before she could answer, he was striding to her. "Damn it, Laura, I don't like having the two of you standing here discussing me as though I were some prize to be awarded to the highest bidder. Marion's a business associate, you're my wife. The two of you are going to have to resolve that."

"I understand that completely." Her voice had changed, hardened to match his. "And you should understand that if I believed you were involved with her in any way I would already have left you."

Whatever he'd been about to say slipped completely away from him. Because he recognized the unshakable resolve in the statement, he could only stare at her. "Just like that?"

"Just like that. I've already lived through one marriage where fidelity meant nothing. I won't live through another."

"I see." Comparisons again, he thought. He wanted to shout at her. Instead, he spoke softly, too softly. "Then I've been warned."

She turned away so that she could close her eyes for a moment. Her head was pounding ruthlessly. If she didn't take the time to draw herself in, she would throw herself into his arms and beg for help. "I didn't come here to discuss the terms of our marriage."

"Maybe you should have. It might be time for us to go back to square one and spell it out."

She shook her head and made herself turn to face him again. "I wanted to tell you that I'm going to see a lawyer in the morning."

He felt the life drain out of him in one swift flood. She wanted a divorce. Then, as quickly as he'd been left limp, the fury came. Unlike Laura, he had never had to prime himself for a fight. "What the hell are you talking about?"

"It can't be put off any longer. I can't keep pretending it's not necessary." Again she wanted to step into his arms, to feel them close around her, make her safe. She kept an arm's length away and stood on her own. "I didn't want to start what will be a difficult and ugly period without letting you know."

"That's big of you." Spinning away, he dragged a hand through his hair. Above him, her portrait smiled gently down. As he stood between them, he felt as though he were caught between two women, between two needs. "What in the hell brought this on? Do you think you can kiss me goodbye at the door, then talk about lawyers a few hours later? If you haven't been happy, why haven't you said so?"

"I don't know what you're talking about, Gabe. We knew this would probably happen eventually. You were the one who told me there'd come a time when I'd have to face it. Now I'm ready to. I just want to give you the option of backing off before it's too late to turn back."

He started to snap at her, then stopped himself. It occurred to him that what he had thought they were talking about, and what was actually being discussed were two different things. "Why do you need to see a lawyer in the morning?"

"Lorraine Eagleton came to the house this afternoon. She wants Michael."

No relief came at the realization that they weren't speaking of divorce. There was no room for it. He recognized a flash of panic before fury replaced it. "She may as well want the moon, because she won't have that, either." He reached out to touch a hand to her cheek. "Are you all right?"

She nodded. "I wasn't, but I am now. She's threatening a custody suit."

"On what grounds?"

She pressed her lips together, but her gaze didn't waver. "On the grounds that I'm not fit to care for him. She told me she'll prove that I was... that there were other men before and during my marriage to Tony."

"How can she prove what isn't true?"

So he believed in her. It was just that easy. Laura reached for his hand. "You can get people to do or say a great many things if you pay them enough. I've seen the Eagletons do that kind of thing before."

"Did she tell you where she was staying?"

"Yes."

"Then it's time I talked with her."

"No." She had his hand before he could stride from the room. "Please, I don't want you to see her yet. I need to talk with a lawyer first, make certain what can and can't be done. We can't afford the luxury of making a mistake in anger."

"I don't need a lawyer to tell me she can't walk into my house and threaten to take Michael."

"Gabe, please." Again she had to stop him. When her fingers curled around his arms, she felt the fury vibrating in him. "Listen to me. You're angry. So was I, and frightened, too. My first impulse was to run again. I'd even started to pack."

He thought of what it would have done to him to have come home to find the house empty. The score he had to settle with the Eagletons was getting bigger. "Why didn't you?"

"Because it wouldn't have been right, not for Michael, not for you or for me. Because I love both of you too much."

He stopped and cupped her face in his hands, trying to read what was behind her eyes. "You wouldn't have gotten very far."

The smile came slowly as she wrapped her fingers around his wrists. "I hope not. Gabe, I know what I have to do, and I also know that I can do it."

He paused, taking it in. She spoke of love one moment, then of what she would do, not of what they would do. "Alone?"

"If necessary. I know you've taken Michael as your own, but I want you to understand that if she pursues the suit it's going to get ugly, and what's said about me will affect you and your family." There was a moment's hesitation as she worked up the courage to give him a choice. "If you'd rather not be involved in what's going to happen now, I understand."

His choices had narrowed from the moment he'd seen her. They'd disappeared completely when she'd first put Michael in his arms. Because he didn't know how to explain, he cut through to the bottom line.

"Where's Michael?"

Relief made her giddy. "He's with your mother."

"Then let's pick him up and take him home."

Chapter Eleven

She couldn't sleep. Both memory and imagination worked against Laura as her mind insisted on racing over what had happened, and what might happen the next day. It was almost a year since she had fled Boston. Now, thousands of miles away, she had chosen to take her stand. But she was no longer alone.

Gabe hadn't waited to make an appointment with his lawyer during regular business hours. He had made a phone call and requested—demanded—a meeting that evening.

Her life, her child, her marriage and her future had been discussed over coffee and crumb cake in the parlor while a low, wispy fog had rolled in from the bay. Her initial embarrassment about speaking with a stranger about her life, her first marriage and her mistakes had sharpened painfully, then vanished. It had seemed as though they were talking about someone else's experiences. The more openly it was discussed, with details meticulously examined and noted, the less shame she'd felt.

Matthew Quartermain had been the Bradleys' attorney for forty years. He was crusty and shrewd and, despite his stuffy exterior, not easily shocked. He'd nodded and made notes and asked questions until Laura's mouth had dried up from answering.

Because he hadn't sympathized or condemned, it had become easier to talk plainly. The truth, spoken in simple unemotional terms, had been easier to face than it had to keep hidden. In the end she hadn't spared herself or Tony

And in the end she'd felt a powerful sense of having been cleansed.

At last she'd said it all, put all the misery and pain into words. She'd purged her heart and her mind in a way that her lingering sense of shame had never permitted before. Now that it was done, she understood what it was to wipe the slate clean and begin again.

Quartermain hadn't been happy with her final decision, but she'd been firm. Before papers of any kind were served or answered, she would see Lorraine again, face-to-face.

Beside Laura, Gabe lay sleepless. Like her, he was thinking back over the scene in the parlor. With every word that played back in his head his fury inched higher. She had spoken of things there that she had never told him, going into detail she had glossed over before. He'd thought he understood what she'd been through, and he'd thought his feelings about it had already peaked. He'd been wrong.

She hadn't told him about the black eye that had prevented her from leaving the house for nearly a week, or about Lorraine explaining away Laura's split lip by speaking of her daughter-in-law's clumsiness. She hadn't told him about the drunken attacks in the middle of the night, the jealous rages if she'd spoken with another man at a social function, the threats of revenge and violence when she'd finally found the courage to leave.

They'd come out tonight, in excruciating detail.

He hadn't touched her when they'd prepared for bed. He wondered how she could bear to be touched at all.

What she had been through was all too clear now. How could he expect her to put it aside, when he was no longer certain he could? No matter how gentle he was, how much care he took with her, the shadow of another man and another time was between them.

She'd said she loved him. As much as he wanted to believe it, he couldn't understand how anyone who had lived through that kind of hell could ever trust a man again, much less love him.

Gratitude, devotion, with Michael as the common ground. That he could understand. And that, Gabe thought as he lay in the dark, was more than many people were ever given.

He'd wanted more for them, had been on the verge of believing they could have more. That had been before all those words had been spoken downstairs while the quiet spring breeze had ruffled the curtains.

Then she turned toward him, her body brushing his. He stiffened.

"I'm sorry. Did I wake you?"

"No." He started to shift so that they were no longer touching, but she moved again until her head rested on his shoulder.

The gesture, the easy, uncomplicated movement toward him, tore him in two. The one who needed, and the one who was afraid to ask.

"I can't sleep, either. I feel as though I've run an obstacle course, and my body's exhausted from it. But my mind keeps circling."

"You should stop thinking about tomorrow."

"I know." Laura brushed her hair aside, then settled more comfortably. She felt the slight drawing away, the pulling back. With her eyes shut tight, she wondered if he thought less of her now that he knew everything.

"There's no need for you to worry. It's going to be all right."

Was it? Taking a chance, she reached through the dark for his hand. "The trouble is, different scenes keep popping into my head. What I'll say, what she'll say. If I don't..." Her words trailed off when the baby started crying. "Sounds like someone else is restless."

"I'll get him."

Though she'd already tossed the covers aside, Laura nodded. "All right. I'll nurse him in here if he's hungry."

She sat up and hugged her knees to her chest as Gabe tossed on a robe and strode to the nursery. A moment later the crying stopped, then started again. Under it, she could hear Gabe's voice, murmuring and soothing.

It was so easy for him, so natural. Sensitivity, tenderness, were as much a part of him as temper and arrogance. Wasn't that why she'd finally been able to admit that she loved him? There would be no cycle of despair, submission and terror with Gabe, as there had been with Tony. She could love him without giving up the pieces of herself that she'd so recently discovered.

No, he didn't think less of her. She couldn't be sure of all of his feelings, but she could be sure of that. It was just that he was as worried as she and felt obligated to pretend otherwise.

The light from the nursery slanted into the hallway. In it she could see Gabe's shadow as he moved. The crying became muffled, then rose in a wail. Recognizing the tone of the crying, Laura leaned back and shut her eyes. It was going to be a long night.

"Teething," she murmured when Gabe brought a sobbing Michael into the bedroom. Switching on the bedside lamp she smiled at him. All of them needed support tonight. "I'll nurse him and see if that helps any."

"There you go, old man. Best seat in the house." Gabe settled him in Laura's arms. The crying faded to a whimper, then disappeared completely as he suckled. "I'm going down for a brandy. Do you want anything?"

"No. Yes, some juice. Whatever's in there."

Alone, she held Michael with one arm and arranged her pillows behind her back with the other. It seemed so normal, so usual, just like any other night. Though there were nights when Michael was restless when her body craved sleep, there were others when she prized these hours in the middle of the night. These were the times she and Gabe would remember years down the road, when Michael took his first steps, when he started school, when he rode a two-wheeler for the first time. They'd look back and remember how they'd walked the floor, half dozing themselves. Nothing could change that.

They needed this, needed the normalcy of it. And, if only for a few hours, they would have it.

When Gabe came back in, he set her glass on the table beside her. Smiling, she lifted a hand to his arm. "Can I smell your brandy?"

Amused, he titled the snifter for her and let her draw in the scent. "Enough?"

"Thanks. I always loved the taste of brandy late at night." Lifting her juice glass, she clinked it against his snifter. "Cheers." He didn't join her in bed, as she'd hoped he would, but turned to stand by the window. "Gabe?"

"Yes?"

"I'd like to make a deal with you. You tell me what's on your mind, ask any question you need to ask, and I'll tell you the absolute truth. Then, in return, I'll ask you and you'll do the same."

"Haven't you answered enough questions for one night?"

So that was it. Laura set her glass aside before she gently shifted Michael to her other breast. "You're upset because of the things I told Mr. Quartermain."

"Did you expect I would take them with a shrug?" When he whirled, the brandy sloshed dangerously close to the lip of the snifter. Laura said nothing as he tossed back half the contents and began to pace.

"I'm sorry it had to be brought up. I'd have preferred another way myself."

"It's not a matter of its being brought up." The words lashed out. He drank more brandy, but it did nothing to soothe him. "My God, it's killing me to think of it, to imagine it. I'm afraid to touch you, because it might bring it back."

"Gabe, you've been telling me all along that it's over, that things are different now. I know they are. You were right when you said I compared you with Tony, but maybe you don't understand that by doing that I helped myself realize that things could change."

He looked at her then, only for a moment, but long enough for her to see that her words weren't enough, not yet. "Things are different now, but I wonder why you don't hate any man who puts his hands on you."

"There was a time when I wouldn't have let any man within ten feet of me, but I was able to start putting things in perspective, through therapy, listening to other women who'd pulled themselves out of the spin." She watched him as he stood in the shadow, his hands thrust in the pockets of his robe and clenched into fists. "When you touch me, when you hold me, it doesn't bring any of that back. It makes me feel the way I've always wanted to feel about myself, about my husband."

"If he were alive," Gabe said evenly, "I'd want to kill him. I find myself resenting the fact that he's already dead."

"Don't do that to yourself." She reached out a hand to him, but he shook his head and walked back to the window. "He was ill. I didn't know that then, not really. And I prolonged it all by not walking away."

"You were afraid. You had nowhere to go."

"That's not enough. I could have gone to Geoffrey. I knew he would have helped me, but I didn't go, because I was pinned there by my own shame and insecurities. When I finally did leave, it was because of the baby. That's when I began to get well myself. Finding you was the best medicine of all, because you made me feel like a woman again."

He remained silent while she searched for the right words. "Gabe, there's nothing either of us can do to change things that have already happened. Don't let it change what we have now."

Calmer now, he swirled his brandy and continued to look out of the window. "When you talked of lawyers in the gallery today, I thought you wanted a divorce. It scared me to death."

"But I wouldn't have— Did it?"

"There you were, standing under the portrait, and I couldn't imagine what I would do if you walked away. I may have changed your life, angel, but no more than you've changed mine."

Pygmalion, she thought. If he loved the image, he might eventually love the woman. "I won't walk away. I love you, Gabe. You and Michael are my whole life."

He came to her then, to sit on the edge of the bed and take her hand. "I won't let anyone hurt either one of you."

Her fingers tightened on his. "I need to know that whatever we have to do we'll do it together."

"We've been in this together right from the start." Leaning forward, he kissed her, while the baby dozed between them. "I need you, Laura, maybe too much."

"It can't be too much."

"Let me go put him down," Gabe murmured. "Then maybe we can continue that."

He took the baby, but the moment he eased off the bed Michael began to cry.

They took turns walking, rocking, rubbing tender gums. Each time Michael was laid back in his crib he woke with a wail. Dizzy with fatigue, Laura leaned over the rail, patting and rubbing his back. Each time she moved her hand away he cried again.

"I guess we're spoiling him," she murmured.

Gabe sat heavy-eyed in the rocking chair and watched her. "We're entitled. Besides, he sleeps like a rock most of the time."

"I know. This teething's got him down. Why don't you go to bed? There's no sense in both of us being up."

"It's my shift." He rose and discovered that at 5:00 a.m. the body could feel decades older than it was. "You go on to bed."

"No—" Her own yawn cut her off. "We're in this together, remember?"

"Or until one of us passes out."

She would have laughed if she had had the energy. "Maybe I'll just sit down."

"You know, I've been known to watch the sun come up after a night of drinking, card playing or...other forms of entertainment." He began to pat Michael's back as Laura collapsed in the rocker. "And I can't remember ever feeling as though someone had run over me with a truck."

"This is one of the joys of parenting," she told him as she curled her legs under her and shut her eyes. "We're actually having the time of our lives."

"I'm glad you let me know. I think he's giving in."

"That's because you have such a wonderful touch," she murmured as she drifted off. "Such a wonderful touch."

Inch by cautious inch, Gabe drew his hand away. A man backing away from a tiger couldn't have taken more care. When he was a full two feet from the crib, he nearly let out a breath of relief. Afraid to push his luck, he held it and turned to Laura.

She was sound asleep, in an impossibly uncomfortable position. Hoping his energy held out for five minutes longer, Gabe walked over to pick her up. She shifted and cuddled against him instinctively. As he carried her from the room, she roused enough to murmur. "Michael?"

"Down for the count." He walked into their room, but rather than taking her to bed he moved to the window. "Look, the sun's coming up."

Laura stirred and opened her eyes. Through the window she could see the curve of the eastern sky. If she looked hard enough she could see the water of the bay, like a mist in the distance. The sun seemed to vibrate as it rose. And the echoes brought colors: pinks, mauves, golds. Softly at first, with the darker night sky still dominating above, the colors spread, then deepened. Pinks became reds, vibrant and glowing.

"Sometimes your paintings are like that," she thought aloud. "Changing, shifting angles, with the colors intensifying from the core to the edges." She nestled her head against his shoulder as they watched the new day dawn. "I don't think I've ever seen a more beautiful sunrise."

His skin was warm beneath her cheek, his arms strong, firm with muscle, as they held her to him. She could feel the light, steady beating of his heart. She turned her face toward his as the first birds woke and began to sing. When love was so easily reached, only a fool questioned it.

"I want you, Gabe." She laid her hand on his cheek, her lips on his lips. "I've never wanted anyone the way I want you."

There was a moment's hesitation. She felt it, understood it, then coaxed him past it. This wasn't the time to think of yesterdays or tomorrows. Her lips softened and parted against his and her hand slipped back to brush through his hair.

"You were right," she murmured.

"About what?"

"I don't think of anyone but you when we make love."

He hadn't meant to ask her for anything. He found there was nothing he couldn't ask.

She was so beautifully open. It made it possible, even easy, to put that part of her life that left him angry and bitter aside. That had nothing to do with where they could take each other. With his mouth still on hers, he moved to the bed. She wrapped her arms around him as he lay beside her. For a moment that was enough.

Morning embraces, sunrise kisses, after a long, sleepless night. Her face was pale with fatigue, but still she trembled for him. The sigh that passed from her lips to his was soft and drowsy. Her body arched, lazy, limber, at the stroke of his hands.

The dawn air was balmy as it fluttered through the window and over their skin. She parted his robe, pushed it back from his shoulders, so that she could warm his skin herself. Just as slowly, he drew off her nightgown. Naked, they lay on the rumpled sheets and made long, luxurious love.

Neither of them set the pace. It wasn't necessary. Here they were in tune, without words or requests. Demands were for other moments, night moments, when passion was hot and urgent. As the light turned gray with morning, desire was deliciously cool.

Perhaps the love she felt for him was best displayed this way, with ease and affection that lasted so much longer than the flare of a flame. She moved with him and he with her, and they brought pleasure to each other that came in sighs and murmurs instead of gasps and shudders.

She felt the roughness of his cheek when she stoked her hand there. This was real. Marriage was more than the band she wore on her finger or the coming together full of need and excitement in the dark. Marriage was holding on at daybreak.

He would have scaled mountains for her. Until now, somehow, the full extent of his feelings for her had escaped him. He'd recognized the need first, the love later, but now he understood the devotion. She was his in a way no other woman could ever be. For the first time in his life, he wanted to be a hero.

When they came together, full light was pouring over the bed. Later, still entwined, they slept.

"I know I'm doing the right thing." Still, Laura hesitated when they stepped off the elevator in Lorraine's hotel. "And, no matter what happens, I'm not going to back down." She caught Gabe's hand in hers and held it tight. Lack of sleep had left her feeling light-headed and primed for action. "I'm awfully glad you're here."

"I told you before, I don't like the idea of you having to see her again, to deal with her on any level. I can easily handle this on my own."

"I know you could. But I told you, I need to. Gabe . . ."

"What?"

"Please don't lose your temper." She laughed a little at the way his brows rose. The tension rising inside her eased. "There's no need to look like that. I'm only trying to say that shouting at Lorraine won't accomplish anything."

"I never shout. I do occasionally raise my voice to get a point across."

"Since we've gotten that straightened out, I guess the only thing left to do is knock." She felt the familiar flutter of panic and fought it back as she knocked on the door. Lorraine answered, looking regal and poised in a navy suit.

"Laura." After the briefest of nods, she turned to Gabe. "Mr. Bradley. It's nice to meet you. Laura didn't mention that you were coming with her this afternoon."

"Everything that concerns Laura and Michael concerns me, Mrs. Eagleton." He entered, as Laura could never have done, without an invitation.

"I'm sure that's very conscientious of you." Lorraine closed the door with a quick click. "However, some of the things Laura and I may discuss are private family matters. I'm sure you understand."

"I understand perfectly." He met her level gaze with one of his own. "My wife and son are my family."

The war of wills was silent and unpleasant. Lorraine ended it with another nod. "If you insist. Please, sit. I'll order coffee. The service here is tolerable."

"Don't bother on our account." Laura spoke with only the slightest trace of nerves as she chose a seat. "I don't think this should take very long."

"As you like." Lorraine sat across from them. "My husband would have been here, but business prevented him from making the trip. I do, however, speak for both of us." That said, she laid her hands on the arms of her chair. "I'll simply repeat what has already been discussed. I intend to take Tony's son back to Boston and raise him properly."

"And I'll repeat, you can't have him." She would try reason one last time, Laura thought, leaning forward. "He's a baby, not an heirloom, Mrs. Eagleton. He has a good home and two parents who love him. He's a healthy, beautiful child. You should be grateful for that. If you want to discuss reasonable visitation rights—"

"We'll discuss visitation rights," Lorraine said, interrupting her. "Yours. And if I have anything to say about it, they will be short and spare. Mr. Bradley," she continued, turning away from Laura. "Surely you don't want to raise another man's child as your own. He hasn't your blood, and he only has your name because, for whatever reason, you married his mother."

Gabe drew out a cigarette and lit it slowly. Laura had asked him not to lose his temper. Though he wouldn't be able to accommodate her, it wouldn't do to let it snap so quickly. "You're very wrong" was all he said.

She sighed, almost indulgently. "I understand you have feelings for Laura. My son had them, too."

The first chain on his temper broke clean in half. The rage could be seen in his eyes and heard in each precise, bitten-off word. "Don't you ever compare my feelings for Laura with your son's."

Lorraine paled a little, but went on evenly. "I have no idea what she may have been telling you—"

"I told him the truth." Before Gabe could speak, or move, Laura put a hand on his arm. "I told him what you know is the truth, that Tony was ill, emotionally unstable."

Now it was Lorraine who moved, rising deliberately from her chair. Her face was flushed and pinched, but her voice was held at the same even pitch. "I will not sit here and listen to you defame my son."

"You will listen." Laura's fingers dug hard into Gabe's arm, but she didn't give way. "You'll listen now the way you never listened when I was desperate for help. The way you never listened when Tony was screaming for it in the only way he knew. He was an alcoholic, an emotional wreck who abused someone weaker than he. You knew he hurt me, you saw the marks and ignored them or made excuses. You knew there were other women. By your silence, you gave him approval."

"What was between you and Tony was none of my concern."

"That's for you to live with. But I warn you, Lorraine, if you open the lid, you won't be able to handle what comes out."

Lorraine sat again, if for no other reason than the tone of Laura's voice and the fact that for the first time Laura had called her by her first name. That one change made them equals. This wasn't the same frightened, easily pressured woman she had known only a year before.

"Threats from someone like you don't worry me. The courts will decide if some loose-moraled young tramp will have custody of an Eagleton or if he'll be placed with those who can give him the proper upbringing.''

''If you refer to my wife in that way again you'll have more than threats to deal with.'' Gabe blew out a long, narrow stream of smoke. ''Mrs. Eagleton.''

''It doesn't matter.'' Laura squeezed his hand. She knew he was on the verge of losing control. ''You can't make me cringe anymore, Lorraine, and you won't make me beg. You know very well that I was faithful to Tony.''

''I know that Tony didn't believe that.''

''Then how do you know the child is his?''

Absolute silence fell the moment Gabe spoke. Laura started to speak but was held off by the look in Gabe's eyes. Color flooded into Lorraine's face again when she found her voice.

''She wouldn't have dared—''

''Wouldn't she? That's odd. You intend to prove that Laura was unfaithful to your son, and now you claim she wasn't. Either way, you have a problem. If she had had an affair with anyone. Me, for example.'' He smiled again as he crushed out his cigarette. ''Or haven't you wondered why we were married so quickly, why, as you've already asked, I accept the child as my own?'' He let that thought take hold before he continued. ''If she had been unfaithful, the child could be anyone's. If she wasn't unfaithful, you haven't got a case.''

Lorraine clenched and unclenched her fingers on the arm of the chair. ''My husband and I have every intention of determining the child's paternity. I would hardly take someone's bastard into my home.''

''Be careful,'' Laura said, so quietly that the words seemed to vibrate in the air. ''Be very careful, Lorraine. I know you have no concern for Michael as a person.''

Fighting for control she so rarely lost, Lorraine settled again. "I have nothing but the gravest concern for Tony's son."

"You've never asked about him, what he looks like, if he's well. You've never demanded to see him, even a picture or a doctor's report. You've never once called him by name. If you had, if I'd seen in you one ounce of love or affection for the baby, I'd feel differently about what I'm about to say." The courage came without the need to muster it. "You're free to draw up the papers and initiate a custody suit. Gabe and I have already notified our attorney. We'll fight you, and we'll win. And in the meantime, I'll go to the press with the story of what my life was like with the Eagletons of Boston."

Lorraine's nails dug into the material on the arm of the chair. "You wouldn't have the nerve."

"I have that and more when it comes to protecting my son."

She could see it, the calm, unshakable determination in Laura's eyes. "Even if you did, no one would believe you."

"But they would," Laura told her. "People have a way of recognizing the truth."

Lorraine's face was set when she turned to Gabe. "Do you have any conception of what this kind of gossip could do to your family name? Do you want to risk your reputation, your parents' reputation, over this woman and a child who isn't even of your blood?"

"My reputation can handle it, and, to be frank, my parents are looking forward to a fight." There was a challenge in his voice now that didn't have to be feigned. "Michael may not be of my blood, but he's mine."

"Lorraine." Laura waited until they were face-to-face again. "You lost your son, and I'm sorry for you, but you won't replace him with mine. Whatever the cost to protect Michael's welfare, I'll pay. And so will you."

Putting a hand under her arm, Gabe rose, keeping Laura beside him. "Your attorney can contact us once you've made your decision. Remember, Mrs. Eagleton, you're not pitting yourself against a lone pregnant woman. You're up against the Bradleys now."

The moment they were in the hall, Gabe pulled Laura against him. He could feel the tremors coursing through her, so he held her a moment longer. "You were wonderful." He kissed her hair before he drew her away from him. "In fact, angel, you were amazing. Lorraine still doesn't know what hit her."

The flush of pride was as warm and satisfying as anything she'd ever felt. "It wasn't as bad as I thought," she said with a sigh, but she kept her hand in his as they walked to the elevator. "I used to be so terrified of her, afraid to speak two words. Now I can see her for what she really is, a lonely woman trapped by her own strict sense of family honor."

Gabe gave a quick, humorless laugh as the elevators doors opened. "Honor has nothing to do with it."

"No, but that's how she sees it."

"Tell you what." He pressed the button for the lobby. "We're going to forget about Lorraine Eagleton for the rest of the day. In fact, we're going to forget about her completely before long, but for now there's a little restaurant a few blocks away. Not too quiet, and very expensive."

"It's too early for dinner."

"Who said anything about dinner?" He slipped an arm around her waist as they walked out into the lobby. "We're going to sit at a table over the water, and I'm going to watch everyone stare at my gorgeous wife while we drink a bottle of champagne."

She loved him for that. Then her heart skipped a beat when he brought her fingers to his lips. "Don't you think we should wait to celebrate until Lorraine gives us her decision?''

''We'll celebrate then, too. Right now I want to celebrate being witness to an angel breathing fire.''

She laughed and walked outside with him. ''I could do it again. In fact . . .''

''What?''

She swept her gaze up to his. ''I'd like to.''

''Sounds as though I'm going to have to watch my step.''

''Probably.'' She was giddy with success, but she was still practical. ''I really shouldn't have champagne. Michael—''

''He'll love it,'' Gabe assured her, and signaled for his car.

Chapter Twelve

Y ou look exhausted.'' Amanda gave a quick shake of her head as she stepped into the house.

"Michael's teething.'' The excuse was valid enough, but more than a fretful baby was keeping Laura from sleeping at night. "He's been down all of ten minutes. With luck, he might make an entire hour straight.''

"Then why aren't you napping?''

Since Amanda was already stepping into the parlor, Laura followed her in. "Because you called and said you were coming over.''

"Oh.'' With a faint smile, Amanda took a seat, then tossed her purse on the table. "So I did. Well, I won't keep you long. Gabe's not home?''

"No. He said he had something to see to.'' Laura sat in the chair facing her and let her head fall back. Sometimes small luxuries felt like heaven. "Can I get you some coffee, or something cold?''

"You don't look as though you can get yourself out of that chair. And, no, I don't need a thing. How is Gabe?''

"He hasn't been getting a great deal of rest, either.''

"I'm not surprised. No word from Lorraine Eagleton or her attorney?''

"Nothing.''

"I don't suppose that you're able to take the attitude that no news is good news?''

Laura managed a smile. "Afraid not. The longer this goes on, the easier it gets to imagine the worst.''

"And if she takes this to court?"

"Then we'll fight." Despite her fatigue, her newly dis covered power came through. "I meant everything I said t her."

"That's really all I wanted to hear." Sitting back Amanda adjusted the pin on her lapel. A little too thin, little too pale, she thought as she studied Laura. But, all i all, she thought her daughter-in-law was holding up wel "When this is over, you and Gabe should be able to tie up few loose ends."

Laura caught herself before she dozed off. "Loos ends?"

"Yes, little things. Such as what you intend to do with th rest of your lives."

"I don't know what you mean."

"Gabe has his art, and you both have Michael, and how ever many other children you choose to bring into th world."

That was something that made Laura sit up straighter More children. They'd never discussed the possibility o more. As she began to, she wondered if Gabe even wante any. Did she? She passed a hand over her now flat stomac and imagined it filled with another child—Gabe's child thi time, from the very first moment. Yes, she wanted tha Glancing over, she saw Amanda studying her quietly an with complete understanding.

"It's difficult to make decisions with so much hangin over us."

"Exactly. But it will pass. When it does, what are yo going to look for? Since I spent more than two decades un der the same roof as Gabe, I know that he can, when th muse in on him, lock himself in his studio for hours an days on end."

"I don't mind. How could I, when I see what he can ac complish?"

"A woman needs a solid sense of accomplishment, as well. Children can be the best of that, but..." She reached for her purse, opened it and took out a business card. "There's an abuse clinic downtown. It's rather small, and unfortunately not well funded. Yet." She intended to correct that. "They need volunteers, women who understand, who know there can be normal life after hell."

"I'm not a therapist."

"You don't need a degree to give support."

"No." She looked at the card on the table as the idea took root. "I don't know. I..."

"Just think about it."

"Amanda, did you go to the clinic?"

"Yes, Cliff and I went there yesterday. We were very impressed."

"Why did you go?"

Amanda lifted a brow in a gesture Laura knew Gabe had inherited. "Because there's someone we both care about who we wanted to understand better. Don't get up." she said as she rose. "I'll let myself out. Give Gabe my love and tell him his father wants to know if they're ever going to play poker again. The man thrives on losing money."

"Amanda." Laura pushed off her shoes before she curled her legs up in the chair. "I never had a mother, and the one I always imagined for myself was nothing like you." She smiled as her eyes began to close. "I'm not at all disappointed."

"You're coming along," Amanda said, and left Laura sleeping in the chair.

She was still there when Gabe came in. He tilted the bulky package against the wall. When she didn't stir at the rattle of the paper, he walked over to the couch. He didn't even have the energy to wish for his sketchpad as he stretched out his legs and almost instantly fell asleep.

The baby woke both of them. Gabe merely groaned and pulled a throw pillow over his face. Disoriented, Laura pulled herself up, blinked groggily at Gabe, then put one foot in front of the other to get upstairs.

A short time later, he went up after her.

"My timing's good," he decided when he saw that Laura was fastening a fresh diaper.

"I'm beginning to wonder about your timing." But she was smiling as she lifted Michael over her head to make him laugh. "How long have you been home?"

"Long enough to see that my wife has nothing better to do than lounge around all day." He plucked Michael from her while she pretended to glare at him. "Do you think if we kept him awake and exhausted him with attention he'd sleep tonight?"

"I'm willing to try anything."

At that, Gabe sat on the floor and began to play nonsense games. Bouncing the Baby, Flying the Baby, Tickling the Baby.

"You're so good with him." Finding her second wind, Laura sat on the floor with them. "It's hard to believe you're new at this."

"I never thought about parenthood. It certainly has its compensations." He set Michael on his knee and jiggled him.

"Like walking the ten-minute mile at 2:00 a.m."

"That, too."

"Gabe, your mother came by."

"Should I be surprised?"

She smiled a little as she leaned over to let Michael tug at her hair. "She left a card—from an abuse clinic."

"I see." He reached over himself to untangle her hair from Michael's grip. "Do you want to go back into therapy?"

"No...at least I don't think so." She looked over at him. Michael was chewing madly at his chin. All the therapy she needed was sitting across from her. "She suggested I might like to volunteer there."

He frowned as he let Michael gnaw on his knuckle. "And be reminded day after day?"

"Yes—of what I was able to change."

"I thought you'd want to go back to modeling eventually."

"No, I haven't any desire to go back to modeling. I think I could do this, and I know I'd like to try."

"If you're asking for my approval, you don't need to."

"I'd still like to have it."

"Then you do, unless I see this wearing you down."

She had to smile. He still saw her as more fragile than she was or could ever have afforded to be. "You know, I've been thinking...with everything that's happened, and everything we've had to think and worry about, we haven't had much time to really get to know a lot about each other."

"I know you take entirely too long in the bathtub and like to sleep with the window open."

She took the stuffed rabbit Michael liked to chew on and passed it from hand to hand. "There are other things."

"Such as?"

"The other night, I said that you could ask me anything and I'd tell you the truth, and then I'd ask you something. Do you remember?"

"I remember."

"I never had my turn."

He shifted so that he could rest his back against the daybed. They were avoiding speaking of the phone call they were both waiting for. And they both knew it. Perhaps that was best, Gabe mused as the baby continued to rub his sore gums against his knuckles.

"Do you want to hear about my misspent youth?"

Though she was plucking nervously at the rabbit's ears, she smiled. "Is there time?"

"You flatter me."

"Actually, I'd like to ask you about something else. A few days ago, when it rained, I went into your studio to close the windows. I looked through some of your paintings. Perhaps I shouldn't have."

"It doesn't matter."

"There was one in particular. The one of Michael. Your brother. I'd like you to tell me about him."

He was silent for so long that she had to fight back the urge to tell him that it didn't matter. But it mattered too much. She was certain it was his brother's death that had sent him to Colorado, that was preventing him, even after all these months, from having a showing of his work.

"Gabe." She laid a tentative hand on his arm. "You asked me to marry you so that you could take on my problems. You wanted me to trust you, and I have. Until you can do the same, we're still strangers."

"We haven't been strangers since the first time we laid eyes on each other, Laura. I would have asked you to marry me with or without your problems."

Now she fell silent, as surprise ran through her, chased frantically by hope. "Do you mean that?"

He shifted the baby onto his shoulder. "I don't always say everything I mean, but I do mean what I say." When Michael began to whimper, Gabe stood to walk him. "You needed someone, I wanted to be that someone. And I, though I didn't know it until you were already part of my life, needed someone, too."

She wanted to ask him how he needed her, and why, and if love—the kind she'd always hoped for—was somehow mixed up with that need. But they needed to go back further than that if they were ever to move forward.

"Please tell me about him."

He wasn't certain he could, that he wouldn't trip over the pain, and then the words. It had been so long since he'd spoken of Michael. "He was three years younger than I," he began. "We got along fairly well growing up because Michael tended to be even-tempered unless backed into a corner. We didn't have many of the same interests. Baseball was about it. It used to infuriate me that I couldn't outhit him. As we grew older, I turned to art, and Michael to law. The law fascinated him."

"I remember," she murmured, as some vague recollection stirred. "There was something about him in an article I read about you. He was working in Washington."

"As a public defender. He set a lot of tongues clucking over that decision. He wasn't interested in corporate law or big fees. Of course, a lot of people said he didn't need the money, anyway. What they didn't understand was that he would have done the same thing with or without his stock portfolio behind him. He wasn't a saint." Gabe set Michael in the crib and wound up the mobile. "But he was the best of us. The best and the brightest, my father used to say."

She had risen, but she wasn't certain he wanted her to go to him. "I could see that in the portrait. You must have loved him very much."

"It's not something you think about, one brother loving another. Either it's there or it isn't. It isn't something you say, because you don't think it needs to be said. Then all you have is time to regret."

"He had to know you loved him. He only had to see the portrait."

With his hands in his pockets, Gabe walked to the window. It was easier than he could have imagined to talk to her about it. "I'd badgered him to sit for me off and on for years. It became a family joke. I won five sittings from him in a poker game. A heart flush to his three of a kind." The pain clawed at him, no longer fresh, but still sharp. "That was the last time we played."

"What happened to him?"

"An accident. I've never believed in accidents. Luck, fate, destiny, but they called it an accident. He was researching a case in Virginia and took a small commuter plane to New York. Minutes after takeoff it went down. He was coming to New York because I was having a showing."

Her heart broke for him. This time there was no hesitation as she went to him and put her arms around him. "You've blamed yourself all this time. You can't."

"He was coming to New York for me, to be there for me. I watched my mother fall apart for the first and only time in her life. I saw my father walk through his own home as if he'd never seen it before, and I didn't know what to say or do."

She stroked his back, aching for him. There was no use telling him that being there was sometimes all that could be done. "I've never lost anyone I've loved, but having you and Michael now, I can imagine how devastating it would be. Sometimes things happen and there's no one to blame. Whether that's an accident or fate, I don't know."

He rested his cheek on her hair and looked out at the flowers she'd planted. "I went to Colorado to get away for a while, to be alone and see if I could paint again. I hadn't been able to here. When I found you, I'd begun to pull myself back. I could work again, I could think about coming home and picking up my life. But there was still something missing." He drew back and cupped her face in his hand. "You filled in those last pieces for me."

She curled her fingers around his wrist. "I'm glad."

When he held her, she closed her eyes. They would make it, Laura told herself. Whatever happened, they would make it. Sometimes need was enough.

"Gabe." She slid her hands down until they gripped his. "The paintings in your studio. They don't belong there." She squeezed his fingers with hers before he could speak or turn away. "It's wrong to keep them there, facing the wall and pretending they don't exist. If your brother was proud enough of you to want to be there for one of your showings, it's time you had one. Dedicate it to him. Maybe you didn't say the words, but there can't be any better way to show that you loved him."

He had started to brush it aside, to make excuses, but her last words hit home. "He would have liked you."

Her lips curved. "Will you do it?"

"Yes." He kissed her while she was still smiling. "Yes, it's time. I've known that, but I haven't been able to take the last step. I'll have Marion start the arrangements." She stiffened, and though the change was only slight he drew her away to study her face. "Problem?"

"No, of course not."

"You do a lot of things well, angel. Lying isn't one of them."

"Gabe, nothing could please me more than you going ahead with this. That's the truth."

"But?"

"Nothing. All of this has really put me behind schedule. I need to give Michael his bath."

"He'll hold a minute." He kept her with him by doing no more than running his hands down her arms. "I know there's some tension between you and Marion. I've already told you there's nothing between us but business."

"I understand that. I've told you what I would have done if I thought otherwise."

"Yes, you did." Amusement moved over his face. She would have packed her bags and headed for the door, but she would have gotten no more than five feet. "So what's the problem?"

"There is no problem."

"I'd prefer not going to Marion with this."

"So would I." Her chin came up. "Don't push this, Gabe. And don't push me."

"Well, well." He brought his hands to her shoulders as he nodded. "It's a rare thing for you to get that look on your face. Whenever you do, I have this deep-seated urge to drag you down on the floor and let loose." When color flooded her face, he laughed and drew her closer.

"Don't laugh at me." She would have twisted away, but his hands were firm.

"Sorry. I wasn't, really, more at the situation." He thought that perhaps delicacy was called for, but then he rejected the idea. "Want to fight?"

"Not at the moment."

"If you can't lie better than that, we'll have to keep you out of poker games," he murmured, and watched her eyes cool. "I overheard your discussion with Marion at the gallery."

"Then you obviously don't need me to spell things out for you. She believes I'm going to hold you back, prevent you from reaching your full potential, and she took steps to stop it. I realize that the Eagletons would have found us, probably in a matter of days, but I won't forgive her for calling them. The fact that you're associated with her gallery means I have to be polite to her in public, but that's the extent of it."

His hands had tightened on her shoulders, and all amusement had been wiped from his face. "You're telling me that Marion called the Eagletons?"

"You just said you'd heard us, so—"

"I hadn't heard that much." Deliberately he relaxed his hands, then took a step back. "Why didn't you explain this to me before so that we could have told her to go to hell?"

"I didn't think that you—" She stopped and stared at him. "Would you have?"

"Damn it, Laura, what more do I have to do to convince you that I'm committed totally to you and Michael?"

"But she said—"

"What difference does it make what she said? It's what I say, isn't it?"

"Yes." She folded her hands but didn't lower her gaze. It was what he said. And not once had he ever said he loved her. "I didn't want to interfere when it came to your work."

"And I won't tolerate Marion interfering in my life. I'll handle it."

"How?"

Exasperated, he tugged his hand through his hair. "One minute you talk of my work as though I had an obligation to mankind to share it, and the next you act as though I'd have to go begging to find another gallery."

"I didn't mean... You'll take your paintings out of Marion's gallery?"

"Good God," he muttered, and took another turn around the room. "Obviously we need to talk—or maybe talking's not what's called for." He took a step toward her, then swore when the phone rang. "Stay here." With that he turned on his heel and strode out.

Laura let out a long breath. He'd said something about dragging her to the floor and letting loose. That was what had been in his eyes a moment before. And what would that have proved?

She moved to the crib to hand a fretful Michael his favorite rabbit. It would only have proved that he wanted and needed her. She had no doubts about that. Why shouldn't she be surprised that he would cut himself off from Marion for her? But not for her, really, Laura thought as she leaned over to nuzzle the baby. For himself. Marion had made the mistake of interfering.

Reasons didn't matter, she told herself. Results did. A great deal had been accomplished here this afternoon. He'd finally trusted her with his feelings about his brother. She'd been able to say the right things to convince him to show his work, and Marion was out of their lives.

"That should be enough for one day," she murmured to Michael. But there was still an ache in her heart.

She wouldn't think about the Eagletons.

"He needs us, Michael." That, too, should have been enough. Perhaps they were a replacement for someone he had loved and lost, but he had already given the baby unconditional love. He had given her a promise of his fidelity. That was more than she'd ever had, more than she had come to believe she would ever have. And yet it wasn't enough.

"Laura."

She turned, annoyed because she was feeling weepy and dejected. "What is it?"

"That was Quartermain on the phone." He saw the fear come first, then saw it vanish to be replaced by determination. "It's over," he told her before she could ask. "The Eagletons' attorney contacted him a few minutes ago."

"Over?" She could only whisper. The strength she'd built up, layer by layer, began to slip.

"They've pulled back. There'll be no custody suit. Not now, not ever. They don't want anything to do with the baby."

"Oh, God." She covered her face with her hands. The tears came, but she wasn't ashamed of them, not even when Gabe gathered her close. "Is he sure? If they change their minds—"

"He's sure. Listen to me." He drew her back, just a little. He wasn't entirely certain how she would feel about the rest. "They're going to file papers claiming that Tony wasn't Michael's biological father. They want him cut off legally from any future claim to the Eagleton estate."

"But she doesn't believe that."

"She wants to believe that."

She closed her eyes while relief and regret poured through her. "I would have tried to be fair, to let them see Michael. At least I want to believe I would have tried."

"He'll lose his heritage."

"The money?" When she opened her eyes, they were dark and damp. "I don't think that will matter to him. It doesn't to me. As far as family goes, he already has one. Gabe, I don't know how to thank you."

"Then don't. You were the one who stood up to her."

"I did." She brushed the tears away, and then there was laughter as she threw her arms around him. "Yes, I did. No one's ever going to take him away from us. I want to celebrate. To go dancing, have a party." She laughed again and squeezed him hard. "After I sleep for a week."

"It's a date." He found her lips with his, then held them there as she melted into him. Another beginning, he thought, and this time they'd take the first step properly. "I want to call my parents and let them know."

"Yes, right away." She pressed against him for a moment longer. "I'll give Michael his bath, and then we'll be down."

It was nearly an hour before she came downstairs, bringing a more contented Michael with her. The baby, fresh from his bath, was awake and ready to be entertained. Because her jeans had gotten wet, she'd changed into a pale lavender shirt and slacks. Her hair was loose around her shoulders, and both she and Michael smelled of soap and soft talc. Gabe met her at the foot of the stairs.

"Here, let me have him." He curled his arm around the baby and tickled his belly. "Looks like you're ready to go field a few grounders."

"So do you." Envious, Laura muffled a yawn. "You haven't had any more sleep than I have. How do you manage it?"

"Three decades of clean living—and a body accustomed to all-night poker games."

"Your father wants to play. Maybe Michael could sit in."

"Maybe." He tipped her chin up with his finger. "You really are ready to drop, aren't you?"

"I've never felt better in my life."

"And you can barely keep you eyes open."

"That's nothing five straight hours of sleep wouldn't fix."

"I've got something to show you. Afterward, why don't you go up and take a nap? Michael and I can entertain ourselves." His thumb traced along her jawline. Until Laura, he hadn't known that the scent of soap and powder could be arousing. "Once you've rested, we can have our private celebration."

"I'll go now."

He laughed and caught her arm before she could start back up. "Come see first."

"Okay, I'm too weak to argue."

"I'll keep that in mind for later." With the baby in one arm and the other around Laura, he walked into the parlor.

She'd seen the painting before, from the first brush strokes to the last. Yet it seemed different now, here, hung over the mantel. In the gallery, she had seen it as a beautiful piece of work, something to to be studied by art students and patrons, a thing to be commented on and discussed and dissected and critiqued. Here, in the parlor, in the late afternoon, it was a personal statement, a part of all three of them.

She hadn't realized just how much she resented seeing it in Marion's gallery. Nor had she known that seeing it here would make her feel, as nothing else had, that she had finally come home.

"It's beautiful," she murmured.

He understood. It wasn't vanity or self-importance. "I've never done anything in my life that compares to this. I doubt I will again. Sit down, will you?"

Something in his tone had her glancing over at him before she settled on the couch. "I didn't know you intended to bring it home. I know you've had offers."

"I never had any intention of selling it. I always meant it for here." Resting the baby on his hip, he walked over to the portrait. "As long as I've lived here, I haven't done anything, or found anything, that I wanted to hang in that spot. It goes back to fate again. If I hadn't been in Colorado, if it hadn't been snowing, if you hadn't been running. It took what had happened to you, and what had happened to me, to bring us together and make this."

"When you were painting it, I wondered why you seemed so driven. I understand now."

"Do you?" With a half smile, he turned back to her. "I wonder just what you understand, angel. It wasn't until a little while ago that I realized you have no idea what I feel for you."

"I know you need me, me and Michael. Because of what happened to all of us, we're able to make things better."

"And that's it?" He wondered if he was pushing too far, but he thought that if he didn't push now it might be too late. "You said you loved me. I know gratitude's a big part of that, but I want to know if there's anything more."

"I don't know what you want me to say."

"I want you to look." He held out a hand. When she didn't move, he walked over to her and drew her to her feet. "Look at the portrait and tell me what you see."

"Myself."

It seemed to be the day for showdowns, Gabe thought. He quickly carried the sleeping Michael upstairs to the nursery and put him in the crib. Going back down to Laura, he took

her by the shoulders and, holding her in front of him, mad
her face the portrait. "Tell me what you see."

"I see myself as you saw me then." Why was her hea
hammering? "I seem a little too vulnerable, a little too sad.

Impatience had him giving her a quick shake. "You don
see enough."

"I want to see strength," she blurted out. "I think I do
And I see a woman alone who's ready to protect what'
hers."

"When you look at her eyes. Look at them, Laura, an
tell me what you see."

"A woman falling in love." She shut her own. "You mus
have known."

"No." He didn't turn her toward him. Instead, h
wrapped his arms around her so that they both continued t
face the portrait. "No, I didn't know, because I kept tellin
myself I was painting what I wanted to see. And what I wa
feeling myself."

Her heart leaped into her throat and throbbed there
Whatever he could feel, he could paint. That had been he
own conclusion. "What are you feeling?"

"Can't you see it?"

"I don't want to see it there." She turned to grip the fron
of his shirt. "I want to hear it."

He wasn't sure he had the words. Words came so muc
less easily than emotion. He could paint his moods, and h
could shout them, but it was difficult to speak them quietl
when they mattered so much.

He touched her face, her hair, then her hand. "Almos
from the first you pulled at me in a way no one ever had be
fore and no one ever will again. I thought I was crazy. Yo
were pregnant, totally dependent on me, grateful for m
help."

"I was grateful. I'll always be grateful."

"Damn it" was all he could manage as he turned away.

"I'm sorry you feel that way." She was calm now, absolutely, beautifully calm, as he glared at her. She'd remember him like this always, she thought, with his hair tousled from his hands, a gray shirt with the sleeves shoved up to the elbows and his face full of impatience. "Because I intend to be grateful for the rest of my life. And that has nothing to do with my intending to love you for the rest of my life."

"I want to be sure of that."

"Be sure. You didn't paint what you wanted to see, you never do. You paint the truth." She took one step toward him, the most important step she'd ever taken. "I've given you the truth, Gabe. Now I have to ask for it. Are your feelings for me tied up in that portrait, in that image, are they an effect of your love for Michael, or are they for me?"

"Yes." He caught her hands in his. "I'm in love with the woman I painted, with the mother of my child, and with you. Separately and together. We could have met anywhere, under any circumstances, and I would still have fallen in love with you. Maybe it wouldn't have happened as quickly, maybe it wouldn't have been as complicated, but it would have happened." She started to move into his arms, but he held her back. "When I married you, it was for purely selfish reasons. I wasn't doing you any favors."

She smiled. "Then I won't be grateful."

"Thank you." He lifted her hands to his lips, the one that wore the old wedding band, then the one that wore the new. "I want to paint you again."

She was laughing as his lips came down to her. "Now?"

"Soon."

Then his hands were in her hair, and the kiss became urgent and seeking. It was met equally as her arms went around him. Love, fully opened, added its own desperation.

There was a murmur of pleasure, then a murmur of protest as he drew her to the floor. Her laugh turned to a moan when he unbuttoned her blouse.

"Michael—"

"Is asleep." He dragged her hair back, leaving her face unframed. Everything he'd wanted to see was there. "Until he wakes up, you're mine. I love you, Laura. Every time you look at the painting, you'll see it. You were mine from the first moment I touched you."

Yours, she thought as she drew him back to her. Gabriel's angel was more than a portrait. And she finally belonged.

* * * * *

WHERE WERE YOU WHEN THE LIGHTS WENT OUT?

SILHOUETTE

SUMMER Sizzlers '93

This summer, Silhouette turns up the heat when a midsummer blackout leaves the entire Eastern seaboard in the dark. Who could ask for a more romantic atmosphere? And who can deliver it better than:

**LINDA HOWARD
CAROLE BUCK
SUZANNE CAREY**

Look for it this June at your favorite retail outlet.

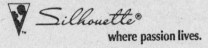

Silhouette®

where passion lives.

SS93

If you've been looking for something a little bit different,
a little bit spooky, let Silhouette Books take you on
a journey to the dark side of love with

SILHOUETTE® Shadows™

Every month, Silhouette will bring you two romantic,
spine-tingling Shadows novels, written by some of your
favorite authors, such as *New York Times* bestseller
Heather Graham Pozzessere, Anne Stuart, Helen R. Myers
and Rachel Lee—to name just a few.

In May, look for:
FLASHBACK by Terri Herrington
WAITING FOR THE WOLF MOON by Evelyn Vaughn

In June, look for:
BREAK THE NIGHT by Anne Stuart
IMMINENT THUNDER by Rachel Lee

Come into the world of Shadows and prepare
to tremble with fear—and passion....

SHAD2

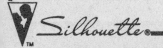

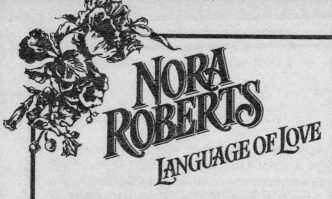

NORA ROBERTS
LANGUAGE OF LOVE

FREE Floral Stationery

Just mail us four proofs-of-purchase from any of the
NORA ROBERTS Language of Love titles 25 to 36, plus
$2.75 for postage and handling (check or money order–
please do not send cash) payable to Silhouette Reader
Service, send to:

In the U.S.
Language of Love Stationery
Silhouette Books
3010 Walden Avenue
P.O. Box 1396
Buffalo, NY 14269-1396

In Canada
Language of Love Stationery
Silhouette Books
P.O. Box 609
Fort Erie, Ontario
L2A 5X3

(Offer expires November 30, 1993)

Please allow six weeks for delivery.

ORDER FORM

Name _____

Address _____

City _____ State/Prov _____

Daytime Phone # _____ Zip/Postal Code _____

♥ Silhouette®

LANGUAGE OF LOVE

PROOF-OF-
PURCHASE

097 LOLPOP1R